If you fall
I will catch you

If you fall
I will catch you

Eifion Jenkins

seren

Seren is the book imprint of
Poetry Wales Press Ltd
57 Nolton Street, Bridgend, Wales, CF31 3AE
www.seren-books.com

ISBN 978-1-85411-456-3

A CIP record for this title is available from the British Library.

Cover design by MO-design.com

Inner design and typesetting by books@lloydrobson.com

Printed by Cromwell Press

The publisher works with the financial assistance of
the Welsh Books Council.

For JJ, who always believed

Book One

I have been in many shapes before I attained a congenial form
– *The Romance of Taliesin*

chapter one

'Have you ever been in love?'

Gwidion felt suddenly dizzy. He and Cai were sitting dangling their legs over the wall of the Ruins. Gwidion looked up at the blue, blue sky – so blue it seemed to have the power to pierce his body. So blue he had to close his eyes and steel his stomach against the rising terror which gripped him. His hands tightened on the blocks of limestone beneath him, blanching his knuckles so they appeared as part of the Ruins themselves.

It is coming again, he thought.

The heady scent of aviation fuel hit him first, making the muscles of his gut contract, then the flames which engulfed that beautiful blue, blue sky in an awesome blaze of red and orange. And finally the black pall which hid the twin towers from view like a shroud suddenly descending over them. Then the falling began...

'Have you ever been in love?' Cai's repeated question jerked his eyes open, and with a kind of relief he saw the blue sky still above his head and felt the solid stones beneath his fingers.

He looked at Cai without replying, then looked down, watching his feet blot out a huge area of grass ten metres below them. This was as high as the two could climb, a crumbling perch which gave them a panoramic view over the countryside. It was the highest point anywhere around. The remains were two or three feet thick in places, and where they were sitting looked down on a large rectangular patch of grass bordered by four walls. At its highest point Gwidion calculated it must have been three storeys high – and at one corner where they now sat, a tangle of rusted and twisted metal jutted out angrily as if the structure had been torn apart by some great force. Sometime in history, a long, long time ago, this great building had risen higher than Cai and Gwidion could imagine. Sixteen floors some said. More, said others. Countless floors, said Cai, with his talent for exaggeration. So countless floors it was.

Their current perch was even higher than three storeys and seemed to be at the top of a great shaft, the front of which had collapsed but which Cai said must originally have housed an elevator, a box which carried people up and down the unimaginably high building at unimaginably high speeds. Gaping holes, which had once been windows, allowed light and sunshine to flood the open space which now remained. With a single foot held in front of him, Gwidion could block out a window, its form framing the shape of his foot almost perfectly. Cai nudged him and Gwidion had to snatch at a protruding piece of metal in the mortar beneath him to keep his balance.

The question had been in Welsh – and Gwidion didn't always trust his brother when he spoke to him in Welsh. Especially a question like that.

'I bet you have,' said Cai.

His brother was right, of course. It was such a shocking experience to fall in love for the first time. It had happened on the last day of spring study term. There was a sort of party atmosphere that day. They had done some drawing and even some maths, but in general the mentor had been easy on them. When he was in a good mood it soon spread throughout the class. He paced slowly from port to port, looking at their work, occasionally nodding or sounding a soft 'hmm' of approval, or if need be a quiet click of his tongue against his teeth. Even his corrections were made gently, as if today they didn't really matter. He seemed to move closer to the children than normal, his thigh might brush against a shoulder as they sat on the floor, his breath might tickle the hairs on the nape of a neck as he hovered, bent deeply from the waist, a fraction longer than was really necessary. In the mentor such small things passed for happiness.

Lauren was sitting across the room – only a port or two away, far enough so that they could look at each other easily without too much head-turning, close enough so that the meaning of their glances was unmistakable. Gwidion yearned for her in a way he had not known possible. They were classmates and friends – and more than that. In such a small community children knew each other from birth. As soon as they were old enough to leave the security of their mothers' arms, their lifelong relationship with the others began, and it continued until they either left the village, or until they died. In such an extended family it was difficult to imagine how from one day to the next mere familiarity could breed love – but he had never had these feelings about her, or anyone else, before. The strength of his emotion was so palpable and seemed so obvious, he feared that others might be able to touch it too. It was also incredibly delicious – and it took him by surprise. He could hardly keep his mind on his work at all. He wanted to touch her there and then, to kiss her even. And when she smiled at him it was as if the rest of the room, his classmates, the study, everything, melted away into the background.

Of course Cai would have noticed. It wouldn't be like him to miss that sort of thing.

'I have,' said Cai. 'I have been in love.' Gwidion was finally forced to look at him. 'Ce'nder Lauren. Did you see the way she was looking at me, the last day of study at the end of term?'

Cai could no longer stifle the huge grin that now spread across his face. Gwidion blushed and held more firmly onto the wall beneath him, to stop himself falling and, more importantly, to keep his hands from wrapping themselves around his brother's neck.

'I'm going to marry her,' Cai leered. The challenge was enough, it was just enough to make Gwidion lose patience and release his grip – and in that same moment Cai twisted in a grotesque mockery of someone being attacked, his arms flailing upwards, his body twisting sideways. And he jumped.

'Cai,' shouted Gwidion, tears, terror and hate already mixed in his voice. But it was too late. Gwidion grabbed his safe hand-hold on the wall again to stop himself from following his brother. Cai fell expertly, landing like a parachutist, knees bending, rolling onto the grass, rolling and rolling over and over until he came to a halt, spreadeagled like the chalk outline of a dead body in an old murder spool.

Gwidion prised a piece of mortar loose from the wall beneath his hands, releasing a small cloud of dust into the air. It smelled old and damp and the fine powder seemed to cling to the inside of his nostrils. He took aim carefully and threw.

He moved his foot so that it blanked out Cai's motionless body from view, waited for the scream and was relieved to hear only the thud of stone on grass echoing around the four walls. Without looking again, he stood up on the ledge and picked his way carefully back down. The jagged outline of the wall they had climbed, worn, he guessed, by generations of disobedient children, provided a sort of staircase to follow. His hands and feet were familiar with the route and he moved fast without hurrying, balancing momentarily in thin air before alighting safely on the next small ledge below, turning his body – now looking out over the green fields towards the village where they lived, now looking down at Cai's still prostrate body on the grass.

He wondered for a moment what it would be like if this time he had judged it wrongly, if this time Cai had really hurt himself. He imagined telling his mother, he thought about the questions of the adults, he thought about the tears. He imagined a funeral such as he had read about in some books, or the sort you got in those old spools they weren't supposed to watch, where the widow stood before the grave in a black veil. It would be quite a scene, the whole village gathered in the roundhouse, the words of the mentor ringing out into the silence. He imagined Lauren being there watching him, admiring his small handsome figure, feeling for him in his grief. He felt the tears welling up in his throat as the coffin was lowered into the ground – and with a shock realised he was so moved by his own fiction that in reality he was about to cry as he, Gwidion, stepped up to drop a final well-aimed stone into the deep, deep hole in the earth.

Clunk. And clunk, clunk, clunk in a rapid diminuendo went the echo around the the tiny confines of a grave.

The final part of his descent took him to the outside of the Ruins and he had to go back through the entrance to reach the room where Cai lay. By the time he stood on the grass of the floor inside, his brother's body had gone and Cai was running – running and laughing across the fields towards home.

'It's lunch time,' shouted Cai. 'Come on, lover boy, I've invited Ce'nder Lauren for lunch.'

He was already a hundred metres or more in front, ploughing

straight through the field of fast-growing sweetcorn which bordered the Ruins. Gwidion stopped and watched the tall plants part and sway as his brother followed a straight furrow through the crop. He gave up the chase. They were not supposed to cut across the fields which grew the village's only source of staple foods. Only water was more precious than their harvest, and even in the boys' few years on Earth, both had known hunger many times. Not just hunger, but desperate hunger. Hunger that burned at your insides and screamed at you throughout the day so that you could not watch a spool or play a realie without it tearing at your thoughts and making you miss the plot. It was hunger which made your clothes grow big and ramshackle and hid your body in folds of cloth. It was a feeling of desire like no other. Until now.

It occurred to him that hunger for food only existed in the short-term memory. Once satisfied, it took cover in the recesses of the mind, until drawn out again. It was possible to remember being hungry, yes, but it was not possible to feel hungry when you had just eaten. Desire for a girl was something different. It did not go away when he saw Lauren or spoke to her or feasted his eyes on the many things that fascinated him about her face, or the way she looked, or that endearing flick of the fingers with which she tidied her hair out of her eyes and behind her ears. None of these things sated his love. If anything at all, it made it grow stronger and demanded more. What could possibly satisfy the craving of love? Consumed by such passion, he was sure he could forget food.

Gwidion sauntered back along the path which led through the fields to the village. The hedges on either side were of birch and ash and the irrigation channels at the foot of them smelled damp. This year's new growth sprang young and straight and fresh towards the sunlight. On these hedges the villagers tied small pieces of string on particularly promising young straight shoots – branches that would one day be suitable for stakes or building poles, or even walking sticks. These would be spared at hedge-cutting time for two or three years, sometimes more, before they were finally harvested and taken to be dried in the low barns around the village, themselves built out of wood harvested in previous years. Gwidion found one or two marked branches and stopped to admire them, stroke their straightness and check that they were developing well. It would soon be time to cut them.

It was beginning to grow warm, especially here in the double shelter of the hedges on each side of the path. There was not exactly a breeze, but the air moved in those light gusts typical of early summer, eddies of moist breath. It was going to be hot today. An explosion of insects drifted close to the lush growth of the trees, the biscuit smell of the gorse flowers hung in pockets on the air. At the end of the path, just before it opened onto the village enclosure stood the menhir. Gwidion stopped and rested his hands on its cool lichen-covered surface and felt the throb of the earth resonating through it. The standing stone was a good metre taller than him, though if he wrapped his arms around it he could just – only just – join the tips of his fingers together. He let his fingers wander the grooves of the ogham carved into its corners. Dŵr, he read. Water. If he put his ear flat against the stone, he could hear the underground river swishing way below, its voice deep and muted by the rock and soil above it. The level was low. In June that was not good. A wood pigeon rose from the trees behind him, its great wings whirring in annoyance at the effort of take off, drawing Gwidion back to the surface.

Smoke from the low duggs of the village rose into the air and brought with it the memory of food. But the memory of love was more powerful and Gwidion still loitered, wishing to daydream a little longer. Cai would probably have arrived home by now, but it didn't matter. There would be no inquest, no row from his mother. Just as Gwidion would say nothing about Cai's dash through the sweetcorn crops. For however cruel and mean his brother was to him, and however much he stretched the boundaries of the acceptable, Gwidion knew him better than anybody. If Cai was lawless towards his brother, then he was even more so a rebel against adult authority. Cai would never tell. And Gwidion would never tell.

They were brothers, after all.

They were, after all, twins.

chapter two

The other children were leaving the main roundhouse as Gwidion walked towards the wafts of cooking coming from his own dugg. Lauren was in the first small group of girls, talking excitedly. The sight caused his stomach to give a small contraction and forget its interest in food. She stopped when she noticed him and detached herself a metre or two from the others. Gwidion walked towards her until he was close enough for her to speak.

'The mentor asked where you were. He went to see your mother,' she spoke American as they were accustomed to do in study.

Their faces met briefly in a formal kiss of greeting, then Gwidion gestured past the village enclosure. His reply was in Welsh. 'The Ruins. I was playing in the Ruins.'

'By yourself?' asked Lauren. She looked nervously towards her friends who had now moved some distance away but chattered and glanced back now and then to watch the two of them. Nothing was missed, nothing went unremarked.

Gwidion shrugged. 'I like the Ruins, you can see for kilometres and kilometres. You can see everything, all the fields, the duggs, everything. You can see as far as there is, where the sky comes down to the land, and that's as far as you can see. You can come with me.'

'My mother says not to,' said Lauren. 'She says it isn't safe.'

'Do you do everything your mother says, Ce'nder Lauren?' Gwidion asked with a nervous smile. She combed her fair hair behind her ears with her fingers and smiled back.

'It's OK, really,' he persisted. 'You just have to be careful. Come this afternoon.'

Lauren looked towards her friends again. 'We have to be in study.'

'After study, then.'

Lauren started to go to rejoin the other girls. 'Maybe,' she said with a backward look to Gwidion. He smiled and gave a half-hidden wave of the hand and Lauren smiled too.

As Gwidion walked down the earthen steps into his dugg the smell of soup met his nostrils. His mother was bending over the central fire, her long black straight hair falling dangerously close to the pot she was stirring. Gwidion's eyes adjusted to the dim light and the haze of smoke and steam. The dugg was really just a small version of a roundhouse, sunk into the ground for insulation so that the grassed roof ended only about half a metre above the ground. The various sleeping and living areas were arranged around the central open fire which provided enough heat to warm the entire space, even in winter. At this time of year the fire would not be kept in all day.

His mother looked up when she sensed him approaching. She put down her spoon and came forward to hug him.

'Gwidion, where have you been? The mentor came. You didn't go to study this morning.'

'I was in the Ruins,' said Gwidion taking his seat at the low wooden table next to the fire.

'But study is important. All the other children go.'

'But Mam, I know everything.'

She straightened herself and could not help laughing loudly, holding onto the bowl of steaming soup in her two hands to keep it from spilling.

'That's no answer, Gwidion. And if you do know everything then you should be helping the others to learn it too.' She put the soup in front of him with a rough hunk of maize bread. 'Now eat your soup and tell me why you didn't go.'

Gwidion dipped the bread into the bowl and sucked on it greedily. 'I was with Cai. He knows everything as well.'

For the first time his mother gave a tut of annoyance. 'Cai is as naughty as you and Cai shouldn't miss study either.' She brought her own bowl to the table and sat opposite her son.

'Now tell me why you didn't go to study.'

There was a pause. 'It was history,' said Gwidion in American.

'And you know everything about history,' said his mother softly, still speaking in Welsh.

'We know nothing about history.' The next pause was even longer. 'Were the Ruins a skyscraper once?'

His mother looked up from her bowl in alarm. It was not the question which bothered her, but the tremor she recognised in his voice. His breath came in short hard bursts as if he was filling his lungs after exercise.

'Cai says so. Cai says it once had countless floors.'

She measured her reply. 'Maybe it was, but I don't think it had that many storeys. Cai exaggerates, you know that. What did you do there?'

'Oh, played.' He took a spoonful of soup but his next words were just audible. 'Cai jumped.'

His mother stopped eating and waited for him to continue.

'He likes to frighten me,' Gwidion added quickly.

'And were you frightened?'

Gwidion had stopped eating too, though he still held his wooden spoon which was dripping soup on the table as it shook in his trembling hand. His eyes filled with tears.

'Mam, why don't we build skyscrapers any more?'

She leaned across the table, taking his hands in hers. She knew too well the note of panic in his voice. She knew where this was heading, but how to stem this tide of sadness, or where it came from, was still a mystery to her.

'Hisht,' she said gently, her face close to his. 'Gwidion, ssh, don't put yourself through this again.'

She knew her words were useless. She knew the pain she felt served no purpose either, but she could not stop herself. She thought back to his childhood and asked herself the question mothers have posed countless times. Was it my fault? Was it something I did? She had learned the long and hard way by now that the questions were fruitless and largely rhetorical. How many times in his thirteen years had she tried to reach inside her son to find this pain and help soothe it? But only he could know where the hurt lurked, and until he could discover it for himself, all she could do was... what mothers do. She tried to coax him back to his food, she held him tight. She talked about his friends at study. She promised him a realie instead of going to study in the afternoon. Anything. She would offer anything to help hold him back from the abyss of this sorrow. But now the tears had begun falling they were not about to be rescued. She moved to his side of the table and took him in her arms and sat down and waited for the grief to subside. She knew she would wait a long time.

Gwidion heard the mentor arrive later that afternoon. His mother had put him to lie on his bed next to hers in the sleeping area at the western side of the dugg opposite the entrance. It was a low wooden bed raised only a few centimetres from the floor and he lay on the mattress he had woven from cordyline leaves the year before. In that time it had slowly begun to compress into a thick piece of cardboard, flat except for two indents where his hip and shoulder had imprinted their weight. In a few months, after the crops had been harvested, there would be time to weave new mattresses from the leaves they picked. And he and Cai would also weave one for their mother as was the custom.

He was dozing when the mentor came in, and still whimpering softly to himself after his prolonged bout of crying. As the conversation went on a few feet away, he began to tune into it. There was another man with the mentor this time, too. One whose voice he did not recognise. The mentor and his mother talked softly for what seemed like ages. He knew from his mother's tone of voice that she was trying to put the mentor off, but the mentor's voice was urgent. Gwidion could not catch everything, but he guessed it was to do with his study and the fact that he had gone to the Ruins again that morning.

Listening to the three of them in that insubstantial state between sleep and waking, it seemed to him that the inside of his head began to swell with a chorus of a hundred jabbering voices. His own breathing became uncomfortably loud like that of a large warm beast. Soon his head seemed to expand to fill the whole room, filled with chattering, chattering and his own terrible breath. He felt as if he might explode.

His mother's voice broke the nightmare. 'Gwidion.' She came and sat on the bed beside him. 'Gwidion, the mentor has brought someone to see you.'

'Is it about my study?' he asked. The two men had followed his mother and stood slightly behind her.

'Where were you this morning, Ce'nder Gwidion?' asked the mentor kindly.

'The Ruins.'

'Was Cai there?'

Gwidion remained silent. Cai was his brother, Cai was his twin.

'This is Colonel Jiménez. From the Academy in Madrid. He wanted to meet you.'

Jiménez stepped forward, almost giving a small bow. He smiled at Gwidion's mother but she did not return it.

'I am very impressed with your work in study, Gwidion. You have a great gift.' His Welsh was faltering, with a heavy Spanish accent.

'I like to know things,' said Gwidion.

'Tell me about Cai,' said Jiménez, moving closer and squatting so that he could see eye-to-eye with the boy. He moved like a bear whose eye had been caught by a telltale ripple in the water. But he had moved too fast, a little too eagerly, and Gwidion averted his gaze quickly. Cai was his brother, Cai was his twin.

'I have a brother,' said Jiménez, relaxing his posture a little but remaining at the boy's eye level. The unusual admission brought Gwidion fully awake. 'I hardly ever see him, he works a long way away in Peru. You are very lucky.'

'Do you miss him?' asked Gwidion.

'Often. We were close. Not twins, but very close, nevertheless.'

'Is he older than you?'

'Two years older.' He laughed softly. 'It's not always easy having an older brother. He's bigger, he's stronger, he bosses you about. And he's always getting you into trouble.'

'But you don't tell,' said Gwidion solemnly. Jiménez laughed again and was forced to agree with the boy.

'No, you don't tell. But I'm not really here to talk about brothers. I'm here to talk about your study.'

'You came all the way from Madrid just because I missed a history study?'

Now everyone laughed and the atmosphere in the room relaxed. His mother let go of his hand while Gwidion sat up cross-legged on his mattress. The mentor sat down on a low bench against the wall of the dugg.

'It's not the first time, is it? Don't you like history?'

'Not all of it. We learn about the dome, how it works, our customs, our rituals, how we live. All this I know.'

'So what do you like?'

'I like the time before history, the time of the menhir, before our life was measured and calculated. When we lived in the open. I like to know things about that.'

'What other sorts of things do you like?'

'I like books. Real books, not the optik books they use in study. I like books you can open at any page, or books which fall open at pages where other people have bent them from reading them over and over. I like books where you can read the end before you get in too deep.'

There was a pause. 'Have you read many books?' Jiménez asked.

Gwidion's expression had changed. As the suspicion dropped from his expression, the colonel saw a bright animated thirteen-year-old boy again.

'We don't have many. I have read them all. I know the endings of some great books,' he said proudly. 'I know the end of Jude and Arabella in *Jude the Obscure*, that's very sad. I know the end of *Ulysses* and Mam says I'm too young to read that sort of thing. I know the end of *A Prayer for Owen Meany* – that's really shocking. I'd like to write a book with an ending like that one day.'

'I'm sure you are capable of it, Gwidion,' said Jiménez. 'I am sure you are capable of many things. And Cai?'

'He, of course, loves optik books. They are created by people who want to stop you jumping back and forth. Cai likes his mysteries to be revealed slowly, bit by bit. He likes tension and fear and surprise. I like to know where I am going.'

Once Cai had been optiking *The Inheritors* by William Golding. Gwidion had already read it. 'Don't you want to know what happens?' Gwidion had asked.

'I'll find that out anyway,' Cai said. 'And besides it doesn't have to end that way.'

'What do you mean it doesn't *have* to end that way. Of course it does, that's the way it ends. That's the way it was written.'

'No it doesn't have to,' he had said simply. And that was that. The conversation could go no further, it could only end in a fight.

Cai was a shaper of the universe. Gwidion was its dreamer.

'Gwidion.' His mother was shaking him gently by the shoulders. 'Gwidion.' He opened his eyes again slowly and found himself lying on the bed. It took him a moment to re-adjust. The mentor was there and another man. Jiménez. From Madrid. He had a brother too. The two men and his mother were looking at him with an expression of kindness and concern. The colonel's bald head caught the light from the central roof-hole for a moment and Gwidion looked for the first time at his uniform. Grey and gold. Grey and gold and, on his lapel, a pair of golden wings. He would like to have wings like that.

'Would I become a pilot at your Academy?' Gwidion asked trying to sit upright, pointing at the wings.

'Take your time,' Jiménez said kindly. 'You drifted off there. I am not a pilot, but my job is to find boys like you who maybe could become a pilot – of sorts. Of a special sort. Do you have dreams?'

'Everybody dreams,' said Gwidion simply.

'Tell me about yours.'

Gwidion appeared to be rousing himself from a deep sleep.

'We went to the Ruins, Cai and I, so we could see where the sky touched the earth. Cai jumped.' The tears were beginning again, starting deep in the throat and rising. He tried to stop them but he could not breathe at the same time as stifling the sadness in his mouth. His mother stood up suddenly and spoke firmly.

'No. No more. Not now, not today.'

The mentor began to object gently. 'Ce'nder Ana, the colonel has come from Madrid...'

But Jiménez stood and held up his hand in a gesture of acquiescence. 'No matter.'

Ana aimed her words at the mentor with unusual force. 'The colonel has come from Madrid, the colonel can also go back to Madrid. Where does the boy have to go?'

Jiménez bowed slightly. 'Indeed I can go back. And I will come again with your permission.' He turned to Gwidion. 'I am sorry to have caused you upset, that was not my intention. You are a young man of many talents, Gwidion, and that is a rare thing. The Academy could be a great place for you to learn and grow. I will talk to your mother and we will see each other again if you wish. But only if you wish.'

There was no reply. Only the soft breathing of a child fast asleep. Jiménez took Gwidion's mother lightly by the elbow and turned to the mentor. 'I would like to talk to Ana alone.'

The mentor didn't have time to answer before Ana answered.

'That won't be necessary.' She moved away from both men and made towards the entrance, signalling that they were to leave.

The colonel hesitated and looked from the mentor to Ana and back. His hand was hanging still in mid-air, still grasping an imaginary elbow. He let it drop to his side.

'Very well.'

'Colonel, I am sorry,' the mentor spoke as soon as they were out of earshot of Gwidion's dugg.

Jiménez shook his head.

'I should have had things better prepared. If he hadn't gone off to the Ruins today, I am sure his mother would have reacted differently.'

Jiménez answered with a light snort. 'That's something I wouldn't bank on.'

'Colonel?'

'But you are right that this has been a wasted visit. And I have come all the way from Madrid. You must prepare the boy. He is already thirteen and we need him at the Academy.'

'Colonel, the village needs him too.'

Jiménez stopped walking. The mentor was the taller of the two and at first glance when they stopped and stood toe to toe it seemed obvious who was in charge. On the one hand was the stocky, solid frame of the military man, pugnacious in contrast to the ascetic stoop of the mentor. In simple physical terms it might appear to be an uneven contest, but perhaps the willowy build of the mentor was flexible enough to have withstood many of these onslaughts from Madrid.

'You have a privileged position, mentor. Your village is also privileged. In return the Academy requires... ' he let his hands fall away from his broad shoulders in a careless gesture, '... what it requires.'

'In this case the boy.'

'Yes.'

'And how on earth am I supposed to persuade him? Not to mention his mother.'

'You'll find a way. There is always a way.'

'Why Gwidion?'

The pair continued their face-off, neither of them showing any signs of aggression, neither one prepared to turn away. Jiménez was used to being obeyed without question, but he had a sort of respect for this thin, slightly bowed man, an uncomfortable go-between who shuffled his allegiance between his village and the might of the Republic. A Catholic priest of a man in an outback mission.

'We have been watching Gwidion since he was seven, since the very first time you told us of his potential. That is your job and you have done it well. Now the time is right. Gwidion is special.'

The mentor's inward struggle continued as he listened to the colonel's words. It was true it had been he who had singled out Gwidion. He had been proud to tell the Academy of the boy's achievements and potential. Six years ago it had seemed obvious that the village would have more sons. At the age of seven, the prospect of Gwidion going away to Madrid had in any case seemed an eternity away. Eternity had a habit of turning up sooner than expected.

'There is the question of this twin... ' the mentor began slowly. 'This is something I haven't told Madrid about, and it is something that worries us all.'

Jiménez laughed. 'Oh yes, the imaginary friend. Hardly surprising, really. A young boy, an outsider in his village, separated from the others by his gender, his intelligence... '

'This is different.'

The mentor stopped. He had not mentioned Cai to the Academy before for fear of spoiling Gwidion's chances, in the hope that it was a phase which would pass. Now he wanted to say more and yet Jiménez seemed completely untroubled by mention of it. A chicken was scratching nearby, sending a light spray of dust over their feet as they spoke. The mentor shooed it away then indicated to the colonel to walk.

'You can stay in the roundhouse tonight. We will feed you and make up a bed for you there. You will be able to talk to Gwidion again in the morning before you leave.'

The colonel stepped into the gloom of the roundhouse and smiled.

'I can't remember the last time I slept on a cordyline mattress, mentor.' He stopped. That was a lie. He could indeed remember the last occasion. And being back in this village now, in Ana's village, he remembered it all too well. And not without a great deal of pleasure. He shook himself back to the present.

'But I'm sure I'll enjoy the experience. After enough mead.'

chapter three

Gwidion's mother bent low over her sleeping son. She passed her hand over his forehead and felt the sticky clamminess of a fever. She could make no sense of the low muttered words coming from his mouth. These episodes had begun two years ago at about the same time as he had shown the first signs of entering puberty. Like the mentor she had put it down to the stress of the changes going on in his body. She had shown patience, she had been understanding, she had not asked too many questions of him or tried to deny his experiences. But it was hard. It was especially hard now when she sat with him, trying to comfort him, trying to calm him.

Outside she could hear the preparations being made for the meal. A visit by someone from anywhere was a rarity. A visit by someone from Madrid was both a rarity and an honour. Though the village chose to live its own life cut off as far as possible from a Republic it had little trust in, it could not escape the connections which bound it to Madrid.

It needed technology, it needed know-how. Most of all it needed an answer to the fertility plague. All the world needed an answer to that.

She walked to the entrance of the dugg and looked over towards the roundhouse to where the villagers were now gathering. It would be difficult to avoid going. She could ask a friend to sit with Gwidion, but that would mean denying someone else the chance to chat to an outsider and catch up on the latest news of the Republic.

She looked back at her son. Perhaps she was simply worrying too much. Then something caught her eye, something about the lump of bedclothes in the gloomy corner of the dugg. She peered harder, letting her eyes re-adjust to the lack of light.

A burst of air left her mouth in shock, followed by a scream of terror which silenced the party beginning in the roundhouse.

'He's gone.'

Tabitha, a well built woman who was talking animatedly with Jiménez near the entrance, was the first to speak. 'It's Ce'nder Ana.'

A number of women ran towards her dugg. From within came Ana's loud wails above the attempts of the other women to calm her and explain what had happened. At first Jiménez chose to ignore the drama as best he could, not wishing to interfere in any private village matter, but his ears had pricked at the mention of Gwidion's mother's name, and putting down his drink he began to move closer to her dugg.

'He was here. He was here. He's gone. It's not possible.'

The colonel moved up alongside the mentor as the women again came to the door of the dugg. Ana's face was distraught.

'My boy. He was here, asleep. I turned my back for a moment. It's not possible. I didn't leave the dugg. It isn't possible.'

She fell weeping into the arms of the other shocked villagers. Those who could not give immediate help walked stupidly into the dugg and looked again at Gwidion's bed as if somehow his mother might have missed him.

Jiménez edged gently through the crowd of women to stand in front of Ana. He took her hand and she looked at him. His voice was low and calm but intent.

'Tell me exactly. I can help.'

Ana breathed deeply in through her sobs and constructed the sentences carefully.

'He was there on the bed asleep. Feverish. He was murmuring things in his sleep, dreaming something.'

'Yes, yes. Go on.'

Ana's eyes looked madly at him for a moment, opening wide with disbelief at what she was about to say.

'I went to the door and looked back. And he was gone. Help me. Look for him.'

The wailing began again, but Jiménez spoke firmly over it.

'Was there anything he said? Anything you could hear. Anything you recognised?'

Gwidion's mother shook her head at him, her eyes full of tears now, but her mouth was fighting to say something.

'Cai.' It was nothing but a hoarse whisper.

'Cai? His twin?'

Ana nodded. Jiménez straightened and looked around him. The villagers waited for him to speak.

'The Ruins,' he said finally. 'Take me to the Ruins.'

The mentor led the search party but it was the colonel who found him asleep, spreadeagled at the foot of the tower, almost as if he had fallen. There was no sign of injury, his breathing was deep and peaceful.

Jiménez lifted him in his powerful arms and carried him the long walk back, stumbling now and then in the failing dusk light and through unfamiliarity with the path. He cursed occasionally under his breath, his face set in grim expression of determination. It was a feat of considerable strength and perseverance, stubbornness even. But no-one else felt the need to offer to take his turn.

Back at the dugg he laid him tenderly on the bed, pulling the rough blanket over him and smoothing the hair out of his eyes before allowing his mother to take over his care.

When he was satisfied Gwidion was comfortable, he stood back. The dugg was empty now, the other villagers having satisfied themselves that all was well and returned to the party. The mentor hovered nearby until a look from the colonel indicated that he too might leave.

'Thank you,' Ana said looking into the colonel's face when they were alone. Then she added quietly: 'You cannot take my boy like this'.

Jiménez looked back at her equally earnestly.

'Ana, we need him more than ever now. And he must come of his own accord.'

She turned away from him. 'He will never do that.'

Jiménez took her by the shoulder and turned her towards him. For the first time there was a familiarity about the way he touched her. For the second time that day he remembered that night on a cordyline mattress fourteen years ago. His voice dropped to a whisper.

'Ana, he is my son too.'

She shook herself away from his hand and turned back to her son. 'There is no need to remind me of that, Colonel.'

The flatness of her voice, its utter absence of emotion, woke him from his pleasant memories more sharply than if she had doused him with cold water. Jiménez bowed slightly and left the dugg.

chapter four

Gwidion was back at his port in study the next morning with the other children. The lesson was Spanish, the language of the Republic of Hispania, of which this corner of Bretaña was a small part. The children were sitting cross-legged in a semi-circle facing their ports which illuminated them in a ghostly fashion in the gloom of the roundhouse. Most of the inhabited buildings in the village used woven plant materials for their floor coverings such as the waste from maize and the virtually indestructible leaves of the cordylines and flax which colonised great swathes of rough ground.

The profusion of elegant tall flower spikes on the flaxes provided an exotic display of orange and brown and creamy yellow in the summer, like so many giant pin cushions, and after flowering they were harvested for their fibrous leaves which were woven into hard-wearing mats for the duggs. But the roundhouse, the main communal building of the sixty-seven domers who lived here, used their most precious resource – wood.

The floor was laid in large rectangular planks, cut in various sizes from the trunk of a felled tree to make the most efficient use of the timber, and laid like a patchwork of irregular flagstones from wall to wall. Here were ash, beech and sycamore side by side, hazel and birch providing thin strips to fill those awkward gaps near the walls. In the centre of the building, some five metres in diameter, was the most impressive feature of all. Set into the floor, like a giant piece of marquetry, was a star shape made from the largest planks of oak, stained dark with woad and blackberry.

The sound of footfalls was different here from in a dugg – softer and more reverential, warmer. The smell of the roundhouse was always changing, according to what it was being used for. Today the slightly acrid smell of hot technology hung in the air, mixed with the scent of a huddle of children. The mentor, his hair greying, his long face drawn and gaunt, but not stern, moved from one child to the next, squatting beside them to examine their work. His ease of movement belied his years as he prowled around the room, occasionally pouncing on something that needed correcting, or praising, or sharing with the rest of the class. The children were working on translating a short technical essay on the principles of solar power acceleration, written in American. The mentor said little, stopping here and there to point something out, occasionally asking a child to read a sentence aloud. Gwidion had already finished and was looking patiently at the mentor, waiting for him to arrive at his port.

The mentor became aware of his gaze and gave an almost imperceptible sigh. He skipped the next child and came over to Gwidion. He gave his work the most cursory of glances.

'Good, good, well done,' he murmured. 'You can tackle another one, you'll find plenty in the same datafile. That's very good.'

The comment was something of an understatement. He had often thought that sometimes it was a little too good. Gwidion had a precocious habit of correcting the original, not from the language point of view, but on its fundamental science. By the age of ten he was comfortable with the field theories of general relativity, not to mention the highly complex equations which governed the infinite multi-dimensional universes of Einstein's successors.

'Why is the speed of light constant?' he had demanded during one translation exercise.

The mentor had not seen the danger signs. 'Because it has been measured experimentally.'

'I don't trust constants. They never work.'

The mentor couldn't help smiling as he remembered the boy's petulant conviction. He should have gone over to talk to him alone. Instead he chose to conduct the argument in front of the class. 'It's true they don't always survive, Ce'nder Gwidion.'

'If speed is measured as a function of distance and time, and time and distance are both measured as functions of the speed of light, then the speed of light is just a function of the speed of light. It's absurd. Why shouldn't distance or time be the constants? Or why shouldn't they all be variable?'

It was such a beguiling argument that the mentor had not been able to think fast enough to answer it. He felt the eyes of Gwidion's studymates on him, uncomprehending, but curious to see how this was going to turn out. The science or the mathematics were not what was at stake here. Something much more ancient was happening, the challenge of the young to the old, the child to the parent. Gwidion was growing up.

The mentor felt his own primordial anger rise in his breast. He bluffed. He pulled rank. He used his age and his verbal sophistication to gain an advantage. He told Gwidion to concentrate on the assignment and not to get sidetracked. He suggested, not without a cutting sarcasm, that they would have a private lesson in logic at a later date. It was a fundamental mistake for a teacher and in the quiet of his dugg that evening he regretted it. He could not in all conscience as mentor argue that any material in study was purely a linguistic exercise and that the science could be left for another time. To translate, the material had to be understood. And once understood it was open to challenge.

As Gwidion's grasp of technical matters and his facility for mathematical acrobatics began to outstrip his own, his only option was to sidestep the conflicts. He encouraged Gwidion to formulate and develop his ideas and passed the results on to the Academy in Madrid. And it wasn't long before the Academy had started to take a serious interest in the boy. Now he hoped that Gwidion's mother could be persuaded to let her son go to the capital to carry on his studies. There were many things he could still offer his pupil as mentor, but he had learned enough to know that he could not fulfill all the needs of the boy's intellectual growth. Such a huge talent in such a small world should not be allowed to go to waste.

But it wasn't going to be easy. There was the question of Cai, for one. And there was an even bigger question from the community's point of view. He looked around the ports. Daisy, Lauren, Amy,

Bethan, Rosa, Angelica, Rhiannon, Boa, Julia, Megan... Girls, nothing but girls.

The community's need for young males was important, but the mentor's memory was long. Fatherhood was a taboo subject, but he remembered well enough the colonel's night on a cordyline mattress all those years ago. Who would not in such a small community? Jiménez was not a colonel then of course, but even so he bore the marks of one destined for success.

The mentor could not argue against such great considerations. He too had served his time in the capital, he knew its workings and he had been lucky, or cunning, enough to survive the harsh politics of a crumbling Republic and get himself sent home.

The price of his sinecure could occasionally be high indeed, the uncomfortable and balancing act of being a friend both to the village and Madrid, and in the process giving up all hopes of finding real friendship.

Gwidion was, as usual, last to leave his port when study ended. As he emerged from the roundhouse into the surprising afternoon sunshine and the sudden heat of a summer's day, he saw Lauren loitering a little apart from the group of girls. She was no more than a few months his senior, but she seemed to Gwidion to be much older. It was partly the way young girls hung around together in tight groups talking easily among themselves and partly the way they giggled when he spoke to them. His mother said that was just the way of girls, that their giggles hid their own nervousness and that it didn't mean they didn't like him. On the contrary. But when faced with having to talk to one of them, especially Lauren, that was difficult to believe. What drove him on this time was his new-found emotion of adolescent love. He remembered what Cai had said, how he had jeered at him. And he remembered Cai's threat. The choice of boys was not exactly plentiful; a girl might be expected to plump for what she could get. He couldn't allow that to happen.

When he was within a metre or two of her he spoke. 'Are you going home?'

Lauren looked towards the other girls who were now some distance away, glancing back towards the pair, curious to see the development of this romance. They chattered and laughed and their hands flew back and forth from hair to faces to mouths, touching themselves, making contact with each other. He envied them their easy pantomime of communication and their apparent freedom from the awkwardness he felt as he stood stiffly before Lauren, his heart beating, his hands unable to find a place to hide.

In answer to his question she looked directly back at him. She wore the same plain smock as the others, clasped around her waist by a cloth belt. It made the upper part of her dress bulge slightly, but as they touched briefly in a formal greeting he noticed that the surplus material was no longer totally empty. There was flesh beneath it, not much perhaps, but enough to suggest that some shape was developing inside the rough fabric. She smoothed the sides of her dress, pulling the skirt tighter below her belt and breathing in as she did so, heightening the effect Gwidion was so fascinated by. Her light curly hair was held back from her face by a silver hairband. It was unusually beautiful, a filigree of fine metalwork.

'I like your headband.'

She smiled. 'My mother made it for me. For my passage.' She blushed and looked down at her bare feet for a minute or two, then back at Gwidion. It was a moment of closeness, a personal revelation shared. It told him she was moving into womanhood, it told him that she wanted him to know it. She pulled the band off with a single movement, tossing her head so that her hair bounced lightly on her shoulders, and handed it to him.

'Look, Ce'nder Gwidion. This is my father's bond, the hawthorn,' she said pointing to one of three strands which made up the main body of the knotwork.

'The sixth tree,' said Gwidion, gravely.

Lauren nodded. 'It is unlucky. It is my father's bond.'

Unlucky perhaps, thought Gwidion, but the scent of may blossom was also the scent of female sexuality – at one and the same time the tree of enforced chastity, and the tree of orgiastic sex.

'And here,' said Lauren pointing at the second strand. 'My mother's bond, the rowan, the tree of life.'

'And yours?' Gwidion asked, although his quick eye had already recognised Lauren's bond as the bramble. But in poring together over this beautiful ornament the pair had forgotten their shynesses and Gwidion's hands had found something to do in caressing the delicate interweaving of the smooth silver braids, so close to her own fingers. He had no wish to break the spell or cause her to move away from him.

'The blackberry. Joy, exhilaration and wrath.' She laughed lightly for one who bore so much in her bonds. Perhaps she took it playfully, as many took zodiacal signs. Perhaps she was too young to feel the full weight of its significance. Perhaps in the face of such portents, her only option was to laugh lightly.

Gwidion turned the hairband over and over in his hands as if searching for something he had missed. 'Ce'nder Arianrhod is a flawless silversmith,' he said finally.

It was true, Lauren's mother was the finest craftsworker in the village in any material. She worked with magnifiers, hot irons and tiny, tiny tools which were fascinating to touch. Some were so small that you could not even tell what they were with the naked eye. Sometimes she even used microscopes.

'I remember once she came to study, when one of the ports broke,' he added, returning the ornament to Lauren. As she took it from him and put it back in her hair, the spell of those close moments was weakened. Gwidion wanted it to last for longer. There was no alternative but to talk.

'She came with her tools strapped around her in a belt and opened up the port there in front of us, do you remember?'

'The belt belonged to her mother too when she was technician.'

What was revealed inside the port was not unlike Lauren's hairband, a tiny network of silver, gold and black, a thing of intricate magic. But not merely in two dimensions this time. The port was built layer on microscopic layer, filaments too thin to see with the naked eye weaving forwards and backwards, up and down.

'But she had to take it away to complete the repair after all because she couldn't do it in the roundhouse,' said Gwidion. Lauren nodded and smiled.

And Lauren had been allowed to go with her, for one day it would be her role also to repair the village's ageing technology. Her eyes were strong and, like the other girls, her fingers were nimble and sensitive. Just one more thing that divided Gwidion from his studymates and made him feel clumsy and stupid in their presence.

'One day perhaps I will be the repairer like my mother. I would love that. Perhaps I will make you a wrist clasp as practice,' she added shyly, and for the first time in ten minutes she looked away to see what had happened to the other girls, although they had long gone, to see if this conversation was being noticed, to see if she should go too.

'No, stay Ce'nder Lauren,' said Gwidion, answering her unspoken question. 'Come with me. Come to the Ruins.'

'I can't. I am not to,' she answered, unsure.

'Then come and see where the sky touches the earth.'

'It is a long way.'

'Not so far, a couple of kilometres.'

Lauren hesitated, looking around again.

'You won't be too late home.'

Again she hesitated. Gwidion urged her.

'I promise.' He took her hand.

Her next words fell like four cold stones into the pool of Gwidion's emotions, breaking the surface, sinking towards his heart, sending the ripples outwards, outwards, waking up his every insecurity, undermining the trust that had been so painstakingly constructed over the last few minutes, tying his tongue again.

'Will Cai be there?'

And suddenly she was frightened. She pulled her hand away.

'No, I can't, my mother... I'm sorry. It's too far.'

And she was gone.

Outwardly Lauren's dugg was almost indistinguishable from Gwidion's. Her mother looked up from the broken port she was working on and smiled briefly as her daughter entered.

'I've nearly finished,' she said.

Rather than going to her sleeping area, Lauren picked a strawberry from a bowl lying on her mother's work-table. She waited. Her mother looked up from her work again.

'Come and give me a cuddle, then,' she said. Lauren put the

whole strawberry in her mouth, then gave her mother a kiss full on the lips, sharing the red sweet juice with her like a pair of lovers. They both laughed. A bright red stain spread over the logic array she was mending.

'Oh damn. That's not going to help. I have enough trouble repairing some of these parts as it is.'

Lauren moved away. 'Sorry.'

But her mother's annoyance wasn't directed at her. 'That's OK.' She put down her work and placed another strawberry in her mouth. 'You're early. Didn't you go to play with the other girls today?'

Lauren shook her head. Her mother gave her a questioning look.

'I was talking to Ce'nder Gwidion after study. The others went off.' She took another strawberry from the bowl and climbed up to sit on her mother's knee. There was a silence while her mother studied her face and Lauren appeared to concentrate on eating her strawberry.

'It's nice of you to talk to him. He must feel a bit lonely sometimes with so many girls around. At his age he needs company.'

'He's very strange,' said Lauren.

'Ce'nder Gwidion is a very bright boy.' She waited. 'Do you like him?'

'He asked me to go to the Ruins.'

'What did you say?'

'I said I couldn't.'

'Did you want to go?'

'I don't know. He asked me to go and see where the sky touches the earth. What does he mean?' She paused. 'I was frightened. Cai frightens me.'

'You should not let your fear stop you. You will come to no harm. When you were both younger you played together a lot. I can remember when the pair of you tried to go swimming in the hydroponics bay and you got a mouthful of nutrients and came home saying you were turning into a banana.'

Lauren squirmed with embarrassment. 'I never did.'

'You did.' She tightened her grip on her daughter to stop her climbing down. 'And I remember the time when you had chicken pox.'

'He's very serious,' Lauren cut in.

'Ce'nder Gwidion is unique among us. One day he could be a

leader of our village, he will certainly be very important to our future.'

She shot her mother a nervous glance and then ventured again. 'And then there's Cai.'

Her mother stroked her head gently. 'You are still very young, there are still many things you cannot understand. Ce'nder Gwidion is different, but he's not dangerous. Try to accept him as he is, in time you may come to understand him, or you may not. Be with him, spend time with him. I am sure he likes you a lot.'

She brushed Lauren's hair back from her face with her hand and said lightly. 'And who wouldn't. Look at you. Look at how pretty you are. You are going through your passage, Lauren. Many things are changing within your body and it is not always easy to know what is right and what is wrong. But if it feels right, then it probably is. And if it isn't, then you will have learned something useful.'

Lauren jumped off her mother's knee. 'He admired my hairband. I said I might make him a clasp. Will you show me?'

Her mother pushed the broken strawberry-stained port away.

'Come and sit here, I will show you. If you're a fast learner perhaps you will get this port mended for me anyway.'

chapter five

People will tell you all sorts of fantastic stories about twins. The incredible coincidences that litter their lives. Twins who have been separated for years, living on opposite sides of the world who dream of events in each other's lives. Or who wake in the middle of the night, sharing the same thought about some family matter or some crazy idea. Or the twin who shares the pain of some tragedy which has happened to the other one, countries or continents apart.

Cai could relate many more fascinating things about twins. They were such a rare phenomenon that the birth of twins to a community like theirs would be a cause for unusual celebration.

'The chances of having a one-egg twin are about the same wherever you are,' Cai had pronounced importantly once, cocking his head as if challenging Gwidion to contradict him.

'Two egg twins used to be more common in Belgium, but rare in Japan. Triplets are about eighty-six times as rare as twins. And quadruplets are about eighty-six times as rare as triplets.'

He reeled off the statistics with pride.

'If the frequency of twins to singles is one to eighty-six, then that of triplets is one to eighty-six squared, and quadruplets one to eighty-six cubed.'

Fascinating, the mathematics of multiple births, but potentially lethal.

'Twins are five times more likely to die in infancy than single children. More than half are born prematurely and are therefore more likely to be injured at birth. The chances of us being born at all are virtually nil.' Cai ended his lecture with a strange note of triumph in his voice.

But as for the strange telepathic connections which are reputed to exist between twins, Gwidion could recall nothing in his own life that might be cited as an example of a single personality in two bodies. On the contrary. Except for one occasion, in fact – when it mattered most, when it was a matter of life or death.

'Let's play blind man's buff,' said Cai. He and Gwidion were loitering along the walls of the Ruins again. It was their ninth birthday. 'Do you remember that fairy story Mam used to read us when we were little, Gwidion? The one about the blind harper?'

'That was no fairytale,' said Gwidion.

'What's it like to be blind?' continued Cai, ignoring him. 'I wonder what it's like to be disabled, missing a sense?' This wasn't cruelty. This was merely Cai – thinking the unthinkable, trying to know the unknowable.

'I've got an idea. Let's close our eyes and walk along the wall as long as we can, trying to be blind. And you've got to stick to it right? No cheating. No, I know, we'll tie something over our eyes and do it. Then you can't cheat.'

They were near the highest point of the Ruins. Below them, ten metres away was a rectangular patch of grass. Cai pulled the cloth belt from around his waist and wrapped it over Gwidion's eyes, pulling it tight behind his head and tying a knot.

'Can you see anything?'

'Nothing.'

'You go first.'

'Feel the wind,' he said as Gwidion walked nervously forward. 'Let your other senses take over. Listen to the space around you. Smell it, taste it.'

And it was true, Gwidion's other senses seemed to sharpen as the adrenaline rushed through his body. He held his arms out to balance himself. Below, on the grass, unknown to him, he cast a huge shadow, like a bird soaring in the air. Gwidion explored the void. He could feel the difference between the wall and space under his fingers. It was tangible – something about the difference in air pressure, he supposed, something barely perceptible, and yet in a strange way perceptible. He put one foot gingerly in front of the other as he began to pluck up the courage to inch his way along the wall.

A sudden chill went through him as his foot stepped on a slightly loose piece of rubble and he lost confidence. His hands went automatically to his blindfold, but then he steadied himself and was calm again. Cai was there, Cai wouldn't let him fall.

'You'll tell me if I'm going to slip?' said Gwidion.

Cai laughed. 'You won't slip. You can fly with your arms out like that.'

Gwidion hesitated. 'Go on, go on,' urged Cai. 'I was only joking.' Gwidion took another step. His foot felt nothingness. Perhaps it was the ledge, perhaps the wall was just a little bit lower here. He breathed deeply to steady himself, practising the meditation techniques he had been taught in study. Feel the wind, listen to the space. Smell it, taste it.

Then: 'No, Gwidion, stop, stop'.

He pulled the blindfold off his face and opened his eyes. What he saw shocked him so much he froze on the spot. He was staring directly down to the ground, his foot dangled in mid-air, his shadow filled the green rectangle far below him. A few more centimetres... No, not even that, merely enough shift in his weight so that he had been going forward, forward and downwards. He took a sharp breath and pulled his foot back onto the safety of the wall, his heart pounding, a sweat of stark terror breaking out on his forehead as he realised how close he had been to plunging to the grass below.

He looked over to Cai who was also frozen to the spot. For once his customary composure and arrogance had disappeared. He stared at Gwidion in disbelief.

Finally: 'Gwidion, are you all right?'

'Thank goodness you stopped me,' Gwidion panted. 'Thank goodness you saw me and shouted.'

Cai looked at Gwidion for a moment. His normally mischievous, ambiguous face had never been so serious.

'Gwid, I never saw you. I never said a word.'

chapter six

It was Friday, the first day of the weekend, and every Friday meant a communal meal in the roundhouse followed by two days when the village lived as one family. Many people would sleep in the roundhouse rather than in their own duggs, unless perhaps they were young lovers seeking a little private time. It was not frowned upon, but it was not encouraged either. It was often the way of adolescents experiencing their first sexual and romantic awakenings, but it was not the custom of the village. Sex might be private, romance was not. This summer solstice gathering was one of the most important of the year when only the most essential tasks were carried out. Midsummer was the traditional opportunity for all sorts of liaisons to be forged, and couplings, sexual or otherwise, to be made. If Gwidion was to declare his love for Lauren, he knew there was no more opportune moment.

He had not been to the Ruins today, but instead had wandered through the village from dugg to dugg. Most domers had already gone to the roundhouse – either to help with the preparations or to begin soaking up the atmosphere. It was the part Gwidion enjoyed best. He liked to look on as the women laughed and chattered and chided as they prepared the special dishes, and they in turn enjoyed the chance to talk with the few men of the village. The rarity of the occasion and their own scarcity meant the men could almost get away with doing nothing but sitting around, sucking gently on datura pipes and throwing jibes and comments back and forth with the women. But most of them enjoyed taking part in the preparations and busy-ness as much as anyone else. There were fires to be fed, vegetables and meat to be chopped. There was even music to be played if they were able, or a dance to be danced.

The sun was in the west, a good hour or more before it would begin to get dark, and Gwidion's bare feet could still feel the warmth of the day in the dusty paths between the duggs. The hot air, lifeless for so much of the afternoon, had begun to move with the coming of evening. Chickens scratched here and there in the red dirt, hollowing out a shallow bowl where they could sit. Pigs ruffled the earth occasionally, but preferred to take things lying down at this time of day. The irrigation channels which ran this way and that, scarring the ground with a maze of ruts, were silent and dry. The duggs had no doors, but many domers were accustomed to hang a piece of gaily striped cloth in front of the entrance, partly to deter animals from wandering in, although that was more or less a lost cause, and partly to prevent dust being kicked up. It gave the simple bare structures a sudden and incongruous note of joviality, like a collection of circus tents.

The village was arranged in a series of concentric circles with the roundhouse at its heart. The living duggs formed the next two circles while the working duggs were around the outer edge. Beyond those lay the fields of crops, and here, at the north-western edge where the ground began to rise and where a series of natural springs bubbled to the surface, were the hydroponics bays. They took up a relatively small area but were by far the most important part of the villagers' food production. Avocados, salad crops, bananas could all be grown here almost the whole year round. This was another of Gwidion's favourite haunts and it was his habit not to join these social occasions too early, but today he was unusually keen to get back to the roundhouse. Girls of his age had their passage. Tonight Gwidion would take his own first steps to manhood as master of the solstice fire. He dawdled a little, teasing himself with the expectation and excitement. He considered going the long way round to see the windmill farm outside the village but settled for a diversion on enticing a pig away from one of the duggs and soon found himself at the entrance to the roundhouse.

The sound of the party was already audible from some distance away. He caught high-pitched laughter above the sound of a violin. That would be the mentor. It was one of those sweet tunes he loved so much, waltz-time, minor key. Later on, once he had had enough mead, and if Tabitha would let him get away with it, he would probably start singing.

The front of the roundhouse had been opened up to accommodate the tables where the food was to be prepared. Gwidion stepped in and pushed through the tangible wall of body temperature which was mixed with the smells of herbs and cooking. Tabitha, a large woman who tended livestock, was in the centre of the six large tables, a huge goose laid out in front of her. Its feathers were more or less plucked and lay in chaos around her and over her, clinging to her smock and the fine hairs on her plump red arms. Her face was even more flushed than usual and she blew now and again out of the corners of her mouth at strands of hair which had escaped from the bun on top of her head and lay across her cheeks.

'Speed it up,' she cried at the mentor who was still lovingly drawing gentle melodies from his instrument. 'If you want this goose cooked tonight, you'll have to play quicker than that.'

The other women laughed and the mentor stopped completely. Gwidion saw his mother at one of the tables chopping vegetables deftly, her face lit up with amusement.

'Don't stop, man. Put some elbow in it,' Tabitha shrieked with laughter. The mentor looked mildly put out but continued his slow airs regardless. Tabitha returned to her bird with renewed vigour, pulling it about the table like a terrier with a dead rat. All the while she maintained a largely one-way conversation with her helpers.

'Carrots,' she muttered. 'Have we got enough carrots? I thought we would have sweetcorn but Ce'nder Lloyd tells me they are not ready.'

Gwidion's mother called out as she scraped at the potatoes. 'There's plenty of carrots, Ce'nder Tabitha. Don't you worry about the carrots. The goose is what needs doing.'

'That'll be the shortage of water,' said Tabitha as if she had not heard. 'Midsummer and no sweetcorn. I can't remember the last time that happened.'

'Last year,' said Michaela, a small timid woman who was attempting to help Tabitha pluck the goose but found herself constantly elbowed away by the big woman's wild movements. The other women laughed.

'Yes,' said Tabitha thoughtfully. 'Last year. Oh well. Where are those rye cakes, are they ready yet?' And she attacked her bird again as if punishing it for the lack of vegetables.

The fire for the meal was to be prepared outside, it would otherwise make the roundhouse unbearably hot. In fact it already was. Sixty-plus people working, talking and laughing together generated a lot of heat.

No-one overtly noticed Gwidion's arrival or greeted him. They did not need to. The communal warmth and good humour drew him in like a pair of open arms. His mother looked up and smiled at him. A group of children was playing slightly apart from the main cooking activities, but others were helping too. Lauren was near his mother who was preparing vegetables.

He hesitated while he watched Lauren's small delicate fingers moving swiftly to pull the shells off hard-boiled eggs. His mother made it easier for him.

'Come and help us, Gwidion. There's always room for more hands.'

He joined them at the table, squeezing in next to Lauren. They smiled shyly at each other. Gwidion reached for his mother's mug of mead and took a draught, then offered it to Lauren. She shook the hair back from her face and wiped her hands on her apron, taking the mug in both hands before emptying it. The work on the tables slowed as others became aware of this little cameo. Tabitha pulled the goose aloft by its legs and slapped it down again, sending a cloud of down into the air.

'Some midsummer's night this will be with the children at the mead,' she said loudly. Then to the mentor, 'is this what you teach them all day in study?'

Her words released new peals of laughter from the tables. They had heard it all before, of course, many times. But they enjoyed this traditional party piece – as ancient and traditional as any morality play or myth-telling – all the more because they also knew the evening would end with the mentor and Tabitha wrapped in each other's arms, as unlikely a pairing as you could imagine, even in a village where lovers were obliged to take what they could get as often as what they might choose. If they could stay off the mead. The mentor, meanwhile, ignored the badinage and played on.

'And didn't I tell you to put some effort into it? How do you think we are going to get this goose cooked tonight to three-four time?'

The mentor finally stopped playing, took a drink of mead and stood up.

'And if you do get it cooked tonight, Ce'nder Tabitha, it will be the first time I can remember since I was a boy,' he replied. 'Unless you think we're going to eat it with its feathers still on.'

Tabitha had already left her post and was standing opposite him, her fat arms on her fat hips. 'The only reason you can't remember it is because you've usually passed out with too much mead by the time anything gets to the table,' she shrieked.

The mentor was a tall man but he seemed to shrink in front of this Amazon of a woman. She grabbed the fiddle from his hand.

'If you think you can do any better, carry on. Because I'm very sure I can punch out a tune better than you.'

With that she cradled the violin in the crook of her arm and began scraping out a fast reel. It was rough at first and the beat faltered, but as the efforts of plucking the goose fell from her muscles, the tune settled down. The mentor shrugged with a reluctant smile and made his way towards the bird, rolling up his sleeves as he went.

The work on the tables picked up again as the music rolled along. Gwidion and Lauren laughed at each other and set to their eggs. The tune Tabitha played was simple, yet it wove its way insidiously into the brain, its unusual phrasing drawing the workers along with it. As she warmed up she hit other open strings with her bow, allowing them to resonate like drones and pushing the tune into new territories. Its lines became tangled and confused in Gwidion's mind, moving it into three dimensions. It reminded him of the complex twists and turns of Lauren's hairband, and even more of the arcane maze of the logic arrays he had seen inside the ports.

Gwidion's thoughts were interrupted by the arrival of Rhisiart, a small, dark, silent man in his thirties. His squat frame and broad shoulders were skilfully balancing the summer birch pole which he had felled and brought from the Outlands after his work at the solar accelerator banks. There was a cheer as he heaved the slender ten-metre trunk onto the ground in front of the roundhouse.

'The ribbons,' he shouted with a broad smile and an obvious sense of pride. This had been his role for as long as Gwidion could remember, although it was said that once nine men of the village would be despatched to cut the *bedwen haf* in the woods surrounding the dome. Gwidion looked around – the mentor, Lame William, Lloyd, Giant Paddy... one man to do the work of nine, that was the way of things.

A number of girls ran to the birch and attached a wreath of flowers with long coloured strips of cloth to the top. The wreath was mounted on a silver cap which bore the unmistakable hallmarks of Lauren's mother's handiwork, and allowed the wreath and its ribbons to turn freely. Gwidion joined some women in preparing to lift the pole into place.

'Lift,' ordered Rhisiart. 'And walk towards me.' The socket had already been dug and while Rhisiart kept the bottom end steady and guided it into the hole, the others walked the birch into the air from the far end. After only a few steps the pole had risen out of Gwidion's reach and he rushed to help Rhisiart wedge the pole into place with chocks he had neatly prepared during his daily wood-cutting duties.

'*Bedwen haf,*' said Rhisiart under his breath as he stood back to admire their handiwork. Then out loud and looking meaningfully towards Gwidion, 'The fire'.

This was indeed Gwidion's moment. A circle of about two metres had been cut in the ground outside the roundhouse and scraped out to a depth of some ten centimetres. Around it Gwidion arranged small piles of kindling that he had gathered from the hedges – oak, holly, beech, birch, ash, rowan, hazel, gorse and bracken. Each stick of kindling was cut to the same size and he laid out the nine separate piles in three layers, each layer crosswise to the one below it, like a three-dimensional noughts and crosses game.

The ritual took some time, and as the villagers watched their talking and chattering subsided, for this was also Gwidion's first fire-making and what they were watching was much more than merely a boy lighting a bonfire. His hands trembled as he took two sticks from the oak pile and knelt next to the bracken. He steadied one branch against his thigh and began to run the other back and forth on top of it. His brow furrowed in concentration and he felt the stick on his leg digging into his flesh as he worked. The food preparation had slowed to a halt and the music had stopped. It seemed as if the whole village held its breath for fear of blowing out the fire. Still Gwidion rubbed, his small hand no more than a flash of pale skin on his thigh. After what seemed like an age he felt the oak begin to warm and light whiffs of smoke brought the smell of fire to his nostrils. His arms and legs ached with the effort, his sweaty palms slipped on the tinder twigs and he thought he could carry on no longer, but the eyes of the villagers willed him on. He managed to look up without interrupting his rhythm and saw his mother at the table. She had stopped her work, but her hands gripped each other tightly in front of her as if they too might begin rubbing themselves together at any moment, her forehead puckered in concentration. Lauren watched too.

He sensed Rhisiart at his shoulder and his light breath blowing on the sticks.

'Good,' he breathed as he blew. 'Good, good.'

The smoke grew thicker and Gwidion brought the sticks close to the bracken. Just at the point when his muscles screamed at him that he could do it no more, magically there was a yellow flame. And at the same moment it seemed the whole village breathed out, fanning the fire into the bracken. The music began again, there were shouts and laughter and suddenly people were running here and there, bringing wood to the fire. Gwidion knelt back and wiped the sweat from his face. He felt Rhisiart's hand on his shoulder and his back relaxed.

By the time darkness fell, the scene was of a party in full swing. People left the tables to pick up drums or flutes or to take hold of a ribbon from the summer birch and dance around it, weaving their way between the other dancers. Rhisiart was squatting on a small stool wrestling with a set of bagpipes made from a goat bladder. He fought and struggled with them, and they repaid him with an uncanny eerie sound, as if the spirit of the goat were still alive. The mentor had long left his goose and was accompanying Tabitha on a second violin. The villagers picked at the raw vegetables and the fruit and the cakes that had been prepared in advance. And if they still felt hungry, they drowned the pangs with mead. The mentor was right. The goose would not be cooked that night.

Gwidion and Lauren walked out into the warm evening air. Behind them the sounds of the party faded slowly, lingering in the mind like an intoxicant. They walked in silence, holding hands, breathing in the enjoyment of each other's company and the relief of being alone. They took the path towards the Ruins until they came to the menhir. They stood either side of it and stretched so that they joined hands around it, their bodies pressed hard against the cool surface, both shocking and welcome after the heat of the day, their faces turned upwards to the purple-blue sky where the first stars were now appearing.

There was a sudden noise behind them as a group of people came out of the roundhouse and the party began to spill from its confines. The dancers left the birch pole and joined hands as they snaked in and out of the roundhouse, around the tables and between the musicians, who complained good-naturedly when their arms were jostled as they played.

'You should see the sunset from the Ruins,' said Gwidion. Her answer took him by surprise.

'Come on, then,' said Lauren, releasing one hand and leading him by the other. There was not room for them side by side on the path, so Lauren went slightly ahead, looking back and giving him a tug.

'Too much mead,' she shouted. 'Come on.'

They broke into a trot, unsteady at first, but faster as the evening air in their lungs, moistened here by the rich vegetation, dispelled the light-headedness of the party they had left. They jogged together a little more than two kilometres before they left the maize fields on either side and came out into open pasture. The Ruins were clearly visible on a small knoll some four hundred metres ahead. Now they ran side by side, able to sprint the final section. At the foot of the

Ruins they fell to the grass, rolling onto their backs and looking at the remains of the sunset in the north-west.

Gwidion propped himself up on his elbows. 'What a sight.' It was true, the sunset was fabulous from this angle. The sky was graded from pink to orange in long horizontal strips. One or two stray clouds provided a reflective background which added points of luminescent brightness to the scene. And from this low angle the biodome itself added its own effect. Mostly the geodesic dome faded into the background, the eye became accustomed to looking through the clear ocuspex structure and the filaments of high-tensile alloy which supported it, rather than at it. It began not far from the Ruins themselves and encircled and protected the place they called home – the pasture, the fields, the duggs. Everything.

To all intents and purposes it was invisible in daytime, but from some angles and in some light conditions it had another property. Now as the final edge of the sun's disc flattened itself at the horizon, it cast spectacular rainbows of light in unusual hues of orange and purple around the dome. It was a sight almost as awesome as the aurora borealis, but it also reminded the domers of where and how they lived. It would remind anyone with a knowledge of history of an awful lot of things. A lot of awful things. Perhaps that was why the Ruins were out of bounds. Not for their dilapidated state but for the memories they still housed.

'Does anyone live outside the dome?' asked Lauren. 'My mother says there are some.'

She lay back and he leaned over her. She felt his warm, mead-scented breath on her face for the briefest of moments, then tasted it on her lips. His body weight relaxed onto her, their hips joined bone to bone. The moment was sweet and thoughtless and without fear. And then it passed.

'We ought to go back,' she murmured without making any attempt to get up.

Gwidion wanted to say so many things, but he didn't know how to begin. In the end it was she who spoke first.

'I heard that a colonel from the Academy came to visit you when you missed study yesterday.' She turned her face to him and drew her ankles towards her, raising her knees so that her smock fell back onto her thighs. 'Are you going to Madrid?'

Gwidion shook his head. 'I don't know. He said he would come again.'

'Do you want to go?'

'I would like to go there. My father is there.'

Lauren sat up and examined his face closely. She wrapped her arms around her knees and said nothing.

'He does something important there, we are not allowed to know.'

'How do you know this? Most of us are not allowed to know our fathers,' she said cautiously.

Gwidion shrugged. 'Do you know yours? Is he here in the village?' he asked.

'Ce'nder Gwidion,' she was visibly embarrassed. 'These are questions we do not ask. You know that?' It was a question as much as a statement. Gwidion didn't look at her, but talked rapidly.

'My father came from this village, but he was not happy with this way of life. He wanted to travel. He does very important work.'

She thought fast. She wanted to be honest with him, but it was better that it was not she who told him. After all there were differences in the way girls and boys were treated in matters of family and of passage – and she had no brother from whom she might have got an idea how the secrets of male adolescence were divulged. This was the contradiction which lay at the heart of life in the village – that so much was unspoken, and yet known by all. Almost all, she corrected herself. She decided on a different tack, and one which was also not dishonest.

'I am not happy with this way of life, Ce'nder Gwidion,' she said. 'But I do not want to leave it either.'

'What do you mean?'

'If you didn't miss so many history studies, you would know as well as I,' she laughed. 'It was not always like this. We didn't always lived trapped inside a biodome. In the time of the menhir the world was a big place, it was a place of adventure and hope and many different peoples.'

'And how would you change it?'

'I don't know. That is why I study history. That is what I want to find out.'

'The history we study is not history at all. It will never tell us what you want to know.'

She lay back again. 'What if there are people in the Outlands? What do they do, how do they live?'

Gwidion struggled with the idea. 'It's hard to imagine.'

'They could hunt, they could fish. They could trade.'

She sat up suddenly looking south of the Ruins.

'A few kilometres out there is the sea, Ce'nder Gwidion. Can you imagine what it is like to see the sea? The waves that crash on the shore out there come all the way from America. Imagine that.'

Gwidion could imagine that. He thought he could imagine America as Lame William told him it once must have been, with its countless buildings of countless storeys.

'The mentor says the dome protects us, but from what?' asked Lauren.

'From ourselves, he says.'

'And what is that supposed to mean? Only that we have lost our self-confidence.'

'And you think we can find it again?'

Lauren looked at him with the eyes of a technician, a repairer.

'Yes,' she said.

The sun had finally disappeared and the light display faded, making the night seem even darker by contrast. In the distance another spectacle drew their eyes towards the roundhouse where the fire burned flameless and dark red and they could see dark shapes continuing their unsteady dancing around it. The musicians had moved outside as well and there were shouts of laughter and fright as some of the children jumped over the fire for dares. They began to return slowly, hand in hand, but before they descended to the path back to the village, Lauren spotted Giant Paddy leading a cow. His arrival was accompanied by the loudest shouts of all.

'Come on, let's jump the fire too. I'll race you,' said Lauren, already five metres ahead of Gwidion and sprinting.

When they arrived breathless at the fire Paddy was standing with his cow, a rope around its neck, whispering in its ear.

'She won't do it,' he shouted to the others who were cheering him on as he tottered slightly from too much mead and too little food.

'Well, it's no use talking to her, Ce'nder Paddy,' shouted someone. 'Give her a kick up the arse.'

There were renewed shouts of laughter and a group of four or five children rushed behind the animal and began to push. The poor beast didn't budge but stamped her feet and turned her head from the fire and attempted to lick Paddy's ear.

'Come on, Giant Paddy. She loves you, look.'

There was a loud thwack as Lame William crept up behind and hit the cow's rump with a switch. She started and gave a moo and was over the fire before Paddy knew what was happening, dragging him by the rope he still held and throwing him sideways. Once free his animal continued on through the village and out of sight.

'Hot milk for the morning,' said Paddy as he got up and brushed a few burning embers from his smock.

'If you can catch her,' laughed William.

'I'll catch her if you jump the fire, Lame William,' cried Paddy.

There were loud laughs again, along with a few worried murmurs of dissent from the more sober elements in the crowd. But the challenge had been made and the solstice was not a time for turning down challenges. William turned like a bowler about to take his run-up and limped a few paces back, rubbing his thigh as if to remind the crowd of the nature of the feat they were about to witness. Then he turned and ran with a strange lolloping gait, swinging his bad leg in a small arc with each step. The fire was low now and despite his disability he moved surprisingly fast. He cleared the fire in a single ungainly jump-cum-stride, landing in a heap on the floor and rolling away to safety. Two women rushed to help him from the floor, but he brushed them aside as he stood up.

'I'm all right, I'm all right.' Then turning to Paddy. 'And I didn't need a cow to get me over.'

As the fire died down and fewer and fewer of the villagers could be bothered to get up and feed it with wood, the party acquired a more mellow feeling. The musicians were still playing and – sure enough – the mentor was now sitting cross-legged before the fire, singing sad laments in his thin high-pitched voice. Tabitha, her hair now almost totally freed from its bun and cascading around her face, lay on the ground, her head resting tenderly against his thigh. Others sat around the fire, their faces reddened by the flames, their features cast in shadow so it was sometimes difficult to know who was who. Some had spilled out around the immediate vicinity of the roundhouse and stood talking in groups. Yet others had moved into the shadows in secret clinches, although real secrets were very few in such a small community. It was the custom to sleep in the roundhouse on occasions like tonight and some had already made their beds around the outer edge and lay either already asleep or dozing fitfully to the sounds of the party.

The goose still lay grotesquely shorn and uncooked on the table where Tabitha and the mentor had abandoned it. Lauren and Gwidion found themselves two blankets and a space at the outer edge of the roundhouse and lay down. Pangs of hunger were beginning to surface after a night which had promised so much and delivered so little, but they would have to wait until the morning. Hunger of a different sort also coursed through the veins of the two youngsters – and those pangs helped blunt the edge of their appetite for food. They lay close to each other, listening to the sounds of people around them against the background of the mentor's singing – coughs, snoring, rustlings and fumblings.

And later into the night as they both still lay awake, there were the muted sounds of pleasure, the temporary couplings of people who shared this moment of celebration in whatever way they thought appropriate. The two young lovers had felt the vicarious thrill of those moments in previous years, had learned about love-making and love in such circumstances as these, but never with such keenness as they experienced them tonight. And never with such poignancy. For these were feelings neither of them was ready to realise yet. Not yet. At least not tonight.

chapter seven

It was Saturday, it was midsummer's eve and that meant no study, but it didn't mean that the chickens could go unfed or that the logs did not have to be chopped for the fire. Not that Gwidion minded. He had taken on those two chores at the age of seven, as soon as he could be trusted to wield a sharp tool without hurting himself, and his daily task was now a source of pride. Rhisiart had taught him the skill of preparing wood, as he had taught him the ritual for the solstice fire, but it was the mentor who had developed his mental attitude to the job, encouraging him to look on it as another form of their regular meditation.

Meditation was the start of every day in study and of every activity which required mental and physical co-ordination, which covered just about everything.

'Meditation is life and life is meditation,' the mentor had told him once when he was instructing him in the techniques of relaxation and focus. 'Imagine the most restful place you can, a place with water and sunshine, a place where you can be happy. Focus on the breath and picture yourself taking a single step towards this place. Think only of your breath and not of where you are going. When you are happy with your new position, take another step towards your destination. Be aware of it, but do not think ahead to it. At each step, focus only on your breath.'

'What is this place supposed to be like?' Gwidion had asked.

'That is for you to decide. It is yours alone and it will be with you for as long as you are happy there. Only it must be a beautiful place, a place of calmness.'

The image which came into his mind seemed strange and unrelated to anything he was familiar with. There was a beach, there was sunshine, and there was a figure. A cloaked figure in a brilliant white arched doorway. The rays of a setting sun illuminated the scene and the figure began to ascend a series of steps. One by one, slowly, stepping up with one foot, bringing the other to join it. Until there was only the darkness of the arched doorway. Gwidion wanted to tell the mentor what he saw.

'Do not tell me. This is your private place.'

'I don't know if it's right,' he complained.

'Are you happy there?' asked the mentor. Gwidion nodded. 'It is yours. It is right.'

And there was something else, something he would not have dared tell the mentor. Words. A single sentence which seemed to come unspoken from the figure. 'In paradise I will drink orange and lime.' Gwidion gave an involuntary shudder as he picked a log from the stack lining the outside of the dugg, which allowed them to dry and, in the process, provided insulation for the homes. Although the managed hedgerows themselves produced fuel for the energy units sited just outside the dome, domestic logs had to be brought from the Outlands.

Cutting logs, he had learned from a very young age, was not about strength or power, it was about technique. He stood the log upright on its end and placed the conical splitter at the centre, then took hold of the sledge-hammer. He half-squatted, and swung the sledge. When it reached the highest point of its arc, he relaxed, allowing it to fall on the splitter under its own weight while keeping his back straight. The splitter dug into the wood with a satisfying thud and small cracks radiated out from the centre. He swung again. The splitter sank farther down, the cracks widened. It was now possible to see exactly where the log would split. How long it took depended on a number of things – the type of wood, its dryness, whether it had knots along it where branches had once grown out. Sycamore was easy, even after only a year of maturing it was sometimes possible to split a sycamore log with a single blow, revealing the beauty of the wood – light here, shaded there. Ash needed more time but it burned better. This was hawthorn, a hard wood to saw but often one which rotted from the inside and therefore split easily.

He swung again and as the log fell open in two satisfying clean halves, the splitter buried itself in the upturned section of trunk on which he had stood the wood. He took one half of the split log and continued chopping with an axe. The work was easy and satisfying now and he cleaved the wood effortlessly into fire-sized pieces.

As he warmed up he began to get into a rhythm. Split with the splitter, swing the sledge, chop with the axe. Split with the splitter, swing the sledge, chop with the axe. The pile of ready firewood began to grow around his feet. It was already more than was needed, especially in summer, but there was no harm in stockpiling. One last log. The sledge swung once more onto the splitter and there was a sickening creak. A knot. The splitter came out of the side at an angle and instead of a clean cut, thick muscle-like fibres of wood tore apart but still held the log in one piece.

'Trouble?' Gwidion looked up. He had been so absorbed in the job he had not seen Cai sitting on the woodpile, his back against the outside of the dugg.

'A knot,' said Gwidion. 'And it's ash. And it's still a bit damp.' The axe hung loosely at his side as he spoke.

'You got Ce'nder Lauren to the Ruins last night then?'

'Where were you?' Gwidion returned to his log to cover his discomfort. He placed the blade of the axe against the strands of half-torn fibre and hit it with a smaller lump hammer. It failed to cut through and the two halves of the log closed around the tool trapping it.

'Oh, I was around,' said Cai nonchalantly.

'You're always around. Never there, but always around.'

'We're very different for twins, aren't we?'

Twins are often regarded as the most truly equal of men and women, almost interchangeable. Never Cai and Gwidion. They didn't even look that much alike.

'I saw your dad getting drunk again.'

'*My* dad?' said Gwidion, finally freeing his axe and straightening up to look at Cai. 'And anyway *our* dad is in Madrid.'

Cai snorted. 'Is he? You are such an innocent, Gwidion, what do you know? Who told you about *our* dad?'

'Nobody,' Gwidion was forced to admit. 'Nobody talks of their fathers. But I have seen him.'

'Seen him? Where?'

'In my dreams.'

'Dreams!' Cai stamped his foot in exasperation. 'Dreams! Think about it. Does he ever write to you, does he ever send you things on your birthday? What sort of dad is this?'

'It's not unusual,' replied Gwidion. His voice was even, but his grip tightened on the axe in his hand. 'It's not unusual, here or anywhere. His work is important, it's secret. When I need him he will be there. He protects me. He will save me. What do you know about anything?'

'I know that you're a bit old to still believe in fathers in Madrid.' He had the bit between his teeth now. 'I know that we are not identical twins born from a single divided ovum, an egg with a double yolk, if you like. We are twins born within nine minutes of each other, me first, from two separate ova.'

Gwidion waited.

'Of course, that implies we were also from two different sperm.' He was always the one to know these sorts of things. 'It is conceivable,' he smiled, but it was not at his own unintentional pun which was beyond them both. He smiled because even at the age of thirteen he knew words like *implies* and *sperm* and *conceivable*. 'It is conceivable that these sperm were not even from the same man.'

The thought fell like a drop of water into the early morning silence. Gwidion could not help himself from following the inevitable train of thought.

'You mean... You mean, in nine minutes after making love to one man she was doing it with someone else?'

'Not necessarily nine minutes. It wouldn't have to be nine minutes. In a woman's cycle she is fertile for four, five, maybe six days. It wouldn't have to be nine minutes.'

He was always prepared to think the unthinkable. Compelled. He was always compelled to think the unthinkable.

'Never,' screamed Gwidion, and lunged at him, sending him flying from his position on top of the logs.

'Wait,' Cai cried out, shielding himself from the attack, but maintaining his good humour. 'Not so fast. Do you want to know the truth or not?'

Gwidion stepped back, still panting, wiping his mouth with the back of his hand.

He thought about the image of the father who appeared in his dreams. It was true, neither he nor Cai really resembled him. In Cai's case this was problematic. He not only didn't look a lot like Gwidion, he didn't look a lot like himself from one age to the next.

'When you are born,' said Cai, as if sensing the direction of

Gwidion's thoughts, if not their exact subject, 'when every child is born, they have blue eyes.'

He not only thought the unthinkable; he knew the unknowable.

'I had blue eyes till I was five, and curly blond hair. Then one eye changed to hazel, then the other. But for a while I had one blue eye and one brown. Our father's eyes are grey.' He stressed the word *father* as if putting it inside inverted commas. He stared hard into Gwidion's grey eyes. His grey, always-been-always-will-be-grey eyes.

Gwidion shivered uncontrollably. It was always like this; always by thinking the unthinkable, by knowing the unknowable, his brother tracked his secret thoughts, circled them, sniffed them, pinned them down.

Tears welled up in his throat. Perhaps it was true. Perhaps that was the real reason why he, Gwidion, was the special one, channelled this way and that, about to be offered a place in the Academy, while Cai was left to his own devices. Perhaps that was why Cai was so bitter and so cruel. Perhaps their mother believed she could at least hold on to her favourite one, the progeny of her other lover, her real lover. Perhaps that was why their mother did not want Gwidion to go to Madrid to meet his father, her lover in Madrid.

'So,' said Cai, cold, surgical, sure he had subdued his prey. 'Half a minute ago you fought me for thinking our mother might have had two lovers. Now you are aching with the pain of wanting to believe it.'

chapter eight

Gwidion made his way back to the roundhouse where last night's fire was still smouldering and dumped an armful of firewood nearby. Grown-ups were still strewn around the inside of the house in positions which in some cases told the story of last night's attachments. Some were stirring and returning to their duggs. Gwidion looked briefly around, there was no sign of Lauren or his mother. He continued on to the first encirclement of duggs and ducked down the steps to his own. The mentor and his mother were sitting at the table. They stopped talking as he entered.

The mentor greeted him as his mother stood up.

'Have you chopped the wood, Ce'nder Gwidion?'

He nodded as the mentor took him by the shoulders in a half-hug. It was an ostentatious act, almost too familiar, and it was followed by an uncharacteristically hearty piece of conversation.

'Good boy. Maybe the goose will get cooked tonight after all. You must be hungry. Come and have some breakfast.'

Gwidion sat cross-legged at the low table while his mother went to fetch him some bread and cheese. He took a mouthful in silence, waiting for the inevitable questions about Lauren. They didn't come. His mother busied herself with something at the other end of the dugg.

'We were talking about you, Ce'nder Gwidion,' said the mentor finally. 'About your studies and about your future.'

Gwidion ate on, holding the mentor's steady gaze.

'You have a special talent, Ce'nder Gwidion. You are by far the brightest in our class and... ' He let out a breath as if he had been holding it for some time. 'There is only so much I can teach you here.'

Gwidion looked back at his food.

'You remember Colonel Jiménez who came to see you the other day? He thinks you might do much better at the Academy in Madrid.'

Gwidion looked towards his mother who was watching him across the dugg.

'My father is in Madrid,' said Gwidion.

He caught the glance which went from the mentor to his mother and sensed the nervousness which accompanied it.

'Do you think you might like to go to Madrid to study?'

Gwidion swallowed a piece of crust. 'And leave here for ever?'

'Not for ever necessarily. Who can say how long it might be for? That would depend on a lot of things. You mostly.'

'I don't want to leave here.'

'It wouldn't be easy for you, I know that. But you are a young man – you are turning into a young man. You may not want to stay here for the rest of your life without seeing something of the world. Ours is a small community and it is one that chooses to look inwards rather than outwards. But even we depend on Madrid for certain things and the opportunities we can provide for you are limited. I am your mentor, it is my job to teach you, but you know as much as I about many things. You have the ability to know much more than that if you choose. And the choice is between here and Madrid.'

Gwidion said nothing.

'Will you think about it?' said the mentor. 'Colonel Jiménez would like to come to talk to you again. He can tell you much more about what it will be like.'

Gwidion could not clear the confusion that Cai had planted in his mind earlier. He looked into the mentor's clear grey eyes which reflected his own face back at him.

'Everyone I know is here,' said Gwidion. 'Apart from my father. Do you want me to go, Mam?'

His mother came to the table and pressed his head against her thighs.

'I don't want you to go, Gwidion. I could never want you to leave me, but we are not always able to decide things so simply. You should listen to what the mentor has to say, and to Colonel Jiménez.'

She knelt and held his head so he could not avoid her gaze. 'If you did go I would still love you, Gwidion. And so would everybody here who loves you. We will talk about it, Gwidion. We will think about it.'

Then to the mentor. 'That's enough now. We will talk about it again.'

The mentor nodded and then unfolded his long body into the air so he was looking down at the boy. He opened his mouth to take his leave but his words were interrupted by Gwidion's question.

'Will Cai come too?' The mentor's face gave him no answer, his mother squeezed him gently. Before she could reply Tabitha appeared at the entrance, her huge frame casting a temporary shadow over the scene around the table. She hesitated as she took in the tight domestic scene, but there was no more to be said on the subject now. Gwidion's mother let go of her son and came to meet her.

'You've chopped more wood, Ce'nder Gwidion. Thank you. The goose will be cooked tonight,' she said as she entered, breaking the spell. The four of them laughed.

'It had better be, Ce'nder Tabitha,' said Gwidion's mother. 'The sight of that naked bird first thing in the morning is putting people off their food.'

Tabitha laughed out loud. 'Don't blame the bird. There was enough mead drunk last night to last us till Christmas. But you're right, the bird needs to be eaten before then. I came to ask for your help, Ce'nder Ana.'

The mentor moved towards the door. 'I was just leaving.'

'To practise your fiddle, I hope,' said Tabitha with a mock expression of severity. He smiled.

'Goodbye Ce'nder Gwidion, Ce'nder Ana. Think over what we have talked about.'

Tabitha clicked her tongue against her teeth and the smile was gone this time. 'Another boy to be ripped out of our village, is it, mentor?' She used the final word like an expression of distaste.

'Not now,' the mentor said softly.

'Not now?' Tabitha's voice rose again. 'When then? After you've persuaded him to go anyway? When it's already too late?' Gwidion's mother made no move. Gwidion looked on interested.

'Not in front of the boy,' said the mentor.

'Boy?' snorted Tabitha. 'He's a young man, isn't he? Didn't he light the solstice fire last night? Old enough to think about going to Madrid, isn't he? Then he's old enough to hear what I've got to say as well. What will they do with him at the Academy? How many of our men do they want? And what will we do with a village full of women and girls? Oh, but there'll be you, of course, mentor. The peacock with his harem.'

The mentor flushed and for the first time ever Gwidion saw him go into a rage.

'That's a lie, Ce'nder Tabitha, and you know it.'

'And how are we going to keep our village alive without men?'

'I came back,' said the mentor haughtily.

'The mentor came back.' The tone was one of disgust again. Gwidion found it difficult to believe that these two were capable of putting such mutual contempt aside when it came to the solstice. Or maybe mead just had that effect? 'For what?' she continued, her arms set on her thighs, her large frame leaning forward, then settling back as she delivered her final shot. 'To teach our children to go to Madrid, it seems to me.'

Ana made to intervene but the argument had progressed too far.

'And what is the alternative?' the mentor snarled back. 'How long do you think we can escape the inevitable? Less than half a dozen men among sixty-seven villagers? One pregnancy in eight years? This is not the community you, me or any of us envisaged. It's time to move on.'

'And your answer is to send one of our men away,' Tabitha snapped back. 'What a stroke of genius.'

'And your answer?'

'My answer is only that I know Madrid is no answer at all.'

The mentor's patience gave out as his voice approached screaming pitch. 'Do you think any of us enjoy sending our children away? Do you think it doesn't hurt me? Do you think you're the only one to feel the pain of it? I've seen my own children go too, you know. Don't fathers have a right to be with their children too?'

Tabitha tutted loudly. Ana stood with her eyes closed, but the mentor was in full flood now.

'And the boy, doesn't he have the right to be with his father?'

As he placed his hand on Gwidion's shoulder he realised what he was saying. He saw the expression of both shock and delight spread across the boy's face.

'He is in Madrid. I knew it. I always knew it.' He turned to his mother. 'Who is it, Mam? Tell me who it is? What does he do? I bet he's something important. Tell me.'

Tabitha looked from one to the other. She rubbed her palms against her dress, smoothing out imaginary creases.

'Well that's out,' she said finally. 'And about time too.' She turned and left, plunging the dugg into darkness once more as her bulk filled the doorway.

When the light returned to the dugg, Ana was on her knees by her son. She held his head tight against her breast and sobbed. 'I wanted to tell you, Gwidion. I wanted to tell you everything. But there are so many things you are too young to understand. I would have told you. I was going to tell you. I shouldn't have listened to the others.'

The mentor spoke. 'Ce'nder Gwidion...' But Ana motioned him away with a low hiss.

'Enough. That's enough now. Leave us.'

How did you tell a thirteen-year-old boy who his real father was? What did a mother tell her boy who didn't like history about his own history? But Gwidion gave her no time to find an answer to any of these questions.

'Who, Mam, who?'

Ana stretched her arms out to him in a pleading gesture, but her son kept his distance. 'The colonel who came to see you.'

'Colonel Jiménez? He is my father? And you didn't want me to go with him? He came for me, he wanted me to go to Madrid.'

'I'm sorry, Gwidion. I should have told you when you were younger. I knew you would have to be told one day.'

Now out of the whole unworldy mixture of emotions seething inside, the anger was rising in Gwidion's body above everything. The sobs gathered deep within him, starting in his abdomen and choking his body from the bottom up. Tears ran down his face as his voice turned into an unworldly howl. 'You wanted to stop me going to Madrid. You wanted to stop me.'

Ana cried back at him. 'It wasn't supposed to be like this, Gwidion. Nothing was ever supposed to be like this.'

He bolted out of the dugg, leaving her words of explanation still finding themselves inside her throat.

The mentor found Gwidion where he expected. The boy had watched his long approach from his vantage point on the Ruins. He had followed the mentor's tall, slightly bowed figure as it took the path between the maize fields, disappearing from view now and then where the vegetation grew tall, reappearing, then disappearing. Now you see me, now you don't. Gwidion looked on as he ascended the slight rise to the Ruins, his pace slackening, the bend in his body becoming more acute. Then slowly and laboriously, the mentor climbed up the Ruins, waiting until he had reached Gwidion before saying a word. But no word came. Gwidion waited while the mentor got his breath back from the climb.

The older man would have liked to take the boy in his arms. And

Gwidion would have liked nothing better, but now there was a lie between them. Well, not a lie. Worse than a lie, a great truth which had not been shared.

'I can see why you come here,' he said. 'It was one of my favourite haunts as a boy. Before I went to the Academy.'

'Was it forbidden then?' asked Gwidion.

'Oh yes. As long as I can remember.' He was breathing more easily now and looked around. 'It hasn't changed much in forty-odd years. There's a bit more grass, a bit more moss.'

'Do you know much about this place? There's not much to be found in the optiks.'

'Not much more than you, I expect. It was a place where people lived a long long time ago.'

'A skyscraper?'

The seriousness of the mentor's purpose for coming here suddenly evaporated in a loud laugh. 'Not a skyscraper, Ce'nder Gwidion, not here. And not built out of stone either.'

Gwidion frowned, the hurt showing clearly on his face.

'I'm sorry, I didn't mean to laugh. Whoever told you it was a skyscraper?'

'I dreamed it,' said Gwidion sullenly. 'I've always believed it.'

The mentor fought to control his amusement. 'When? How old were you?'

'I don't know. Every year.'

'Every year?'

'Every year on my birthday. And other times as well. As long as I can remember.'

His intensity evaporated the mentor's amusement.

'Cai said the shaft used to have a lift inside it, a glass bubble which went up and down so you could see the people travelling inside.'

The mentor chuckled more gently this time. 'No, no lift I'm afraid, Ce'nder Gwidion. Not in this part of the world. Just some sort of place to live, probably. There might have been a few families living here perhaps, one on top of the other. I doubt it was ever much higher than where we are now.'

'Why don't they build skyscrapers any more?'

'For the same reason the people who lived here never built one.

They didn't need them,' said the mentor. 'They belong to another time and another place, like pyramids or castles.'

'People were frightened of them.'

The mentor nodded. 'They were abandoned even before people fled the cities. They belong to a time before the dome when we lived in cities of many hundreds of thousands of people, millions of people in some of the very biggest. Can you imagine that? In a place the size of our village there might be hundreds of tall buildings towering above the narrow streets far below. No fields, no greenery. Concrete and glass everywhere.'

'How did they grow food?'

'Ah, that was grown in other parts of the country, outside the cities where there were still fields and forests.'

'And everyone lived in skyscrapers?'

The mentor gave a chuckle. 'No, not everyone. In the big cities perhaps. But mostly they were where people worked. Think of it. Thousands of people working in a single tall building. Every day they would have to go there to work like we go to study every day. Thousands of them. And just across the street would be another skyscraper with more thousands inside. And next to that another one. Each one full of strangers. Most of them wouldn't have known each other nor even have met.'

Gwidion tried to conjure the pictures in his mind. He put himself in an office high up in a huge office block with lots of men and women sitting cross-legged before their optiks and looked across at another equally tall building across the street, full of people he had never met. It was difficult. What did people he didn't know look like? The only stranger he knew was Colonel Jiménez, so he populated his offices with bald-headed colonels. He knew this wasn't right but if he screwed up his eyes and blurred everything together, he got the impression. He brought himself back to the present.

'Why have the Ruins been left? If we aren't supposed to come here, why don't we just take them away?'

'I don't know. Maybe when the dome was first built people wanted a reminder of the way we'd lived before, like we still have the menhir.'

'Then why are we forbidden to come here?'

The mentor could only shake his head sadly. His answer was another question. 'And why do some of us obey and others not? Whoever decided it should stay was a wiser person than us.'

He looked at Gwidion and waited until he had caught his eye. He gestured in a wide sweep with his hand.

'You see this dome, Ce'nder Gwidion? Some people see this as their universe, they look no further. We have the material things we need to survive, we produce everything we eat. We have technology – it creaks and groans, but it works. We have communications if we want, but most of us don't. We have chosen to cut ourselves off here. This is our own square mile, it's where we belong. We know everyone in the dome and everyone knows us. We help everyone when they need help and they help us. We are born, we grow, we learn, we love, we hate, we grow old and we die, and the experience of all those things is as rich and fulfilling as if we owned the entire universe.'

'But that's not the whole story,' Gwidion prompted.

'Nothing is ever the whole story,' said the mentor gravely. 'To others, in Madrid, elsewhere in the Republic, this is no more than a prison, a place for the timid to hide. That picture of our world is outside your experience. You have no way of judging between one and the other. All you have ever known is the safety and warmth of your mother's dugg and our small community, and that is why the Academy could be so important to you – and your village. In that sense Ce'nder Tabitha is right. We send our brightest and best to Madrid and we are left to fumble on as best we can. But Ce'nder Tabitha sees it only from her own perspective. There is another perspective, Ce'nder Gwidion. One of people who want to recover the civilisation that gave us cities of millions with their unbelievable diversity. Their art, their theatre, opera, sport, great thoughts, great science. The civilisation that gave us all the technology we depend on today to keep us alive. Everything born out of that unique mix of cultures and beliefs.'

He stood up on the narrow ledge.

'A million times this and more,' he said raising his arms dramatically. 'And what do we have to show for it? A handful of classic novels, two Humphrey Bogart spools, some Disney cartoons... And there are some on the Women's Council who would stop us watching even those.'

He looked down at Gwidion. 'They gave us buildings that reached to the sky, because *they* were reaching for the sky. All we have left is a small pile of intellectual debris. Just like the Ruins here.' He stopped, and smiled, slightly embarrassed at his display of passion.

'What happened to it all?'

The mentor remained gazing out over the village. 'It still exists. Most of it. More than you could ever imagine. Go to Madrid, Ce'nder Gwidion. Not because your father is there, but go and make the choice for yourself. Don't let Ce'nder Tabitha make it for you. Those who really love you will want you to see for yourself and make your own decision. Your mother, who it hurts more than you can imagine. Me.'

Gwidion bowed his head. The mentor sat down. 'I'm sorry, Ce'nder Gwidion. I'm sorry that you didn't know.'

'My mother could have told me.'

The mentor put his arm around the boy.

'That is not her fault. Fathers are the blood line we do not talk about. If we are all ce'nder, cousins, then at least we are all equal. And sometimes it is better that we are all equal than that we are father or sister or brother. That is the meaning of passage. The time had come for you to know, I am only sorry that it happened the way it did.'

The mentor looked out over the view. What a view. The fields of maize, the tassles stirring in the slight breeze, the glorious colours of linseed and soya, the snugness of the duggs nestling like brown pebbles around the roundhouse. What wasn't there to love about this place?

'Gwidion, we are a sick people. Before Bretaña, when this country was called Wales, it contained more than three million people. This,' he spread out both his hands, 'is what is left. England, forty-nine million people, wasn't so lucky. As far as we know, because we are far from knowing anything about life outside here. Nor France, fifty-eight million, or Germany, eighty million.'

For the second time that day his voice quavered with anger.

'Do the mathematics yourself, Gwidion, you've got the brains.

What incredible fluke saved Wales and its dying language from extinction?'

Gwidion looked at him with an expression of surprise and hurt.

'I'm sorry,' the mentor rubbed his face between his hands then scratched his head. 'Unfortunately we weren't spared everything. We weren't spared the effects of E402.'

Gwidion looked puzzled again.

'Not everyone knows these things, Gwidion, and what I am telling you is knowledge you must guard carefully because there are many here who do not wish to listen to it. It must have struck you that you learn no history from before the dome, apart from the ancient people of the menhir.'

Gwidion nodded eagerly. 'Exactly.'

'This community was set up to escape history, not to take part in it. I am among the oldest here, but even my memory is not long enough to fill in the gaps. What I have learned I have learned in Madrid, or by stealth, or from the stories sometimes told between older men.'

'You knew your father?'

'As you now know yours, Gwidion. In my case too late to know him at all. He died when I was seven.'

Gwidion thought he saw a tear in the mentor's eyes, which he assumed was because of their talk of fathers.

'What was E402?'

'You've heard of the fertility plague?'

'Yes.'

The mentor put his arm around Gwidion's shoulder again and the two gazed out across their corner of paradise.

'It was before I was born, before the dome. E402 was a mumps-related virus developed by a group of Islamic terrorists in Indonesia – but it turned out to be more virulent than they ever dreamed of.'

'So does Indonesia rule the world?'

The mentor gave a grim smile. 'Weapons know nothing of political or national boundaries. It was released simultaneously in livestock markets across Europe and at a number of international airports. Within days farmers and their animals had taken it back to their homes and travellers had taken it across the world. By the time anybody even discovered that the attack had taken place, it was already three months later, three months too late to do anything about it. The first signs were swellings in the glands, particularly in the sexual organs, the armpits and the neck. Victims swelled up to enormous size, as if they had been pumped full of air. Less than twenty-four hours after showing the first symptoms they were usually dead. They say that people died on the streets in a horrible fit. The numbers were too big for the authorities to cope with. Bodies were piled in the streets waiting for collection, but there was no-one to collect them. We can only guess at the panic and the horror in cities of millions of people, which was where it first appeared. At the height of the epidemic plague patrols were formed and anyone exhibiting even the slightest case of acne was shot on sight. Their fate was probably a blessing.'

'Is that why the dome was built, to protect us?'

'There was no protection. Thousands tried to escape to the country or to other countries, but if the plague was not already where they were running to, then they merely brought it with them.'

'Then why was the dome built?'

Far across the fields the mentor could see the figure of Tabitha striding towards the roundhouse. It reminded him that he had said more than he should have said, and perhaps more than he really knew.

'What is the truth? Ce'nder Tabitha is right when she says that Madrid takes our bright young boys and leaves us a community of old men, women and children. She may even be right when she says we are better off without knowing about these things in our past.'

'And what do you say?'

The mentor still gazed out over the village, but he was aware of Gwidion's eyes scrutinising him, assessing him, until he could not bear it any longer.

'We don't know exactly why the dome was built. Maybe it was to defend people from some other sort of threat, maybe it was some sort of experiment, maybe it was just a way of escaping from a world where any stranger was not to be trusted. In here, at least, whatever our differences, we know we are all friends.'

'But we survived. And others in Madrid.'

'No virus is ever one hundred per cent effective. Pockets of people must have survived all over the world. But even those who weren't killed by the plague did not escape some of its effects. We are not free of its effects now – in case you're wondering why you haven't got any male friends of your own age.'

Gwidion shook his head in bewilderment.

'Even those who survive suffer a high rate of infertility, particularly men. And those who are fertile are much more likely to give birth to girls than boys.'

The mentor squeezed him hard. 'That is the reason we do not talk of fathers.'

'Why?'

The mentor looked at him with what seemed like a smile flickering on his lips.

'Fathers are a rare commodity and a village like ours needs children to survive. We cannot belong solely to one woman or to one family. The family we belong to is the whole community.'

'There must have been another way.'

'There might be,' agreed the mentor. 'If we had the medical facilities. If we had the science and technology. But that is not the way we have chosen. What would become of those men who were not fertile? Then we would have men and less-than-men, we would have fathers with huge families. And large families would mean status. And status would mean power. And power would mean resources.'

He gave a grim laugh. 'The dome builders may have escaped from their past, but they did at least learn one important history lesson – that inequality breeds power and that power breeds conflict and that conflict breeds disaster. Perhaps after all it is better to veil our fatherhood in the mists of a midsummer orgy, to celebrate all births as you would celebrate the birth of your own child and to love all as if they were your own family.'

'It doesn't make it feel that much better,' Gwidion said quietly.

The mentor squatted and looked into his eyes.

'No, Gwidion. It doesn't to me either. At least you have the chance to find out the truth, to escape if that is what you want. Go to Madrid.'

chapter nine

The goose fat dribbled down Gwidion's chin as he chewed on a piece of bone which was much too big to fit in his mouth. It was his first food since breakfast but even so he had no appetite. He was eating because everyone else was now gathered around the fire outside the roundhouse and there wasn't much else to do. But the taste of animal fat was having the desired effect on his shrunken and twisted stomach, loosening the tension, lubricating his insides. The truth was that it was easier to digest than anything else he'd had to swallow that day.

Colonel Jiménez was his father. He no longer knew what that meant. Did that mean he loved Jiménez now? Is that what it meant? Did it suddenly, magically transform him? What was he supposed to feel, who could tell him that? For thirteen years *father* had been no more than an amorphous mass of somebody not present, a shadowy figure in a scientific institute in Madrid working on some important but undefined project.

Now *father* was real and physical. And he wanted Gwidion to come to Madrid.

'Is it good, Ce'nder Gwidion?' The mentor's voice could barely be heard over the chatter around the fire. Gwidion's expression acknowledged that it was.

Gwidion looked around at the other children from study. Daisy, Lauren, Amy, Bethan, Rosa, Angelica, Rhiannon, Boa, Julia, Megan. He searched for more evidence of paternity. What did he know about their fathers? His stares were not always unnoticed. Bethan caught his eye. She was a year or two older than he and she smiled at him. Did she know who her father was? Did she know who Gwidion's father was? Was it part of a woman's knowledge passed on to her during her passage? It was the women too who made up the members of the village council. They led the community, they set the rules. They must also be the keepers of the secrets of the dome's family tree.

Suddenly he looked on the women with new eyes. They were ce'nder, kin. Literally so. Now he knew what that meant.

He began to do the mathematics in his head. Sixty-seven people in the dome, five of them men. Probably two, maybe more, would be infertile. Which left, let's say, three. Maximum. Three possible fathers. For an adolescent boy this was a fascinating pursuit. There was Rhisiart, the piper, short and dark, almost Spanish-looking. Rhiannon, maybe. Probably. And her sisters Bethan and Megan. Their mother worked in the hydroponics bays. She was somewhere here tonight but Gwidion couldn't see her. Beyond the blaze of the fire there was a pool of darkness which extended back into the roundhouse. Yes, he could see her. Her prematurely silver hair caught the light from the flames for a moment, then she was gone. So many shadows, so many ghosts.

And there was William. He was already in his sixties and walked with a pronounced limp. It was possible, of course. He would come back to William.

Lloyd. In his thirties, tall and well-built, fair-haired, clear-skinned. Gwidion had seen Lloyd at Lauren's dugg many times.

And Paddy. A great friendly giant of a man, a teller of late-night stories. If he and Tabitha ever got together the results would be unmistakable, thought Gwidion, and he laughed out loud without realising what he was doing. Fortunately it did not attract any attention. There were plenty of things to laugh about around the fire as people talked and ate. The flames seemed to draw them in closer as the evening got darker. He returned to his detective work. Tabitha had no children, that he knew. And none of the children remotely fitted the profile of Giant Paddy.

Gwidion had not progressed very far with his goose but already the others were beginning to break away from their positions around the fire. The mead was passed and music started and drums. He was finding it difficult to hold onto these thoughts now as people moved in and out of view.

Who was left? Amy, Daisy, Rosa, Boa? His mind began to explore other possibilities. What if people from outside came? Say, people from Madrid, like his own father. Or might there be sperm banks? It had been possible at one time to grow human babies outside the womb. Did that technology still exist? The infinite possibilities continued to multiply in his head. And, of course, the mentor himself was old enough to have fathered two or even three generations.

As the mead fuddled his brain the lines of blood and family wove in and out of the village population like the dry red irrigation ruts that snaked along the ground, like the silver braids that were woven into a child's bonds. He tried to bring his focus back to the unfathered children, but his thread of thought was already getting lost in the exponential growth of half-sisters and cousins.

His hand was taken as the growing line of dancers passed by him for a second time. It was Bethan. He dropped his food and got to his feet, shuffling awkwardly to find the time of the other dancers and then he was up, doing the steps they had performed on mid-summer's eve for as long as he could remember, relaxing into the rhythm of the dance.

He tried to find the faces again to continue his genealogical search, but the line stretched far around the fire and out into the duggs. Night brought anonymity. They left the warmth and light of the fire as the dance wound through the first circle of homes, scattering odd chickens who had ventured close to the roundhouse in the hope of finding food. It was a dangerous thing to do on such a night when they were more likely to be taken for food than given it.

The evening air was still warm and as the dance wove its way around the village it opened up new views. The sun was low in the north-west, casting its aurora borealis against the ocuspex of the dome. Outside, to the north-east stood the majestic wind turbines turning slowly and gracefully in the light wind and feeding power to the village. Then as the line of dancers wound farther and farther out away from the fire but still barely in earshot of the music, he could see the glint of the solar accelerators which lay built into the base of the dome from the east around to the west. Farther out, and now only the beat of the drums and the communication of their own bodies kept the dancers in time. To the south they could see the Ruins illuminated by the setting sun. On and on went the dance, into the paths which ran between the fields and into the fields themselves.

Gwidion thought of Lauren and looked for her among the dancers. But they were in the field of maize now strung in a long line, following the furrow. The tassles of the ripening corn brushed against them as they swayed along the uneven surface. He felt Bethan's hand hot and sweaty in his. She gripped tighter and laughed as the dance became more and more chaotic. Gwidion was laughing too. The dancers had lost contact with the beat and as they stumbled through the field they began to lose contact with each other, breaking into smaller lines which dawdled or stopped or ran ahead. Gwidion paused to catch his breath from the dancing and the laughter, stooping over and holding his side where the pain of a stitch cut across his chest. When he straightened up there was only Bethan still holding his hand, looking at him, smiling at him, waiting for him to recover. He looked around. The line had gone off through the maize, broken up into half a dozen separate dances fading into the distance as some headed back to the fire and others petered out into heaps of giggling people or fell into a secret silence.

'This way,' said Gwidion, pointing back towards the roundhouse. But Bethan's warm body was already against his.

'Wait, Ce'nder Gwidion,' she said.

She was almost as tall as him and her hair and eyes were black in the deepening dusk. The simple smocks the domers wore hid many shapes and sizes of people, but with her pressed against him hard Gwidion could feel the fullness of her figure compared to Lauren's. He tasted the sweetness and wideness of mead and goose fat on her lips. It seemed to make the kissing easier as their tongues explored each other. Her breath was still fast and warm against his face and her slightest suggestion of a moustache stroked his upper lip. She broke away and held him at arm's length.

'Let's play a game,' she smiled.

'What game?' Gwidion moved towards her again but she maintained an arm's length between them. She took two sticks from inside her smock and held them behind her back, her chest pushed towards him.

'Which hand?'

Gwidion touched her left shoulder. She hesitated, teasing him a moment.

'Don't swap them,' he said.

She held out the stick he had chosen, its smooth silver and mottled bark was easily recognisable.

'Birch.' She did not need to explain its meaning. You may begin.

'And the other one?' She let the second stick fall to the ground. Hazel. Be wise and stop. Then they were body to body again. His passion had not been meant for her but she owned it now.

'Here,' she said, pushing over some stalks of maize onto the earth to make a rudimentary bed. Her forwardness intimidated him, she seemed vastly more grown-up than him.

The smell of earth reached his nostrils and Gwidion thought briefly of Lauren. And he thought briefly of his father. And he wondered briefly whether, if he was fertile, if she was fertile, whether he wanted to be the sort of father that his father was. Or whether he would like to be another sort of father. The sort of father there used to be, the sort of father he had always liked to imagine he had himself. His head still swam with all he had learned that day. Now as the slight evening breeze cooled them perhaps he too had joined the thrilling mystery of the dance of life.

They walked in silence holding hands, one slightly behind the other down the row of maize until they came to the menhir. They could hear the sounds of the celebration again, the drums that never stopped and the dance which broke and reformed like the waves of the ocean which lay less than three kilometres away outside their dome.

At the standing stone Bethan stopped and kissed him. Gwidion responded but his heart felt heavy with many unspoken thoughts. He thought of Lauren and he thought of Madrid. In his simple, thirteen-year-old way, he thought he would have to go now, his choice was made. The line of dancers stretched out again into the gloom, a parade of gyrating shadows. She pointed to the field.

'I will go and rejoin the dance over here. You go back to the roundhouse. Go through the duggs and arrive from the other side.'

Gwidion hesitated. 'But what about... us?'

Bethan shook her head. 'I was never for you and you are not for me. You will go to Madrid before too long and I... ' she tossed her black hair. 'Perhaps I will have a child.'

'My child,' said Gwidion urgently.

Bethan gestured at the dancers. 'The dance is still going on. I am going to rejoin it, probably you will too. It may be your child, it may be someone else's. We will never be sure.'

'Go now,' she repeated.

'They will know,' said Gwidion.

Bethan's face had grown stern. She took both his hands and faced him with an air of finality as if talking to a child. 'Ce'nder Gwidion, you are very sweet. They will know and they will not know,' she said. 'That is the meaning of passage. That is what a girl learns when she becomes a woman. You are still a boy, barely a man, but you will learn it too. It is what we all learn.' She dropped his hands, turned and ran.

Gwidion did what she had told him and returned to the roundhouse by another route. As he approached the fire, glad of the darkness which helped hide his secret, he noticed there were no men among the musicians. He imagined they were out in the fields, making couples like he had. Tabitha was beating out an ancient tune on the fiddle, a repetitive tune that ground and bounced along above the drumming. His mother was there, and some of the older women. Some played drums, some drank or picked at goose bones.

Tabitha was the first to notice him and called out without breaking the rhythmic mantra of her violin: 'The boy returns. Are you a man yet, boy? Give him some mead.'

His mother got up and brought Gwidion a cup of mead. She had a concerned look on her face. 'Have you been with Cai?' she said softly so no-one could hear. Gwidion shook his head.

'Drink it,' she said with a relieved smile and wrapped his hand around the cup of mead. 'The dance went that way.'

Gwidion looked over the rim of his cup at her. 'Ce'nder Lauren?'

'You will find her,' said his mother. 'Or she will find you.'

He turned to go, but his mother stopped him. 'Remember, Gwidion, she has not completed her passage yet.'

He nodded, gave the cup back to her and headed towards the dancers. As Ana turned to rejoin the women she noticed Lauren's mother looking at her from inside the roundhouse where she sat at one of the tables, her fingers idly plaiting the ends of the belt which tied her smock.

'I fear for your boy, Ce'nder Ana,' she said, half-jokingly as Ana joined her at the table.

'I fear for him too, Ce'nder Arianrhod. In some things he is such an innocent. I expect it is my fault.' Ana pulled her long hair back behind her head and secured it swiftly with a leather tie.

'That is true, it's always our fault.' Arianrhod was like her daughter, fair and blue-eyed, though she kept her hair cut short like a man's. She said it was because of the work she did.

'Lauren is not finding her passage easy. She says she will not complete it.'

Ana reached a cup of mead from the table, took a sip and handed it on. 'Gwidion is in love with her, it's easy to see.'

'Easy enough to see. But Lauren is a hard one to love, take it from her mother. She demands as much as she is prepared to give herself. She's tough and stubborn when she's got an idea in her head.'

'Definitely your fault then,' said Ana softly. The women laughed. 'What will she do?'

'She says she will only lie with someone she loves. She wants a relationship.'

'She will see in time.' Ana peered down into the cup of mead which Arianrhod had returned to her as if searching for something.

'Like you did?'

Ana looked up suddenly as if someone had tapped her on the shoulder. The other woman was not smiling.

'That was a long time ago. And there was no lack of love between us.'

'Things are changing, Ce'nder Ana. I fear we have looked inwards so long we have lost our way. Can you imagine Lauren sitting here in twenty years time like we are now?'

Ana did not answer.

'I can't. I'm beginning to think that perhaps Lauren is right.'

'You've changed your tune.'

'I'm not a teenager any more, Ce'nder Ana. Twenty years is a long time to sit around on midsummer's night being sad and lonely. Hoping that maybe Lame William or Giant Paddy will come back from the dance to fetch us. Ironic, isn't it, that Lauren should have turned out more like you than me?'

'The girl who wanted it to be different, you mean? History repeating itself.'

'I hope not. But then history never does repeat itself. We can never predict how it's going to turn out. The ending we are looking for is always one that hasn't happened yet.'

She pulled her thumb through the knots she had weaved into her belt separating the two strands and letting them hang free once more.

'What will you do about Gwidion when Jiménez comes to take him to Madrid?'

Ana's eyes were full of tears as she looked at the other woman.

'I don't know. I couldn't bear to lose him. He is all I have. But he will go – now that he knows who his father is.'

She felt Arianrhod's arms closing around her and buried her head momentarily on her breast before they were interrupted by the arrival of Rhisiart still panting from his exertions in the dance. He held out his hand.

'Will you join the dance, Ce'nder Ana?'

She looked up, detaching herself from Arianrhod, loosened her hair from its binding, shook it free and smiled back at the other woman.

'Why not?'

It was morning before Gwidion did find her. She was not among the dancers even though he danced for a solid hour in the hope of seeing her return to the line. In the end he was obliged to wander the village in search of her. A hunch took him to the hydroponics bays, housed in a series of greenhouse-like structures. The biodome itself provided a protection from the worst of the weather and enabled the village to grow crops they would not otherwise have been able to contemplate, but despite the dome and the genetic manipulation of plants it was still too risky to grow certain of the more exotic foods.

The greenhouses provided a perfect sub-tropical environment for plants such as bananas, avocados and citrus and here where the springs rose at the foot of the hill outside the dome was a perfect site. The plants were grown without soil, in baths of water mixed with nutrients.

Gwidion opened the outer doors of the bays, closing them behind him before passing through the inner doors which led into the greenhouses. The night was light and it was now not far off sunrise, but he could see nothing through the dense foliage. It was hot and humid and in minutes the sweat was pouring off him. Huge banana leaves towered above him, brushing him occasionally and giving him a shower of warm water droplets. There was a strong heady scent of orange blossom, even more sensuous in the warm, wet atmosphere. He found Lauren beneath one of the banana trees, her hair and clothes drenched with moisture. The roots of the tree delved into the nutrient bath where it stood. They were stunted by their lack of space, twisting and circling in and over one another, growing absurdly fat and stumpy as they were released from the necessity of either supporting the plant or searching for food.

'I looked everywhere for you,' said Gwidion. 'Have you been here all along?'

'Yes.'

He touched her hand shyly, forcing her to look up at him.

'I love it here. I would like to work here one day.'

'I thought your mother was training you to be a technician.'

'She is. But when there's nothing to mend you will find me here.'

'There's always something to mend,' said Gwidion.

'Not when I'm the technician there won't be,' said Lauren mischievously. They both laughed.

'I've been looking for you,' Gwidion repeated.

Lauren attempted to sound nonchalant. 'I thought you were enjoying the dance.'

'Don't you?' Gwidion crouched down beside her, but she did not make room for him to sit.

'I haven't completed my passage yet.'

Gwidion looked at his feet. 'No. But there are lots of things to enjoy about dancing.'

'The vertical expression of a horizontal idea,' she murmured.

'What was that?' said Gwidion, though he had heard every word.

'Something my mother said.' Lauren finally made room for him and he sat next to her, leaning his back against the banana tree, letting his head gravitate towards hers.

'Anyway I will never complete my passage,' she said.

'What do you mean?' asked Gwidion.

'What I say.' She moved away from him a little so she could look him in the eyes. 'I don't want to live like this. We didn't always live like this.'

'Yes, but...' Gwidion's sentence tailed away. He wasn't interrupted, it was more a rhetorical habit – but he had no argument this time. The sentence hung in mid-air for a moment. 'What don't you like?'

'Anything. I don't like any of it. I don't like the celebrations and I don't like the dance. I don't want to give birth to children by somebody I don't like or hate or... just because they are one of the few men left around who are able to *do* it. I don't want my children growing up without a father, not knowing who he is, being lied to. I don't want to be a birth machine. I don't want to do it.'

She was on her feet and her voice had risen to a shout, her wet hair hung in lank strands around her face and her sharp blue eyes screamed at him in the semi-gloom. He took one of her clenched fists.

'Lauren, Lauren.'

She pulled away from him, bursting into tears and hiding her face in her hands. 'Do you think you've earned the right to drop my familial then, Ce'nder Gwidion?'

'I'm sorry. Ce'nder Lauren, so many people must feel like you. You are not the only one.'

'Then why do they do it?' she shot back, her inconsolable grief suddenly changing to fire. And then it was Gwidion's turn to get angry.

'Because they think it's the right thing to do for the village. Because we might not survive if things were another way.' He took her by the shoulders and made her look at him. 'Look, Ce'nder Lauren. Because for some people it's the only way they are going to get anything at all and why shouldn't they have it?'

Lauren looked at him hard. She almost spat the sentence at him. 'Now that's the self-righteousness of someone who's guilty as hell. You loved *me*, you wanted *me* tonight.'

She reached under her smock and took out a beautifully-crafted silver object and threw it to the ground. It was the wrist clasp she had promised to make him. Gwidion recognised the three interwoven strands – his own bond of hazel, the tree of wisdom, his mother's bond of holly and his father's of oak, locked in an eternal struggle for supremacy.

Gwidion stepped back.

'Forgive me, Lauren.'

They were both breathing heavily. Lauren's voice shook as she spoke.

'You have the right, I don't deny you the right. Or Bethan. But listen Ce'nder Gwidion, I don't want children without a father. I don't want children without a relationship. That is not for me.'

There was a pause while they both recovered their breath. Gwidion turned away, thought better of it and turned back.

'I found out who my father is today,' he said. They looked at each other for a long time.

'Oh, Gwidion.' Lauren threw her arms around him and hugged hard.

'You didn't know?' whispered Lauren.

Gwidion shook his head. 'It looks like everyone else did,' he said bitterly. 'Did you? I mean, know yours?'

'Only when I began my passage. Until then I had thought like you. I thought it must have been the way things were in books. I didn't think it could be any other way.'

They stood a long time hugging hard, the tears mixing with their sweat and the moisture of the hothouse, until the glorious sunshine of a midsummer's day began to pour through the ocuspex.

Gwidion returned to the roundhouse alone. He needed to think and he wanted solitude. But more than solitude he wanted the familiarity of the sights and sounds of his home and the people he knew. A few of the adults were stirring as he entered the roundhouse but no-one took much notice of him. He found a space and lay there on his back listening to the comforting noises of people sleeping. These were his cousins after all, related to him in ways he was only beginning to understand.

His mind struggled to accommodate the events of the last two days, crowding in on him, repeating themselves endlessly. And as they competed for his attention they became jumbled and confused. Here was Colonel Jiménez at the Ruins telling him he was his father, but when he looked again he found it was Bethan. His body thrilled again at the memory of her touch and the smoothness of her young olive skin. He looked into the darkness of her eyes, letting them swallow him. Suddenly it was Lauren looking back at him. He awoke from his dozing with a start. Across the roundhouse he could see the morning light flooding through the door, but still most of the villagers around him were not awake. He felt tired but sleep would not come.

He rolled onto his back and tried to relax. He breathed deeply, starting at the abdomen and letting the air fill his lungs from the bottom, expanding his chest and rising towards the collarbone. Then slowly out. The images still came to him – Lauren, Bethan, the mentor, Colonel Jiménez – but he did not focus on them. Instead he concentrated on his breath. He repeated the sequence patiently time after time until the faces began to fade and move away to the periphery. In his mind he conjured the image the mentor had given him when he was first taught to meditate, or rather the image that had arrived in his mind. A cloaked figure, framed by an archway, lit by the rays of a setting sun, ascending the cool wet steps of a cave. Soon he was breathing normally, slipping into sleep.

He found himself at the foot of a high tower. It was a castle, the sort of stone castle you find in ancient fairytales peopled with dragons and princesses and wicked queens. It was narrow and tall with a round pointed roof and as he craned his neck to look up it seemed to grow. He let his gaze wander higher and higher, and as fast as his eyes moved up, the tower grew until it was unimaginably high. From a single window right at the very top leaned a woman. No, a girl. She was crying for help.

He began to climb the outside of the building laboriously, searching meticulously for hand and footholds in the stonework, but as he climbed the walls became smoother and smoother. He looked down. He was already twenty or thirty metres up, but seemingly no nearer Lauren. Yes, of course it was Lauren. He heard her cries in the distance and each one seemed to pierce his heart like an arrow. He was panting heavily and his arms and legs ached from the strain of gripping onto the blank surface.

'I'm going to jump,' he heard Lauren cry.

'No,' he shouted. 'Don't jump. I'm coming.'

He redoubled his efforts, forcing himself onwards despite his screaming muscles. 'Don't jump,' he cried again.

And then she did. Arms spread out like a great bird, her clothes floating around her.

'Save me, save me,' she shrieked.

And as she came within reach, Gwidion jumped too, taking her in his arms so that his body was underneath hers. Falling, falling.

And the more they fell, the higher they rose. Up, up, above the tower, higher into the sky until their biodome was laid out below them. It was the most beautiful sight. The Preseli Hills lay to the north, strangely shaped outcrops of rock which jutted above the thick woodland. Some looked like animals or, from another angle, like figures or household objects. Here was the source of the great Cleddau river with its two silver blades, east and west, slicing through the forest then meandering and widening as they travelled through the flatter land below until they finally melted into the great rolling sea.

Along these the builders of Stonehenge had floated the precious bluestones which once made up two concentric circles within the sarsens on Salisbury Plain. Eighty bluestones weighing up to four tonnes apiece, transported across 385 kilometres. And so humankind's obsession with building to the sky was begun.

The quarries from which they came were no longer visible under the covering of trees which had recolonised the land as humans and their pasture animals retreated. It was perhaps more than a millennium since the landscape had last looked like this, but it had taken less than fifty years after the fertility plague for it to return to that state.

Then here in the south, just a few kilometres from the sea, the land opened out again and below a ridge where the wind turbines chopped the air, the dome could be seen. By contrast with the vegetation around it, it was a colourful place. At its heart, on the unirrigated centre of the village, were the roundhouse and the duggs which appeared like small dark yellow spots against the red sandstone of the earth. To the north-west was the silvery sheen of the hydroponics bays reflecting light back from the sun. And in a great circular swathe around the red inner area were the fields – dark green, lime green, yellow, bare red earth.

In the south where the black banks of solar arrays soaked up the light at the edge of the dome were the Ruins, standing like Norman castles had once stood the length and breadth of this landscape – and still stood for all that anybody in the dome knew.

But as Gwidion looked he saw that the Ruins were no longer a crumbling relic, but a skyscraper scores of storeys high, its steel and glass glinting in the sun like the dome itself and through the windows he could see people working at desks. Some had ports in front of them, others talked with their colleagues, others walked carrying bags and papers. The old-fashioned suits they wore reminded him of scenes from the spools and made them look stiff and doll-like, not at all like humans. He could not count the number of floors but as he looked in each one he saw the same scenes – people after people after people, layer on layer, back and forth, up and down, a huge human knotwork of people.

And there, who was that? Bent over a desk there, turning to smile at him? His father! Not the colonel at all, but his father. The father who worked in Madrid. It was him. It was true.

Now he had noticed Gwidion and was coming to the window with an expression of fear on his face. What was the matter? He was calling, waving his hands, he seemed to be shouting something to Gwidion but he could not hear.

'Dad,' he shouted. 'Dad, I'm here. I'm all right.'

And as his father leaned forwards to open the window of his office high on the 103rd floor, Gwidion fell.

'Dad, help,' he cried. 'I'm falling, Dad, save me.'

But it was too late.

Gwidion shivered. The scent of wet grass filled his nostrils as he woke and he realised he was lying on the ground. He rolled onto his back and looked up at the walls rising into the blueness above him. He shivered again, not from cold this time, but to shake off the remnants of his dream. The sun was already quite high, it must be mid-morning, he calculated, and as he lay peering into the clear sky he could just detect the sepia effect of the photoactive ocuspex which helped control the temperature inside the dome. There were voices too, somewhere nearby. He realised, without any sense of surprise, that he was in the Ruins. They must be out looking for him. He rose slowly, his mouth dry from too much mead and dancing and his head aching slightly from too little water and sleep.

From his vantage point he could see the mentor and his mother coming towards the Ruins along the path from the menhir. They were walking briskly, but not with undue haste. His mother spotted him and waved and Gwidion waved back and began to return to meet them. He ran the final hundred metres into his mother's arms. She smelled of goose, cooking, woodsmoke, the unmistakable scent of the homespun wool they used for making smocks. And she smelled of mother. There were few words said. There were few things which needed to be said right now.

chapter ten

The children were back at their ports as normal on Monday. The roundhouse still smelled faintly of the events of the weekend and the atmosphere retained its holiday air. Bethan and her friends chattered and giggled, casting glances occasionally towards Gwidion. Their conversation was hushed but easily audible in the quiet of study.

'I saw you on Saturday night,' said Amy, gesturing towards Gwidion. She was a small mousey girl, a few years younger than Bethan. 'I saw you leave the dance.'

'Me too,' said Daisy. 'What was it like?'

'Ssh, Amy,' Bethan replied.

'Didn't you have anything better to do then, than watch other people having a bit of fun?' It was Julia, nearly sixteen and the oldest of the class, who spoke. Her hair was black and curly and she spread her long slender fingers languidly in front of her. 'He's not the only man in the village, you know.'

Amy's question was spoken with a note of awe. 'What, you mean, you..?'

Julia pushed her lips out in a superior sort of pout and looked towards Lauren. 'I don't see anything wrong with having a little bit of fun on midsummer's night.'

'Nor me,' said Amy with a giggle which was halted by the mentor's arrival.

Lauren absorbed herself in her work. Her hair was tied back tightly in a pony tail, sharpening her features and intensifying the colour of her blue eyes. She looked efficient, secretarial – except for her age.

After the lesson, Bethan appeared to hang back for a moment as Gwidion waited for the room to empty.

'Are you coming?' said Julia. The question drew the other girls' attention to Bethan and she thought better of it and joined her friends.

Lauren had already gone. Gwidion headed for his own dugg without conviction, kicking the ground with his feet as he walked, sending small puffs of dust into the still air. A flurry of chickens noticed him and made their way over to see if there was any food included in this display of indecision. They came running to within half a metre before slowing abruptly, still a safe distance away and making soft clucking noises. They picked their legs up slowly one by one as if treading carefully over hot coals, turning their heads from side to side, then scratched at the place where Gwidion's feet had disturbed the earth.

Gwidion changed direction and the chickens gathered around his heels. And so the small deputation arrived at the bright striped canvas doorway of Lauren's dugg.

'Henffic,' he called in the traditional greeting of a people whose doorways were, quite literally, always open. He guessed that his visit might not be totally unexpected. 'Ce'nder Lauren,' he called. There was no answer, but after a moment the curtain was pulled back. Lauren's mother greeted him.

'Ce'nder Gwidion. Come in. Will you eat?'

'I came to see Ce'nder Lauren, if she is here.'

'She is here. Come in.'

Lauren was already sitting at the table which was laid with corn pancakes, cheese and fruit. She pushed an imaginary loose strand of hair behind her ear.

'Henffic, Ce'nder Gwidion,' she said, looking up from her food.

'Come in, eat. You are welcome.'

She stood to greet him and Gwidion leaned forward slightly to kiss her. Imperceptibly, and not unkindly, she tilted her head so that his lips touched her forehead. The formality of the two youngsters was almost incongruous after the events of the solstice and Lauren's mother smiled.

They ate in comparative silence. Lauren's mother attempted to fuel the conversation with questions about study, carefully judged comments on the midsummer celebration and Gwidion replied politely and sparingly. He fell on the food like someone who had not eaten for days, feeling nervous and shy but finding a focus in filling his stomach and glad of the company of the women. But he had come here with another purpose and one which was a great deal more difficult to accomplish. In the village, everyone knew everything and like most adolescents he feared that the everything they knew was exclusively about him. Among adults there was a custom of collusion, a tacit agreement that however much you knew the facts and details of someone's life, you nevertheless posed the questions of polite conversation as if that was furthest from being the case. The alternative was that there would be no questions to be asked or no conversation to be had at all.

Lauren's mother finally discovered that she had a call to make in the nutrients lab of the hydroponics bays. She wrapped her tool-belt around her and left Lauren to tidy up the table.

'Does your mother know you're here, Ce'nder Gwidion?' she asked as she left. Gwidion shook his head. 'I will tell her as I pass.'

Now they were alone Gwidion searched hard for something to say, something to keep Lauren from busying herself with the table things. She was already getting to her feet and preparing to gather their bowls and spoons. The pause became a silence and the longer it went on the more difficult it was for him to break it. He tried hard to catch her eye but she saw no reason to make this easy for him. Eventually she found the silence harder to bear than he did.

'Well, Ce'nder Gwidion, do you have anything to say or have you just come to sit at my table?'

Still she failed to meet his gaze and, without giving him an opportunity to answer, swept quickly towards the sink.

'Lauren, I'm sorry.'

It was all he could manage for the moment, but it was enough to soften her demeanour a little.

'Sorry? For what?'

'For everything. For the other night.' In his panic the words blurted out quite unprepared. 'I love you.'

His honesty and passion made up for his lack of grace and she forgave him that, but Lauren was not one to settle for three words – not after the hours of pain and self-searching she had suffered on midsummer night.

'What I told you the other night was all true, Ce'nder Gwidion.'

'You mean, about your passage?'

'And about my children and the man who will be their father.'

'Yes,' said Gwidion fervently. 'That is what I want too.'

She raised her eyebrows and gave a soft snort. '*Now*, that is what you want!'

'What do you mean? Yes, that is what I want.'

'Because of course you've just had your fun with Bethan. It's easy for you to say now. You can't have it both ways, you know.'

'That's not how it happened, Ce'nder Lauren. I've always wanted it. I've wanted it more than anything... I just didn't know.' He trailed off helplessly.

'You are a boy, Ce'nder Gwidion. I am barely beginning to turn into a woman. You don't know what you want.'

'And you do?' He regretted the words as soon as they were out of his mouth. Lauren would not be happy with passion alone. Her repairer's mind required something more tangible than that. First she would take the strands and unpick them, then she would examine them one by one, then she would re-weave them precisely as they were – unaltered, except that now they would be fully comprehended.

'Yes, I do,' she answered. 'I could have joined the dance like Ce'nder Bethan did or like you did. But I didn't. And there is the difference between us.'

Gwidion was not used to losing arguments of reason, not with adults nor with his study-mates. One part of him immediately rose to the challenge as it had once risen to the challenge of the mentor's arguments in study, but that was the product of anger. He dimly understood – but in his boyish and self-centred way did not truly appreciate – the humiliation he had caused her. And he knew that he must now suffer some of the same also, but there was a limit to how far he could be expected to let that go. He had, after all, bared his heart to her in declaring his love.

'I did nothing that is not normal for us to do. And I had made you no promises, nor you to me. The reason you did not join the dance was because you had decided not to complete your passage. How was I to know that?'

Lauren stood up with the bowls in her hand, attempting an air of finality which might bring them back down to a calmer subject. 'You might have guessed,' she said with a note of resignation rather than defiance. Gwidion stood to stop her leaving the table and the moment of possible reconciliation evaporated.

'You say that I can't have it both ways, that I can't have both Bethan and you. Well, I don't want both. I want you. But you can't have it both ways either, Ce'nder Lauren. Either you want me at all or you don't. And if you did, you should have joined the dance, then you would have seen that it was you I wanted, whatever happened later.'

Now it was Lauren's turn to feel the anger rising. She slammed the bowls back down on the table, making the spoons fall out and tumble to the floor.

'So now it's my fault for not joining the dance,' she hissed. 'Well, thanks for putting me right.' She gathered the fallen utensils.

Gwidion sat down again.

'No, I didn't mean that,' he groaned.

'Don't sit down,' she continued almost on top of his last sentence. 'I have got work to do.' And the situation might yet have been saved except for the final, gratuitous remark which escaped her lips almost without her volition. It was a put-down born of too many hours spent alone in a hydroponics bay on midsummer's night when all her friends were enjoying themselves at a celebration. It appeared to believe it had a right of its own to exist.

'Didn't you have something to do in Madrid?' She turned her back on him and went to the far corner where there was a tub of water which served as a sink. She didn't look again until she was sure he had gone.

Her mother returned before she had time to think and rethink her conversation with Gwidion more than two or three times, and found her still at the sink with the bowls and spoons unwashed.

'Has Ce'nder Gwidion gone already?' she asked quietly. Her daughter turned without a word and buried her face in her mother's smock.

'He was with Bethan, Mam, on Saturday,' she wailed. 'I know he was. He never denied it.'

Her mother let the sobs subside. She knew there was nothing she could say which would ease the pain of this passage. It was something everyone went through.

'Lauren, you have your mother's stubbornness.'

'What was it like for you, Mam? Was it so hard?'

'Oh, Lauren, my child.' She kissed the crown of her daughter's head. 'For some it is quick, for others it is slow, but it is easy for no-one. And remember it's not easy for Ce'nder Gwidion either. He bears the burden of the village's expectations already, though he hardly knows it.'

'Did you ever love anyone, Mam? Any one person who you wanted and only him? That was the way it used to be, wasn't it? The optiks we read, the old spools.'

'The optiks come from another time.'

'But we're the same, aren't we? Aren't we the same as the people from before?'

'Not all of us, Lauren. There were more men in the village then when my mother was technician and our growing up did not start so young. She even had a helper, a man quite a few years older than me. He had been sent here to study. He was not a ce'nder and spoke no Welsh when he first arrived, though I taught him a lot. He used to come to our dugg after study every day to learn his skills.'

'Not my father?'

'Not your father, Lauren.' But the question was enough to rekindle some old, old memories. 'How I wish. He was the first I ever loved and I loved him... ' She gave a slightly embarrassed laugh as she emerged from her daydream, then continued with an effort to be matter-of-fact. 'I loved him as much as you love Ce'nder Gwidion. He was tall and handsome and all the girls in study wanted him. Some who were older than me had already succeeded, but I didn't let that bother me. I knew my time would come. Every day he would come to our dugg and I would do anything to be near him.'

Lauren's crying had stopped as she listened intently to the story. She had heard it, or parts of it, many times before, but today she needed to hear it more than ever.

'I pretended to be interested in the repairs and hung around him while he worked. I learned about logic arrays and surprised him with my knowledge. In fact I was faster and cleverer than him. When my mother left him with a particularly difficult job he would get me to help. Subtly, so he didn't show his lack of expertise. He made a game of it and I played the game so as not to appear too clever or forward.'

Now the tears were running down her mother's face and she had to break off to wipe her nose.

'One night he asked me to meet him in the fields. I still hadn't been with another man, even though I was fifteen by then.' She laughed. 'But I'd studied all the optiks and I knew what to do as well as I knew how to repair a shorted logic array – and I knew I was going to do it.'

'And did you?'

'Of course I did. And you will too when the time is right and when you are ready, and don't let anyone or anything make you do what you are not ready for.'

'Even if my time is running out?'

'We live the way we live for better or for worse, and most of us believe it is for the better. But we cannot go forward without change either. If the time has come for us to choose another way, then that is what we must do, however hard it may be. Relationships are not like logic arrays, Lauren. They involve other people. We can't always control them. We shouldn't try.'

'That's exactly what's so frustrating.'

'Or enjoyable, depending on which way you look at it.'

'Frustrating,' said Lauren very definitely.

Her mother smiled and looked down at her daughter's face, still red and puffed from her crying. 'That's a technician talking.'

'What happened to him?'

'He went away soon after. To Madrid.'

There was a silence. And then the tears began again.

'I sent him away, Mam,' wept Lauren.

'Who, what?' asked her mother, furrowing her eyebrows, so caught up in her own story that she did not understand straight away.

'Ce'nder Gwidion. I was angry, I lost my temper. I told him to go to Madrid. And now he will go and never come back.'

Her mother clutched her tight again, stroking her hair out of its pony tail and letting it fall through her fingers like fine sand.

'There, there, Lauren,' she whispered through her own tears. 'There, there.'

chapter eleven

'You blew it,' said Cai in the matter-of-fact voice which he knew pricked Gwidion so deeply. 'Let's face it, you blew the whole weekend. One quick grope with Ce'nder Bethan and her hairy lip, that's all you got.'

It was late and they were back at their old haunt on the Ruins. They lay on their backs staring upwards where the sky was turning dark blue and the first stars could be seen through the ocuspex. As the heat of the day receded they listened to the layers of sound which made up dusk inside the dome. From far away across the fields drifted the sounds of animals, the occasional raised voices of people or children. Overlaid on that was the hiss of the dome vents closing for the night which gave the impression of running water. Above that again was the chatter of birds about to put themselves to sleep. But Cai's words drowned everything else out.

'And then they're trying to tell you Jiménez is your father. You know better than that. Who do you trust?'

'Not you,' said Gwidion sullenly.

'Then trust yourself. Maybe he's my father and not yours.'

'We're twins, Cai.'

'Twins born from separate ova, remember. Me first, you nine minutes later. I'm you're big brother. Trust me.'

Cai sat up, chewing on a piece of grass.

'They want me to go to Madrid.'

'Lauren certainly does,' said Cai with a laugh. 'Anything to get rid of you I'd say. Still, it will leave the way clear for me.'

'I don't know what to do.'

'Ask Mam.'

'She doesn't want me to go.'

'Ask the mentor.'

'He'll tell me to go. He'll have all sorts of clever reasons.'

'And what about you. Will you go?'

Cai shrugged. 'Ask Lauren's mother,' he said.

'Why her?'

Cai looked at his brother long and hard, sucking vigorously on his piece of grass which made a strange whining sound in his mouth.

'Because she will be honest with you.'

The sky was dark purple now and the few stars which had appeared earlier were gone. For a moment Gwidion could not make out what was happening, then he saw large black clouds taking the place of the purple sky. Inside the dome with the vents closed the village was protected from the wind, but now they could hear it in the distance buffeting their ocuspex island. The hiss of the vents which had sounded so much like running water was replaced with real water as rain lashed down the outside of the dome only a few hundred metres away from the Ruins. The air temperature dropped a degree or two, not much but enough for the brothers to notice.

Cai turned to Gwidion excitedly. 'What would it be like to stand outside in that?' he shouted. He was on his feet, bending down into Gwidion's face. His eyes were shining. 'Come on.' He put out his hand to lift his brother up. 'Come on.'

'What? Where are you going?' said Gwidion. Cai was already running south, away from the Ruins, away from the village towards the boundary of the dome.

'To the solar accelerators,' Cai shouted back. 'Come on. We can get outside there.'

They followed a path which wound through the rough ground bordering the far edge of the settlement, barely able to see their way ahead. Bracken and cordylines grew taller than the boys on either side and now they were running they sweated in the warmth and humidity of the closed dome. At last they reached the boundary where the dome disappeared into the ground, cutting off the village from the world outside. Arranged along this southern edge were the solar accelerators, built into the structure of the dome and sloping outwards. In front of them was a cleared area of pastureland where animals were grazed in the daytime – and then the woodland began. Cai found the maintenance exit at the end of the path and swung the door open. Gwidion caught up with him, panting heavily. Cai waited for him to go through.

'Isn't it supposed to be locked?' Gwidion asked.

'Not from the inside,' said Cai.

'But it is forbidden.'

'Lots of things are forbidden,' answered Cai.

Gwidion walked slowly forward in wonder, looking up at the great structure which rose as far as he could see into the sky. In a few seconds they were outside feeling the rain pouring over their heads and faces. It was cold. Colder than Gwidion had imagined. In a few minutes his smock was soaked through and the movement of his feet where he stood had churned up the ground into a small mud puddle. He was no more than a metre outside the dome, within two seconds he could be back inside, warm and dry, but his heart pounded as if he had suddenly found himself on the most remote and wild island.

'The woodland,' shouted Cai over the noise of the rain pounding on the ocuspex of the dome.

'No,' Gwidion shouted back. But Cai was running again, across the clearing towards the impenetrable blackness of the trees.

'No,' screamed Gwidion again. As he turned to go back there was a sudden flash of lightning which illuminated everything for the briefest of moments. Cai was caught in a running pose as if frozen in mid-air. Gwidion only had time to wonder at the image before the peals of thunder began.

'Cai,' his voice broke under the force of his scream, almost inaudible under the sound of the storm. And then he too was running towards the woods, shouting as he went.

He found Cai sheltering under the trees at the edge, laughing at his brother.

'I don't like this,' said Gwidion. 'We've got to go back. We can't stay here.'

'I'm staying,' said Cai. 'This is fantastic. Have you ever been out in a storm before? This is fantastic.'

'Cai, please.'

'You go back if you want.'

Gwidion pleaded again. 'I can't go back without you.'

'Then stay with me.'

'What if... what if... ' Gwidion searched for an argument which would shake his brother out of this escapade, but he also didn't want to think too closely about the dangers that might persuade Cai to come back.

'What if what?' said Cai. 'What can happen to us?'

Gwidion gestured. 'The woods.' The area of land between them and the dome was illuminated again as another fork of lightning struck. 'They say there are some people who still live here. And animals.' His words were drowned by the crack of thunder.

'The eye of the storm is right above us,' said Cai when the sound had faded away. 'The dome is the highest thing anywhere around. We're much safer here.'

As if on cue, lightning struck again, this time appearing to hit the dome itself. Gwidion looked at Cai.

'See I told you. It's all right, the lightning conductor will earth it if it does strike.'

They squatted down on the thick carpet of needles, gazing out towards the dome and breathing in the scent of pine. It was a breath-taking sight. Lights from the duggs and the roundhouse pierced the darkness, providing the only relief to the blackness. It appeared so comforting, so inviting. For the first time Gwidion stood looking back at his world from the outside. It reminded him of the feeling he experienced when he first saw images of Earth taken from outer space. Of course he had seen images of the dome from outside too. But this was different. Here was the cradle of his life, here was the only place he had ever really known. Here was the place he was being asked to leave. He stared at the flickering lights and tried to locate them. The roundhouse was easiest to find because of its central position and its size. But his mother, where was she? And Lauren?

The rain was falling harder than ever and though the thick covering of fir trees gave them shelter, the large droplets falling from above caught them in unsuspecting places, tormenting them with their coldness. The thick clouds bulged as they clipped the dome but the storm passed as fast as it had arrived and the sky lightened a little. In the new quietness the sounds of water dripping from the trees above onto the forest floor became unnerving. They sounded like footfalls and they seemed to come from everywhere. He breathed deeply and regularly, knowing that if he suggested going back, Cai would only come up with some new mad idea – and going further into the forest was the most likely.

Cai finally turned his gaze away from the settlement.

'Let's go,' he said, walking out casually into the open as if it was a bright sunny day, back towards the dome.

chapter twelve

The next day, when the mentor asked Gwidion to stay behind after study finished, he feared the worst. While he waited for the others to leave he had to endure their inquiring looks as they filed out. Bethan at least gave him a smile and the relief of tension which that brought meant he returned it eagerly. In a brief moment he caught Lauren's eyes noticing, assessing and passing judgment on the innocent exchange of looks. Just as quickly she averted her gaze and walked out without giving him a glance. The mentor stood at the doorway to the roundhouse and beckoned.

'Come, let's walk.'

The mentor guided him through the duggs in silence. In some indefinable way he seemed older today, and as they walked Gwidion occasionally felt his weight press on him as his balance shifted on the uneven ground.

'Have you ever been outside the dome?'

Gwidion looked at him, but the mentor had his eyes fixed on the ground. It was a moment before he replied, as evenly as he could, with his heart thumping in his chest. It was so violent he feared the mentor might hear it.

'It is forbidden.'

'Many things are forbidden,' said the mentor. They had left the duggs and were walking along a path through the fields towards the north-east edge of the dome where carrots and other root crops were spraying their foliage over the furrows like sprouts of hair. Even on this cultivated area the ground was beginning to rise and its effect was accentuated by the straight lines of the planting which seemed to take off in front of them. Beyond the fields the ground rose even more steeply, continuing to the wind farm which could be seen through the ocuspex. The wind was still fresh after last night's storm and the great windmill blades were cutting through the air. At the edge of the dome there was a doorway similar to the one Gwidion and Cai had gone out through last night. There was a sudden change in temperature and sound level as they stepped through it and continued to climb. The wind whipped at their smocks and the white silent blades of the turbines could now be heard swishing loudly.

'It's a magnificent sight, isn't it?' said the mentor stopping to look back at their home. 'It's a sight everyone should see.' He turned back again to Gwidion and then continued his climb, bent over into the wind.

'There are not many things which are forbidden in our village.' He sighed. 'Forbidden things invite us to try them. That's why the doors are left open. That's why nobody stops you going to the Ruins.'

'No harm comes from it,' said Gwidion hesitantly.

'No. So can you imagine why they are forbidden?'

'Maybe because there is some danger.'

'Yes, the Ruins could be dangerous. It would be a long way to fall.'

They had reached the outer rim of the wind farm and as they turned again to look at the dome the wind hit the back of their heads. There was a long silence which Gwidion was compelled to break.

'And out here. Is it dangerous too?'

The mentor appeared to sniff the air. 'That's what I want you to find out.'

'What do you mean? They say there are still people living out here, and all sorts of animals.'

'Don't believe all the tales you hear, Gwidion. And anyway I don't mean that you have to come out here to find what you are looking for. I mean it's a project for you this summer.'

Gwidion turned his attention from the fascinating sight of the dome and realised that the windmills stood on a ridge. He wondered what they would see if they climbed to the top and looked beyond. Would they be able to see the sea? And what lay to the north? A memory of his dream came back to him and made him shudder involuntarily. That way lay the bluestone quarries. The mentor interrupted his reverie.

'We don't really know if it is dangerous. But there is fear out here, and ignorance. And there are few things more dangerous than those. Perhaps the most frightening thing out here after all is fear itself. We have lost the habit of exploring. We've lost our sense of adventure. I'd like you to understand why that happened.'

'You mean you want me to study history,' said Gwidion.

The mentor laughed and put his arm around him again. 'You have a wonderful ability to see through things and reduce them to the bare bones sometimes, Gwidion. It is a useful talent for a historian.'

'Why me? Why history? History is so dull. All we learn about is the dome and its construction and how it works. I know that stuff. There are plenty of things I could do which I am much better at – and which would be more useful to the village.'

'History, Gwidion. You've only just begun to understand our history. Even I, who have been to Madrid and learned much more of it than you, am only a student. When... if... you go to the Academy you will be able to find out many things which are not known here, or if they are then they are certainly not discussed. Colonel Jiménez will return in the autumn to see you again and he will ask you if you want to go to the Academy in Madrid. What will you say?'

'I don't know.'

'No. And you cannot know yet.'

'You think I should go.'

'I can't answer for you, Gwidion, and nor can anyone else. I am your mentor – not your commanding officer. But for us to have this conversation properly, you must at least know what I know, and what Colonel Jiménez knows. I will help you if you like.'

The mentor reached inside the satchel slung over his shoulder and pulled out a thick bound notebook. Real books were rare enough, but Gwidion had never seen anything like this. The mentor handed it to him, at the same time sharing and enjoying the appreciation which the youngster showed. Gwidion leafed through it carefully, running his flat hand diagonally up the page to feel its texture or as if his palm could make sense of the text. It was old and dog-eared and yellowing, and each page was covered in the mentor's spidery handwriting. The outside had been covered at some stage in maize fibre to protect it, but inside the pages were made of manufactured paper, thin and fine and reeking of age. The contents, however, were less impressive at first glance. It seemed to consist of an endless list of dates.

'What is it?' asked Gwidion.

'History, but not like we learn in study. It is history from before the dome was built. These are things we are not allowed to see.'

'Before the dome?' There was a note of awe in Gwidion's voice. 'You wrote it yourself?'

'In Madrid I had access to many things. You cannot imagine it, Gwidion. They have all sorts of books. Ideas, philosophies, religions which we have never heard of. I copied it.'

Gwidion was still turning page after crammed page.

'It's huge.'

'It took me many months. Every night I would spend an hour or more transcribing the book I found.'

'But nobody has ever seen this here?'

'No. Until now. There are many people who would prefer that knowledge like this was lost forever.'

'Can I read it?'

The mentor laughed. 'And I was thinking I might have to persuade you to take on this project.'

'You wanted me to read it?'

'I want you to study it. I want you to know what life was like before the dome was built. If you go to Madrid you will have access to knowledge that you can only dream about. You need to be prepared.'

Gwidion nodded. The mentor looked at him sideways to see his expression. A hint of a smile played at his lips as he spoke the next sentence.

'And Ce'nder Lauren, perhaps.'

Now Gwidion looked him straight in the eye, but the trace of humour was already hidden.

'She is a good history student. She has that... ' he searched for the word, '... tidiness of the mind, the ability to follow the plot.'

If such a thing was possible, Gwidion suddenly felt even more excited about the whole idea. He suddenly felt better about a lot of things.

Gwidion hovered in front of the entrance to Lauren's dugg. He was not so naive that he didn't know he'd been fixed up by the mentor, but that didn't make it any easier. He thought about her last words to him a few days ago and wondered how to tackle it. With humour, perhaps?

Something along the lines of: 'You know you wanted me to go to Madrid? Well, here's how you can help.' No. Too cutting. She did have some justification for being angry at him after all. And he did want her to help him. He also wanted her to like him. More than anything he wanted that.

How about: 'The mentor says you are to help me with my summer history project.' No. He didn't want to pull the mentor's rank on her either. That sounded too childish.

He backed away from the dugg, suddenly losing his nerve. There was no rush. The mentor had only assigned the project that day. Perhaps he should leave it until an opportunity presented itself. That would be more natural. She surely wouldn't remain annoyed at him forever. But before he had a chance to do anything, Lauren's mother pulled back the curtain from the doorway.

'It's you, Ce'nder Gwidion. I thought there was someone there. Come in.'

Gwidion was inside before he had managed to stutter anything apart from a surprised 'Henffic' and give Lauren's mother a formal kiss. She returned to her work table, putting a magnifying glass to her eye and bending over an open port.

'Lauren's gone to fetch me something, she'll be back soon. Sit down.'

Gwidion sat cross-legged on the floor and watched her carefully cleaning the inside of the port with a tiny brush.

'Nine times out of ten these things just need a clean. Dust is lethal. It's nearly always dust.' She sighed and straightened her back. 'I'm no more than a cleaning woman really. They weren't designed to operate in these sorts of conditions.'

'Where were they designed for?' asked Gwidion.

'Offices. They were built a long long time ago, Ce'nder Gwidion, when people didn't work surrounded by bare floors and animals.'

'Skyscrapers?' said Gwidion quietly. Lauren's mother looked up at him, puzzled at first. Then she laughed.

'Yes, skyscrapers maybe. Certainly.'

'Have you seen a skyscraper, Ce'nder Arianrhod?'

'Never.' She shook her head. 'I don't think I'd want to.'

'I would.'

'Maybe one day you will, if there are any left. Peru, Argentina, I don't know.'

Gwidion liked Lauren's mother. She was different from lots of the other women. She talked to him differently. And she knew things.

'Will you go to Madrid?'

Gwidion was taken aback by her directness for a moment.

'I don't know.'

There was a silence as she concentrated on her work and Gwidion wondered what to say next.

'My father is in Madrid.' He tried to sound casual as if discussing where he had left some trivial household object, but there was a shiver in his voice which he could not hide. Arianrhod put down her brush, came from behind her work table and squatted beside him. She took his hands in hers and examined them as if looking for dust.

'There is nothing I know that I would not tell you, Ce'nder Gwidion. But when we are young we are protected from this knowledge. We live like one family — a family of cousins, and that is the way we have chosen.'

'And when we grow up and we want to know?'

'Then we may be told. But it is a question for your mother, not for me.'

Gwidion looked up at her, his clear grey eyes wide open, ready at any minute to shed tears – and once more she wished it did not have to be like this.

'Did you know your father, Ce'nder Arianrhod?'

She shook her head. 'When I was a girl there were many more men in the village than now. It was not so easy to know then. And in a way it was not so hard on us either.'

'Ce'nder Gwidion. Henffic.' Lauren's arrival took them by surprise. Arianrhod dropped Gwidion's hands and stood up, tousling his head as she rose.

'Lauren.'

Gwidion rose to greet her.

She gave her mother the bottle of alcohol she had gone to fetch and Arianrhod returned to her cleaning duties. Lauren appeared pleased to see Gwidion although she affected a brusque and efficient manner.

'Have you got the book?'

Gwidion looked at Lauren's mother.

'That's OK,' said Lauren. 'She knows.'

The mentor had obviously prepared the way well. Gwidion reached inside his smock and pulled it out. He carefully unwrapped it from the piece of cloth he had used to hide it and opened it before her.

'It's just numbers,' he said almost to himself. 'Columns and rows of numbers.'

'They're dates,' replied Lauren brightly, attempting to take it off him. Gwidion stopped her.

'No, wait. Look at them. It's virtually every year – 1521, 1522, 1523, 1524. Every year, since history began.'

Lauren read the page he held out before her. '1521, Mexico conquered by Cortes. 1522, Rhodes taken by the Turks. 1523, Swedes expel Danes. 1524, Peasants' War in Germany.'

Gwidion sat down next to Lauren and the two watched mesmerised as their eyes ran over the brief accounts of each conflict. Page after page. He called out dates at random and Lauren flicked through the notebook to see if there was an entry.

'1894, Armenian massacre by the Turks. 1839, first Afghan war.

1680, Louis XIV annexes Alsace. 1648, second English Civil War. 1618, Thirty Years War. 1640, Second Bishops' War.'

So much war, so much killing, so many people dead. Every year. Since history began. They stopped and looked at each other.

'I'm not sure this is what we're supposed to be doing,' said Lauren.

'928,' said Gwidion. Lauren returned to the book.

'Brandenburg taken from the Slavs.'

And the macabre game began again.

'251, Goths defeat Emperor Decius. 43, Roman invasion of Britain. 1904, Russo-Japanese war. 1664, New York taken by the English...'

In the recitation of humanity's appalling habit for getting into war, Lauren and Gwidion's own conflict was soon forgotten. The end of the summer study term was just over a week away and suddenly it seemed to both of them an enticing prospect. Most of the older children would be assigned projects by the mentor but the months of July and August would be busy for all the village. There was much work to be done in the fields harvesting what was now coming to fruition – and the children were needed to help with that. Thanks to the protection of the dome a second planting would also take place in July for harvesting in October or November – and even over the winter many of the hardier vegetables could be grown.

It was late when Gwidion left Lauren's dugg and his head reeled with kings, queens, leaders and battles. He walked to the menhir to clear his head and rest his eyes, and wrapped his arms around the tall coolness of the stone. His fingers found the ogham inscriptions along its sides and rested on the well-worn grooves. He would have liked to think that history had been different in the days of the cromlech builders – that these people who had first dared to commit their thoughts to the permanence of writing might have lived in wiser and more enlightened times. But the ancient Celtic tree alphabet and calendar which his fingers now read represented a war of words – and maybe much worse besides.

He leaned his forehead against the menhir and listened to the hum of his own thoughts echoing back. He began to sing. Nothing at first. A low chant – as you might fall into when working for long periods with a machine, to break the monotony and relieve the mind from its numbing effect. Then it started to change, to become something else, something familiar but too elusive to be discovered. And after a while he was able to name it. It was one of their winter solstice carols.

> *Of all the trees that are in the wood*
> *The holly bears the crown.*

What movement of peoples, what intellectual conflict, what clash of cultures, what bloodshed lay behind that innocent line? For this was the time of the druids, whose sacred oak was the tree of knowledge itself, the undisputed king of their universe. The oak, in whose month they were now, marking the end of the first half of the year and the start of the second. The holly, the holy tree, evergreen twin of the deciduous oak. The holly and the oak. They lay too in Gwidion's bonds, woven into him in an eternal struggle.

Tonight, however, they were at peace as he relaxed his body into the stone. He allowed himself to breathe deeply, pressing his abdomen against the menhir and filling his lungs with its faint lichen-scented breath. Then out, feeling his own breath return to him. His eyes closed and he saw before him the woodland he had visited last night and had seen that morning with the mentor from the wind farm.

In an instant he was there, a few hundred metres from the ridge he had wanted to climb earlier. The light was strange, neither day nor night. Rather it was without colour, like a woodcut or a landscape caught in a flash of lightning. He felt his knees tingling with the effort of climbing the steep slope. The grass was rough where the village's flock of sheep had not grazed and grew in great tufts, some of which were as tall as his legs. He arrived at the ridge panting, expecting to see an expanse of mountains, but there was only a shallow valley and another ridge ahead, no higher than the one he was on now.

He carried on, though the ground became even more rough. Small trees were taking root where no animals from the village came at all. A network of brambles was spreading out in search of new and devilish ways to loop and bind and trip. There were small birches and hawthorn which ripped at his clothes and his skin as he brushed against them. He walked for what seemed like many minutes before reaching the top of the second ridge.

There were no mountains, as he had expected, only a meadow. The sort of meadow he might expect to find in another time and another place completely. Large ox-eye daisies grew among the fescues and tall buttercups. The more he looked, the more he could see – cornflowers, plantains, docks. As he looked the colour returned to the scene. And there, in the middle – it was incredible he hadn't seen it at first – a huge oak tree. It was twenty metres or more high, standing alone in the centre of the field, laden with its semi-glossy leaves, its long gnarled branches reaching out in the most perfect shape.

It was an exhilarating sight. He began to run. He wanted to throw his arms around it before it slipped from his grasp. He got no further than halfway before the grey wash returned. In the sky above him a huge black cloud was chasing the colour from his beautiful meadow. The flowers seemed to bend under the terrible weight of the cloud. He sprinted as fast as he could the last thirty metres to the tree, desperate to keep ahead of the cloud, and threw his arms around it blindly. There was a flash of lightning, a crack and a terrible smell of charred wood. He opened his eyes, holding in his arms the shattered, blackened remains of his once-proud oak, its branches and vegetation gone, its heart broken, its massive trunk gutted and smoking, cleft into a giant V shape silhouetted against the monochrome sky.

chapter thirteen

'You don't know if it's yours.' There was just room for the two of them to walk side by side along the path leading from the menhir to the Ruins. Cai walked slightly ahead, his body half-turned to look back at his brother. 'Fathers never do. You can never be sure. It was the celebration after all.'

He stopped so that Gwidion caught up with him and stood head to head. Gwidion felt his breath on his face.

'Maybe someone was there before you, maybe someone was there after you. There's no point in getting all moony about it.'

Gwidion pushed past him and attempted to fill the path so that Cai had to walk behind him.

'I'm not going all moony about it.'

'Just a flash in the pan, was it?' jeered Cai. 'Just a quick fiddle with a friend.'

Gwidion walked on in silence.

'Don't tell me you didn't feel something when you found out. You must have felt something. A small leap of the heart, maybe? The proud dad. You couldn't help it, could you?'

'I thought you said I wasn't the father,' said Gwidion grimly.

'Maybe not, I said. You don't know. That's the really terrible bit. You just don't know.'

Gwidion turned and faced him.

'You don't know anything, Cai. Whatever you say, for all your cynicism and cruelty, you don't know anything.'

He walked back the way he came, pushing past his brother again.

'If you really want to know, I hope it's not mine.' He turned and faced his brother again. 'Maybe it's yours.'

Cai laughed loudly. 'Bravo, little brother. Maybe it is.'

They had reached the menhir again. Gwidion looked towards the roundhouse where people were already gathering. It was early evening and the work in the fields had been abandoned in the face of the news. This was the dome's first baby for eight years – if it survived, and there was no way of knowing if that would happen. For now it was enough that Bethan was pregnant, even pregnancy was something worth celebrating.

'Maybe it'll be twins,' Cai's jibes distracted Gwidion. He was not ready to join the villagers at the roundhouse. He had to think what he was going to do. What was he supposed to do? Congratulate her? He was a jumble of ill-defined emotions, but he had no precedent to guide him. He was just five at the time of the last birth in the village, he had no idea how he was supposed to behave.

'Twins. That would be good. Like us, Gwidion. Twins of twins. What do you think the chances are of that happening?'

Gwidion looked from the roundhouse to the duggs and back to the roundhouse.

'Leave me alone, Cai.'

'Alone? That's the last thing you want to be, isn't it? Besides I'm your brother. You always wanted a brother, didn't you? Well that's me. We think. Sort of.'

Gwidion leaned against the menhir in exasperation.

'You wanted a father, too. And you got that. We think. Well, he says so anyway. And now *you* are a father. We think.'

Gwidion turned again towards the Ruins. He was trapped. One way lay the roundhouse and a social situation he could not face. The other way lay Cai and his merciless teasing. He was tired after the morning's work and the heat of the day even now was still over-powering. The sweat trickled from his eyebrows into his eyes, interfering with his vision and turning the village into a blur as if mirroring his own feelings.

'OK,' said Cai suddenly. 'Let's ask her.'

Gwidion reacted immediately, grabbing his brother's arm. 'I'll go.' Cai shook himself free, standing aside and letting his hand indicate the way past in an exaggerated display of courtesy.

'Off you go, then.' And he watched Gwidion as he headed towards the roundhouse.

chapter fourteen

Tabitha was at her cooking tables, the centre once more of the preparations. Her face and arms were red from the day's exertions and the heat and she bore both with a look of determination, though there was a lightness for all that. Groups of villagers were congregating outside, while behind the tables Gwidion saw the healer and Bethan's mother kneeling beside Bethan who was propped up against a sack of maize. Gwidion walked resolutely on past the greetings of the others and past Tabitha's table. She opened her mouth as if to say something, then appeared to think better of it. Instead she addressed the company in general.

'Eight years.' She gave a low manly whistle. 'Eight years. I was beginning to think I'd never see the day again.'

It was enough to distract their looks from Gwidion's entry, and once she had their attention she made full use of it.

'So let's get moving if we're going to have a celebration. We're not going to get the poor girl anything to eat by standing around talking. I need people to help here. Thank you, Ce'nder. And where's that mentor with the meat?'

The healer still knelt with her hands on Bethan's womb. She was a stick of a woman, smaller than Gwidion but seemingly wearing the skin of someone much larger and fatter. Both she and Bethan had their eyes closed. Gwidion hovered nearby, almost ready to beat a retreat, but Bethan's mother noticed him and moved aside with a kind gesture.

The healer took her hands from Bethan and knelt upright.

'It is well,' she said. Then to Bethan, 'Eat plenty, stay in good health. You are young and strong, this is a fine day.'

Bethan had opened her eyes and turned them on her new visitor.

'Henffic, Ce'nder Bethan' said Gwidion. 'Are you all right? I heard that you fell in the fields.'

She smiled. 'It was nothing, a little faintness, that is all.'

'It was very hot today.'

Bethan giggled girlishly and placed her hands over her stomach. 'And now I don't have to work again. Thank you, Ce'nder Gwidion.'

The healer and her mother had not moved away. His heart beat fast. He needed to ask her, but the words formed in the churnings of his stomach lay like bile at the back of his throat.

'The healer thinks it will be well,' said Bethan.

'Good. Eight years. It is a great day for you and for us.'

He hoped she might say something else. Something, anything to give him an indication and answer his unspoken question. She was polite and kindly, but she was also distant. He felt like he had felt after their encounter at midsummer – nervous and inferior and naive. He felt he did not have the right.

Behind them Tabitha gave a sudden shout and they all turned to see the mentor arriving with a pig in a wheelbarrow. Behind him came Gwidion's mother who rushed to greet Bethan, putting her arm around her son's shoulders as she did so and pulling him tight against her.

'Go and help the mentor, Gwidion,' she said. 'Ce'nder Bethan needs rest and there are many more people coming to congratulate her. I too would like to talk to her.'

'Henffic,' said Gwidion again to Bethan as he left.

Lauren's mother was becoming exasperated. This was supposed to be a day of unprecedented celebration. She was hungry, the fire was already alight outside the roundhouse and the smell of food wafted enticingly through the duggs. Her daughter still lay on her mattress, unwilling to move.

'Leave me alone. I'm tired.'

Her mother tried for the umpteenth time to cajole her out of this sulk. She knelt beside her and stroked her hair which was laid out on the pillow hiding her face.

'Lauren, we must talk. This is a great day for the village. It is our duty as women to congratulate Ce'nder Bethan. She would do the same for you.'

'Would she?' The last remark had finally pricked her into a response. She sat up, pushing her mother's hand away from her hair, and smoothing it out of her tear-stained face. 'Would she?'

At that moment Gwidion's mother appeared at the entrance. 'Henffic.'

'Henffic, Ce'nder Ana. Come in.'

Ana hesitated. 'If you are sure it is a good time?'

It was Lauren who spoke as the three exchanged kisses. 'Stay. My mother says I must go to the celebration, but I don't want to.'

'It would be kind to greet Ce'nder Bethan.'

'She is no ce'nder to me.'

Lauren's mother busied herself at the table a few metres away.

'She went with your Gwidion. It is his child and yet he loves me. What sort of person can do such a thing?'

Ana shook her head. 'We do not know it is his child. Or rather we know and we do not know. We do not know because we do not ask. We do not ask because it is less painful not to know.'

Lauren gave a tut of impatience. 'No, truth is the least painful. It wasn't always like this.'

'You have great independence of mind, Lauren. That is a good thing, but in this matter we have another way and it has helped us survive. We did not choose it, it chose us. What alternative would you have?'

Lauren thought a minute. 'Well, if I love Ce'nder Gwidion and he loves me, then I should have his children and not Ce'nder Bethan.'

Ana corrected her gently. '*If* it is his child. But if it is not? Or if he is not fertile? Or if you are not fertile? Then there will be no children. And without children there will soon be no community. We have waited eight years for a new baby – and we have no guarantee that it will yet be born. If it does not then we must hope and wait once more. Conception is a lottery and we must find a way to increase our chances of success.'

Lauren would not be placated. 'Then there must be another way.'

'Ce'nder Ana is right. And you are right too, Lauren. You are becoming a woman, like we became women a long time ago and struggled with the same pain that you are struggling with. We are all ce'nder, we are all family, and that is the only reason we have survived. The father of Ce'nder Bethan's child will be shown in the bonds I weave for its birth day offering. He will be holly or oak or aspen or willow and that is all he will be. We can ask no further than that.'

'For the sake of the family,' said Lauren scathingly.

'For the sake of the family,' said her mother.

Lauren pulled her hairband out of her hair with a gesture of anger. Her hands tightened as she threw it on her mattress, beating it with her two clenched fists.

'I will not go to the celebration. And I will not complete my passage. I will find another way.'

The two women looked at each other and waited. When the crying had subsided, Lauren's mother put a hand on her shoulder as if rousing her from sleep.

'Lauren,' she whispered. 'Lauren.'

'What?' she answered petulantly.

'Earlier you said that truth was the least painful. I have not been truthful with you.'

Lauren looked up and wiped her eyes. Her mother exchanged a glance with Ana and spread her hands before her as if examining them.

'If truth is so important to you, then you deserve to hear it.'

'What?' This time there was an eagerness in her voice.

'The story I told you about my mother's apprentice. It wasn't the whole story.'

Lauren's attention was hooked.

'His name was Pablo. Pablo Jiménez.'

'The colonel?' Lauren asked, her eyes wide. 'Ce'nder Gwidion's father?'

Her mother nodded.

Lauren's mind was reeling, she could not help but let out a gasp of surprise. She looked towards Ana then back to her mother.

'But Pablo. You loved Pablo.'

'I loved your father too. In a lifetime we are lucky to be able to love more than one.'

'But Pablo was... special.'

There was both a smile and a sigh in her mother's expression as she took her daughter in her arms. 'I shared his love for a short while and I do not regret that. But I was not the one he really loved.'

'Who then? Is he with her now? I have heard that things are different in Madrid. Who was it?'

Her mother smiled towards Ana. Lauren looked from one woman to the other as the shock of what was not being said sank in.

'You, Ce'nder Ana?'

Gwidion's mother nodded.

'You mean... ? But you are the best of friends. You mean, he really loved you?'

'Just as Gwidion loves you.'

Lauren didn't know whether to laugh or cry or be angry. The three emotions flickered over her face in quick succession and as fast as one appeared it was replaced by another. Ana put her hand on Lauren's.

'You must do whatever you think is right. But if ever you feel, even for a moment, that nobody understands or that you are the only one to go through this, then at least you know you are not alone.'

'And what did you do, mother? When Ce'nder Gwidion was born?'

Her voice shook with emotion. 'By that time I too was carrying a child. And I knew what every mother knows in any place at any time. That there is nothing more important than that and nothing more deserving of celebration. I swallowed my pride and went to Ce'nder Ana, and I was glad that the village was to have two new children.'

She rose and the two older women embraced for a long time in the semi-gloom of the dugg. Without them noticing, Lauren slipped quietly out and headed for the fields where the other villagers had been working that day.

The maize had now been harvested and it was the turn of the solar carts to do their work clearing the stalks and vegetation so new plantings could be made. Lauren watched their slow progress. It struck her somehow as a sad sight. Finally she bent to pick up a billhook from the ground along with a strand of maize stalk. She split it expertly into three long strands, pulling it over the sharp blade in a swift easy movement. After knotting one end she began plaiting the strips quickly into a *caseg fedi*, the harvest mare.

She admired her handiwork for a moment laying the ancient fertility symbol on her upturned palms which she held out before her as if making an offering. She retraced her steps to the village, stopping before Bethan's dugg.

'Henffic,' she said softly, laying the *caseg fedi* at her door. 'It is yours.'

chapter fifteen

If the holidays of childhood always seemed to be over too quickly, the summer of 2084 was by far the shortest in Gwidion's brief life. It was already September and the autumn winds had arrived early, turning the forests around the dome a premature yellow. Bethan's pregnancy was progressing well, the fields around the menhir had been replanted with beet making the Ruins appear nearer. Instead of the majestically colourful view of green and yellow sweetcorn, the large floppy ears of beet gave the fields a soft, plush look.

In Lauren's dugg, the two young history students had grown closer than ever. They had not talked about it directly, but the day of

Gwidion's possible departure was now close at hand, and neither of them believed he wouldn't go.

He and Lauren had reached the end of their project. Though they had memorised its contents and could recite the battles of history across nearly three millennia, the mentor's notebook was incomplete. He had copied it from an old encyclopaedia published in the year 2001. While it did provide a picture of an interconnected and global civilisation, what it didn't explain was what had gone wrong or why the dome itself had been built. The notebook was only the beginning, a tantalising tease for the meat that was still to come. Madrid held out the promise of that knowledge.

'The mentor must have known that when he gave us the book,' said Lauren in frustration. 'I bet he does know more.'

They thought about seeking him out there and then and asking him for the rest of the story, but perhaps they knew they wouldn't get it. Besides, it was September 11, Gwidion's birthday. He was fourteen, there would be a celebration that night in the roundhouse and Colonel Jiménez was here. In fact that was where Gwidion had to go now.

The colonel had fallen foul of one small detail in his plan to take Gwidion to Madrid – and that was that it was not purely a decision for Gwidion or his mother. His failure to observe the etiquette of village decision-making was forgiven, but he was not excused his appearance before the Women's Council.

Ana had a place on the tribunal as Gwidion's mother, along with Tabitha and Michaela, the mother of one of the younger girls in study.

Colonel Jiménez stood before them in his grey and gold uniform, a man of medium height, slightly bowed by the weight of his position, but not one used to explaining his actions to a tribunal of women. He was, after all, the representative of the Republic of Hispania, the last great technological power on Earth. His approach was not going down well.

'Ana, your son is a rare talent. What are you able to offer him out here in Mimosa?'

'Your appeal is to the tribunal, not to his mother,' Tabitha reprimanded him. He turned to her with a look of irritation and bowed his head in an exaggerated gesture.

'Apologies. As I was...'

'What is the Academy exactly, Colonel Jiménez?' Michaela interrupted him.

He turned to her and drew himself up, pulling the jacket of his uniform downwards. 'We are the top scientific research institute in the Republic. Some of our greatest minds have been educated there – and still work there.'

'On what?' asked Ana.

Jiménez appeared non-committal. 'On a number of different projects.'

'And my son? Yes, he is clever but I am sure you have other equally bright students. Why do you want him?'

'We want all the bright students we can get. If Gwidion is to fulfil his potential, he cannot remain here. Look. I don't wish to appear rude or dismissive of your community or patronising, I didn't come here to do either of these things. Your founders chose your niche and we have no wish to interfere with it. Your life here is as successful as it can be, given the problems we all face, but you must acknowledge that it only continues because of the existence of the Republic. You know that is true. There are certain things that neither we nor you can escape. Without our technological help your life here would be extremely precarious.'

'We cope,' said Tabitha.

'You cope,' he repeated. 'And in 2070 when the springs ran dry you were unable to cope without us. In 2074 when the hydroponics bays failed we provided the laboratory support you needed to re-establish them. If the Outlanders ever attacked, you would depend on us for your security. If the structure of the dome was endangered you would need our helicopters to repair it. When the solar accelerators fail you will come to us to replace them.'

He spread his hands wide. 'Shall I go on? Your way of life depends on us – and we in turn depend on you. In return for what help we are able to give you we ask you for your finest brains which we are unable to find elsewhere. And the rest of the time we leave each other alone.'

'We have lost many young people to Madrid,' said Tabitha.

'And many return with technological skills which help maintain your way of life in Mimosa. But apart from that, have you considered what it is your children want?'

'Ah, Colonel Jiménez, this is something you may not understand in your Academy. We are a community here, and every member must sometimes give up a little of their individuality for the sake of everyone else. That is the meaning of community.'

'Even when that is not what is best for them?'

'In return they receive the benefits of living in a community. They do not have to look for help or beg their neighbour for it or worry how to solve their problem. No-one here has a problem that is not everyone's problem. When someone leaves, our world shrinks a little, and those who remain must give up a little more of their individuality to keep the village alive.'

'When someone leaves, that is their decision,' said the colonel. 'We persuade them to come to the Academy, but we cannot force them to stay.'

'You know of Gwidion's episodes, his fits, his dreams, call them what you like? What effect will life in the Academy have on him?' Ana said.

Jiménez was quick to latch onto the argument. 'I owe you an honest answer, Ana. We do not know how he will fit in or even if he will fit in. But we can provide the medical, psychological support which might help him overcome those problems.'

'And you know about Cai?' she asked shortly.

'I repeat. Whether Gwidion stays or returns will be his decision, but our facilities and our knowledge of dealing with what appears to be a childhood trauma are very much more advanced than here.'

'You lie,' said Ana softly. 'Isn't that the very reason you want him? You never answered my question, Colonel Jiménez. What research will he be involved in?'

Jiménez passed the palm of his hand flat across his bald head. 'I am not at liberty to tell you that. He will receive the finest schooling at the Academy in a number of subjects. Where he chooses to concentrate his energies will be as much a decision for him as for us.'

'The Hispania Soma Academy,' said Tabitha.

He bowed. 'To give it its full title.'

'I can remember hearing of the City of Dreamers, Colonel.'

He gave a sardonic smile. 'A colourful description, but not necessarily an accurate one. However you are correct in one thing. Soma involves the study of dream states. I cannot tell you a lot more than that. The truth is we know little about dreaming or the mental forces at work in someone like Gwidion, but we believe that some of the answers to our problems may lie with children like him. And some of the answers he seeks may lie with us.'

He looked at the faces of the women. This was not good. Any hint of secrecy was only increasing the mistrust between them – and he saw the prospects of taking Gwidion away fast disappearing.

'Colonel Jiménez, you know how greatly we depend on our children in the dome,' said Tabitha.

He tried again. 'You are familiar with shamanic healing, you practise it yourselves. The notion that there are certain people able to travel independently of space and time has been fundamental to many civilisations in history. We believe Gwidion may have a unique form of that power, one which could be immensely valuable to us.'

'Militarily, you mean?' said Tabitha.

Jiménez laughed. 'There are too few people left in this world to fight. I wear the uniform of a military man, these are the relics of our terrible history, but my interest is not in aggression or battle. The world is a very big place these days. There are huge areas of once-inhabited land where no-one has ventured for decades. We have no idea whether they are safe, whether there are groups of people still living some sort of non-technological life out there. In the Far East we believe there are pockets of population, there may even be biodomes. North America, the southern hemisphere? We think not, we don't know. What we do know is that what the Republic needs is not soldiers or weapons specialists. We need communicators. If we are to rebuild a world community we need to start talking to the rest of our scattered and cowed world. If there are people out there who have survived like we did then some of them may just hold the key to curing the fertility plague. We don't have a lot of choice – it is that or die the slow pathetic death of a people who have lost their way and their will to live.'

Now in the full flood of his rhetoric, he looked straight into the faces of each of the women. The sight of Ana's face, her long black hair, those aquiline features, reminded him of another period in his life, long, long ago. Despite his years in Madrid, despite his rank and his status, he could not hold her gaze.

'We are not so different, you and I,' he continued. 'Even in Madrid or Buenos Aires or Lima, the birth of a child is a day for great rejoicing.'

Tabitha looked at the two women beside her. 'Will we vote?' Ana shook her head.

'Bring in the boy,' she ordered.

There was a short delay while someone was found to go and fetch Gwidion. Jiménez paced the room while they waited. Gwidion entered hesitantly after some minutes had passed. Tabitha made to address him, but his mother stopped her. Suddenly she wanted to put an end to this hypocrisy, this arguing over shadows. Her son stood before her, and his father was asking him to follow him to Madrid. Sometimes things were absurdly simple.

'Gwidion, do you want to go to Madrid?' she asked.

Gwidion looked from one face to the other around the round-house in search of an answer. He thought of Lauren and his mother. He thought of the village he would have to leave, he thought of the books the mentor had told him about. But most of all he felt the confused emotions of an adolescent whose world has left the secure confines of childhood and has suddenly become incomprehensible, who is embarrassed by his failures and mistakes, to whom escape seems both possible and highly attractive.

'Yes.'

'Then the vote is cast,' said Ana. Tabitha gave a start at her pronouncement and looked quickly to Michaela, but she was already rising to leave. Ana went to her son and took him in her arms.

Jiménez joined the domers in Gwidion's birthday celebration which had suddenly also turned into a farewell party, for they would leave together the next day in the colonel's shuttle. There was little enough time for goodbyes in a community of so many people and Gwidion's eyes constantly searched out Lauren in the crowded roundhouse.

The mentor put his hand on his shoulder and said simply, 'You will do well, Ce'nder Gwidion.'

The boy reached inside his smock and proffered the dog-eared notebook.

'Keep it,' said the mentor. 'I have nothing else to give you. Besides,' he tapped his head and smiled, 'it's all up here.'

Gwidion turned to go, but the mentor held onto him a moment longer and lowered his voice so that others could not hear.

'There are some things I cannot tell you because I do not know them, and there are others I cannot tell you because this is where I live and I respect our customs. But here,' he fingered the chest of Gwidion's smock which concealed the notebook, 'you will find the truth. Not in the bare dates and entries, but between the lines, between the pages. That is the best I can do.'

Gwidion nodded, though he did not understand, and the mentor bent to kiss his head before releasing him to the rest of the crowd of well-wishers.

And then there were the other children from study who greeted him shyly. In their eyes he was already different from them, in some indefinable way he had already moved on, and it made him feel older and wiser and and more sure of what he had decided to do. The older villagers joked with him or embarrassed him with memories of his childhood. Some of the men had themselves spent time in Madrid when they were younger and treated him with the vicarious pride that parents feel when their offspring are about to achieve what they themselves never did. They teased him too, speaking Welsh with a lisp in imitation of a Spanish accent or strutting and saluting like men in uniform. But they were kind and many were genuinely moved.

'Don't forget your poor country cousins when you're in the big city,' they said. 'And bring us back some of that brandy.'

Others winked and nudged him. 'And keep your hands off those city girls.'

The mead and the lack of food and the emotion of the occasion were combining into a powerful intoxicant and Gwidion could do no more than grin or nod in reply.

Bethan, her stomach already swelling – though she still had to pull her smock tight with a belt to show it off to its best advantage – kissed him lightly on the lips. She tasted of mead and he felt again the light brush of her faint moustache with a surprising thrill of pleasure. He tried to find something to say, but she was almost gone before he had managed to utter a lame 'Good luck'. She turned and gave him a quick smile.

In the few moments that he had stopped searching out Lauren among the crowd, she suddenly appeared before him. She pressed her lips against the side of his cheek, pulling his head against hers with one hand while she pressed something cold and smooth into his other.

'Lauren,' he managed to say. But she was already gone. He opened his hand and looked down at the wrist clasp she had made for him at midsummer. The silver bonds were woven in intricate ways, the braids decorated with the leaves of his individual trees. The work was as fine as her mother's. Finer, perhaps, for he knew this had been forged out of her love for him. Holly, oak and hazel. It seemed like a lifetime ago. And the tears began to gather in his throat.

As for his mother, their goodbyes were left to the privacy of their dugg later in the night. There were no words to be said between a mother and son. And yet there were an endless number of words. Words such as, 'Look after yourself,' and 'Have you got everything?' and 'Will you need something warmer?' and 'Time will go quickly,' and 'You will be able to come back soon'. And when she had said all these things in as many possible ways as she could, and then started again until Gwidion began to get impatient, then they held each other as they had when he was smaller, rocking gently on his bed, wrapped up in her, shielded by her curtain of hair, feeling her lips on his head, drinking in her smell, feeling an inexplicable, unfathomable hole at the centre of their beings. Then at last there were very few words. 'I will miss you,' and 'I love you'.

In the brilliant morning sunshine the forests stretched in all directions. North to the bluestone quarries of the Preselis, west to the cleft silver blades of the Cleddau river. Eastwards they rolled unbroken like a thick green carpet. And southwards was the sea. Gwidion remembered what Lauren had said and imagined those blue-grey waves which had travelled so many thousands of kilometres from the other side of the world. Below him as the colonel's shuttle circled in farewell was the shrinking dome. And as the details lost their definition it became no more than a bubble of coloured light, an enormous eye staring up at him. At its centre were the dugg roofs, flecks of browny-green, ribboned with the red of the soil. Around that were the stripes of the fields of crops now growing their second harvests for the winter and beyond those, the metallic glints of the hydroponics bays and the solar arrays.

But this was not one of his dreams. At the southern end, outside the dome, the villagers had gathered to watch him leave. He could not count them all, but he knew they would all be there. Some he could pick out easily even at this distance — Giant Paddy, Tabitha. Others he did not dare look for. These were his people. He was woven into them as securely as the wrist clasp he wore. He let his fingers follow its intricate folds, enjoying its newness on his arm.

Colonel Jiménez turned from the controls of the air shuttle. 'One more pass and we must go.'

Gwidion did not answer. Despite the tears filling his eyes he still stared at his home. Like a painting left in the rain, the scene began to run, colours smudging and mixing into each other, the people blending into the earth. The giant eye closed and then they were gone.

Book Two

It is 99.9999 per cent certain that you are here, in this place and in this time. There is a very small possibility, infinitesimally small, that you are not. Sooner or later that will be true.

— The First Soñador

chapter one

Jiménez' assistant was the first to greet them when the shuttle landed. She smiled a perfect white smile at Gwidion – but that is not what one would remember about Alara Myers. Her colours, the smile, the olive skin, the grey and gold of the Academy uniform, seemed to exist only to emphasise her blackness. She was nineteen, black eyes, black hair cut to the shoulder and styled into a gentle wave, as Gwidion had only ever seen in ancient spools. She smelled of – he wasn't sure what she smelled of. He was unfamiliar with the scents, but they were dark and deep and honest.

'Welcome, welcome,' she said. She held his hand longer than he would have chosen. 'You and I are going to be great friends.'

He believed her immediately. She and the colonel exchanged some words in American, then she took Gwidion by the hand and led him inside the Academy. He had slept aboard the shuttle and had woken up in a wonderland. He had never seen buildings on such a grand scale before, though most of Europe had been famous for architecture such as this at one time – solid square stone buildings from the seventeenth, eighteenth and nineteenth centuries. The bright glare of the Spanish sun flattened the images, sending back a reflection which almost blinded his still sleepy eyes and made them water. But once through the doors, with the coolness of the shiny tiled corridors beneath his bare feet, the atmosphere was comfortable and hushed. He looked up in awe at the high-ceilinged rooms. Shuttered windows lined the walls, allowing shafts of light to fall from high up through chinks in the wood and catching myriad specks of dust in the languid air. The only remaining signs of the wealth of this colonial past were in the structure of the building. The decoration in stone and marble and plaster was a fierce expression of empire but now there were no ornaments or hangings to soften the effect.

Alara led him up a wide curving marble stairway which split to left and right and joined together again, forming a gallery which looked down the sweep of steps to the entrance. She walked briskly, as one who might walk this building in her dreams, following the seemingly identical dark corridors this way and that to the accompaniment of the hard tap of her feet on tiled floors and the soft pad of Gwidion's feet as he struggled to keep up. Door after closed door passed before his eyes until Gwidion lost all sense of where he was, let alone an appreciation of the architectural wonders around every corner. At last she stopped before one of the doors and opened it. They stepped into what might once have been an ante-chamber to some royal reception room. Now its vast emptiness contained nothing but the most basic of necessities.

'I will come to get you at five,' said Alara, still speaking American. 'Make yourself at home.'

'I've never seen anything like it,' said Gwidion.

'You will find it strange here at first, I did too. I'd never seen a room so big until I came to Madrid. I'm sure you're not used to this sort of bedroom either. Enjoy it, it's fun. Rest, look around, though there's not much to see from here. Soon you will meet some of the other students.'

She caressed his head in a sisterly way and left. Gwidion unpacked the very few things he had been allowed to bring with him from Mimosa, the very few things he could call his own – some clothes, his washing things. And something he had slipped into the bag without anyone noticing. He looked around the room, then enjoyed the novelty of bouncing on a sprung bed for a while. Then he sat again. In contrast with the silence of this large space, he remembered his going-away party. The faces were clear in his mind, the aftermath of tears was fresh in his eyes, but nevertheless it seemed an age ago. He thought of the warm snugness of his dugg and wondered what his mother was doing. He imagined her bent over some cooking and he felt a lump rising in his throat. He tried not to think of Lauren. And then there was the flight. First there was the huge expanse of sea, rolling towards Bretaña from America, and it had taken a long time to cross it, so that his initial excitement at flying had gradually faded to a vague contentment such as one feels after a good meal. Then there were the dense forests of Galicia and the endless desert scrubland of Extremadura. Then had come fatigue, and finally sleep. Now he was tired and hungry and the lump in his throat was becoming harder to swallow.

'There, there, Gwidion. Don't be sad.' The shock of hearing his name without the familial ce'nder from someone he barely knew was still something he had to get used to. In his village such a form of address could mean only two things – intimacy or insult. It was Alara's voice. He had not heard her come in. She was carrying a grey and gold uniform.

'I've brought you this to wear. You will feel very out of place in your smock when we go to the great hall to meet Soñador Martín.' She sat on the bed and he raised his tearful eyes to her. She took his face in both hands.

'I know it's strange. I know you miss your family. But we will be your family for a while until you are ready to return. You are as important to us here as you are to your village. You have valuable work to do. And I am here to take care of you.'

Important work meant nothing to him. He buried his face on the bed and cried again.

So they were late for Gwidion's first dinner at the Academy. As he followed Alara once more along the corridors he flexed his body inside the grey and gold uniform and let the sharp tap of his hard-soled shoes chime with Alara's brisk rhythm. His uniform was tight and stiff in places he was not used to tightness and stiffness, but it also asked things of him which made him forget any discomfort. To wear the uniform of the Academy required him to be bigger and taller. It required precision and purpose. It required him not to cry. These first hours were like a dream. In fact he had dreamed so much and so vividly in his life that he no longer knew for sure that it was not. They entered a huge dining hall where tables were laid end to end on either side and, backs to the aisle, sat boy after boy. They were about Gwidion's age and older, as old perhaps as seventeen or eighteen. And opposite each one a young woman. Their own Alaras, he guessed. Fair-haired Alaras, small Alaras, big Alaras, Alaras almost like his own.

'Stay by me,' she whispered as they began their huge walk down the aisle towards the top of the room. Gwidion trotted to keep up with her, trying at the same time to look at the lines of boys, all dressed in the neat light grey and gold suits of the Academy. None of them appeared to notice as he passed.

It was hardly light enough to see the details of the room clearly. Along the base of the walls small lamps projected their beams up towards the vaulted ceilings. By halfway up the effect of the illumination had faded to nothing but his eye was drawn upwards into the mysterious darkness of the vaults. Occasionally, from a certain angle, the light penetrated high enough to briefly reflect the gilt which covered the vaults. The effect was of a shooting star seen through the corner of the eye – a fuzzy yellow disc which was gone before it had been properly seen. He looked again at the boys waiting patiently at their tables, heads bowed.

'Are these all to be pilots?' he asked Alara in wonder and a little too loudly.

'Ssh. Very few, Gwidion. Very few.'

They reached their place near the top of the room and as he sat down he saw the only other face he knew in all those hundreds of faces – Colonel Jiménez, sitting with some other officers at the top table. Next to him was the man Alara had already told him about – Soñador Martín. He alone was not wearing the grey and gold of the Academy uniform, but a black cloak which accentuated the carefully combed greyness of his hair and the huge unkempt eyebrows which flitted about his face like two unruly caterpillars.

Of the others Jiménez stood out even then. His bearing was severe, but there was a lightness in the eyes which radiated friendliness and engendered trust. He smiled at Gwidion, and the boy could not help but smile back. And next to him – maybe it was his imagination, maybe it was not – Alara too returned his smile.

Someone else was watching the exchange with a less friendly expression. For the briefest of moments the soñador's eyes met Gwidion's. There was a hint of something, recognition, a connection at least, before the caterpillars met in the middle and he looked away. Gwidion's attention was soon taken by the other boys in the hall. After thirteen years in the village, Gwidion had grown accustomed to the company of girls. He looked at the boy alongside him at the table and then to Alara. 'Where do all these boys come from?' he wanted to ask. But before they had left his room she had instructed him to be quiet and to observe how the others behaved, so he remained silent. There was a slight commotion far at the other end of the room where they had come in. He looked up the aisle – it was all so far away he couldn't see what was causing it. The other boys did not react to the sound but kept their eyes on the table before them.

Soon he realised what was happening as plates of food were passed from hand to hand along the lines. Silently, wordlessly like some giant human conveyor belt.

After the richness and glory of the building, the food on his plate came as something of a disappointment. There was no meat or vegetables as Gwidion knew them. There were two squares of a textured substance, almost like meat, and some cubes of what could conceivably be vegetable matter. And over all of it a dark red sauce. Alara looked across at him and whispered.

'Textured protein,' she indicated the squares of meat-like matter. 'The sauce contains a full range of synthesised vitamins and minerals. Do as I do.'

Colonel Jiménez stood up at the top of the room. 'For the pride of our Republic, the pride of our produce. That you may one day lead us again to a land of plenty.'

The boys to his left and right immediately fell on the food before them. Gwidion copied Alara as she picked up a fork in her left hand and held a square of meat-matter firm to the plate with it, cutting through it with her knife. Then she lifted the fork to her mouth and ate.

The food must have been somewhere near hot at the beginning of its journey down the dining room. Now it barely steamed as he lifted it to his mouth. But Gwidion was hungry, and with the appreciation of one who has known real hunger, he found it tasted surprisingly good.

At the end of the meal, as the other boys and their keepers filed from the room in tidy pairs, the soñador caught his eye again. He stood.

'Stay. And you, Colonel, please.'

The four waited in silence until the hall had finally emptied and the echoes of hundreds of shoes faded into the distance. Jiménez still sat, his hands folded over his stomach, a light expectant look on his face.

'A new boy-mmm.'

Jiménez nodded. 'Gwidion. He is from Mimosa, I have high hopes of him.'

Martín stepped towards Gwidion and Alara. He was a tall man and as he moved his cloak made him look like a large black bird. '*You* have high hopes-mmm?'

Jiménez smiled at the peculiar verbal twitch which punctuated his sentences and gave the effect of a small motor struggling to start. It was endearing enough, almost charming, but also a sure indicator that Martín was rattled. Then to Gwidion. 'Welcome, Gwidion.'

Their eyes met again. The same flicker passed between them, Gwidion was sure. The emotions swelled inside his breast. He was here, in Madrid, with his father. He was bursting to reveal the secret, to have the colonel know he knew, to be allowed to call him father, to hug him even.

'Mimosa.' Then suddenly. 'Do you have a brother-mmm?'

Gwidion looked embarrassed. He glanced from Alara to Jiménez and back again. The soñador smiled.

'No matter. Here you will have many brothers. Hundreds of brothers.'

Gwidion could contain himself no longer. 'My father is in Madrid.'

Martín nodded slowly and chose not to ask the obvious question. As if continuing on his own tack, he added kindly: 'the colonel speaks highly of your abilities. Do you think you will live up to the colonel's expectations?'

'I want to be a pilot.'

The soñador smiled even more widely and the caterpillars played at the edge of his hairline. 'All small boys want to be pilots. Even the colonel can fly a shuttle. That is easy. I believe you will be more than that.'

Jiménez maintained his air of relaxed contentment. Gwidion remained silent. His spirit wilted. He had hoped for something from Jiménez, some small sign at least. Martín put a hand on his shoulder. 'We will talk again soon. If you want anything you must ask Alara, we want you to be happy here-mmm. Take good care of him, Alara.'

He gestured with his hand to show that the interview was over and the two turned to begin the long walk out of the hall. As they went they could hear the slowly fading conversation between the two men behind them.

'What is the meaning of this? I was not told of a new arrival-mmm.'

Jiménez still sat. He looked rather pleased with himself. 'Impressive, isn't he?' He knew the soñador's interest had been aroused.

'He may be, Colonel. He may not. That is why I assess all prospective students personally. Nobody is admitted to this Academy-mmm without my knowledge.'

Jiménez feigned surprise. 'I've only just brought him here, Soñador. He hasn't been in Madrid more than a few hours. You are virtually the first to meet him.'

'And how long before that have you been watching him?'

'Oh,' Jiménez said vaguely with a shrug.

'This isn't the first time this has happened, Jiménez.'

The colonel stood up at last, pulling his uniform straight. 'Does it matter? Part of my job is to find promising new students.'

'Your job-mmm is to report promising new students to me.'

Jiménez shrugged again. 'Do you want to send him back?'

'You are an insolent man, Colonel. What I want is for you to follow the procedures of the Academy. This is not some sort of production line for the ambitions of the Republic-mmm, nor is it a route to high power for people like you.'

Jiménez began to walk away. Martín called out after him.

'And it is not an ego trip for proud fathers and their offspring either. I will take this up in Buenos Aires.'

Jiménez turned and spread his arms wide open. 'Yes, Soñador. Try the president, he's an old friend of mine.'

Martín's voice quivered with suppressed anger. 'I set the rules in this Academy.'

'You set the rules, Soñador.' Jiménez turned and continued down the hall. His disappearing figure was illuminated briefly at intervals as he passed the floor-level lamps. His words reached the high ceiling and bounced back to Martín. 'I set the pace.'

'What will be our work here?' Gwidion asked. He wanted to ask so many things. He wanted to ask about the food and the other boys and where they came from. And the other Alaras. And Colonel Jiménez.

Alara sat with him on the bed that first night and ran her hand over his brow, her sweet white smile and her blackness consuming his questions.

'The soñador was angry. Why was he angry? Did I do something wrong?'

'There are too many questions to be answered all at once, Gwidion. Understand that you are here to learn, but more than that you are here to discover. The things we cannot teach you – that is what we wish you to learn.'

Gwidion shifted uncomfortably. 'These are riddles like our story-tellers tell us in the long winter nights.'

Her smile and her soft hand again soothed his impatience. 'Then there is hope for you.'

Gwidion pouted. 'I thought I was to be a pilot.'

'Maybe you will be. You are young, you may be many things. What we offer at the Academy is learning of all sorts. This is the greatest of all the Republic's educational institutions. Here we train technicians, historians, linguists, farmers, philosophers – you name it.'

'And pilots?'

'And pilots.' She laughed and smoothed his hair. 'First you must sleep. You are tired and tomorrow you will have many things to do.'

Gwidion nodded. She kissed him and for the first time since he had arrived Gwidion was able to breathe in her smell. Such proximity to a woman made him think of his mother and he hung round her neck tightly as if that might shut out the thought, as if that might strangle the tears bursting up from his stomach. They stayed like that motionless for a long time before she gently released his arms, kissed him again and drew herself away.

'Sweet dreams.'

She left, but sleep was not going to come that simply. In the tranquillity of his Academy room the events of the last days ran through Gwidion's head. In June, only a few months ago, the summer had stretched before him and there seemed so much time to think about his life, the village and the Academy. There were so many things he might have said to so many people. And yet suddenly, before he had had time to consider any of that, he was here in Madrid. Events seemed to sweep him along, just as Bethan had swept him into his first act of love and, in the process, tarnished his hopes of a relationship with the true object of his affections. And when that was all but repaired, along came the Academy and Jiménez. Another wave had knocked him off balance and taken him wherever it wanted to go.

And he was alone. There were none of the familiar snuffles and rustlings of someone sleeping nearby, there was no-one to talk to, no-one to share a joke with in the middle of the night when a storm whistled outside and sleep would not come, no-one with whom to share the spectres which prowled his dreams. Certainly he had known solitude in the village, had sought it even. But this being alone was different.

He turned his wrist back and forth to admire his treasured clasp which glinted and flickered by the light of his table lamp as he followed once more the intricate weave of its three bonds.

He went to the drawers where he had stashed his small collection of belongings, took out a close-woven cloth bag and undid the tie-strings. He brought the open bag to his nose and breathed in the smell. It was fading fast, but then the scent of gorse was notoriously difficult to preserve. The healer had given it to him as a symbol of the young sun and a talisman against evil of all sorts. And he appreciated it for that. But he valued it more because it was the scent of home. It smelled of his mother cooking biscuits and of his mother making honey. It reminded him of being ill and being comforted, it reminded him of being put to bed, his mother's hands still dusty and floury from her cooking. He tried to conjure up a picture of his mother, but it was not easy. The mentor, yes, or Lauren, certainly. But his mother, that image formed in the first few hours after birth, the most important image of a child's life, the one which enabled him to distinguish between safety and danger, the one which ensured food and comfort, the image of which he was more certain than anything else in the world, dissolved to the mind's touch like a reflection in a pool of water. It was warm and kind and loving. The image smelled of gorse. And like the scent of gorse, it did not travel well.

Then he thought of the mentor and reached inside his uniform to pull out the notebook he and Lauren had spent so much time poring over. He rubbed the flat of his hand against the wrinkled brown paper covering. Alara had said they trained historians. He wished Lauren was here with him. She would love the Academy. Himself, he wasn't sure.

chapter two

Alara was there when he opened his eyes again. She smiled at him and sat on the bed.

'Did you sleep well?'

She noticed him pushing his bag of gorse below the covers where no-one could see it, but said nothing. The job of surrogate mother came easily to her, but it was not without its pain. She watched his waking face come to terms with his surroundings as he realised where he was, felt with him as his stomach tightened and churned. 'You dreamed last night,' she said quickly.

'You knew?' he asked, curiosity helping to brighten his thoughts.

She nodded. 'I looked in to see you were all right. Look at the bed.' She pointed to the twisted heap of sheets and covers which Gwidion had emerged from. 'You were talking in your sleep.'

'What did I say?'

She smiled. 'Something in Welsh. You will have to learn to dream in Spanish or American if you want me to tell you that.'

'It was frightening.'

'You must learn to control your dreams. You must learn to dream what you want, not to be taken wherever your dream takes you.'

Gwidion appeared puzzled. 'But I just dream.'

'The soñador will help you.'

There was a knock on the door and Colonel Jiménez appeared. He smiled first at Alara, then at Gwidion.

'*Gysgaist ti'n dda?*' Did you sleep well.

'*Do, diolch,*' he nodded and he laughed out loud at the sound of his own language. He wondered fleetingly how many languages Colonel Jiménez spoke. He wondered how many languages there were. He felt better and with a look at Alara's patient face, 'Tonight I will dream in Spanish and at weekends in American.'

It was the turn of the two adults to laugh and as they did so they moved closer, almost as a couple might if posing for a family portrait. 'Yes, in American, that's the way,' said Colonel Jiménez. 'Spanish is the language of the soul and of the heart, but American is the language of technology.'

'Do I begin my study today?' asked Gwidion.

The colonel nodded and looked intently into his face. 'You have everything you need here. You have only to dream a little. Search and dream and the answers will come to you.'

The puzzled look returned to Gwidion's face. 'What do you mean?'

'An hour's learning then you will have breakfast,' said Alara. Gwidion remembered his meal the night before. The thought of food was not overly appealing.

'But how do I learn?' he asked her. 'What do I need to know?'

'We will start with mathematics,' she said, rising to go. 'I will come back to get you for breakfast.' She indicated the port and followed Colonel Jiménez out of the door.

Gwidion looked around the room – at the bed raised off the floor with its strange combination of material and springs, a wardrobe, a chest, a chair at a port. He took the port from the desk and placed it before him on the floor and sat cross-legged. It was smaller than those in the village and had no touch panels. The screen appeared to be on, but remained blank.

Perhaps it was voice-activated. 'Right,' he said aloud and rather self-consciously. And, ignoring Alara's suggestion, 'history'. He thought he detected a slight flicker on the screen, but nothing happened. He was tempted to open it up, to see if it was the same as the optiks he was used to. He thought of Lauren's mother and what she would say. He thought of Lauren. She would know what to do. She would flick her hair behind her ears as if switching off her surroundings and she would begin. He wished she were here with him. The screen and Gwidion stared at each other. He looked around vaguely, without expectation, to see if Alara and the colonel might still be nearby to ask for help.

He adjusted the port in front of himself again, and when he was happy that it was in just the right position he got up and opened the wardrobe. It still contained nothing but a spare uniform, the smock he had arrived in and his cordyline travelling bag. The chest contained his underclothes just as it had done before. He examined the mattress again and bounced on it three or four times, then went to the door. He poked his head outside, hanging on the frame so he could pull himself back in at a moment's notice, and saw the corridor stretching far into the distance towards the stairs which led down to the ground floor and the dining hall. He guessed that the other boys, his fellow students, were in the rooms along this corridor, but the doors were all closed and he did not dare venture out yet.

He returned to the optik. It was early and he was still tired from yesterday's travelling. He was unsure what he was supposed to do. He prepared himself as the mentor had taught him, breathing deeply and focusing his concentration.

The optik flickered into life and Gwidion's excitement rose. But it was not history after all. It was mathematics. And it was very familiar. He could not pretend it wasn't a disappointment. The graphics were certainly better than in the roundhouse, the presentation was slicker, but without any controls there was nothing he could do but watch an explanation of matricular maths which was meant for someone much less advanced than he. And he missed the feeling of classmates around him.

When Alara returned he could not hide his disillusionment. He hadn't needed to leave Mimosa to learn what the optik had taught him today. He tried to talk to her as they walked down the corridors to the dining room. But the silence which pervaded the building seemed to have begun to permeate him also like a cold fog. It cloaked conversation and intimidated him. Again he wondered at the presence of so many boys – there were more here than the complete population of his dome. There were so many questions he wanted to ask, but it was dawning on him that he would get no answers from Alara or Jiménez.

'Will there be more lessons afterwards?' he whispered over breakfast, which seemed to be identical to yesterday's dinner except for the colour of the sauce. She motioned him to be quiet and this time he saw Colonel Jiménez glance at him sternly from the top table.

'We'll try something a little more challenging. Now you must be quiet,' she whispered.

After eating they filed once more along the corridors behind similar pairs of boys and their Alaras. Occasionally Gwidion would turn his head and try to meet their eyes, but they kept their gaze on the ground or on some faraway spot in the distance. None of them spoke.

'What do we do next? I would like to see Madrid,' Gwidion said eagerly, going to the window of his room and attempting to move the heavy oak shutters. They did not meet properly in the middle, allowing a shaft of thin rectangular light to fall across the room, widening as it stretched and faded towards the opposite wall.

'They don't open.'

Gwidion turned round in surprise.

'Everything here is made as conducive as possible to the learning process. Distractions such as the outside world might interfere with that. Besides, there is not a lot to see of Madrid.'

'You're not expecting me to study now?'

'That is why you are here, Gwidion. That is why all the other boys are here. When you have been here for a little while you will begin to understand.'

'Am I allowed to talk to them? Ever?'

'It is not forbidden, but it is not usual. It is not why we are here. When you have been here for some time you will come to understand that too.'

'But I don't want to study now. The lessons are too easy.'

'Good,' said Alara simply. 'Then you will progress all the more quickly.' She sat cross-legged on the floor in front of the optik. 'Your mentor taught you techniques of meditation. Use those now before you start.'

Gwidion did as she asked. He began as they had begun every study day in the village, filling his lungs with air from his abdomen to his collar-bones, calming the breathing, filling his body with light. After some time, when the rhythmic movement of his lungs had dropped to two breaths a minute, Alara spoke again.

'Your mentor taught you well. Now we will start the lesson.'

'History,' said Gwidion eagerly.

'American,' she corrected him. Quietly she unfolded her legs and brushed his head gently and briefly with her hand. Then she left the room, closing the heavy panelled door behind her.

'Alara.'

She re-appeared.

'Don't close it.' She shrugged and smiled and left again, leaving the door ajar.

The lesson was even worse than mathematics. It was obviously aimed at Spanish-speakers, and although Gwidion had spoken that language almost as long as Welsh, he had spoken American even longer. His concentration faltered, his eyes closed and he began to drift.

He dreamed of home, but it was not the home he knew. There was no dome, no duggs, no roundhouse. But there were no sky-scrapers either. There were fields and hedges and stone-built houses, clustered together in groups. There were wide roadways too and the ridge was bare of trees. Except for one perfectly shaped ash tree, standing alone, silhouetted against the sky. Or was it a tree? As he stared at it, Gwidion was sure it was a figure. It seemed to be waving to him in the light wind. He could not escape the thought – Cai. It sent a chill down his back. Then suddenly it was neither an ash tree or a figure, it was a sentence. Of course, he saw now, the branches were the shapes of the letters in a sentence, jumbled up together one on top of the other so it was impossible to read. There was a letter E, its arms enmeshed in an O. There was a noun and there was a verb – he could tell it was a verb because it was doing something. And what it was doing it to, was the object. And...

Alara was shaking him gently by the shoulder. Gwidion sat up with a start and found a lesson in American grammar still droning on the optik in front of him.

'It's all right.'

'Where am I?' He rubbed his eyes and took in the unfamiliar room.

'Madrid. You are at the Academy. Remember?'

He looked at the light falling across the floor and heard the coo-ing of doves.

'It's evening.'

'It's dinner time. You slept all afternoon and I decided not to wake you. You had a tiring day yesterday, everything is new.'

'Are you annoyed with me?'

'Why?'

'I did not follow my American lesson.'

She laughed, opening her mouth and showing her white teeth. 'You already speak American well enough. Better than me.'

'Does anyone else speak Welsh here?'

'I don't know. Occasionally there is someone. We sometimes have students from Patagonia, or your village of course. Colonel Jiménez speaks some.'

Gwidion nodded. 'His accent is funny.'

She laughed again. 'It's not an easy language.'

'And you, where do you come from?'

'Puno. In Peru.'

'I don't know it.'

She sat on the bed and tucked her legs underneath her. 'Then you must study your geography too. It is high in the Andes on the shores of Lake Titicaca. The air is so thin you can barely breathe.'

Gwidion looked at her in wonder, but her face was still smiling.

'Do you miss it?'

'Yes, and no. I missed it very much when Colonel Jiménez first brought me here. I missed my mother and my sisters, but we were very poor and life was not easy there either. At least here I am able to send money to my family and they can have many things they would not otherwise be able to buy. I missed my language too at first.'

'You speak another language?'

'Aymara. It is one of the languages of the native South Americans. But no-one speaks it here. Not even Colonel Jiménez.'

'Say something to me in Aymara.'

Alara laughed again. 'What shall I say?' She thought for a moment, suddenly coy like a young girl. 'It must be years since I've spoken Aymara.'

'Shall I tell you the days of the week?'

Gwidion cocked his head at her.

'Say... I don't know, say something.'

She thought for a moment. '*Waliki jutax, jichax akan qamannani.*'

It was Gwidion's turn to laugh. 'It sounds like...' The giggle took hold of him. 'It sounds like someone struggling to breathe. What does it mean?'

'It means I hope you will be happy here. I would like us to be friends. Now you. In Welsh.'

'*Dw i'n mo'yn bod yn ffrind i ti, hefyd.* I want to be your friend too.'

Alara tried to repeat it, but her efforts ended in more laughter.

'What does it sound like?' asked Gwidion.

She screwed up her eyes and rocked her head back and forth. 'Stone. It sounds like stone.'

They burst out laughing again. Gwidion looked suddenly serious. As he spoke his smile froze, then wavered. 'I miss hearing Welsh.'

Alara touched his arm. 'I know.' Then more brightly. 'But you speak American and Spanish so well.'

'We speak all three in the village. Some things, like study, in American or Spanish. Other things in Welsh. Or we mix them up for fun. Or if you can't think of a word in one, it just comes out in another. Or sometimes it just comes out anyway.'

He looked down at the wrist clasp on his arm and turned it around. He was about to speak, but something in Alara's expression stopped him. She seemed to take the words out of his mouth.

'It is like the strands of your bracelet. Our life is woven with all three languages, and we never think about it. That is the way it is. And now one of them is missing.'

'It is very lonely here with no-one to talk to.'

Alara put her hand on his clasp. 'It is very beautiful. Such workmanship.'

Gwidion's voice dropped a decibel or two. 'I miss my mother.'

It was a natural movement from handling the clasp to let her arm

wrap itself around his shoulder and he let his head drop against
her breast.

'You must do. I miss mine. It is not easy at first.'

'I miss the mentor, I miss Ce'nder Tabitha and Lame William and
Ce'nder Rhisiart and...' His voice tailed off. 'I miss them all.'

'I'm sure they are all very proud of you. You will be a good student,
I know that.'

'I miss Lauren.'

'Is she your sister?'

Gwidion shook his head.

'Ahh,' she said, understanding. And held him tighter. 'You must
tell me about her one day. I would like to know everything.'

He tried to answer, but the sadness which rose through his body like
a tide shook him harder against her and drowned his words.

chapter three

Gwidion's door was open when Alara returned to his room. For a
moment her heart skipped a beat at the thought that he might
have gone somewhere after his unhappiness the night before. She
found him already settled in front of his optik, the shutters wide
open, a flood of sunlight in the room. He turned to greet her but she
motioned him not to lose his concentration. It was too late.

'Look, Alara. Look at the view. You said there wasn't much out
there.'

'Gwidion, you're supposed to keep them closed.'

'Why?'

'To help your concentration.'

'This helps my concentration.' He pointed outside. His window
looked out on a tiled inner courtyard of the building a floor below.
The raised central area was planted with palms, small citrus and aloes.
From somewhere beneath the structure water was fed upwards and
spilled over into a narrow channel which ran through the courtyard
and out of sight. The scent of damp earth rose from the tiny garden

and the sound of doves perching in the trees drifted into his room.

'This helps me concentrate,' he said.

'I suppose it might,' said Alara. 'But enough of it. Concentrate. You should be studying by now.'

'I don't need to study. Anyway I was too excited,' he said, sitting on the bed and bouncing. 'I've got something to tell you.'

'What's that?'

'I've decided to go home,' said Gwidion, grinning and bouncing some more on the bed. His high spirits were slightly deflated by Alara's silence. For her part she was taken aback by his behaviour and it took her a moment to re-order her thoughts.

'I like it here, it's fine. But I miss the village, I miss the fields and the sky. And the people. I don't want to live here alone.'

'You're not alone. You have me.'

'I like you, Alara. But for me, that is alone. I am used to many more people. And the others here, well, I am not allowed to talk to them. Don't you miss people too?'

'I do, but... Gwidion, it's not that simple. It's not easy for you to get home.'

'The colonel brought me. I am sure he will take me back.'

'I'm not so sure,' said Alara.

'I'll ask him then.'

'As I said, Gwidion, I don't think it's going to be that simple.' She took him by the hands and looked at him earnestly.

'Why don't you give it a few more days? Everything is strange here for you, I know. But you only arrived two days ago. Believe me, I know how you feel – Peru is a lot further away than your village. But give it some time. Give it a week and in the meantime I will ask Colonel Jiménez about it. I am sure he would like to talk to you first.'

Gwidion pulled his hands away, unable to hide his disappointment. 'I thought you would help me. I thought you would understand.'

'I do understand, Gwidion. I do understand. But you have come to Madrid, to the old capital of the Republic of Hispania, to its finest academic institution. You have been chosen out of thousands of boys. To return to your village now would look like... Well, however it would look, what would your mother think, or your mentor? What would *you* feel like after a few days back at home? There would be no turning back then.'

Gwidion avoided her gaze. 'I want to go.'

'You have come a long way to take your place at this Academy, Gwidion, and it is the Republic's greatest honour. At least give it a fair try. At least give it some time. And I will talk to the colonel.'

'I want to go home.'

There was a pause.

'Is it Lauren?' Gwidion looked at her with frightened eyes. Alara took his hand again. Her voice was low and soft. 'What would Lauren think?'

Soñador Martín came to see him that afternoon. He perched on Gwidion's bed, his eyebrows knitting together in the middle of his face. They looked at each other and the same recognition passed between them. But now Martín was sure. This was something deeper, more fundamental, the meeting of like minds.

'Alara-mmm tells me you are unhappy here?'

'I find the lessons boring.'

Martín nodded slowly, but said nothing.

'Even in the village we could study the same material. The optiks are a bit better, but... '

'Do you prepare yourself properly for the lesson?'

'As our mentor taught me. But it's not the preparation.'

The soñador completed his thought. 'It's the lessons-mmm.'

It was Gwidion's turn to nod.

'Many students who train here go on to greater things. There are many projects in South America that demand highly-skilled and highly-trained technicians. Others return to their villages as mentors or with valuable technical abilities, whatever particular role they choose to play in their communities.'

'I want to go home.'

'You told me you wanted to be a pilot.'

There was a pause. 'Why were you angry on the first day you saw me?'

The caterpillars jumped. 'Not with you, Gwidion. Don't let yourself think that. Not with you at all. The colonel and I were having–mmm... well, we were having an argument over procedures. We have, let us say, different visions of life at the Academy, sometimes they clash. Nothing of any importance to you.'

'You asked me if I had a brother.'

The soñador agreed. 'I did.' There was a long silence which Martín was the first to break. 'But you do not.' The silence began again.

'I would like to go home.' There was less conviction this time.

Martín smiled. 'It must be a very nice place, your village. Perhaps I should go there one day.'

He lifted himself to an upright position as if his joints were hydraulic, barely leaning forward or shifting his centre of gravity from his sitting position.

'Perhaps, Gwidion, you did not come here after all to be a pilot. Perhaps you came here in search of your father and now you are disappointed that things are not how you expected. I can do nothing about that. The young men and women who come here come from many different cultures and many different backgrounds and sometimes it seems, even to me, that things are not how they should be. That is a pity, but it is not something I can do anything about.'

He squatted and took both the boy's hands in his own and looked into his eyes.

'My job is to find people with special abilities and you have that talent, Gwidion. But I cannot make you do anything you do not want to do. It seems that we do not have your trust. That is a pity.'

There was a pause and the soñador rose again. 'I think for now we should increase the difficulty of the lessons and we will see. And if not I will take you back to see this village of yours for myself. What do you think?'

The caterpillars demanded a reply. Gwidion nodded.

As he reached the door, he turned back again. 'You are properly prepared for your study?' Then. 'Yes, of course. You said. As the mentor taught you. Search and dream, as we say.'

Gwidion watched his cloak follow him out of the door. He felt thoroughly confused and slightly silly, as if he had embarrassed himself. Yet at the same time the soñador did not seem to mind at all. He ran to the corridor.

'Soñador Martín.'

The older man turned.

'Why are you called a soñador?'

He laughed and continued down the corridor. 'Search and dream, Gwidion. Search and dream.'

Soñador Martín leaned back in his leather chair as Jiménez entered his office, then let it rotate gently from side to side, mirroring the arc of his bow-shaped desk.

'Take a seat-mmm.' He gestured towards an upright upholstered chair in front of the desk and leaned forward onto his elbows. Jiménez moved the chair to the side so he sat at an angle, his hands relaxed across his stomach and his eyes taking in the heavy wood-panelled walls of the office.

Martín smiled mischievously under his dark eyebrows.

'Another one leaving us? You always seem keen to inform me about the ones who are going home-mmm.' He coughed as if to clear his throat of his hum. 'It seems to be the only time I see you these days.'

Jiménez let the comment pass. Martín straightened himself. 'But that's often enough, Jiménez. Not losing your touch I hope?'

Again the colonel ignored the implied criticism. 'Xavier. You're familiar with his case, I take it? He was a bright student. I admit I had high hopes of him. Didn't we all?'

Martín sucked on his lower lip. 'High hopes-mmm. Always high hopes. Xavier. Buenos Aires. Never really took to Madrid. I'm sure he will be happy to go back.'

'His family will be happy too.'

'And what about us, Colonel? The third in a month, I believe.'

'You know as well as I do, Soñador, people like yourself are not easy to find.'

The soñador's eyebrows rose almost to his hairline. 'Flattery. What-ever next? You must be desperate.'

'Concerned, I hate to see failure, but not desperate.'

Martín leaned forward again as if to avoid being overheard. 'How many more can we afford to send back? Eh?'

'The Republic is interested in results, Soñador. As you know I am always searching for new students who show promise.'

The reminder of the Gwidion episode was enough to make

Martín stand suddenly, his avuncular expression turning to one of anger. 'Results! What do your political masters know about results?'

'They know them when they see them,' replied Jiménez evenly.

Martín sat down again with a sudden bump. 'I despise people like them, Colonel-mmm.'

'You've never made a secret of it,' Jiménez agreed. 'Unfortunately your line of work does not come cheaply.' He gestured at the large ornate room which served as an office. 'You have a nice place, your acolytes are brought from all over the Republic, housed, fed. And then there are the keepers. From some points of view that is an awful lot of luxury for an arcane pursuit such as soma research.'

'All right, all right, Colonel, it's an old argument. Tot up the pesetas if you want, if that is what interests you-mmm. My interest is not in the bricks and mortar, it is in the incalculable value of the minds of these young people. Agoreros, soñadores. They are not born overnight. This Xavier, he has some talent, despite what you say.'

'But not enough.'

'Not enough for you because you are not prepared to wait. You are interested in the one-in-a-million, the freak. I am interested in them all. Every single boy who has passed through these doors has left with a new knowledge, a new skill of the mind, however small that may be. Each one of them has been part of a community of minds. Each one takes that new way of thinking home with them. In time it is they who will change the world.'

Jiménez crossed his legs and brushed an imaginary speck of dirt from his knee. 'We may not have that long, Soñador. The generation ship is nearing completion.'

Martín almost spat out his disgust. 'And you talk to me of the luxury of arcane pursuits. Generation ship. Escape. It's madness.'

'Not if the right people are on board, Soñador. Don't treat me like your enemy, I've worked for the success of this Academy for too long to allow you to do that.'

Martín leaned back in his chair and breathed deeply. 'Forgive me, Colonel. You are a man of integrity, but you have chosen your masters badly. There is no place to run away to. Luis, Fernandez, Lorca, even yourself. The Republic is in the blood of people like you.'

'You make it sound like a sickness. Dangerous words. You are fortunate to be in a privileged position.'

Martín met Jiménez' threatening gaze and laughed. 'Don't worry, Pablo. You frighten me. You frighten me plenty and I know that pleases you-mmm. I don't wish to die and I don't wish to lose my Academy, but I don't think there is any danger of that yet. Eh?'

The two men looked at each other. Despite their frequent outbursts of animosity, their relationship stretched back over many years. They relied on each other more than either cared to admit. If the price of having the Academy at all was a political minder, then Jiménez was as good as any, and better than most.

'Very well, Jiménez. Send the boy in. Let's have a little chat with young Xavier.'

Gwidion sat staring at the optik. It seemed that after the soñador's visit everyone had forgotten about him. Alara had not returned, the optik was blank before him.

It was hot in his room. The sunlight fell in shafts through the shutters and the air was still and humid. It reminded him of the hydroponics bays, and memories of the village returned him to his dream of the night before and he felt the tingle down his spine once again.

Search and dream. First Jiménez, then Martín. What did they mean? And preparation. They always asked him about his preparation. He breathed deeply, pulling the light up his spine. His eyes began to close as he stared at the screen for inspiration, and as his breathing deepened and his body relaxed he slipped into the dim twilight between sleep and wakefulness. Search and dream. He focused on the mid-point just above the bridge of the nose, watching the fractal patterns grow and divide in shades of dark red, and sent the light out to the world.

Search and dream. He saw a figure in a cloak, framed in an arched doorway and lit from behind by the rays of a setting sun, ascending the cool white steps which rose into the darkness. His eyeballs flickered wildly behind his closed lids but the mind remained clear. Control the dream.

At an optik screen in the huge soma hall which housed the boys' keepers, Alara smiled to herself. 'He's done it,' she whispered, and looked around for someone to share her excitement with. Across the room she saw the figure of Soñador Martín look up from another girl's screen and catch her eye. In a moment he was on his way towards her. She tried to control the desire to laugh out loud which filled her stomach and pushed her chest upwards and her hands trembled slightly as she returned her attention to the optik. It was vital to monitor every step of these first stages.

Martín let his eye rove over the other optiks as he walked towards Alara. They showed nothing of obvious interest. Some were blank, others displayed the easily-recognisable hallmarks of a standard Academy optik lesson. He was behind her now, leaning over slightly, his breath disturbing the hair which lay across her shoulders. He looked at the panel in the right-hand corner of the screen.

On this the brainwave readout showed clear REM sleep patterns but without loss of major motor control. There was no mistaking it. Gwidion was in soma.

Martín gave a low whistle and straightened himself. He put his hand on her shoulder. 'Two days. A record, I think, Alara.'

His quiet calmness was in such contrast to the story they were watching on the screen that Alara could not contain her laughter any longer and it exploded in a nervous peal which echoed around the huge hall. What they saw on the optik was very different from an Academy optik lesson. Behind the palettes which monitored various physiological data was a hotch-potch of images which flooded the optik, too fast to follow or to make sense of.

Back in his room, Gwidion was in history. Not watching an optik history lesson or a documentary. He was in history.

It began with the Big Bang. The beginning, he supposed, because he had been no more precise than 'History'. At first it was just like a dream – a chaotic kaleidoscope of images and information which left him almost breathless as it jumped backwards and forwards. In his head clusters of revolving gas coalesced into the nuclei of stars, matter was formed, there were huge explosions.

Search and dream. It was beginning to make sense. And Alara had told him he must learn to control his dreams, not to be led this way and that by them. He returned to his meditation techniques, concentrated on the breath, centred his being. At first the assault of images and information was too much, but gradually he discovered that navigating his way around this massive textbook was an easy matter. This was not a mere picture or representation of the physics of the universe, this was its essence. Each image that he held in his mind's eye contained its own explanation, its beginning, its growth, its maturity, its ultimate fate. And this knowledge was neither in words or pictures. It was pure knowledge. Knowledge was its substance. Seek and you shall find.

Like a child with a new toy he drank in the information greedily, crazily, jumping this way and that. And he discovered that he was not confined to one subject at a time. Dinosaurs, the Greeks, landing on the Moon (he would have to come back to that one), the Incas, Einstein, all reeled before him. It was so easy. Names, dates, facts came to him as if they had always been there. Here was Kruschev, there Stalin, and here an unknown soldier James Wilkins, aged twenty-two, wife and child in Battersea, London, lying shattered in the mud of the Somme. He survived, but he would rather not have.

He began to understand what the mentor had been trying to tell him about Madrid, although not even he had realised exactly how fantastically true it was. Here were all the answers he had been seeking. One could spend a lifetime wandering here as easily as – easier than – living a life outside.

Thoughts of the mentor brought him to 43, the Roman invasion of Britain. He smiled at the familiarity of the date from the notebook the mentor had given him. But this was something different. It was almost as if he was watching it happen. Here were the first Roman legions arriving, the native Britons daubed with woad preparing for battle. He could, if he wished, hear the terrifying sounds of battle, the screams of the dying, crushed by the wheels of chariots. He could just as easily choose to ignore them.

There was a sort of flash in his head as his excitement mounted. New destinations flooded into his mind. He was about to access Mimosa when he was woken by Alara shaking his shoulders. For a moment he did not know where he was. He was lying on the floor, his breathing was fast and shallow, around his mouth a light scum was forming where his saliva had dried. Her face was stern – and anxious.

'Gwidion, wake up. Leave it now. That's enough.'

He stared at her groggily, annoyed at being pulled from his wonderland.

'You must not go in so deep. It's all so new to you. You must learn to control your dreaming.'

'I'm starving,' he said, his breath rasping against his dry throat.

She laughed her bell-like laugh and helped him stand up. 'Come on, let's go. Let's go and get something to eat.'

Gwidion could barely contain himself over dinner. His experience on what Alara called 'the loom' had unleashed an avalanche of new questions and he wanted them answered now.

'You don't need me to tell you. You know where all the answers are to be found.'

'But I want you to tell me. Can anyone access the loom?' he moaned, a fourteen-year-old child again, as they filed down the corridors among the silent pairs of boys and keepers.

Alara sighed and smiled. 'Yes, in another format anyone could access it on the optik. It was recorded on optical fibres many years ago.'

'But it's not like a normal optikopedia. It's not at all like the lessons we have in study.'

'No. What you are learning is soma, a dream world. There are very few who have the ability to access it in an ordered way.'

'It isn't like a dream at all.'

'It is. And it isn't.'

'Where is it, this dream world?'

Alara looked at him. 'It is in your mind.'

'But how? It wasn't there before.'

'It is in your mind and it is in the mind of Soñador Martín.'

'And nowhere else?'

'Gwidion, your questions.' He looked at her pleadingly. She chose her words carefully. 'It was created by other soñadores many years ago, and it resides in a network of crystals. But you have come much closer to it than that. In time you will understand.' She pushed him playfully. 'If you dream in American.'

'But the loom was in Welsh.'

Alara shook her head. 'The loom is not in a language, Gwidion. It is a language.'

Gwidion nodded towards the procession in front of them. 'And the others, do they all dream too?'

They were entering the dining hall. 'Sssh.'

'But I thought we were here to become pilots.'

Alara dropped her voice so Gwidion could barely hear. 'There is more than one way to travel.'

'Will you be a great dreamer, Alara. Will we dream together, you and I?'

She looked quickly at his young open face and there was genuine sadness in her voice. 'No, I will not be a great soñador, that is not my talent. But I will help you. That I can do.'

chapter four

The next morning Gwidion was in front of his optik early. He directed his attention to the screen, but the word which came to his mind once more was history. Once more the flood of information and images washed over him, some of them familiar from the mentor's notebook, others obscure and meaningless. Once more they came in random waves, jumping backwards and forwards, a fantastic jumble of events, but as the novelty of it all wore off he began to develop a way of ordering his searches.

He brought himself back to his breathing, centring his being, stilling his mind. And the waves lessened, the flow of information slowed, until finally after what seemed at the same time like many hours and like no time at all, there was nothing but a single point of light. He held it on the optik screen, let it grow intense like the flame of a candle. And when it had stopped wavering and its rainbow colours had fused into a photon of pure whiteness, he was ready to begin.

'Fertility plague,' he thought. At that moment Alara re-entered the room. Still he held onto his point of light, allowing his awareness to envelop her entry but not letting it disturb his concentration.

'It is time to eat,' she said softly.

His flame flickered as he realised how much time must have passed. But now that he had found this place he did not want to leave. He shook his head gently, all the while maintaining his hold on the flame.

'Hold the light,' said Alara. She touched him on the shoulder. The flame wavered again. 'Let your breath hold the light. But you must eat.'

He rose while maintaining his state of meditation and together they joined the column of boys and Alaras going to the dining room. This time he did not attempt to meet their eyes, nor barely saw them. He fixed his eyes on his feet, picking out their unique rhythm from all the sound of hundreds of shoes on tiled floors, and allowed them to take him where Alara led.

'Good,' whispered Alara. 'Very good. Now you begin to understand.'

There was a light knock on the door. 'Gwidion-mmm.' It was unmistakably the soñador.

Gwidion moved to rise from his meditation position, but Martín indicated that he should stay seated. The soñador joined him on the floor. His movements reminded Gwidion of a marionette. His long legs appeared to cross while still standing, then in a single movement he descended, splaying out as he came down, so that by the time he touched the floor he seemed already to be sitting cross-legged. His billowing cloak joined him a moment later.

'You-mmm. Alara tells me you have many questions.'

Gwidion nodded.

'I am here to answer them.'

For a moment the boy could think of nothing to say. The soñador smiled.

'First I expect you will want to know why I hum when I talk.'

Gwidion laughed out loud at the absurdity of the remark, and at its honesty, and at the fact that it was indeed one of the many things that perplexed him.

'That is easy-mmm. The rhythms of our breath are the rhythms of our mind. You will know this because your mentor has taught you well.' He indicated the optik. 'This I can already see-mmm. The rhythms of speech also affect the rhythms of breath and vice versa.

Italian, they tell me, was a wonderful language to sing in.'

'Welsh too,' Gwidion piped up eagerly.

Martín smiled. 'Welsh too, of course-mmm. But, Gwidion, breathing is not something we do in order to meditate, breathing is something we do in order to live to the fullest extent possible. Your mentor will have told you this. That is why I hum.'

Gwidion looked dubious, he could not decide if the soñador was serious.

'You should try it. Next you will be wondering why my eyebrows are dark and bushy when my hair is thinning and grey.'

Gwidion laughed again.

'I can see no purpose in it. But my students are amused-mmm.' This time the both of them laughed. 'Now. Your questions.'

'Why are there only boys here?'

'For every boy there is a keeper. Do not underestimate your keeper.' He paused. 'Anything else?'

'What questions cannot be answered on the loom?'

The caterpillars danced. Gwidion laughed and Martín was gone.

The fertility plague. Gwidion was sitting in front of the optik, holding the light steady on the screen. It bent, as if blown by a light wind, and suddenly he was assaulted by the screams of the dying. His body convulsed as if in agony and the images of bodies in mass graves burned his eyes, misting the light. He breathed again and the pain subsided. Again he focused on the light. He listened to the screams this time and watched the images, but still they hurt, still they buffeted the light. Perhaps Alara was right, perhaps he should be attempting American first. But he had already compromised by not dreaming in Welsh. As Jiménez had said, Spanish was more liquid, it flowed over him, it was sensual and it was painful.

Again. He let go of the effort, he relaxed, he breathed, he held the light steady. Narrative. Narrative was what he wanted.

The fertility plague. E402 was a genetically-modified mumps virus developed by the United Christian States of America government of 2021 in their war against the Spanish-speaking majorities of the southern states.

This was not the history the mentor had taught him. The light shimmered. Again the images and the screams assaulted him. Again he let go of the effort, he relaxed, he breathed, he held the light steady.

Designed to produce infertility in men and women of Hispanic origin, it was first used in 2023 in California following a series of terrorist attacks allegedly masterminded by Hispanic Catholic leader Pedro Suavez, and was later released in several major cities in the Federation of Latin American Republics including Lima and Buenos Aires.

Its effects proved to be lethal, highly contagious and not confined to the Hispanic population. In the United Christian States and Europe the scientific community was decimated even before it had an opportunity to react to the crisis. Within a year of its first use, world population had been reduced from more than nine billion to an estimated two and a half billion.

Survivors enjoying some immunity to its most deadly effects nevertheless suffered extreme fertility problems, particularly among men.

Gwidion shifted his attention to the shaft of light coming through the shutters and gazed at the tiny particles of dust which swam and floated in its thermal eddies. Mostly the temperature inside the building remained remarkably constant, but the yellowing light told him that it was already evening. Alara would come to get him soon, he imagined, and she would be angry that he still had not tackled the subject she suggested. Since arriving at the Academy he had felt sad and lonely, he had felt awe and surprise. Now, for the first time, he felt frightened. The plague was a disaster on a scale like no other in recent history. How was it possible that there were two explanations of it? The new version of events shocked him. The mentor had been to Madrid, and although there was no loom then, surely he would have had access to the same information Gwidion was now discovering. Or had he been involved in some other project altogether? He went to the door and stood for a few moments in the cool marbled silence of the corridor then returned to his room, closing the door behind him. He threw himself on the bed, enjoying again the madness of a sprung bed, lying while the mattress moved up and down in smaller and smaller cycles, until they were almost imperceptible, until they returned to complete stillness. There was no way to answer his questions right now. Right now all he wanted to do was sleep. American would have to wait.

chapter five

The air in the soma hall was cooler and the polished wooden floor gave off a familiar smell, but even after the best part of three years at the Academy, Alara found the atmosphere of this place, more than any other, both intimidating and awe-inspiring. Before her, arranged as if in an exam room, stretched row after row of optiks, each with its own two-metre radius of personal space. And in front of each one sat the keepers, young women like her, each one dedicated to the care of a single boy at the Academy, each one linked to the loom, monitoring the progress of their individual charges.

It seemed to take an age to reach her own place as she walked as quietly as she could down the central aisle, anxious not to disturb her colleagues. Above her she could see the high vaulted ceiling where a magnificent baroque fresco, faded with the centuries, told a complicated story of the nature of heaven. The intricate hierarchy of cherubim and seraphim hovered in layers among clouds of yellowed-white, drawing the eye towards a cupola at the far end where a fierce and bearded God sat in flowing splendour on his throne.

Below the fresco, and high above the floor of the hall where her fellow keepers maintained their link to their hundreds of individual dreaming charges, ran a colonnaded gallery. Colonel Jiménez was leaning against the balustrade, looking down. When he saw her arrive, he gestured to her and began to make his way towards the stairs. Alara settled herself before her optik and waited for him to arrive.

'I didn't see you after breakfast. Problems?'

'His first few days. You can imagine.'

'He's a fast learner.' His face betrayed nothing.

'Oh yes, he's a fast learner. But not necessarily an obedient one.' This time Jiménez grinned. 'I like the boy. We'll cope.'

'He's fascinated by history, that's all he accesses at the moment.'

'That's understandable, given where he comes from. These are not people with the same outlook on the world as us. They have lost touch with much of their past, they have turned their backs on the Republic. But the Republic has not turned its back on them. They have provided us with some of our most promising students. When he has got over the novelty of it, and satisfied his curiosity about his history, he will want to find out more. We need to be on our toes.'

'I have never seen anyone able to access the loom so fast. On his first attempt he went in so deep I was worried he might harm himself. At least he's started dreaming in a language I can understand.'

Jiménez nodded and put his hand on her shoulder.

'I'm sure with your guidance he will adjust. And I am sure he will repay our efforts.' He indicated the rows on rows of optiks and keepers. 'You see Rosa, your sister? She has had her new boy for two months. So far, nothing. He barely seems capable of linking to the loom.' He swept his arm wider. 'María, the same. And Ana-Marie. And so on, and so on.' He sighed. 'Soon we will have to send them back and start again with a new intake. If we have the time.'

'What do you mean?'

Jiménez passed his hand over his balding head as if measuring himself against something at his back. 'I mean politics. I mean money.'

He raised his arm off her shoulder and let it fall again. 'I mean we need a success.'

Alara was waiting for Jiménez when he got back to his office after breakfast. He greeted her cheerily. He was feeling pleased with himself. But Alara failed to smile back.

'What's the matter?'

'It's Gwidion. He still wants to go home.'

His good mood evaporated instantly. 'He can't,' he snapped.

'I don't know if I can persuade him.'

In front of Alara the diplomat in him vanished. To her he was prepared to show anger – all traces of that charming friendliness in his eyes had disappeared.

'I thought Martín had sorted this one out. He made the leap onto the loom, didn't he?'

Alara looked helpless. 'He still wants to go home.'

'Come on Alara. Why are you bothering me with this? He's been here four days. This isn't the first time one of them has broken into tears and asked to go home. We've always kept them before.'

'This one's different.'

Jiménez turned on her. 'Yes, this one's different. This one looks like my best chance in three years.' He corrected himself but the subtlety was not lost on Alara. 'This one looks like our best hope ever. We can't let him go.'

'It's not my fault, Pablo. We can't force him to stay either.'

The colonel softened and threw himself at his chair. 'I'm sorry, Alara. It's Martín. He may be an academic but he is an influential man. He's not happy with the numbers we're sending back and neither am I.' He gave a loud sigh. 'We need a success, Alara, and this boy looks like the success we need. And no, we can't force anybody to do anything. Least of all what we're asking them to do.'

He tapped his fingers irritably on the table. 'What's the problem. Mother, girlfriend?'

'Both, I think.'

Jiménez pulled his fingers down his forehead, squeezing his eyes shut. 'Well, mother, girlfriend. Isn't that where you come in?' He opened his eyes to look directly at her.

She held his gaze and when she spoke he had to strain to hear her. 'What are you suggesting, Pablo?'

It was he who had to look away first. 'Very well. What, then? What else have we got?'

Alara threw him a contemptuous glance, hesitated, then decided to say it anyway. 'You're his father, maybe you're the one who should know.'

There was a silence. Finally Jiménez replied. 'I'll pretend you didn't say that.'

Alara got up with as much dignity as she could, but she could not hide the hurt. 'Then there's not a lot else we've got, in my opinion. I'll leave you to think about it.'

Before she had quite gone out of the door, he stopped her.

'Alara. Has he mentioned anybody called Cai?'

She shook her head. 'Why?'

'Nothing. Just an idea. You're right, I'll have to give it some thought.'

She lingered a moment at the door.

'Alara, I'm sorry. I didn't mean... I'm not sure what I meant. It hasn't been a good day.'

'The day has hardly begun.'

He smiled. 'I didn't intend to take it out on you.'

She closed the door quietly behind her.

It was an idea, thought Jiménez. Getting at Gwidion through Cai. Any adjustment to the loom would mean another interview with Martín, which was a drawback, especially after his meeting over Xavier. But first he had something else to attend to.

'Vidcom.' The optik port on his desk illuminated. 'The President.' There was a slight delay as his secure line was established and the beaming face of Jorge Luis appeared in his room.

'Pablo. Long time. Problems, I suppose?'

Jiménez shook his head. 'Nothing too serious.'

'Martín giving you a hard time again?'

'Something like that.'

Luis raised a glass of brandy and turned it slowly in his hand. 'Not turning you into a monk, is he? You need to get out more often. Cusco is fabulous this time of year. We'll have to find an excuse for you to come over.'

Jiménez smiled back. 'Thank you, Jorge. That would be a great release.'

'So what can I do for you?'

'I'm sending another one back.'

The president suddenly looked serious. 'Third in a month.'

Jiménez nodded. 'Martín's unhappy.'

'Martín's always unhappy. That's why we set up the Academy in Madrid, remember?' His smile faded again. 'But three in a month.'

'I didn't see an alternative. You wanted the programme moved along, Jorge.'

'This is hardly moving in the right direction, Pablo. I can do without any trouble in the villages right now.'

'I wouldn't worry about that.'

'I might, Pablo. How long before some disgruntled student of yours goes back to his village and decides to open his mouth or even just lets something drop out? It might not pose a serious threat, but it could make life extremely uncomfortable.'

'We do take precautions, President.'

'I'm sure you do. Put my mind at rest, it helps me sleep at night.' He took another draught of brandy and beamed again.

'They don't know much because we don't tell them much. What they learn is learnt through access to the loom. The boys we are talking about are, after all, failures. They are going back because they are not suited to the work. They cannot have gleaned much from their very limited access. We've been here before.'

'We certainly have,' agreed Luis.

'Look at it from their point of view. None of these boys wants to return to their village as a failure. They've been to Madrid, they've studied at the Academy. They want to return as heroes.'

'Hardly very heroic.'

'These villages which worry you so much. What do they want, what are they screaming out for? Technology. They want someone to fix their decrepit machinery and optiks. Our students go back, not as Academy drop-outs, but as mentors or technicians, trained at the Republic's finest institution. It works because it suits everyone. As far as anything else goes they have little to tell and even less reason to tell it.'

Luis looked askance. 'For a military man your trust in human nature has always surprised me, Colonel.'

Jiménez shrugged. 'On the contrary, it is our most powerful weapon. Trust people to do what is good for them. And make what is good for them, good for us as well.'

There was a long pause as Luis swirled the brandy round his glass. 'How many more, Pablo?'

'How fast do you want your results?'

'I don't want more trouble than we can handle.'

'By the time there's any trouble, we may well be gone, President.'

Luis looked doubtful. Jiménez cut in quickly. 'Most of all, we offer them guaranteed fertility. A relatively simple operation. By our standards at least.'

'And the price is silence?'

Jiménez nodded. 'And the penalty would be to lose their fertility. And, of course, any children which might have resulted from it.'

'An ambitious threat, Pablo.'

'The threat is usually enough.'

'Usually?' asked the president, emptying his glass.

'In ninety-nine per cent of cases the gift of fertility is a perfectly acceptable trade for a few months' absence from home.'

'And the other one per cent?'

Jiménez was not a man for wasting much time on hypotheticals. In his experience there were an awful lot of possibilities in the world and often reality was the one scenario you hadn't thought of in advance. The last thing on his mind was letting the head of defence, or any other military bureaucrat, anywhere near his project. But if that thought satisfied the president, well...

'Fernandez.'

The name was a synonym for crude, cruel, but very direct and effective action. Luis made an expression of distaste and poured himself some more brandy as if to wash the word out of his mouth.

'Get me some results, Pablo. We need a target planet for the ship.' He turned away, and then had second thoughts. 'And don't forget that invitation to Cusco.'

Jiménez smiled. 'I won't, Jorge.'

Gwidion's small bag was already packed on the bed, the shutters were now allowing a low yellow half-moon to flood his room with light. He went to the window and strained to see outside of the complex in which the Academy was situated, but it was impossible from this angle. His face wore the determined grimness of a teenager who has been told he cannot do what he wants and has decided to take matters into his own hands. He had asked to go home, to see his mother. In his village that was a simple, straightforward request. It could not possibly be denied. True, Alara had promised to talk to Colonel Jiménez, but that was more than a day ago and nothing had come of that.

He took a last look around the room, checked his wrist to see if he was wearing his clasp, felt his smock to make sure his notebook was next to his chest, then opened the door. The corridor stretched emptily away into the blackness, as it always seemed to do. This was not going to be difficult. He had left his shoes behind so that his walk down the corridor would be as quiet as possible. As he passed the fourth door on his left, he smelled something he had not smelled since he left home. Smoke. For a moment he could not believe it. It surely could not be coming from within the building. Then he thought that perhaps it was drifting in from outside. He stopped and sniffed. He did not recognise it, it was like the smoke of a wood fire, but different. Sweeter, and at the same time more acrid. He examined the door and breathed gently around the frame. It was undoubtedly coming from inside the room.

He looked up and down the corridor. Everything was dark and quiet. He knocked at the door.

'Just a minute.'

There was the sound of someone opening a window, and then the door opened. A boy of about seventeen or eighteen came out to meet him.

'I smelled smoke.'

The boy looked at Gwidion, then gave a wide grin and leaned casually against the door frame. 'You're the new boy. I saw you at dinner when you arrived.'

'Gwidion.'

'Hola, Gwidion. I don't get many calls in this place. Come in.'

Gwidion hesitated. 'I smelt smoke, I wasn't sure where it was coming from.'

The boy gestured at the room. 'Everything's OK. Come in,' he repeated, then noticing Gwidion's bag. 'Unless you're going somewhere.'

Gwidion followed the boy's eyes. 'I'm going home.'

The boy laughed. 'Are you? You're a strange one. How are you going to do that?'

'I don't know yet.'

The pair stood for a moment in the corridor. Gwidion picked up his bag. The older boy clapped his hands together.

'Sounds good. I'll come with you.'

They descended the grand sweeping staircase leading to the dining hall and made their way through to the far end. It seemed gigantic now, empty of its students and its ceiling was in darkness. At the far end of the hall two large doors led out into an entrance hall, and two further large doors would lead them to the outside world.

The night was warm and the crickets drilled their tuneless song into the still air. In his mind was a picture-perfect memory of a map of central Madrid he had located on the loom. It showed that the Academy was located inside the Museo del Prado, one-time repository of a fabulous collection of art works.

Gwidion's new friend stopped and pulled a packet out of his pocket, took out a cigarette and lit it. He breathed in deeply and let the stream of smoke float out into the night air.

'What's in it?'

The boy looked at Gwidion and looked at the cigarette.

'Tobacco.' Gwidion's brow furrowed. 'Want one?'

Gwidion took it and examined it, feeling the smoothness of its length then letting his nose run along it. The boy lit his lighter. Gwidion breathed in the smoke and tasted it in his mouth before letting it out as he had seen the boy do.

'What do you think?' His face bore a detached expression of amusement.

Gwidion puffed again letting the smoke come out of his mouth in small clouds as he answered. 'OK. How do you get them?'

The boy shrugged. 'You can get anything you want. Even here in Madrid.'

Gwidion looked up and down the Paseo del Prado. Beneath the lopped plane trees which lined the road, hovered myriads of tiny insects. Apart from them, the street was deserted. He picked up his bag and the two walked again, the older boy letting Gwidion lead the way. The Paseo's two fountains, Fuente de Neptuno and Fuente de Apolo, were silent. The third, Fuente la Cibeles, was gone. Then suddenly, Madrid ended.

Gwidion left his mental map of the city and brought himself back to the reality. The scent of citrus reached his nostrils. In front of them was a forest of small trees – oranges, lemons, this time left to grow prickly and unkempt like the thorn bushes they really were, and plane trees, unlopped, branching into the sky and casting an impenetrable shade. He stopped. It was like an optical illusion. One minute there were the regular slabs of the pavement, the wide open stretch of tarmac. Then there was forest.

He crossed the Paseo and peered into the gloom. He could make out buildings still beyond the tree line. Some of them rose above the level of the tallest trees, but their facades were pale and peeling and their windows bereft of light.

He retraced his steps, running back down the Paseo zigzagging as he went, hoping to see a way through, but before he reached the Plaza del Emperador Carlos V he was stopped again by the sprawling wilderness which had once been the botanical gardens.

He put his bag down on the pavement and breathed in slowly. This, then, was Madrid, nominal capital of the Earth's major power. A couple of square kilometres. The Museo del Prado, now housing the Academy, the Palacio de Comunicaciones, the Bolsa, two fountains and a stretch of paving.

The other boy made his way towards him, stubbing out his cigarette on the pavement as he approached. 'I wondered whether you knew.'

'No wonder escaping was so easy.'

The older boy held out his hand to take Gwidion's bag. 'Come on, I'll go back with you.'

Alara sat in her room at a small dressing table in front of the shuttered window. It was sparsely stocked – a hairbrush, a comb, some pins and slides. She brushed her hair over her eyes to find the parting, then with a start, felt someone's hands on her shoulder. She flung her head back, sending her hair showering over her shoulders and saw Colonel Jiménez reflected in her mirror.

'Pablo. I wasn't expecting you.'

He smiled and slid his hands down her arms, bending to kiss the nape of her neck. It was an unwelcome advance at that moment and rather than please her it made her feel ticklish. She squirmed and he straightened himself.

'I'm sorry.' Despite the apology, his tone of voice was surprised and hurt. 'I thought you might fancy some company.'

She swivelled on her seat to face him and yielded a little. '*I'm* sorry. It's just that... '

He took her by the shoulders and turned her back so that they could carry on their conversation in the mirror. 'Just what?'

'Gwidion. You upset me.'

'I didn't upset you. I didn't mean to upset you – it was just news that I didn't want to hear, that's all.'

'You upset me. You virtually suggested I should seduce Gwidion.' He laughed. 'Seduce him, how did you get that idea?' His hand returned to her shoulders but she shook it away.

'Don't try that with me, Pablo. You always mean something. Nothing comes out of your mouth unless it means something.'

'I'm sorry. I didn't really mean anything. I hadn't thought it through. I didn't know what I was saying.'

'That doesn't sound like you.'

He was obliged to let his hands drop again. 'Well, I'm prepared to apologise. But if you'd prefer to be angry, I can go.'

She turned to him as he took a pace or two backwards.

'Yes, I'm sure I'm not the only young girl you have to visit on your evening rounds.'

This time he was stung. 'Now that is not true, Alara. And you should know better. Ever since I found you in Peru, and ever since you have been here, I have never, ever, loved another woman. That is the truth.'

'The others, then, were just for the sake of the Republic?'

He squatted beside her chair and took her by the shoulders.

'We are required to do some things we may not wish to do. Not for the sake of the Republic, never for the sake of the Republic. But if it is for the sake of our survival, then yes.'

Her silence was more hurtful than her contempt. He got up and walked towards the bed. It was a four-poster in the grand colonial style, though now it was without its curtains and the heavy dark wood was pitted with the tell-tale holes of woodworm. He sat on the mattress and the structure sighed gently.

'Alara, I'm worried. For the first time I'm really worried. I've got the president pushing me for results as hard as he is washing his hands of the whole business and I've got Martín still chasing some romantic ideal about, I don't know about what.'

Alara spoke softly, 'About a community of minds connected through space and time.'

Jiménez snorted. 'Exactly.'

'They were your words once, Pablo. Three years ago they were the sort of words you used to persuade me to come here.'

'People are losing faith with the whole idea, Alara. And losing Gwidion would be one failure too many. I was speaking out of desperation, without thinking.'

She looked at his bent figure, elbows on knees, chin on hands, framed by the enormous bed, and she softened. 'You are really worried.'

'It's like I said. We need a success.'

She came to the bed and took his head in her hands, lifting it towards her.

'I'll talk to Gwidion tomorrow. I'll do my best.'

'Yes,' he said, circling her hips with his arms. 'He should be back by then.'

'Back?' cried Alara in alarm. He squeezed her tighter.

Jiménez grinned. 'He took a walk tonight, probably planning to escape. He won't get far.'

'Poor boy.'

'Maybe not so poor. Perhaps, just perhaps, he knows more than any of us. That's what I'm counting on.'

'I ought to go and see him.'

He looked up into her beautiful face. It was not a Spanish face, and yet not a native South American one either. It had something of the flatness and wideness of the Aymara about the eyes and cheeks, but the nose and forehead bore the aristocratic fineness of the Mediterranean peoples.

Dishonesty was part of the life of a man in his position, or if not dishonesty, then at least he was sometimes obliged to tell less than the truth. But he was not lying when he told her he loved her. She, more than anything, had kept him at the Academy, at the outside edge of what was left of the civilised world when all his political instincts told him he needed to be in Cusco or Buenos Aires. He was no longer a young man, yet he lusted after her with a young man's lust. There was only one thing he feared more than losing

Alara, and that was losing his credibility.

He took her in his arms and kissed her tenderly on the lips. 'I love you, never forget that.'

He felt her soften in his arms. 'There is one thing I've thought of,' said the colonel finally.

'Mmm.'

'About Gwidion.'

'Mmm.'

'It can wait, though.'

But he had succeeded in tickling her curiosity.

'No. Go on.'

'You remember I mentioned Cai?'

'Ah, yes. What was that about?'

'An imaginary twin, has been ever since any of his family can remember.'

'I remember having an imaginary friend, when I was very young, for a short while.'

Jiménez extracted himself from Alara's arms and sat on the edge of the bed looking up at her.

'Me too, but this seems to be different. Gwidion was always a brilliant scholar, I'm sure he would have been brought here on the strength of that alone, but it was when his mentor mentioned Cai that I began to think there was something that might be of use to our work. Apparently he appears to Gwidion in a sort of trance or dream state.'

'What does Gwidion think about it?'

'That is the weird thing. He knows Cai is imaginary and yet at the same time he believes he is real. And he fails to see the contradiction. What is even more unusual is that his dream states have been associated with unexplained absences.'

'What do you mean?'

'Sometimes he has been found in different parts of the village, or even outside it. He doesn't know how he got there, and no-one else knows either.'

'Soma travel?'

Jiménez shrugged. 'It's all anecdotal, but how many explanations are there? Out-of-body experiences, journeying, astral travel, alien abduction, it's had many different names at different times. But it could be what makes Gwidion so special.'

'You believe that?'

Jiménez looked almost affronted. 'I've spent nearly ten years of my life at this Academy in the political wilderness when I could have been enjoying all the trappings of power and privilege in Buenos Aires or Cusco. What do you think?'

'Do you believe it is possible? For someone to move through space in a way which breaks all the accepted laws of nature, I mean?'

'There was a time when I didn't believe the loom was possible.'

'But you believe soma travel is possible.'

They looked at each other for a long time. Alara's half-smile let him know that she was teasing him, that she would let him off if he did not want to answer. But she was not Luis. He had no reason not to be truthful.

'I never have until now.'

Her smile turned into a full-blown laugh.

'You are not so different from Martín after all, then. Despite your politician's replies.'

There was another long pause.

'What are you thinking?' asked Alara.

'Only that if Gwidion thought Cai was part of the loom, it might be enough to keep him here.'

'The soñador would never allow it.'

Jiménez closed his eyes and let his head rock gently from side to side. 'Martín is as keen to see this project succeed as we all are.'

'You've talked with him about it?'

He shook his head. 'Not yet.' There was a pause. 'I don't know if I dare ask after that business with Gwidion arriving here. And then there was Xavier. Alara, the generation ship is nearly ready to leave. All it needs is a target, a habitable planet to aim for. Can you imagine that?'

He stood up and paced his enthusiasm around the room. 'You can laugh and say I'm no different from Martín if you like. But, Alara, the man is living in the past. He thinks we can still rebuild the world. He thinks that once we have a cure for the plague somehow things will get back to normal.'

'But we can already make people fertile again.'

'Yes, Alara. But it's not enough. The plague didn't just affect our bodies. We still have to deal with the blame and the recriminations. Everybody has a different scapegoat. The Indonesians blame us, we blame the Christian Americans. It's as if the trauma was so great, the calamity so huge, that we've damaged humankind's psyche. You would think that after all that people would want peace at any price.'

He sat again and let his hands tidy her hair about her face. 'Maybe Gwidion and his people have got the right idea. Maybe we should all go home to Mimosa.'

'That's why you believe in the loom, isn't it?' Alara asked.

'Sure, the loom is a brilliant creation, but this community of minds he wants to build... this idea that we can change the world by churning out technicians and mentors enlightened by their contact with the loom, it's just... mysticism. He doesn't know what he's got here and what's worse is that without another soñador to take his place, it is dying with him.'

'There will be others.'

'There is Gwidion. Gwidion cannot be allowed to leave.'

'What are you suggesting?'

'Could you plant Cai on the loom?'

'Pablo!' There was as much sadness in her voice as outrage. 'Now you want me to lie to him?'

'Not lie, Alara. Cai already exists in his mind, he finds him... wherever he finds him. All I'm saying is that if he finds him on the loom, so much the better for us.'

'He's just a boy, Pablo. You don't know what damage you might do to him. You also don't know if he'd be fooled by a trick like that. And where would that leave us?'

'It might only have to be for a little while, Alara. Just to get him to stay, to help him get over the first few days or weeks, until he's settled down here and can appreciate what we are doing.'

'Will you ever really tell him what we are doing?'

He looked at her as seriously and earnestly as he had looked at her three years ago on the shores of Lake Titicaca when he had first convinced her to join the project.

'Oh yes, Alara. I will tell him.'

Her question fell like a stone into the silence. 'Have you lost your faith too, Pablo?'

He banged his fist into the palm of his hand. His sudden violence startled her, though she had seen it many times before. His face was red as he turned to her.

'Faith! What is faith but another set of lies to believe in? It has taken thirty years for the Republic to build a generation ship. Thirty years without resources, without technical skills, without a fraction of the population that the United Christian States once had. But we did it. Think of it. A new start for humanity, without war, without the fertility plague, without the decaying weight of years of history, without hate, without revenge. That is what I call faith. That is something I can believe in. I don't know where my final resting place will be, Alara, but I vow it will not be under these stars.'

'Then why are you in Madrid?'

'Because this is where I may find the final piece of the jigsaw.' He strode across the room and punched the headboard of the bed. 'Listen, Alara, can you hear the insects running? The world is riddled with lies and petty conflict, underhand schemes and plain stupidity, just like this bed and its rotten woodworm. When we find a way to start again we will leave all that behind. And believe me, the first thing we will ditch is the lies.'

Alara listened to the words without fully understanding them. But the passion that lay buried beneath his worldly exterior, the desire to get something done, she did understand. There were men like Martín whose belief was so strong that they ploughed their furrow single-mindedly whatever the world thought or required of them, and there were men like Jiménez whose strength of belief was never diminished by the wheeling and dealing, the compromises of getting things done. She loved him for it, and yet it frightened her too. For it begged the question of what was essential to the belief and what was only a compromise, a deal that had to be done. When he had achieved what he needed to do, what would become of her?

Alara was cowed by his outburst. She could not say what she wanted to say. But she could not stop herself thinking it.

'And meanwhile we'll tell just one more lie to help it all along. To the fourteen-year-old boy who's supposed to be our saviour.'

chapter six

Alara watched Soñador Martín as he strode the gallery of the soma hall, his head bowed. Despite herself, she was thinking about what Pablo had said to her. Even the mere suggestion of interfering in the loom made her feel guilty, although she had no intention of trying it, and her hands shook slightly on the desk before her. Her screen showed no activity. Keepers were chosen for their empathic qualities, their role, she knew very well, was as surrogate mothers to the adolescent boys who came to Madrid. But in three years at the Academy, patiently watching the optik which monitored the brainwave patterns of her charges, she had had time to dream a little too.

She had even dreamed of being a soñador. It was not unknown in the part of the world she came from for women to show unusual talents as shamans or healers. And she knew there had been female soñadores in the early years, in the golden age of soñadores immediately after the fertility plague. Since then the numbers, men or women, had dwindled. Martín was the last in that line and already he was getting old. There was no sign of a successor. Now all the Academy's efforts were concentrated on pubescent males.

She had approached Martín about it on a few occasions and he had never discouraged her. He had taught her the techniques of meditation and in those long boring hours of watching the perfectly usual brain activity of her boys, she had practised them. After all, surely it was like any other skill: like playing a musical instrument or doing mathematics. Practice might make perfect.

Occasionally, very occasionally, she thought she perceived a way of accessing the loom. When Martín himself was on the loom, for example, there was something, something she could not put into words or images, but something. Sometimes it was like a ripple in her head, a wave that swept over her mind and brought her glimpses of knowledge she did not have before. At other times it was as if there was a new channel in her brain, a new connection, a new way of thinking which seemed to exist at the very outside edges of her perception, like something half-seen from the farthest corners of her eyes. Again it might be like an extra sense, a smell that had no obvious cause, for example, or even more bizarrely, a smell that was not a smell at all.

All too often, however, there were her duties to be attended to, boys who needed attention or entertaining or mothering, and her focus was turned to her emotional resources to the detriment of any other activity. And then there were the long, interminably long, boring hours of watching the optik.

She jumped as Martín put his hand on her shoulder.

'Dreaming?' It was a joke, but Alara's recent thoughts of Cai and the loom still made her flush. He looked at the screen.

'What's the matter?'

Alara stuttered.

'With Gwidion?' he said in explanation.

'He's unhappy. He wants to go home. We thought when he actually made contact on the loom, that might be enough to make him forget.'

Martín looked unsurprised. 'Perhaps you should be with him.'

'Colonel Jiménez went to talk to him, Soñador.'

The caterpillars closed together, there was a suppressed note of fury in his voice. 'That is not his place.' He swung around, his cloak following behind him, then reconsidered.

'Is Jiménez there now?'

'I don't know, I don't think so.'

'Go and fetch Gwidion. I think it is time I showed him something.'

Some minutes later the sound of two pairs of feet told Martín that Alara and Gwidion were coming back. Gwidion stopped at the entrance to the soma hall, his mouth open. The rows of other Alaras turned their heads to see the unprecedented sight of a student in their midst. As Martín strode towards him they returned to their screens. He held out his arm in a grand sweeping gesture.

'The heart of the matter-mmm. Impressive, don't you think?'

As Gwidion looked around the huge room, question after question forming in his mind, the soñador held out his hand and led him past the rows of keepers.

'Gwidion, you may go home any time you want. We have no right to keep you here, and you will not be of any use to us if you do not wish to stay. But before you make up your mind I want to show you something.'

As they walked, Martín considered the enormity of the risk he was taking. He was about to break the colonel's fundamental security rule that none of the students knew the details of the soma project. It was their ignorance that made it possible one day to send them back to their villages – and he had just promised Gwidion that he could go back any time he liked. As for the other bribe to silence, fertility treatment, he was not sure that carried much weight at all in Gwidion's case.

It was a slightly perverse thrill to be here, in the inner sanctum as it were, with the colonel's most prized protege. For a moment he experienced the feeling of power that he imagined Jiménez must enjoy so often. In any case, he reflected, and as the colonel had so glibly said, it was the soñador who made the rules.

'These are the keepers of the loom. Each one is assigned to a single student as long as he is here.'

'Is that how Alara knew what I had dreamed?'

'Not exactly. Her soma powers are not that fully developed.' He smiled back at her, for in the silence of the soma hall his words could be heard almost everywhere. 'But we have high hopes of her, given the time.'

'Then how does she know?'

'The loom is a telepathic construct created over many years, by some of the greatest soñadores. I am the only survivor in that line, though we have a number of agoreros or diviners who may one day aspire to that title. They, along with the best of our keepers, are capable of maintaining the loom.'

'And it is stored on these optiks?'

Martín shook his head. 'These optiks can give your keeper an inkling of what goes on inside your head, but they are not for storage. When we are talking about the loom we need to think differently. The technology is, if you like, an interface between the loom and the brain. Not the other way round. It is useful, it may even be necessary. For now anyway. Come with me.'

Gwidion studied the vision of heaven which looked down on them from the cupola as they walked to the far end of the hall. In a small alcove many metres beneath the fresco stood a metre-high statue of a figure dressed like Soñador Martín. The cupped hands cradled a glass ball no bigger than a man's head.

'Soñador Saval. The first soñador, the creator of the loom fifteen years ago.' Martín pointed at the globe.

'You see the network of lazurite crystals?' He picked up the globe and turned it reverently in his hands. 'Beautiful, isn't it? Lazurite is the main component of lapis lazuli, but in its crystalline form it is extremely rare.'

Gwidion gazed at the incredibly intricate structure. It was azure, almost translucent.

'The loom?' said Gwidion. 'That's all it is?'

'As I said it is a telepathic construct, not a physical one.'

'Then why does it need crystals at all?'

Martín breathed deeply. 'Why is a candle an aid to meditation? If we understood in the way you are asking to understand, then perhaps the search for soñadores would not be my life's work.' He smiled. 'Perhaps one day you will tell me. The loom exists at many levels, but not all of them are accessible to everyone. In its purest form only a soñador is able to completely connect to it. Those people are very few, and sometimes their links to it are very erratic. Sometimes, in particular during the early years of puberty, boys who show no signs of other soma abilities are nevertheless able to connect with the loom for brief periods. That is why we have concentrated our research here on boys.'

'So why the optik in my room?'

'Obviously so that we can monitor your progress and your safety. But also you may think of it as a meditation device, a method of concentrating the mind, like the flame of a candle or a mantra. All our students come from places where meditation of one sort or another is part of their culture. Only here there is one important difference. Since all trance or dream states are associated with certain changes in brainwave patterns and other motor control functions, we are able to observe those. Each optik contains a special crystal sensitive to changes in those measurable factors which we are able to record.'

'So Alara can see what I am dreaming.'

Martín hesitated. What he and Alara had seen on the screen the day before had been unusually lucid for a student accessing the loom, but it was hardly typical.

'Not exactly. But over the years we have identified many patterns and have come to know what they might signify. It is like a real loom, and each keeper oversees the progress of a single thread. At first she will see only random movements, backwards and forwards, in and out. But in time she will see a pattern, some hint of the complete design. So it is with us.'

Gwidion looked at the rows and rows of optiks again and imagined all those minds attempting to link to the loom.

'What will happen if you do not find a new soñador?'

Martín sighed. 'I don't know. We will find an answer.'

'I would like to be a soñador.'

Martín smiled and put his arm around the boy's shoulder. The boy's simplicity and straightforwardness made him feel lighter and happier than he had felt for many months. Jiménez might be a thorn in his side, but it was true that he had brought him Gwidion.

'I would like you to be one too.'

As they walked back. Gwidion remembered something from his earlier talk with Jiménez.

'Soñador, who released the fertility plague?' And before he could reply. 'I don't believe what is on the loom.'

Martín stopped and looked around, then walked on again. 'Come, I will take you back to your room.'

Once outside the hall, and out of the earshot of the keepers, the soñador stopped again. The boy still looked at him questioningly. Today seemed like a good day for taking risks.

'Empires built on truth are a rarity, Gwidion. The history you find on the loom is only the history as written by the Republic of Hispania. There are other histories.'

'Why would anyone lie about history?'

He squeezed the boy tightly.

'Why would anyone want to lie about anything? History starts so simply. It begins with a single story, the present, the here and now. And in no time at all it is a skein of different strands. Strands of truth, strands of fiction, strands of fact and strands of deceit. We desperately want it to be one and whole again. But it never is.'

'Truth.' Gwidion pronounced it treeth. The caterpillars questioned him.

He spelled it. 'T R U T H. In Welsh it means rigmarole.'

The soñador smiled.

'Then why do you not alter the loom?'

Martín's face clouded. 'What to, Gwidion. Mmm. What to?'

When Jiménez got back to his desk there was a message waiting for him. He swivelled the optik towards him.

Resolution 1024 of the High Council of the Republic of Hispania. Buenos Aires, September 16, 2084.

In view of the deepening economic crisis and increasing evidence of pockets of technologically-active insurgents in Asia and parts of Eastern Europe, the Soma Academy is requested and required to channel all resources towards a series of travel simulations to be undertaken within six months.

The academy director is therefore required to submit six possible life-supporting targets to the Council.

Well, thought the colonel, when things get bad they get worse. As a military man who had spent more time in the debating chamber than on the battlefield, he wasn't used to being wholly dependant on others for his survival. All he could do was hope that Alara's efforts were enough to keep Gwidion at the Academy. But there was something worthwhile he could do in the meantime, and that was renew his friendship with the president face to face.

Before that he had one more duty to complete.

'For the pride of our Republic, the pride of our produce. That you may one day lead us again to a land of plenty.' The colonel's familiar benediction rang out into the dark spaces of the dining hall as the hundreds of patient faces waited to tuck into their textured protein with its sauce of the day. He held up his hand.

As Gwidion looked at the colonel he noticed someone else in his line of vision. Just a table away was the boy he had met on his abortive escape attempt the night before. As if feeling Gwidion's eyes on the back of his neck, the other boy turned. He looked first at Alara, then at Gwidion. There was the briefest of acknowledgements, a suggestion of approval, a hint of a smile before the colonel's voice rang out again.

'The time of plenty may be sooner than you think. Many of you will have become aware of the nature of our work here, though very few will have an inkling of its purpose. Many of you will know that you have left your families and friends, the people and the places you love, to be engaged on one of the Republic's most valued scientific projects.'

Behind him the impressive figure of Soñador Martín sat slightly apart. He hated the colonel's pep talks, they struck him as the worst sort of chauvinism. What linked the three hundred or so boys and keepers who made up the Academy was a bond of the mind, not Republican propaganda.

'You may also know that there are those who scoff at the adjective 'scientific' in connection with what we are doing here. But I also know that any of you who have made even the most fleeting contact with the loom... ' he paused a gave a slight bow towards the seated figure of Soñador Martín who returned the gesture in an exaggerated fashion... 'You will appreciate that those notions are fuelled either by blindness or ignorance. True, when we deal with matters of the mind, we are at the edge of our understanding. We may stumble, we may trip, we may take wrong turnings. But still we go forward, because we know that real science, great science, the science that may save us is just ahead in that dark void that the cynics and detractors find so frightening to enter.'

He looked down the ranks of young faces turned towards him, making eye contact with one after another. The soñador began to hum, so softly that it was barely audible. The colonel looked around only to be met by the sight of two slightly surprised caterpillars.

'Forgive me, I will not let your food become even cooler.' There was a ripple of laughter, but the soñador's antics had succeeded in taking the wind out of his sails. 'I believe we are nearer our goal than we have ever been and the next few months will be critical to our success or failure. For all your work, for all your sacrifice, for all your hope, I wish to thank you.'

Martín ostentatiously took up his knife and fork and began to eat.

'To you, the pride of our Republic. To you, the pride of our produce. That you may one day lead us again to a land of plenty.'

He sat down to a mixture of stunned silence and suppressed giggles. Then somewhere far back in the depths of the dining hall, some brave soul put his hands together in a quiet clap, which echoed up to the vaulted ceilings. And as it travelled forward to the top table it collected other braver claps, and others braver still. Until at last, when it reached the grey and gold-clad officers of the Academy and their grey-haired soñador it was a wave of hundreds of boys, standing, clapping, shouting, cheering.

chapter seven

Alara usually hated it when Jiménez was away. Diversions at the Academy were hard to come by and at any other time she would have jumped at the chance of a trip to Cusco. As it was, she was rather glad it had not been possible.

He was under pressure, she knew that, though she might not know the full details of how great the pressure could be, but that did not excuse his behaviour since Gwidion had arrived at the Academy. He had made light of his suggestion that she should introduce Cai on the loom when he saw her dismay at the idea; but she feared it was not something he would leave alone. She loved Pablo, she was a conscientious worker and wanted to please – two reasons why, once planted, the thought grew like a cancer inside her. She was sure, in the first place, that she could not do anything so crass and deceptive. Secondly she was sure that nothing she could achieve on the loom was anywhere near what Gwidion was capable of. The notion of fooling the boy was absurd.

And so the cancer grew. Was Pablo really so blind that he could not see that was the case? How deep, in truth, was his understanding of the loom, how genuine was his commitment to it? Or if it was not blindness, how desperate was he? And desperate for what, exactly? It was like watching an amoeba divide and grow under a microscope, suspicion and doubt multiplying exponentially and endlessly. One thing was more important to her than anything, and that was trust. For the first time in their relationship she dared to think that Pablo was not being totally honest with her.

Besides, she had a new protege, and no ordinary new protege either. Gwidion had done more than just engage her mothering instinct, he had revived some of the initial enthusiasm she had once felt for exploring the loom herself. At her optik in the soma hall she found herself practising the techniques of meditation that Martín had taught her whenever she could. She had begun to ask her sister, and her close friends among the other keepers, about it too. The more she made her own tentative attempts at linking with the loom, the more she imagined she was making a connection. And the imagination turned to certainty, and the certainty fuelled her efforts again.

It was late, the day was over and there was no Pablo to expect. She took off her shoes and padded her way along the corridors until she came to the soñador's room and lifted her hand to knock on the door. Then her courage failed her. She was being silly. She was just another keeper among a hundred and fifty keepers and Martín had more important things to attend to than her feeble efforts at soma. She retraced her steps to her own room, then changed her mind again. If she could not practise her meditation then at least she wanted someone to talk to. Gwidion might still be awake. She pushed open his door.

'Oh. Excuse me.'

The soñador and Gwidion were both sitting cross-legged on the floor facing each other. Between them on a small brass bowl was the crystal globe from the soma hall.

'I'm sorry, Soñador. I thought Gwidion was alone. I came to see that he was all right.'

The soñador beckoned her in. 'Come in, come in, Alara. We were sharing some meditation. You may find this useful.'

She stepped into the room and he made room for her so that the three of them sat at the points of an equilateral triangle.

'Alara has been practising her meditation,' said Gwidion with all the lack of guile of a boy who believes that all the world is as talented as he, and probably more so.

'Yes, I know,' said Martín. Alara flushed. 'Don't be embarrassed, it is not beneficial for freeing the mind. Joint meditation is a technique practised by all soñadores. So huge a construct as the loom could not have been built by one mind alone. In the writings of the first soñador we find many references to multiple soma sessions as a method for training pupils.'

'Did you know Soñador Saval?' asked Alara.

'Yes, I knew her.'

Gwidion looked surprised. 'She was a woman?'

Martín laughed. 'It's difficult to tell from her statue. Oh yes. She was a woman.'

At first Alara could not recognise the expression that flitted across his face at the mention of Soñador Saval's name. Or perhaps it was that she just could not believe it. But yes. It was unmistakable. Affection, lust even. It was almost incongruous on so respected and senior a figure, a man who she had watched every day for three years walking past a hundred and fifty girls of all shapes and sizes in the soma hall without so much as the suggestion that one of them might even be to his taste. She was shocked by it, but more than that she momentarily shared the emotion. Then just as quickly they were soñador and keeper once more.

Martín composed himself. 'Saval was a great teacher. There are many ways to access the loom, and very often the best way is through one of the senses. It seemed to her no accident that many of the great soñadores had one or more of the usual five senses which were acutely developed. She herself likened accessing the loom to listening to a strange and wonderful piece of music. At first it was chaotic and shapeless, indistinguishable from the normal mental jabbering which fills our days. But in time it acquired form and became harmonious. And in more time it was possible to distinguish the individual instruments and the rhythms and the melodies, and the counter-melodies. But there is no end to the process, she said.

For every instrument, every note, creates an infinite number of harmonics, and these too are part of what we hear. So that infinite interweaving, which is a piece of music, is also the loom. And on it may be stored an infinite amount of information.'

He paused to allow his students time to digest the metaphor.

'It is only like a language,' Gwidion broke in excitedly. 'Except that there are no words. It is like a language before there are words.'

Alara could not help laughing out loud at the apparent contradiction. Martín smiled too.

'Yes, Gwidion. Saval put it rather more helpfully, but what you say is also true. You must study her works.'

Martín placed his upturned hands on his knees, indicating that it was time to meditate. Alara suddenly felt rather awkward, but the soñador's gentle humming helped her to overcome her nervousness and concentrate on her breathing. She stared into the globe, admiring its infinite surfaces and angles, the refractions and reflections. She felt a frisson of excitement at the thought of being here. Then her eyes closed as she felt the pull from Martín, something she had occasionally experienced when he was on the loom. Except now, with Gwidion present, the intensity seemed much greater.

Alara was not the only one who was affected by it. As Martín felt his eyeballs beginning the crazy gyrations which signified the onset of REM sleep, his body stiffened. At first the fine line between sleep and wakeful meditation was always difficult to hold, but gradually he brought it under control. It moved still. Like a snake it slithered backwards and forwards attempting to tip the consciousness this way or that. It was like balancing on a tightrope, never absolutely motionless, always a delicate balance, a dynamic interplay.

He was about to suggest a meditation on some aspect of Saval's writings, but that line was impossible to maintain. Something much more powerful tugged at him. It was easy to guess where, who, it was coming from. When he was able for a moment to achieve the ultimate counterpoise between awareness and dreaming, he spoke.

'Very well,' he said softly. 'Take us home.'

Immediately the dome of Mimosa was spread out before them. It was remarkable. Even Martín, in a lifetime of soma, had seldom experienced such clarity and precision. They seemed to be standing

on the ridge above the dome and from there they could look north
to the hills of the Preselis glowering against a dark blue sky. Large
white fluffy clouds were making their way towards them, their
bottoms flat in the air as if they were going to land where they stood.
South to the crashing shoreline of the Atlantic, the sky was lighter
and the filtered rays of sunlight caught the highlights of the waves like
a pulsating patchwork of diamonds. They stood a moment, taking
in the enormity of the view, gathering their breath, maintaining
their control.

They moved in. The concentric circles of duggs, their striped
canvas doors lifting in a slight breeze, were laid out before them
with the roundhouse at their centre. The remnants of September
sun cast long shadows across the vibrant red earth, the longest of all
belonging to the Ruins.

Here was the mentor, standing at the doorway of the roundhouse,
taking a moment to stare out across the fields with their new crops
like a rich green blanket across the soil.

Here was Bethan, her proud pregnancy needing no emphasis
now. Here was Gwidion's mother, her dark figure bent, as ever, over
the fire of her dugg. For whom was she cooking now? And here,
somewhere, was Lauren. Where else but before her optik? Her hair
scraped back behind her ears, her face set on her task. It seemed as
though they might watch this scene indefinitely. And then, as if the
clouds and rain were finally closing in on them, the image faded.

As the soñador opened his eyes he found Gwidion in tears,
violent sobs wracking his body. Beside him Alara was taking the
gentle rhythmic breaths of someone peacefully asleep. Martín wiped
the tears from his own eyes and took the boy in his arms.

Gwidion woke up with a start. He might have been dreaming,
but he was sure he could smell smoke. As his eyes adjusted to the
darkness and the contents of his room came into focus, he heard a tap
at the door. It opened slowly and a familiar figure leaned itself against
the frame, an unlit cigarette in his mouth.

'Fancy a smoke?'

'It's you,' breathed Gwidion.

The boy he had met earlier on his escape attempt, walked in and closed the door behind him.

'I couldn't sleep.'

He looked around the room with a vague curiosity, logging its furniture.

'Same as mine.'

He picked up the mentor's notebook which Gwidion had been reading before going to bed.

'You had a lot of visitors tonight. The soñador, no less. You must be a star pupil.'

Gwidion shrugged. 'I don't know. I barely know what I'm supposed to be learning here.'

The boy sat on the bed. 'I'm Xavier.' He held out his hand. For a moment Gwidion did not know what to do. It seemed a strange gesture between two boys in the middle of the night. They shook hands.

'Nobody knows what they are supposed to be learning here. We're not supposed to meet, we're not supposed to talk. I'm not even supposed to be here now.'

'Will we get into trouble?'

Xavier shook his head and lit his cigarette. 'No. Me, maybe. It doesn't matter, I'm being kicked out anyway.'

'Why?'

'No reason I know of. I mean, they don't say that to you. They told me I'd done very well, that I can practise medicine. Well, once I've worked in a clinic for a while, anyway.'

'But you're going home?'

'There's nowhere else to go.'

'Where is home?'

'Buenos Aires.'

'You come from the city?' Gwidion's voice contained a note of wonder.

'Yes. It'll be great after this place, believe me. Proper food, girls.' He puffed on his cigarette. 'And plenty of other diversions. Tobacco's fine, you know, but there's better things on the market.'

'I'd like to see a big city.'

'Where are you from?'

'Mimosa.'

Xavier shook his head. 'Don't know it. What's it like?'

'It's a small village in the country.'

'Not for me, then.'

There was a pause. Xavier got up and threw the end of his cigarette out of the window. He reached in his pocket and took out the packet.

'Do you want them? They're easy to get where I'm going.'

Gwidion didn't want them, but he liked Xavier.

'Thanks. Thanks a lot.'

'You're welcome.'

Xavier stretched and yawned.

'Well, I just thought I'd come and say goodbye.' He turned to go.

'I wish I was going home,' said Gwidion.

'Me too.'

Gwidion hesitated. 'What do you mean? I thought you were.'

Xavier tried to make a joke of it. 'I meant I wished you were going home.' He laughed, but Gwidion did not join in.

Xavier came back to the bed and took the cigarettes off Gwidion again. 'Lend us one.'

'Of course.'

He lit it. 'I lied about going home. Well, not quite, Buenos Aires is where I am going.' He looked around conspiratorially. 'Look, don't tell anyone this, OK, I could get in a lot of trouble.'

'OK.'

'They've got me this job at a clinic aboard a spaceship.'

'Wow.' Gwidion sat up with a bounce. 'That's almost as good as being a pilot.'

'Maybe. But this ship isn't coming back. They're planning a voyage to find a new planet to settle. Hundreds of top people, technicians, medical people, scientists, artists, politicians, all sorts. All especially chosen for the journey.'

'That's fantastic. I thought they were kicking you out.'

'Like I say, it just felt that way.'

'Why do they want to leave?'

Xavier shrugged. 'Who wouldn't? I mean, some people say the Indonesians have developed a photon bomb.'

'Photon bomb?'

Gwidion felt suddenly stupid. He had spent so much time studying history, it appeared he had no notion of what was happening here and now.

'But where are they going?'

Xavier's voice dropped to a whisper. 'That's the really amazing thing. They don't know yet. I mean it could take sixty years or more. I may not even see the new place. But maybe my children will.'

The two paused to imagine what an endless journey sixty years might be.

'What about your family? Won't you miss them? I mean, going away forever like that?'

Xavier shrugged. 'Yes, I'll miss them.' He laughed nervously. 'They'll think I'm a hero anyway. Big brother going off to Madrid and landing a place on a spaceship. I don't know, it's better than going back a failure.'

'A failure?'

'And they sort out any fertility problems for you as part of the deal. I mean, I'm all right. But, you know, if you've got them. That could mean a lot to a lot of people.'

'Yes,' said Gwidion.

Xavier got up again and went to the window to dispose of his cigarette. 'Anyway, I've got to get up early tomorrow. It's a long flight.'

'Good luck. I think you're really lucky.'

'Don't tell anyone, will you? I just wanted to say goodbye, anyway. And meet the star pupil.'

Gwidion blushed and smiled. Xavier had reached the door.

'I don't expect I'll see you again.' He made a final effort at levity. 'Not unless you're going past Alpha Centauri in a few weeks.'

They laughed.

'Thanks for the cigarettes,' said Gwidion.

'You're welcome.'

Gwidion couldn't sleep after Xavier had gone. Thoughts of home were never far from his own mind, and now they seemed to be cropping up all over the place. He took hold of his clasp and twirled it gently around his wrist. He picked up the mentor's notebook from the bed where Xavier had left it and rubbed the front cover flat.

As he did so, the clasp snagged a corner, ripping it open. He gave a gasp of annoyance. Then something caught his eye. Inside the covering, pressed flat against the original cover of the book, was another piece of paper. He reached out and brought the lamp closer so he could see to carefully lengthen the rip he had already made. He slipped the sheet of paper out gently. It was folded in quarters and as he opened it he realised it was a cutting from an old newspaper. It was fragile, but the covering on the notebook had preserved some of its pristine whiteness and the type was clear. He had read about newspapers, but this was the first time he had ever seen one and his heart beat fast.

In his excitement he had a sudden urge to rush to Lauren's dugg and show her his find, or the mentor's, but with just as sudden a stab of sadness he realised that was not possible. He laid the cutting on his mattress, smoothing out the creases as best he could, and peered at the type. His heart pounded so loudly it seemed to fill the room with its beating and his hands trembled as he followed the words. It was a newspaper front page, dated September 20, 2001.

A fourteen-year-old Welsh boy miraculously survived a fall from the 103rd floor of one of the two towers of the World Trade Center in New York after September 11th's terrorist attacks, it was revealed today.

Cai Williams, from Pembrokeshire, was found cradled in his father's arms among the rubble, unconscious but otherwise unhurt. Police said it appeared his father, who died instantly, had broken the boy's fall.

David Williams, a financial consultant with the Welsh Assembly, was in the World Trade Center to attend a meeting aimed at raising finance for a new electronics factory in the South Wales valleys.

He had taken his son along on the American trip as a treat because it was his 14th birthday. Police believe that when the second of the hijacked passenger jets struck the tower, David Williams leaped out of a 103rd floor window in a desperate attempt to save his son.

'This looks like a remarkable story of self-sacrifice,' said NYPD spokesman Lou Vincetti.

'The enormity of this outrage meant that many tragic human stories will never be known or told, but this must be one of the most fantastic.

'Even more fantastic is that the boy survived. When he was found by rescuers they just couldn't believe what they were seeing.

'The father was on his back, crushed on the rubble with the boy wrapped in his arms and lying face up on his stomach.

'We just can't imagine what it must have been like inside that building when the plane exploded.'

The teenager was taken to hospital but was expected to be flown home to his mother in West Wales yesterday.

The world watched in horror, live on their television screens as, shortly after 9am on that Tuesday which changed the world, two hijacked passenger jets were flown into the twin towers of the World Trade Center, financial hub of the economy of the Western world and two of the world's tallest buildings.

Against the backdrop of a clear blue sky, in scenes which for all their sharpness, clarity and drama could have been plucked from a Hollywood movie, the explosions ripped through the buildings leading to their collapse in one of the city's busiest business areas.

Many people were seen throwing themselves from the upper floors in a desperate attempt to escape the unimaginable heat and horror of the inferno.

It is thought that more than five thousand people of all nationalities died as a result of the attack by a handful of dedicated and suicidal terrorists linked to Muslim fundamentalist Osama bin Laden, though the final death count may well be higher.

Gwidion's heart beat fast. He re-read the article. Then he read it again. It was as if he had stumbled across something he had always known and yet even now he did not know it. The images of his dreams came and went in his head. Skyscrapers, offices. Falling, always falling. As fast as he followed a train of thought, it fell away from him. Only the images remained. And the fear. The smell of fear.

Gwidion lifted the piece of newspaper to his nose and breathed in the faint, faded aroma of newsprint and ink. As the light from his lamp shone through the thin paper he caught sight of something written on the back. He turned it over and placed it once more on his mattress. In the unmistakable scrawl of his mother's handwriting he read:

Cai Williams, my father. Died May 8, 2051.

And again he unfolded the newspaper cutting and read. And re-read. And turned it over and read again. Cai was his brother, Cai was his twin. Cai was his grandfather, Cai was his twin. He lay on the bed, still clutching the scrap of paper in his hand, and tried to calm his breathing. He could still feel the tears in his eyes from the soñador's visit, as if they were covered with a thin layer of grit, and he let his lids close over them. Breathe. Control the breath.

The implications of what he had discovered still raced around his mind, a hopeless jumble of ifs and what-ifs. It was as though he was trying to rerun his whole life history through the lens that this new information had given him. But it wasn't that simple. Cai was his grandfather. Cai was his twin. And the mentor. Had the mentor planted this information for him?

As soon as he had re-adjusted one strand of his life, it looped around and another strand came loose. As fast as he was able to answer one question, a hundred other questions sprang from it. And it was not only the unanswered questions but the unanswerable questions too. It was like the loom, an intricate network of reflection and refraction in which one new grain of information was bounced around, changing other pieces of information, which in turn were bounced around and changed other pieces of information, which in turn... which in turn...

He needed answers. His breathing was coming in gasps now and the more he gasped, the more he fought for air. He tried to read the cutting again but his panting had become so violent he could hardly sit up on the bed. Beneath him the mattress shook, magnifying the spasms of his body, accelerating the sense of panic. He felt a pain around his chest as if someone had wound a rope around it and was twisting the ends together.

Desperately he tried to think. Perhaps Xavier could hear him. He tried calling out but his voice was no more than a strangled squeak. He lay on the bed until the pain in his chest was so great he did not dare breathe. And suddenly, as suddenly as it had come, the pain was gone. His breath began again, filling the abdomen, then the chest and finally the collarbones. He stretched out his arms and legs and relaxed them. And breathed. Pulling in the light, sending it out through his pained muscles. Pulling in the light. His pulse slowed and his breaths dropped to a rate of about two a minute. He focused above the bridge of his nose. He was tired, so tired. His eyeballs began moving rapidly to and fro under his heavy lids. Search and dream. Control the dream.

Gwidion looked out over the graveyard before him. Here and there old headstones covered in lichen and moss lurched at ugly angles. Others, more upright, bore the unsightly ageing spots of organic material on wet stone. Behind him was a small stone-built church, its tower newly renovated and shining almost white in the low winter sun. Each side bore a blue clockface with gold lettering and a series of narrow windows were cut into its sides. He entered its cool and quiet nave through an arched doorway at the opposite end. It smelled of polish and damp and decaying mortar, but its pews shone and hassocks were laid out neatly in rows.

The sun shone through the tinted windows casting shafts of dust-filled rose and yellow light across the aisle. He opened a small doorway to one side of the main nave and climbed up the circular stone steps until he reached the top of the tower. He shivered as the cold air reddened his cheeks and ears and looked out over the flat moor to the west. The view was magnificent. And familiar.

As he gazed at the patchwork of fields divided by hedges or stands of trees, a single cloud marched across the landscape picking out the houses which were scattered across the moor, half-hidden by trees. Some were isolated, a cluster of barns and outbuildings attached to them. Others were huddled together, set along wide dark grey roads. He shivered again. Not from cold this time, but because he knew this place. It was his village. Mimosa.

He looked north expecting to see the ridge crowned with its familiar forests, but there were none. But it was unmistakable. Further north again lay the familiar shapes of the Preseli Hills. Gwidion focused on his breathing and relaxed once more into the loom.

He was about to turn to descend the tower steps again when he heard the voice.

'In love again?' The tone was unmistakable, the wide grin was audible in his voice. 'Alara this time? You don't half pick them.'

'Cai.' Gwidion turned but saw no-one.

'It took me a while to find you. Nice place you've got here, just up your street. Dates, facts, figures, theories.'

'Cai. Where are you?'

'On the loom, where do you think? Weaving in and out of all this garbage you call history. Alara's a bit of all right, though. No wonder you didn't want to bring me along. Reckon you'll get anywhere with her?'

Gwidion's initial excitement evaporated at the hectoring tone. 'Alara's nice.'

'I reckon old Jiménez got there first though, don't you?'

Despite himself, Gwidion felt the hurt.

'Cai, get lost. I'm busy.'

'Busy doing what? Saving the world? That's the colonel's story, isn't it? Can't see it myself. Still it left the field clear for me and Lauren.'

Suddenly Cai was perched on one of the tower's turrets, his legs dangling into mid-air, his face still set in a wide grin.

'Cai.' Gwidion refocused on his breathing.

'She is something. isn't she? Not that you'd know. Not after that business with Bethan. But Lauren was happy enough to get her own back on you. Never trust a woman. Never trust anyone for that matter.'

'Cai, get out.'

'You don't mean that, Gwidion. I'm your brother, I'm your twin. Remember? Where would you be without me?'

Gwidion gave up the battle and turned his focus on Cai.

'OK. Tell me. Where would I be without you?'

There was a pause.

'Cai. I'm serious. Where would I be without you?'

'You're ready to know?'

'I'm ready to know.'

'Take a look.' He indicated the view before them. 'See, this is how we used to live when there were many more people.'

'Are these their houses? They're huge. And the paths are huge.'

'Roads,' said Cai. 'For vehicles like cars. And the fields were individually owned. People kept animals there or grew crops.'

Gwidion stood in wonder as he tried to lay his own memories of home over the view before him. 'I never imagined it could look like this.'

Cai put both hands on the stone wall beneath him and lifted his body into the air.

'Why did you bring me here?'

Cai shrugged non-committally and continued to grin at him. 'Oh, to get away from it all,' he said airily.

And the thought struck. 'Cai. Cai Williams.'

Cai still grinned. 'Now you've got it, little brother.'

'You?'

'The very same.' He looked out over the moor again. 'The miracle boy. The survivor.'

Gwidion felt dizzy. His head reeled and he was obliged to catch hold of one of the turrets for support. Cai laughed again.

'Careful. I wouldn't want you to fall.'

'But why here?'

'This is where I came. This is where I built the dome.'

'You built the dome?'

Cai nodded.

'Why?'

'To escape.'

'To escape what?'

Cai bent his head over his feet and stared directly down to the gravestones beneath him. 'Can you have any idea what goes through your mind when you fall a hundred and three floors from a skyscraper? No, you can't. Of course you can't. I've got very little idea myself and I relived those moments for decades. Every night, in every dream. There's the terror, first. There's always the terror. There are things you see on the way down. Smoke, flames, a blue, blue sky. So blue it was perfect. I often think – when people say that something came out of the blue – I often think of that blue. It was such a terrifying blue for something to come out of. And windows, flashing past. One hundred and three floors is a long way, and yet it's a very short way too. Hundreds of windows, each one framing some perfect nightmare. Each one frozen in an instant of horror, running past your eyes like a moving film, each frame the same. And reflections of horror. And other people falling on the same terrible journey. The air rushing past, the smell of aviation fuel, a heady smell. Heat and cold. Screams. Fear. And my father's arms clasped tight around me. He was warm in the coldness of the air. I could feel the cloth of his suit, his arms gripping me tightly, his tie flailing upwards. He smelled of sweat. Sweat and fear. He said, 'Cai, I love you. Tell your mother I love her too.' He said it many times. He kept on saying it and I felt... despite everything, I felt... ' he looked at Gwidion again. 'Safe. And then... '

He looked away again and there was a long silence. A buzzard wheeled high above them searching for some tiny movement in the acres of fields, cultivating the currents of air, spreading its feathered fingers as if playing some delicate piece of music on the wind.

'And then?'

'And then, nothing. Just nothing. For a long time, nothing.'

He swung his feet back within the tower and Gwidion breathed out.

'I bought this church many years later when the congregation had grown so small that they could not afford to keep it. And I bought the land for the dome, and some of the farms. I was a living miracle, I was the boy who came back from certain death, and there was money to be made from being a celebrity in those days – chat shows, quiz shows, magazine articles. And I thought I would be able to escape.'

'From what?'

'Oh, from everything. From politics and war and terrorism. From the world, mainly. From a world which couldn't find room for my father to live in. From myself, because I had lived and he hadn't. From my nightmares, from my memories. From people's fascination with my story. In those days, if I could have lived those moments over again, I would have gladly died if it had meant my father could be saved. Or even if not. I would just gladly have died.'

The hectoring tone had disappeared.

'I can't imagine it.' It was all Gwidion could think of to say.

'The dome was my new Patagonia, my new Pennsylvania, a colony for people who felt the same disgust for humanity and its sad history. In my soured mind, I felt nothing but distaste for life. What did Wales have to do with all that? What did a peaceful rural people speaking an old and venerable tongue have to do with hate and rage? What did my father have to do with it? Yes, there was always that above everything. Why my father?'

'And did you escape?'

Cai gave a strangled laugh and shook his head. 'It seemed like it for a while. It seemed for one glorious moment as if I had. It seemed that I was invincible, that I could do anything. And then came the fertility plague. There was no escaping that.'

The two of them stared out across the fields. Gwidion thought of his own father, and his mother. And Lauren.

'Do you remember the Ruins?' asked Gwidion suddenly.

Cai gave his brother a questioning look. He grinned again and patted the stone wall they were both sitting on. Gwidion looked down and saw his foot blot out the gravestones far beneath them. And it dawned on him.

'These are the Ruins, aren't they, Cai? There never was a sky-scraper.'

Cai's grin was his only answer.

'Were you really there? I mean, at the Ruins, in the village, all those times? Or did I just dream you?'

'That depends, little brother. That all depends on how you look at it.'

Jiménez was in a bad mood. First there had been the long flight in his personal shuttle, then there was the fact that he had been obliged to make the trip on his own. He had been looking forward to bringing Alara with him this time and showing her some of the sights along the way. With Gwidion at such a delicate stage in settling down at the Academy, that had not been possible. Shame. Cusco was a sight to see after the spartan life of Madrid.

It was almost the start of the wet season, but the nights were still cold and clear. Its ramshackle development had made the city an untidy sprawl of humanity, but the mountains that encircled it set a natural boundary to its growth, and tonight, with its many lights twinkling in the sharp frosty air, it was like looking down into the depths of a magic cauldron. Jiménez checked the time. Despite his fatigue, in his time zone he was up and about and raring to go.

The presidential offices of Amarucancha lay below him on the city's central plaza, a squat bulldog of a building reconstructed from the Incas' huge polygonal stone blocks.

He brought his shuttle down on the rooftop landing pad and left his luggage to be taken to his suite. He needed a walk before he met the others. From the restaurants around the colonial arcades of the plaza came the sound of music and the smell of food. He strolled across the square where the crowds were now gathering after their evening meal. At the centre an illuminated fountain rose almost thirty metres in the air, a shower of gold which speckled the spectators as the light wind circled the bowl in which the city lay. Couples and families strolled around with no particular purpose, on the benches lovers sat holding hands or kissing. Through them all moved the mass of people with something to sell. Snacks, sweets, trinkets, beads. Gangs of small children were out too, practising their trading skills. To them 'no' was not a sufficient answer.

His uniform spared him many of these approaches, it had other effects too. He reached the far side of the plaza and entered the arcades where women sat offering their textiles and leathers and knitted alpaca wares. Here too were the kick sellers, marked out by an orange and green striped patch on their coats, peddlars of a herbal high to those for whom chewing coca was not enough. At the sight of the colonel they glided away into the shadows.

Inside the comforting Inca walls of Amarucancha the style was unmistakably Spanish. In the yellow glow of the huge open fire, President Luis leaned back in his large leather-upholstered chair and swung his cup of mint tea in a slow gentle arc before him, raising it in a languid toast.

The Council members were ranged in a horseshoe around Jiménez – he took it wryly as a sign of luck. He knew them all – Juan Fernandez, head of defence, was a personal friend, a veteran, like himself, of few conflicts and many interminable political meetings such as this. Antonio Lorca, now head of internal affairs, had been a tele-writer, a scourge of the government before the days of Luis. The president himself was a short, dapper man who had come to power in the darkest years of the fertility plague. A former tele-paper editor, like Lorca his cynical attitude towards the military aspirations of the Republic's politicians had won him the admiration of a population jaded with impossible election promises. As president he had managed to turn his cynicism into a realistic programme of hope. But there was someone new at the table.

'Colonel Jiménez, I do not believe you have met Pepe Bascato. Of course as Soñador Martín is fully engaged on the Academy project at the moment, I have asked him to represent the scientific view.'

The words sent a shiver up his spine as they exchanged curt nods. Bascato was younger than he, late twenties maybe, it was not easy to say. His gaunt, predatory look might even make him look older than he was. But it was neither his youth nor his demeanour which caused the hairs on his neck to bristle. As the last survivor of a line of great soñadores, Martín commanded enormous respect and, naturally, was a powerful advocate of the Academy's research. Despite the excitement and incredulity of the early years of soma investigation, it was increasingly looking as if, rather than being a new branch of the science of the mind it was no more than a blind-alley. Entertaining, intriguing, but still way outside the mainstream. And science, just as much as clothes and drugs, was subject to the vagaries of fashion.

As the Republic struggled with the economic realities of supporting a technological society with a dwindling population, so power had reverted to the centre. Madrid, no less than soma research, was at the fringes of the modern Republic. It was extremely unlikely that any young career-minded scientist would share either Martín's or the colonel's faith in its future. Still, Jiménez consoled himself, he'd seen them come and he'd seen them go, and no doubt he would see a few more go the same way.

The president addressed Jiménez. 'So, Pablo, it is good to see you back. And with hopeful news too. You are claiming to be close to a breakthrough after all these years. The generation ship is in orbit, the crew has been picked. Since events are moving fast, when can we expect your results?'

'You will appreciate, Jorge, that we are operating at the frontiers of conventional science, if not outside its bounds. But we do anticipate we will be able to meet your six-month deadline for a list of targets.'

'Forgive me.' It was Bascato who spoke. 'I have studied the Academy's research intently.' He gave Jiménez a laconic grin. 'What verifiable scientific data there is available, that is, which does not amount to much. And it seems to me, and many of my colleagues, that given the new urgency of the situation those resources at Madrid would be better used in more conventional fields of astronomy.'

Lorca smiled slightly to himself. He had expected just another boring council meeting followed by some pleasant eating and drinking, not a cock-fight. This was getting seriously interesting. Sometimes he thought it was a shame to have had to leave journalism in order to get really close to the seat of power.

Jiménez straightened himself and spoke quickly. 'President, I appreciate that Pepe is new to the considerations of the High Council, but we have been over this ground many times. Conventional fields of astronomy, for all the resources they currently command, have yet to offer any better hope of a solution.'

The president held up his hand. 'Pepe *is* new to the considerations of the High Council. So maybe we should not take everything for granted.' He turned to the newcomer. 'Pepe?'

'Thank you.' Jiménez watched Bascato's Adam's apple rise and fall in his throat as he swallowed. 'As I was saying, what we are seeking here is a list of planets capable of supporting human life and within theoretical reach of a generation ship. That is no mean feat at the sort of distances we are looking at – more than four light years to the nearest star.'

'Exactly,' interposed Jiménez, leaning forward with a growl.

'And that is why conventional fields of astronomy have failed. We do not have the instruments on Earth or off it which can investigate single planets at those sorts of distances. Hubble is a wreck, Earth-based telescopes do not have a hope of resolving the problem and all our space resources have been engaged on building the ship. Conventional astronomy doesn't have the answers now and it won't have them within six months, or six years, or sixty years.'

Bascato let the colonel's words fall into the silence as he appeared to fiddle with his handcom. There was a whirr as the blinds of the windows descended and a three-dimensional holographic image appeared on the table in front of him.

'What we like to call our top one hundred. I think this gives a good idea of what we are talking about.'

He let the men take in the miniature planetarium before them. At its centre was Earth and around it were arranged a hundred solar systems in which, like some intricate toy, tiny planets revolved around their stars. Bascato was enjoying his moment in the limelight.

'This represents everything we currently know about solar systems which may contain planets capable of supporting life. It also gives an idea of their relative positions. All within five hundred years travelling time at one fifth the speed of light.'

He pointed to a small star close to Earth with three planets circling it.

'Eridani, the closest, could take less than fifty-five years.'

There was a barely detectable frisson around the table. Suddenly the universe didn't seem such a huge place after all.

'All of them, colonel, with planetary systems, all of them showing the presence of oxygen, ozone and water vapour. All of them located using gravitational lensing and infrared spectrometry.' He sat down to join the group of men admiring the holograph, his last comment almost, but not quite, inaudible. 'Not bad for conventional astronomy.'

Jiménez crossed his legs and avoided the interested looks of his colleagues. He studied the labels on the graphic for a moment, leaning forward, his lips pursed.

'No surprises there,' he said, looking up. 'All of them predicted as possible targets by Soñador Saval more than ten years ago. Are you familiar with her work?'

Bascato's Adam's apple rose and fell again. 'Naturally. Sadly the soñador is no longer with us, and as far as I'm aware no-one has been able to replicate her analysis.' He gestured with his hand, cutting a small swathe through the outer reaches of his graphic which for a moment flashed on his skin like a rainbow. 'What we have here however is reliable scientific data. It's repeatable and it's refinable. What's more once the ship is outside our solar system its own satellite array will be able to analyse the nature of these planets much more exactly.' He spread the long fingers of his hands on the table. 'Pity Saval cannot be with us.'

Jiménez thought fast. He didn't need the detached body language of his former friends to tell him he was in a corner. He needed to offer something better, but he was far from able to. He also had the uncomfortable feeling he'd been stitched up. This was supposed to be his opportunity to unveil Gwidion's talents to a hungry audience. The long flight was catching up with him. He felt sick.

At the end of the horseshoe Fernandez lit a cigar and blew a cloud of smoke across the space that divided them. His fat jowls spilled over the stiff collar of his uniform as he spoke between lips that barely appeared to move.

'Are you all right, Pablo? You're looking a bit the worse for wear.'

Jiménez uncrossed his legs and leaned back in his seat.

'Thanks, Juan. I've been working hard.'

'Too much dreaming and not enough sleep, eh?' The stream of smoke hid the thin smile. Lorca laughed, not unsympathetically, and came to his old friend's aid. He liked a good set-to as much as anyone, but this was looking a little like humiliation.

'Great graphics, lovely toy. But let's not deceive ourselves about the time frame. If Eridani doesn't work then it's on to Indi, and if Indi's no good we're off to Ceti. This is a voyage of exploration you're suggesting, my friend. We could find ourselves zigzagging across the universe for some time.' He turned to Jiménez. 'Tell us about your new boy. What's his name? Gwidion?'

Jiménez swallowed hard and ploughed on. 'He's very new, but neither Martín nor I have seen anything approaching his soma powers. Not since the days of Saval.'

Luis kept his head bent down, avoiding the colonel's eyes.

'Between them we believe he and Martín could provide a cast-iron target to head for.'

'By dowsing for it?' Bascato switched off the holograph which obscured his view of Jiménez.

'Something more sophisticated than dowsing.'

'What are you suggesting? That we send the finest specimens of humanity, the cream of our Republic on a five hundred-year journey planned by a community of social misfits?'

Lorca allowed himself another laugh. Gruffer this time.

'Dreamers, Bascato, not misfits,' Jiménez replied evenly and glanced mischievously at Lorca. 'It might do you good to dream a little yourself. And why not? We've shown the loom works. It has been maintained consistently for more than a decade by our soñadores while conventional fields of science are still struggling to explain how we do it.'

Luis finally lifted his head. 'Frankly this doesn't seem to take us all that much further, Pablo. If the astronomers and your Gwidion agree on the best option, all well and good. But if they don't, then we're no further forward. I was rather hoping your breakthrough might be more substantial than that.'

The colonel's heart beat fast. What he was about to say was extremely premature, and in the present company it might expose him to even more ridicule than he was already suffering, but he couldn't let Bascato get away with his triumph.

'There is another possibility and I have to stress that it's too early to be anything more than speculative at this stage... '

The president indicated that he was giving him his full attention.

'We are currently working on an experiment in soma travel that could bring us back definitive information on planets across the galaxy.'

'Soma travel? Are you suggesting Gwidion is going to visit outer space?' The rising tone in Bascato's voice indicated the extent of his incredulity. Lorca obliged him with another snort.

Jiménez decided his only option was to keep it simple. 'Exactly.'

'Physically visiting outer space?' Bascato stressed each word as if giving dictation.

It was the colonel's turn to be off-hand. 'Physically, mentally, we don't know. As I say we are only at the edge of what may be a radical new way of exploring the universe. The implications are enormous, both for gathering information and, who knows, for ways of travelling through space that we've never even considered.'

'Magic.' Bascato said it softly. Jiménez did not acknowledge it, but he did not let it pass. He directed his words to the room in general.

'As magic as a holograph might have seemed a hundred years ago. As crazy as the Stargate project might have seemed to the American public in the twentieth century.'

The president intervened. 'Enough, gentlemen, enough, this isn't getting us anywhere. Pepe's presentation is impressive enough but it seems to me that two strands of research are always better than one. As things stand, Pablo, you have six months to come up with something stunning. I'm sure everyone around this table hopes you can do it.'

He looked from one person to another so that they each met his gaze. Lorca nodded. Fernandez leaned forward through his screen of smoke and blinked his small eyes. Jiménez leaned back easily. Bascato's Adam's apple rose and fell as he fingered his handcom. He couldn't resist a final jibe. 'We might as well use a ouija board.'

Jiménez grinned at him. 'I got to you, didn't I?' he said quietly. 'I got to you.'

Jiménez' feeling of relief was shortlived. In the privacy of the president's suite, Luis raised his brandy glass.

'Salúd. I am glad you did not have to rush back, Pablo. You would have come a long way for such a short meeting.'

Jiménez raised his glass. 'It's just as well I did. Young Pepe was in need of some supervision.'

The president laughed. 'You should stay the night.'

Jiménez drank again. 'I will. It's a long flight when you're drunk.'

'Well, don't take it so fast. We have a number of other temptations to keep you. And too much brandy makes you go a bit soft, you know.' He grabbed his groin in a crude gesture to illustrate his meaning. 'Come, you don't get the chance to enjoy city life much these days.'

Jiménez smiled. 'Madrid has its compensations.'

'I'm sure it does. Tell me, how are they all, your collection of teenage girls?'

Jiménez leaned forward. 'Jorge, we have known each other a long time and I would not deceive you. We are close to success, very close. Maybe for the first time I actually believe we can do it. And so does Martín. Don't let the likes of Bascato get in the way of it now. Holographs are bewitching, but they're not any more real than... I don't know, our dreams.'

The president stared down into his glass, cradling it like a crystal ball. 'You are getting serious in your old age, my friend. So, you have not come here to be entertained. Well, maybe you are right. The entertainment is not what it used to be.' He gestured to the window. 'Go, see for yourself.'

Jiménez obeyed. The Plaza des Armas lay before him, illuminated by the floodlights outside La Compañia. The ornate baroque church, which had once rivalled Cusco's own cathedral, had not been rebuilt since the last earthquake had reduced it to a few crumbling Christian turrets on a foundation of Inca stones, but it was still a magnificent sight.

'You see the colonnades?'

Jiménez looked around the square. Yes, he saw them. A few hours before they had teemed with life. Peasants selling their produce or their materials, or their weavings or crafts. Drug peddlars, musicians, cripples, blind people, beggars, street urchins, choclo sellers, sad-eyed women with babies bound in blankets on their back, who sat and chewed coca and waited through the night. They were empty now but for a few armed guards pacing in pairs around the central park area. The colonel turned around.

'The curfew,' said Luis. 'The closer the generation ship gets to completion, the more crew who are taken on, the harder it is to keep it under wraps. The rumours spread. They hear stories about a huge ship being built in space and they know they won't be aboard it, they think their leaders are about to desert them and leave them to their fate. They want to know where is the seed for them to plant their land, or where is the fertiliser. They want to know why, if we have rid the land of Americans, they are still poor. They want to know where the money is. They think we have it.'

'What are you telling me, Jorge?'

The president rose and joined him at the window. He put his hand on his shoulder.

'Everyone wants a place on that ship, Pablo. The peasants. You. Bascato. I am telling you what you already know. That we are running out of time, old friend. We are running out of time.'

Jiménez did not reply.

'Pablo, do you hear what I am saying?' The colonel turned his head to look at the president. 'It may be sooner than you think. It may be much sooner than six months. Much sooner. Have you thought about basing yourself here, in Cusco or Buenos Aires?'

'I have to go back.'

'You can direct things as effectively from here. And at least you'll be able to keep a closer eye on your friends.'

'Friends? I thought you were going to say enemies.'

The president's eyelids closed languidly.

'I have to go back, Jorge. I can't be seen to be distancing myself from Madrid. Not now, above all. Besides I want to be there.'

'There may not be time to do whatever it is you have in mind. Not in Madrid at any rate.'

'What do you mean?'

The president walked back towards the fire, swilling his brandy as he went. 'You know how politics works, Pablo. Sometimes one has to change tack to carry on going in the same direction. Events may be playing into Bascato's hands today, but who knows? It need never be too late if we have the loom aboard the generation ship.'

'I don't even know if Martín will take up his place any more. He would never let us take the loom without him.'

The president's voice chided him again, but the edge was harder this time.

'The academic life is making you go soft, my friend. Bascato will not think like that.'

'Bascato is a thug. It is he who should be staying behind.'

'Come, come, colonel. Bascato is one of my closest advisers.'

The words were innocent enough, but Jiménez knew what the president was saying. Perhaps he had gone soft in Madrid after all, or maybe he was just that fraction slower to the finish line than he used to be. Was it a mistake to have dedicated himself to Madrid while leaving others to win influence in the places where it mattered most?

'This is very difficult for me, Pablo. Believe me, I want you on that ship. But...' There was a silence.

'No loom, no ship? Is that what you're saying?'

'You can carry on your work there as easily as anywhere else. And if Martín doesn't want to join the party?' He sat down. 'Well, you tell me you have a boy who will.'

'Jorge.' Jiménez spread his hands wide, sending his brandy curling dangerously close to the edge of his glass. 'It's hard enough to keep him in Madrid at the moment.'

Luis shook his head. 'Don't give me the problems, Pablo. Give me the solutions. Come, we will talk about it in the morning at Machu Picchu.'

'I have to be back in Madrid.'

Luis nodded. 'Yes, yes. Tomorrow. Machu Picchu.'

chapter eight

Alara looked across the rows of girls. No-one else seemed to be noticing anything unusual going on, but her optik was giving readings like she'd never seen before. She beckoned to her sister.

'Rosa, come here.' Even a whisper seemed loud in the silence of the soma hall. In the gallery, out of the corner of her eye, she could see the black crow-like figure of Soñador Martín. He was pacing back and forth, his hands clasped behind him, making his dark cloak flare out like a pair of unfolding wings. Rosa bent over her screen, she let out a soft stream of air through her lips.

'I've never seen anything like it,' said Rosa. 'Not even my best students. Never.'

Alara stood up.

'Soñador Martín.' Her words rose to the gallery like a shout. There was a sudden buzz around the hall from the other keepers. Martín stopped his pacing and swung round, his cloak following a few microseconds later. He came to the balustrade.

'Return to your work, please.' Within a few minutes he too was bending over Alara's screen. His face was flushed and beads of sweat broke out along his upper lip, either from his rapid descent to the hall floor, or from his excitement at what he saw.

'A sonãdor. A true soñador.' Alara made room for him and he sat down before the optik, closing his eyes and breathing deeply for a few seconds. He remained motionless and concentrated for what seemed like an age. When he looked at Alara again, his expression had turned to a deep frown.

'This is not on the loom,' he said. 'There are two of them, Gwidion and Cai.'

Alara panicked. 'But I thought... '

Martín was already getting up.

'We'd better get to his room. Now. Hurry.'

They ran through the empty corridors, the soñador a few paces in front, his wings flapping behind him while Alara struggled to keep up. Gwidion was lying on the floor, his eyes closed, his body spreadeagled as if he had fallen. Martín pulled open his uniform and felt his heart.

'I think he's all right. Help me get him to the bed.'

The two laid him out on the mattress and Martín checked his pulse again.

'I think he's just sleeping. He may have had some sort of shock, he is not used to the loom yet.' He let Gwidion's wrist drop to his side and turned to Alara.

'What happened?'

'He was on the loom. I'd never seen such active readings, never with any other student. But everything was normal.'

'And the other readings? From Cai?'

'I didn't know what they were. That's when I called you.'

'How did this Cai get in there?'

'I don't know. I thought you... I thought Colonel Jiménez had talked to you.'

The soñador looked at her angrily.

'Yes, he did talk to me. I did not think he would have talked to you.'

Alara held his gaze as steadily as she could. 'I am Gwidion's loom keeper.'

The soñador looked at the prostrate figure on the bed.

'Of course you are. You would have been told at the appropriate time.'

'You mean you didn't alter the loom?'

He snorted. 'No. Even if I was willing I barely know how. Stay with him. Check his pulse regularly, and his breathing. If there are any signs of irregularity or if he wakes, call me. Immediately, any time of the day or night. And no-one else is to see him without my permission? Understand? No-one.'

Alara nodded. 'I will look after him.'

He smiled. 'I'm sure you will.' He went to go, then turned back.

'You did well, Alara. You did the right thing.' And then, with a deliberate dramatic swirl of his cloak, he was gone.

Memorandum from Colonel Pablo Jiménez, director of the Madrid Soma Academy, September 18, 2084.

In accordance with resolution 1024 of the High Council of the Republic of Hispania, I hereby submit the intended extra-terrestrial targets to be explored for possible life-supporting planets. Pilots will be chosen to undertake simulated missions to each of the following star systems:

1. *Tau Bootis*
2. *Vega*
3. *Sirius*
4. *Mizar*
5. *61 Cygni*
6. *Unman*

Within minutes of Martín receiving his copy of the memo, he was on the vidcom. His eyebrows told their own story.

'Unman. What's Unman? A new galaxy?'

Jiménez chuckled. 'Not unless they discovered it last night.'

Martín's eyebrows were unamused. They repeated their question.

'It's Welsh for anywhere.'

The soñador allowed himself a rare smile of his own.

'It's your name on the memo, Jiménez. Let's hope your friend Bascato doesn't count languages among his many talents.'

'It may keep him occupied for a while. It may even keep his mind off the fact that so far we don't appear to have anything resembling a soma pilot in the Academy.'

Martín did not reply.

'How are things in Madrid?'

Martín considered bringing him up to date, then thought better of it. If the colonel was sending memos from Peru, then it was likely that things were happening that he was not aware of.

'Jiménez, I have every respect for your political skills, but this is a dangerous game. Gwidion is a breakthrough, I'd be the first to say that, but what exactly are you claiming he may be capable of?'

The colonel spoke with precision. 'Putting it simply, Soñador. We need to identify a habitable planet as a destination for the generation ship. We have star maps of the galaxies most likely to contain such a planet already on the loom. Maybe his powers can tell us something about them. All we need is for Gwidion to investigate them.'

'All we need?' Martín gave a tut. 'We've never attempted a simulation on that scale. We have no idea if he is capable of that, or whether we can rely on any answer he comes back with. What we need is time, at least long enough to construct some preliminary experiments.'

'Soñador, in six months' time, the Academy will be closed. Planet or no planet. Time is what we don't have. We've run smaller simulations before, the principle is no different. If we want a place on that generation ship, then it's time we unwrapped the loom from its cotton wool and put it to good use.'

Martín sat at his desk and eyed the colonel for a long time. 'If that's meant as a threat, I'm not convinced. I've got no plans to take a place on that ship, Jiménez.'

'Your prerogative.'

'And it's also my prerogative to decide what goes on at this Academy. This isn't what the loom was developed for. I'm not going to let you destroy years of careful research for the sake of a mad gamble with a mythical galaxy.'

Jiménez considered the soñador. The time had undoubtedly come for a few home truths.

'You may not have that option.'

Martín's eyebrows rose in angry unison.

'The loom is nothing to you without me. You know that.'

Jiménez felt the frustration and anger rising inside him as they stared at each other across thousands of kilometres.

'Do you seriously think you are going to be left here to carry on as normal when the generation ship leaves? Imagine the shock when the world wakes up to the fact that we have left.'

'All events – however shocking they may seem at the time – begin to look understandable with the benefit of hindsight, Colonel. The world will survive.'

'You're more naive than I imagined, Soñador.'

'Naive-mmm? You're meddling in things you don't have the capacity to understand. Without me the loom means nothing.'

'The loom used to be nothing without you,' Jiménez corrected him. 'Until Gwidion, that is. Until I came up with Gwidion.'

His face lit up, but the sarcasm was heavy in Martín's voice. 'Ah, that's it. Your boy, your protegé, your ticket to fame and fortune.'

The grains of truth in the comment riled Jiménez. But he had just spent a gruelling few hours in the company of the Republic's hardest men. It was time to get a few things off his chest. 'A little hypocritical, Martín, don't you think? For someone whose own fame and fortune dates back fifteen years to the creators of the loom. You are the last survivor in a line of soñadores and you've had the privilege of that unique position for a long time. I expect you rather like it. It rather suits your idea of your own grandness, doesn't it? Whereas I am a mite more humble than that. I've spent my time finding people. Hundreds of students, hundreds of keepers, drawn from around the world. From the Andes and the Amazon basin, from Bretaña, from Galicia. I've spent my time persuading and cajoling, wheeling and dealing, cultivating and nurturing while you've sat back on your fat laurels and dreamed of glory. Well, my search is over. It seems I'm the one who's found the next great soñador. And now is when we need to use him. Whether you like it or not.'

'We'll see about that.'

Jiménez ended the transmission.

'Yes, we'll see.'

Night was falling over the reconstructed city of Machu Picchu and the massive peak of Huyna Picchu loomed above the colonel. It was a breathtaking place. Thousands of metres below him, the Urubamba River wound its way like a silver thread through the near vertical mountainsides, and thousands of metres above him the snow-capped Cordillera Vilcabamba caught the last rays of the setting sun, making the range look as if it was capped with fire.

Jiménez immediately regretted his outburst at Martín. He'd already found one new adversary in Bascato in the last couple of days and he didn't need another enemy. Still it was done and he had said some things that needed saying. There was nothing like a bit of pressure to concentrate the mind. He comforted himself with the thought that he was always good in a crisis, it brought out the best in him.

Finally, Luis arrived, looking tired and rather flustered.

'Forgive me, Pablo. There have been some developments and we are at a critical time. Every day a rocket shuttle leaves to take crew to the generation ship in orbit. It's not easy to keep that sort of thing quiet, even on the Paracas Peninsula. Sit down.'

The two men took their seats at a large table overlooking the central plaza. The president stared out.

'I'll be sorry to leave this place.' He turned to Jiménez and smiled. 'But we have a responsibility to the future also. Every civilisation must come to an end, Pablo, and I fear the sand ran out for ours long ago.'

He gestured at the view.

'Fabulous, isn't it? Exactly how it might have looked centuries ago. But appearances can be deceptive. We can reconstruct the buildings, but still we cannot recover the way of life which gave them meaning. We have lost them all, the Incas, the Aztecs, the Egyptians and God knows how many before them. We may have some remains, we may even have some of their writings, but it is no more than a glimpse of the greatness that once was. We have lost the wisdom of countless great civilisations and that is a mistake we must not make again.'

He looked at Jiménez.

'Do you understand what I am saying, Pablo?'

'The loom.'

'Exactly. We must have it on board the generation ship. You may be right, it may be possible to explore the universe with the loom. One day. But here and now it represents something rather different.'

The colonel shifted uncomfortably in his chair.

'We must have it. That is our only option. Without it we are a people without a history. We must ensure this time that everything we have achieved here is not lost again.'

'We are very close, Jorge. I believe we can identify a target planet through a careful simulation. Martín is working on the details now.'

Luis shrugged. 'Maybe you can. But, Pablo, I cannot sell that. Yesterday I went out on a limb for you in the High Council. The truth is I have my own position to consider. This is a critical time. Whoever goes on board that ship as its leader carves himself a niche in history. There are a lot of people who would like the statues to bear their name.'

Jiménez exploded. 'Bascato is an upstart. Fernandez, Lorca, they may not agree with me, but that doesn't mean they're ready to come down on his side.'

'It's not only Bascato, there are many others who think like he does.'

'And you?'

'It doesn't matter what I think. Let us say you are right. Let us say your new boy can identify a habitable planet merely by examining star maps on the loom, or that he can even claim to have visited it. Who will believe it? Who will set out on a centuries-long journey across space guided by a telepathic hunch?'

'This is not telepathy, Jorge.'

The president began to lose patience. 'I know, I know. This is not telepathy or dowsing, this is soma. So you say. But the fact remains that I've got more important things to worry about than trying to sell untried technology for the sake of an old friend.'

Jiménez passed the flat of his palm over his head. The sickness in the pit of his stomach returned. 'Jorge, this is about more than friendship. I've spent years working on this. You can't throw it all over because of whizzkids like Bascato. I thought you believed in it.'

Luis brought his hands in front of his lips in a gesture of prayer.

'I believe the loom is among the Republic's greatest achievements and, who knows, maybe it is all that you think it can be. Maybe one day we will all have to eat our words. It has been an invaluable tool for training our people. Without it I am sure the generation ship could not have been completed and crewed. And if along the way we have begun to explore these new facets that you and Martín are so dedicated to, then all well and good. But for today and tomorrow and the day after that it is the most valuable repository of history and knowledge that we have. That is all it is. And it must be on the ship.'

'That will not be easy.'

'What do you need?'

Jiménez looked at him without understanding.

'Men? Weapons?'

The colonel swallowed and held his voice steady. 'That won't be necessary.'

Luis waited.

'That won't be necessary.'

'Very well.'

chapter nine

'Colonel, you're back mmm. I expected you yesterday. How are the pleasures of the city?' Martín leant back in his chair and let it circle his bow-shaped desk watching Jiménez closely.

The colonel sat down opposite him. It was as if those words they had exchanged across the Atlantic had never been spoken. They were just two close colleagues, meeting again after a short absence. 'We need to talk.'

The soñador spread his large hands. 'We are talking. Bascato not happy with the targets?'

'It's too late for the targets, it's too late for anything.'

Martín leaned forward, his eyebrows knitting into a straight line.

'That suits me fine-mmm. It's never been part of my work here to go careering around the universe for President Luis and his cronies.'

'They want us on board the generation ship. With the loom.'

Martín shook his head gravely. 'Never-mmm.'

'You don't have a choice.'

'There is always a choice. What are they going to do, send in a special services team?'

'If they have to.'

'And what good will the loom be to them with a dead soñador?'

There was a pause.

'There's always Gwidion.'

Martín sat back. 'I'm tired of your threats, Jiménez. I'll destroy the loom before I let you have it.'

'You would never do that.'

The soñador's eyebrows stood still.

'At least run the simulations.'

'Not under these conditions.'

The colonel felt the hollow in his stomach rising again. Two long flights in as many days had drained his energy and fuddled his mind. He was running out of arguments and he was running out of options.

'Send in the troops. Although knowing Luis I'm sure they are already on their way. He was never one for trusting people, not even his old friends. You should watch your back, Colonel.'

The comment was not meant unkindly, but it hurt. Jiménez was on his feet in an instant, the sweat beginning to show on his upper lip.

'You arrogant bastard.'

'Send in the troops. It will be interesting to see which side you are fighting on.'

The colonel left.

'I wasn't planning on taking sides.'

Alara was at her optik as Jiménez strode into the soma hall. Despite his pleasure at seeing her, his expression was serious. He bent down to kiss her, but her attention was riveted on the optik. His eyes took in the information on the screen quickly.

'Gwidion?'

'He's dreaming again.'

'Does Martín know?'

'I was just going to tell him.'

'Where is Gwidion?'

'He's with Cai.'

'Cai? What do you mean. Already? You put him on there?'

Alara shot back at him in an aggrieved tone. 'No.'

'What's going on?'

'I don't know. It happened when you were in Cusco. I thought Martín had planted Cai like you said, but he was as surprised as anyone. We had better tell him.'

Jiménez put her hand on her shoulder.

'You don't need to do that.'

'He asked to be told if anything happened.'

'I'm sure he did. Where are they?'

'This part of the loom they've created has not been mapped. It's very difficult to see what is happening.'

'You should have called me in Cusco.'

Jiménez straightened himself up. What the hell was going on? Was it just paranoia or was everybody suddenly drawing a large exclusion zone around him? It was understandable perhaps in Martín or Luis. But Alara? Still, there was really only one ally he needed right now and that was the one he was going to concentrate on.

'I'm going to see him.' Before Alara could ask who, his eye caught the flash of an incoming message on the optik. It was orange. High-level emergency.

The heads of a hundred keepers turned as his expletive burst into the silence of the hall. Jiménez looked at Alara's port. He accessed an empty optik and skimmed the text.

Emergency resolution of the High Council of the Republic of Hispania. Cusco, September 18, 2084.

Following a photon attack by an unidentified force on military installations and oilfields in Venezuela, all research establishments have been placed under the direct command of the Defence Department. All computing and scientific resources are henceforward under the control of Acting Scientific Director Pepe Bascato.

Jiménez felt the sweat breaking out on his body. He was a fool. Luis had been trying to warn him, and he hadn't been ready to listen. He looked at the memo again, this time reading between the lines. Photon bombs didn't come in battlefield sizes. A photon bomb didn't take out military installations. A photon bomb took out a complete country.

His voice echoed around the soma hall with a roar. 'Everybody leave your optiks.' The turned heads looked at Jiménez in surprise, but no-one moved.

Alara looked at him. 'Pablo?'

'Now is the time, Alara. It's now.' He turned back to the keepers.

'Everybody leave, except Alara.' Still no-one moved. He singled out one or two girls by name. 'María, Jeanette.' They got up and began to leave, then the others copied.

Alara stood up with the others. 'What are you doing?'

Jiménez indicated the message on the screen. 'There's no time. Trust me. It's now or never.'

Despite the colonel's order, groups of girls still hesitated at the doors, looking back to see what would happen next.

'Pablo. What are you doing?'

Jiménez spoke with exaggerated clarity as if to a child. 'Martín may be happy with an academic exercise in soma, but I am not and neither, it seems, is the president. We need to run a simulation.'

Alara looked at him in surprise. 'Without Martín?'

'We haven't got time to argue.'

'If it doesn't work... '

The colonel exploded as his patience finally ran out. 'If it doesn't work, that's my career over. But you'll survive, and if you're lucky – really lucky – so will the loom. But I wouldn't bet on it.'

Alara's hands trembled on the desk in front of her.

'Locate astronomy. All star systems within five hundred years travelling time at one-fifth the speed of light. Feed them into Gwidion's optik.'

'Pablo.' Her eyes were pleading. 'He needs to be briefed, he's completely unprepared.'

'Trust me, Alara. Or if you can't trust me, take it as an order.'

'Pablo.'

He ignored her. 'Locate astronomy. All star systems within five hundred years travelling time at one-fifth the speed of light. That's an order.'

Alara nodded and turned to her screen.

Cai and Gwidion were back at the church. The scene was already very different. A huge area had been cleared, hedges had been up-rooted to allow for the new field system, the small number of properties which fell inside the perimeter were being demolished and the foundations for the dome itself were being sunk. The work was attracting a crowd of sightseers every day.

'How did you decide who came in?'

'It was difficult,' said Cai. 'The idea had attracted a huge number of people – New Agers, extreme Welsh nationalists, eco-groups, intellectuals, artists and people who were just fascinated by the dome. It was incredible, so many people with so many agendas. It was almost impossible to get anything done. I spent days and weeks sifting through applications, trying to put together a community of people who thought like I did. In the end that was the only criterion I could go by – people I'd be happy to have in my family. As simple as that.' He clicked his tongue against his teeth. 'It was all irrelevant anyway.'

'What do you mean?'

'The fertility plague. Suddenly from having thousands to choose from, I had next to no-one. There was nothing else to do but open up the dome as a refuge for any survivors living in the area. Whoever was still alive and wanted to come in, they came in.'

'Do you know who released the plague?'

Cai laughed. 'Take your pick, little brother. Which version do you want? You can have the terrorist theory, or the conspiracy theory or the pest control accident theory. You can have the United Christian States of America official history of the plague, or the Republic of Hispania's. Or perhaps you prefer a minority view, like the Indonesian Islamic Nation's. Or the remnants of the Japanese, I'm sure they'll have an angle on it. Or New Zealand, if anybody is left, which is quite possible, but they're certainly not shouting about it. I can't say I blame them.'

'But it's our history.'

'It's not history and it's not ours. It's like a mirror. It reflects the truth of what we are now, not the truth of what we used to be.'

Gwidion joined his brother on the turret of the tower and let his legs dangle below him, blotting out the gravestones far below. He had a sudden urge to get his own back on Cai for all those times at the Ruins and jump from the tower. See how he liked the shock of seeing someone fall. But he couldn't. It would be a mean trick on the Cai he now knew. Then through the gate, just beyond a large yew tree, he saw a strange shape. The tears ran from his eyes as he focused hard on it and the rest of the scene began to fade into a watery impression. It was like a painting at first, then as he looked more closely it became a series of dots. As if he was zooming in on a pointillist picture, the detail dissolved into the minute brushstrokes of the artist.

'They want me to do something,' said Gwidion.

'What?' The question was in Welsh.

'I don't know.'

He looked away to the fields spread out below and then back again, hoping both to rest his eyes and catch the image unawares. It was not a picture at all, Gwidion realised. The points were not the marks of an artist's brush. It was a cluster of stars. As he stared the image began to resolve itself further. It was a single star, a single yellow disc of light which grew as he leaned into it. And smaller points of light began to appear around it. A solar system. It was a solar system.

'It's beautiful,' whispered Cai.

'I don't understand,' said Gwidion.

Cai put his arm on Gwidion's shoulder. 'Feel the wind. Let your other senses take over. Listen to the space around you. Smell it, taste it.'

Gwidion could smell gas and cold. The absolute cold of inter-stellar space.

'What is it?' asked Gwidion again.

'In the Middle Ages the Church declared it the crime of *curiositas* – a passion for knowing unnecessary things,' said Cai. 'Imagine the unimaginable, know the unknowable. Dream.'

The fourth planet from the star looked different. It was blue and green and white. And warm. It was warm and it smelled of... It smelled of gorse. Gwidion laughed with pleasure at the absurdity of it. It smelled of home.

Cai wrapped his arms around his twin and the scent of sweat and fear mixed with the rough warmth of his woven smock.

'I will save you, Gwidion. I will not let you fall.'

And Gwidion jumped. But he did not fall. It was as if he dropped gently into a pool of warm water. It felt indescribably good. And suddenly there was no blind leap into the unknown, there was no act of faith or trusting to luck. In that moment, cradled in the arms of his twin and his grandfather, he knew where he was going and he knew he was going to get there. He was going home.

Jiménez left Alara crouched over the optik as he turned towards the final group of keepers who were still hovering near the door. At the entrance he stopped to look down the long hall towards the small alcove where the heart of the loom lay cradled gently in the arms of the first soñador. Then he made his decision.

His shoes clip-clopped past the huddles of keepers who now filled the corridors.

'There's nothing to worry about,' he said. 'The soñador has everything under control. Go back to your students, make sure they are OK. Bring them off the loom. If there are any problems, report them to Soñador Martín.'

He carried on unhurriedly, but his calm exterior hid both his excitement and his fear. He passed his hand flat over his head, feeling his palm warm and sweaty on his bald pate. The effort of appearing unworried was as great as he if he had sprinted up the corridor. His mouth was dry as he opened the door to Gwidion's room. It was as he thought, but the reality was nevertheless a shock which caused him to bite his lower lip as he breathed in sharply. Gwidion was not there. He double-checked the room, though he was well aware there was nowhere for the boy to hide among its sparse furnishings, then turned and retraced his steps as calmly as he could to his office.

The orange alert on his optik told him the president was waiting to talk to him. He sat down, attempted to compose himself and switched on the secure connection. It was a minute or two before Luis himself appeared. He smiled.

'Time is up, Pablo. Twenty four hours. That gives you just about enough time to get here and board the shuttle.'

It was just what he didn't want to hear, but Jiménez knew there was no point in arguing.

'There's a place for you and Martín, the boy and his keeper. We want the loom on board too.'

Jiménez grimaced. 'That may not be possible. We think the boy has jumped.'

There was a silence.

'Bad timing, Pablo. Bad timing.'

'Jorge, you don't know what this could mean. We were in the middle of running a simulation to target possible habitable planets. The implications could be enormous. Is there any way you can delay the ship?'

The president's face remained unmoved.

'We need you aboard. With the loom. The simulation can be continued aboard the ship.'

'Jorge.'

'Pablo, I held back on the troops because of you. Don't let me down.'

'I can't leave him out there.'

'Colonel. This is your president speaking.'

Luis ended the communication.

The soma hall was empty now apart from Alara. She turned as Jiménez came back. There was a gleam in his eyes.

'I think we have a jump. I think something incredible is happening.'

Alara turned, fear and excitement in her face. 'I think it is. I can't find Gwidion anywhere. He just seems to have left the loom completely.'

'Is there anyone else on the loom?'

Alara checked. 'The soñador.'

Jiménez put his hand on her shoulder.

'Get to my shuttle, we haven't got long.'

'But what about Gwidion?'

'Trust me, Alara, I know what I am doing. The soñador authorised the simulation, he will be doing whatever he can to get Gwidion back. Martín and I will join you at the shuttle. With a bit of luck Gwidion will be with us too by then.'

As Alara got up he slipped into her chair, but she hesitated again.

'Somebody needs to be monitoring what's going on,' he said over his shoulder. 'Let me see if I can make anything of it.'

'I don't like this, Pablo. What's going on?'

'No time to explain, Alara. Get your belongings, anything you want to take with you. We'll be right behind you.'

After a few seconds of fruitless fiddling at the screen he gave a tut of annoyance and strode towards the far end of the soma hall. Her questions about the generation ship were superseded by a new set as Jiménez reached the alcove where the first soñador still held the precious globe. Jiménez lifted it from her hands. It was lighter than he had imagined. Alara was a few metres behind him now, surprise and concern written on her broad open face.

'What are you doing?'

Jiménez held the globe in one hand and took her arm with the other as he continued to walk. 'We need this if we're to get Gwidion back. There'll be plenty of time to explain aboard the generation ship. A couple of hundred years probably.'

'What about Soñador Martín?'

'Go now, Alara, hurry. Grab a few things. Go to my shuttle and wait for me. I am going to fetch Martín.'

They had reached the entrance to the soma hall and Jiménez turned to take a final look at the heavenly scene which gazed darkly down over the rows and rows of empty optiks. He held up the globe as if making a toast.

'You can't just leave your son,' said Alara.

He felt the impact of her words in the pit of his stomach.

'We're not leaving him behind. We're taking him with us.'

And yet, somewhere deep inside him, secretly, he was glad Gwidion was not here to witness this sorry mess. Somehow, he thought fleetingly, it might even be better if he was far beyond the grasp of either them or the loom.

Jiménez found Martín seated in front of the optik in his office. His head was bowed, his breathing was deep and regular. He appeared to be concerned as if encountering something he had not met before.

'What are you doing?'

Martín maintained his concentration, his eyes closed, his eyebrows flickering with the effort.

'What do you think, you fool. Trying to get your boy back.'

'Can you do it?'

What appeared like pain flitted across the soñador's face.

'I don't know. You should never have attempted anything like this. He's gone. I don't know where. Far beyond the loom.'

The strain of maintaining the conversation was clear in his voice.

'Get out, Jiménez. You've done enough damage here.'

Jiménez raised the globe in both hands and tested its weight as if mesmerised by its intricate folds and facets. Alara should be in the shuttle by now waiting for him. He didn't have much time.

'Get out, you idiot.'

The colonel hesitated. He'd screwed up badly and it wasn't his fault. There was a loud crash from outside, sharp shouts and the sound of heavy boots running in the corridors. A shot was fired.

So, thought Jiménez grimly, the troops had never been that far away after all. The rush of adrenaline brought his anger and frustration to a head. He didn't deserve this, he wasn't someone to be pushed out of the way when things were difficult. He'd promised the president the loom, hadn't he? And no troops. If Luis thought he was just another minion to be manipulated, he was wrong. All his life he had been a reasonable man. He had been silent when he might have spoken up, he had even been loud when he didn't really feel much enthusiasm. But he had got things done, that was the important thing. If he couldn't achieve what he wanted then at least he could want what was achievable. And he had stayed loyal. And this was how he was repaid, by being made to look a fool. Luis, Bascato, Martín, the whole rotten lot of them. One was as bad as the other. He didn't deserve to be treated like a nobody by an old friend.

Martín opened his eyes in startled amazement at the sounds outside, but what he saw shocked him even more. Jiménez lifted the globe above his head and brought it down on the back of the old man's neck with a sickening crack. Martín slumped forward, his forehead hitting the port in front of him with a second lighter crack, as if the room had an echo.

'Sleep well, Soñador,' he said quietly.

Books three
and four

book three chapter one

And this is the myth of Jemin, that he was born
bald-headed and died bald-headed.

In the galley, deep in the bowels of the Spaceliner Tierra Nueva, Alara was feeling a fool. The remains on the stainless steel plates before her were depressingly familiar. Textured protein and sauce. She loaded them one by one into the sonic cleaner and recycler. It filled the machine. It filled her time. The duties of a domestic assistant in the food kitchens were something of a shock after the privileged lifestyle of a keeper in the Academy. More than that, they felt like a punishment, and that perfectly suited her mood.

It was more than a week since she and Jiménez had taken off in the shuttle from Madrid, leaving behind them the chaotic and farcical sight of troops storming the Academy in search of a loom which was already safely in the colonel's possession and on its way to the spaceliner. The undemanding nature of her job gave her plenty of time to remember those long hours on the flight to Peru. It seemed as if the two had barely exchanged a word.

Soñador Martín had decided to stay, so Jiménez told her. And as for Gwidion, no-one knew the answer to that. She had cradled the loom in her lap endlessly, searching its intricate interior for some clue, admiring it, wondering at it, hoping against all hope that somehow Gwidion would simply appear out of it like a genie out of a lamp if she wanted it badly enough. And she did want it badly enough. She wanted it with the passion of someone who had lost everything. Surrogate mother she may have been, but there was nothing surrogate about her feelings at losing her charge. Only the loss of her own child could possibly be more devastating.

There were other losses too. She would never see her family in Puno again. Nor the soñador – the trace of blood on the outside of the globe she turned and turned in her hands told her that. And this time all the colonel's protestations that Martín had simply not wanted to come, that he was safe in the Academy, that he still planned to attempt to retrieve Gwidion even without the loom, all his lies washed past her numbed mind unchallenged, unquestioned and unbelieved.

For three years she had wanted nothing more than to be with him. No matter where. He was the man she loved and spending an eternity with him in the darkest reaches of space had seemed as attractive to her as a life in any other situation she could think of. No matter what. But then it was not in her nature to conceive of all the 'whats' that Jiménez was capable of. The loss of Gwidion was the single most painful thing she had suffered. The loss of trust in someone she loved was something much more subtle, more poisonous and in a way more dangerous. It was possible, barely possible, that Gwidion was either safe somewhere, God knew where, or that he would one day come back. Trust, once lost, seemed irredeemable. And always in her ears rang the words of her mother whenever she had believed in something too passionately as a child. 'You silly girl. With your head in the clouds how will you ever see where you are going?'

The end of her shift was getting close. She shook herself out of her daydreaming and made a last effort to pile the sonic cleaner high with the waste of a day aboard the Tierra Nueva. Then in her mind she walked the decks which led her back to her tiny quarters and prepared herself for the daily ritual which marked the beginning of each evening aboard the ship – playing back her internal vidcom messages. There was only ever one message, and only ever one sender. And there was only ever one response. Delete.

Today would be no different.

Colonel Jiménez sat in his suite reviewing the reports from the various areas of the ship on the vidcom. He groaned. The one message he really wanted above everything to see was not among them. Somehow it still surprised him. Women could be so stubborn.

Well, he mused, she was still a long way from talking to him, let alone listening to his side of the story, but she was, at least, within his sphere of influence. Time and patience were his speciality. And time was one thing everyone aboard had more than enough of.

He looked at the loom, lying in its new home in the corner of his quarters. Time and patience had been at the heart of his quest for Gwidion too, but in that case time had run out on him. He wouldn't make the same mistake again. In fact there were lots of mistakes he wouldn't make again, but he had no room in his life for regrets. He hadn't wasted much mental effort in going over the events of the last few days at the Academy. He had done what he needed to do and that belief was sustained by all the busy-ness and jostling for power which went with the first few weeks aboard the Tierra Nueva. Above all, after that particular farrago, he needed to absolve himself from blame, consolidate his position at the centre of power and deflect any awkward questions.

Whether Martín was alive or dead, he did not know, though a man in his position could have found out if he wanted. The inquiry might even be irrelevant in the wake of the photon bomb attacks on various targets in the Republic. The political reality was that neither Luis nor Jiménez was keen to draw too much attention to what had gone on. In retrospect the president's special services assault on the Academy appeared close to the hysterical. For his part the colonel had to admit the whole episode – apart from being criminal – was something of an embarrassment. So, and this was where old friends really came in useful, they were both happy to bury the details of the operation in the past.

There would be time for post-mortems, though Jiménez had about as much regard for them as he had for hypotheticals, but for now the future was calling. And the colonel was suddenly developing a radically new vision of his place aboard the Tierra Nueva. If it was time for him to start again, then perhaps the same applied to everyone.

Jiménez found himself in a privileged position aboard the ship. The official version of events was straightforward enough; his old colleague Soñador Martín, a man already in his seventies, had chosen to spend his last days on Earth. Jiménez had, with great sadness, accepted Martín's post as head of science, while his old friend Fernandez, formerly head of defence, was responsible for security. Antonio Lorca, head of internal affairs, Fernandez, Jiménez and the president himself now made up the inner chamber of the High Council.

Bascato had paid the price for being too young, too dangerous and too clever. What Luis needed at the start of their historic voyage was a shield of trusted and loyal friends around him. Bascato had, with great grace, swallowed his pride and agreed to become Jiménez' deputy with special responsibility for medicine and pharmacology.

The other members looked up in surprise when the new head of science floated his suggestion. Luis stuttered. His view that the loom was the ultimate record of human history on Earth had been voiced often enough. And now here was Jiménez suggesting it was time for a break with the past.

'President, we've already had to ban communications with Earth. Quite apart from the fact that our vidcom systems can't cope with demand for calls to friends and family, the whole business is having a very destabilising effect. What we need is a crew dedicated to looking forwards, not fretting about whatever new crisis is hitting their loved ones at home.'

'But the loom is priceless. It's the story of thousands of years of civilisation,' Lorca protested. 'We can't just turn off our history.'

Jiménez raised his eyebrows. 'Can't we? Isn't that precisely why we came on board?'

The president opened his mouth, but Jiménez beat him to it.

'I know, Jorge. You're going to tell us about how important the loom is to this mission. The priceless knowledge we've lost in the past from our greatest civilisations. Well, fine. The loom is there for the day when we want it, but if we open it up to public access what will happen? What will happen when a wave of nostalgia hits the crew? Quite apart from the effect on morale, what happens if a bunch of people suddenly get the idea they would like to go home?'

This wasn't the line the president was expecting – and Jiménez knew it. His reputation behind the closed doors of Cusco and Buenos Aires was, not a yes-man exactly, but at least a man who checked which way the political wind was blowing before choosing his hat. To his old colleagues on the Council this suggestion looked a bit like going out in a storm with no clothes on.

Luis looked around the table. Lorca was eyeing Jiménez curiously. 'You've changed,' he said simply.

Jiménez met his gaze. 'Who hasn't? How many of us have the same opinions at forty as we did at, say, twenty? If we do then we are either extremely clever to have been right all along or extremely stupid never to have been right at all. Most of us are neither. We're either mostly clever or mostly stupid. I was mostly stupid until now.'

Fernandez was staring into his lap. Among old friends revolutions took their first steps in slippers rather than army boots.

'Juan?' The president chose Fernandez for his support.

Jiménez waited for the large man to raise his head. There was a brutishness about the former head of defence which was accentuated by the close-crop on his head and his virulent facial hair which seemed to spring out almost as soon as the razor had left his face.

'We have the loom, President. That is one issue. Public access is another. As for history, what good is it?'

There was a barely suppressed ripple of laughter from Lorca. It was Jiménez' turn to stare into his lap now. His words had signalled a subtle change in their relationships. It would take some time for their new positions to harden and become clear, but the process had begun. Fernandez knew the effect his words were having, and once started he warmed to his theme.

'There are an infinite number of histories which might have led us more or less to the position we are in now – and an infinite number of positions which might have been arrived at from our own history. We have no way of knowing which events were the ones that really mattered. It might have been the day on which the United Christian States crumbled, it might just as easily have been the day a butterfly landed on a leaf deep in the heart of the Amazon.'

Vintage Fernandez, thought Jiménez. A thug with poetry in his soul. Old friends could be so useful, and so difficult to dispose of. As for Luis, that old friendship had been fatally damaged. The president had called on his loyalty and then pushed it too far. He had sent in the troops when it was Jiménez' call and he would never forgive him for that. Old friends were there to give you enough rope.

That's what old friends were for, even if it meant you ended up hanging yourself in the process.

There would be a time for the loom. The loom was not the real bone of contention here, and everyone knew it. The fact that it might represent the only hope for retrieving Gwidion was a tragedy, Jiménez had to admit, but great men and great enterprises could not avoid tragedy. Perversely, Gwidion's loss was almost a justification of the colonel's vision, a sobering reminder that progress is often built on sacrifice.

As for Martín. The sweat broke out on his bald head and he passed his hand across it. As for Martín. What was it the soñador had told him once? In retrospect all shocking events appear inevitable. And what was escape, what was the Tierra Nueva if it wasn't a chance to wipe the slate clean?

The generation ship had barely waved goodbye to Jupiter before the problems began. Without doubt the Tierra Nueva was a triumph of engineering. Work on its construction at a space station orbiting the Earth had begun in the glory days of the Republic of Hispania. It now housed more than nine hundred scientists, technicians and a disproportionate number of leading politicians who occupied the upper deck in luxurious apartments reminiscent of the great days of the ocean-going steamers of the twentieth century.

Its three living decks were each the size of two football pitches; it housed classrooms, laboratories, medical units, supermarkets, corner shops, bars, cinemas, churches, theatres and takeaways. It was a small city floating through interstellar space. Though built by the Republic, it was a homage to a distinctly American way of life. It was the way things should have turned out.

It housed plants and gardens, hothouses and hydroculture labs. The greenery which decorated the public spaces and the shopping malls did not consist of aspidistras and Swiss cheese plants – they were soya plants, sugar cane, peanuts or sunflower. Maybe it was not possible for the travellers to pretend they had never left home, for home had never been quite as good as this. But it was enough to help them not mind. They earned money, they paid for their goods. The internal TV station carried news from around the ship – pronouncements of the government, interviews, speculation on the future. But emphatically not a word about the world they had all left behind.

It was all a sham, of course. But a sham specially constructed with the aim of preserving the elements of human social culture through a voyage which was to take an unimaginable length of time. Longer, in fact, than many a civilisation had lasted on Earth.

The on-board computers knew the ship's course, could make corrections, could calculate the best way to gain momentum from the orbits of the huge planets of the outer solar system. Once these delicate manoeuvres had been completed and once they and the power of the photon sails had brought the ship out of the solar system and up to its maximum design velocity of one-fifth the speed of light – a pilot was scarcely necessary.

The planners had put their best efforts into devising a piece of engineering which needed human intervention only for maintenance. Yet human intervention was the one problem the ship's authorities still had to solve – how to replace the teams of highly-skilled scientists and technicians through countless generations. The technology itself had been solved by a previous civilisation, the task for those aboard the Tierra Nueva was less technological and more to do with maintaining their own civilisation through hundreds of generations.

Alara keyed in her security number at the galley entrance. Day ninety-six. She laughed grimly. How long were they going to keep that up for? How long before the read-out told her it was day one hundred and fifty thousand and something, she was ready to retire and they still hadn't reached anywhere? Her laugh turned to a sob. There was no way out of this place. There was no way for her ever to get access to the loom. She was trapped not only by the ship itself but also by what she knew. Jiménez would never let her out of the galley unless she compromised with him. And that was not an option. She might be lucky to be alive, but just now it didn't seem like any luck at all.

'Make yourself at home, you're going to be here some time,' said a voice at her shoulder.

She realised she was still standing in the doorway staring at the display. She turned and looked up at the man through tear-blurred eyes.

'Hola. Are you easy?' His voice was suddenly concerned. He leaned against the door frame in a way which struck her as familiar.

'Oh, hola. Yes, I'm OK. I can't get any decent entertainment on this screen. Just a life sentence.'

He chuckled. 'Alara, isn't it?'

She wiped her eyes and looked at him again. He did look familiar, and he knew her name. But then that wasn't so surprising. She nodded.

'That's the stuff.'

She smiled at his ship's patois. 'It's the stuff?'

He looked apologetic. 'Look, no deal. You want to be alone, I can leave you alone.' He put down a plastic box near the sonic cleaner.

'It's from the nursery. Pretty messy I'm afraid.'

'What's your name?' asked Alara.

'Xavier.'

'Xavier,' she said with a smile of recognition as it finally dawned on her. He looked different in his white medical uniform. 'You were at the Academy.'

He nodded and smiled back. 'I didn't know if you'd recognise me. I didn't want to... ' He shrugged, '... say anything out of place.' The smile broke his face again. 'You have to be careful what you say.'

Alara began loading the feeding bottles into the cleaner, suddenly animated at finding a link with the life she had left behind. 'I didn't realise this was where you were coming.'

'They promised me a place in the medical unit. This wasn't exactly what I had in mind.'

Alara laughed. There was a pause as he watched her working.

'I don't expect this is what you had in mind either.'

'No.'

He made to go. 'That's easy. I didn't mean to pry.'

Alara stopped working, straightened and pulled her hair back behind her ears. 'That's OK. Another time maybe.' She nodded towards the security display. 'There will be plenty of it.'

He smiled again. 'I'll be back for the bottles later,' he said over his shoulder as the door swished closed behind him.

By the time the Tierra Nueva was on its way out of the solar system, someone had got the bright idea that the president was due for re-election. The notion made its first appearance as a series of fly-posters on the shop malls which appeared overnight. They were removed just as quickly. Then the campaigners attempted something a little more permanent. The message 'It's time for a vote' began to appear in a variety of paints on the shop windows, and even gouged deeply into the alloy structures.

The anodyne feature items on internal TV which came regularly from the shopping malls and interviewed people about the range of items on offer and extolled the virtues of the generation ship were suddenly scrapped. They were replaced by music and stock shots of the interior of the ship. In the shopping malls themselves there was no hiding the change in atmosphere. Security presence was increased. There was no way in or out without passing through a screening process. Numbers inside the shops were restricted. Queues built up as shoppers waited for their turn to get in. And still the messages appeared.

In the matter of the unrest aboard the ship, Jiménez and Lorca took the hawkish position.

'President, we cannot afford to have this disruption,' Lorca was saying. 'We are in the most delicate of positions, any weakness shown at this stage will cost us heavily.'

The president looked at Jiménez.

'I am in agreement. We are the first generation on a mission the like of which has not been attempted before. We can't tell what unexpected problems there may be either from within or from without. Whatever happens we need to deal with it quickly and effectively. Our situation demands a strong authority structure. We are, if you like, in a constant state of war. We can't afford the unpredictability of a peacetime population.'

'It's the old argument, isn't it?' sighed the president. 'The ultimate truth always recedes a step; visible remains only the penultimate lie with which we have to serve it.'

Lorca and Jiménez exchanged a glance.

'Koestler,' said the president.

'A writer from the twentieth century. No matter.'

Lorca tried again. 'Imagine. In the next generation, in the one after that, our people will have come to accept life aboard the ship as normal. They will know no other, the dangers will be past.'

'They will know no other,' the president mused. 'And they will not know democracy and liberty. What sort of a people are we breeding?'

'A people who are going to survive.' Jiménez left it at that.

Luis nodded. He was not so much of a hypocrite as to try to pretend that he had not been just as hard-headed and ruthless in the past, but in the claustrophobic confines of a spaceship there were other considerations. As leader of a sparsely populated and scattered republic, misinformation was easy to spread and blame was easy to divert. He wasn't sure if the same rules applied here. And more than that, Luis was getting on, and he had at least one eye on posterity. They had written off the blotted history of Earth and he rather wanted this new blank page to reflect well on him.

The president himself addressed the problem in one of his weekly speeches to the people. He tried to appear reasonable.

'I know there is a feeling among some of you that the time has come for an election. Let me put it to you why your government resists this. We are embarked on humankind's ultimate voyage – to find a new planet and so ensure the survival of our race. Your politicians have not been put here for reasons of personal power or preferment, but to serve that single, most important end.

'Aboard the Spaceliner Tierra Nueva we each have our role – scientists, technicians, linguists, experts in every field who have been chosen to accomplish this greatest of tasks. You must not be distracted from your particular duty by the circus of politics, your work is too important. Our role as politicians is only to make sure you are able to achieve your goal. That is our primary aim and it is one which even over-rides our normal political processes.

'Our mission must be maintained over unimaginable generations aboard this ship – long after you and I have gone, order and stability must be ensured. And so we must accept a political order which we would not normally accept – these are not normal times. The structure of command and authority which serves our ultimate goal best is therefore also the one which serves us as individuals. The ideals which gave us a democratic society are noble ideals. Let us not forget the sacrifices our forefathers made to achieve them. Let us not forget the sacrifices we now have to make to ensure the survival of our people.'

The benign face of President Luis froze and faded on the tele-screens around the ship. A faceless voice spoke.

'People of the Tierra, survivors of Earth. Does our president seriously ask us to believe that our noble ideals of democracy will survive centuries of military rule? Does he ask us to accept that on arrival at our destination we will magically regain what has already taken mankind its whole history to achieve? If we are to give birth to a new planet, let us make sure it inherits our greatest gift. Keep the spirit of democracy alive, for the sake of the millions who have died for it...'

The screens went blank while gentle music played.

It was ten minutes before shift change when Xavier walked into the galley. A group of workers waiting to take over the sonic cleaners were milling around the door as he pushed his way through.

'Ola. That's easy. Thank you.'

Alara spotted him immediately.

'Everything easy?'

Alara stood upright and wiped a hand across her cheeks. 'I'm bored. I'm hot. I'm tired.' She smiled. 'Yes, everything's easy.'

Xavier gave a look of mock apology and gestured at his box. 'I should have brought it after you'd finished.'

Alara grinned. 'I'm glad you didn't.'

'Did you watch the president's speech?'

Alara nodded. 'It's compulsory viewing, isn't it?' She took the box from him and started loading the cleaner. 'What does it all mean, do you think?' She looked at him so directly, so honestly that he could not help but answer honestly too.

'Trouble, I guess. It means that the excitement and the good intentions have worn off. People are suddenly wondering what exactly they've done.'

Alara looked thoughtful. 'I suppose some of us will never even reach the place we're going to. It requires a lot of trust.'

Xavier looked around him, then lowered his voice. 'Somebody told me we didn't even have a destination yet. Someone else said one of our people, you know from the Academy, had helped find us one. Do you know anything about that?'

She looked for any sign of guile or deceit, but could see none. Just his open face questioning her, his head cocked to one side, interested but friendly.

'There's always someone with an imaginative story. I wouldn't worry about it.'

It disturbed her. It disturbed her that she'd had the thought, even fleetingly. She had mistrusted him. She had chosen not to answer him as she might. And she knew that it was her guilt that had made her doubt him. Nothing to do with him. Even in such small beginnings, truth was tainted. She even felt guilty about that. The punishment had begun.

'Have you seen what's happening on the shopping malls?' Xavier asked. 'Posters, protests, graffiti on the walls calling for elections. You can hardly go shopping with all the security people about. It's as if we haven't really left Earth behind at all – we've brought all the conflicts and arguments which led to us leaving there in the first place. We've just brought them on board the Tierra.'

'And we're barely out of the solar system. Still no-one said it was going to be easy.'

'You sound like the president.'

'I mean in a generation or two we will have adapted. The scientists must have foreseen the initial problems.'

'You worked at the Academy. Did you foresee the problems?'

'Now you're the one who's sounding cynical. Anyway I wasn't really a scientist. I knew nothing about all this.'

She handed him the empty box.

He hovered a moment longer, for the first time a nervousness in his voice. 'My shift finishes in an hour. Can I see you?'

It was Alara's turn to avoid his gaze. 'I don't know.'

There was a pause. Xavier looked down at his feet and reached inside his trouser pocket as if checking something was there. Alara watched and waited.

'What?'

Xavier looked up and opened his hand in front of her. Two small orange and green striped wafers lay on his palm, shaking slightly.

'There's always these.'

She picked one up. 'What are they?'

'Kick.'

'Kick?'

'You haven't come across them? You live a sheltered life.'

'What do they do?'

Xavier shrugged, still a little unsure.

'Relieve the boredom for one thing.'

'Do you take them?'

'Everybody does.'

'Are they safe? Are they legal?'

'They're safe as far as anybody knows. They stimulate the optical and pleasure centres of the brain. You feel good. As for legal, well... nobody's been arrested yet.'

Alara put the wafer back on his palm. 'I don't know.'

Xavier stood up and slipped them back in his pocket nervously. 'That's easy. You don't have to. We can always get something more conventional. Chocolate. It rots your teeth, stimulates your nervous system and it's highly addictive.'

Alara laughed. 'That sounds good.' Her expression changed quickly to a frown. 'But I can't. I mean, I don't think I ought to.'

'Why not?'

Xavier couldn't hide his disappointment. 'That's the stuff. Another time maybe.'

Alara stopped him from going. 'I don't think you ought to, either. You know. With me.'

He looked at her hard.

'Yeh. That's easy.'

In the shopping mall the authorities appeared to have given up the battle to keep the walls and windows free of posters and graffiti. Xavier showed his ID as he entered. The inspector looked at him.

'It closes in half an hour.'

Xavier nodded. 'I'm just going to wander around for a break.'

He moved on into the central piazza where a fountain set in a giant bowl stood in the centre of a small plantation of banana trees. The water jet almost reached the huge arched glass dome of the mall before spreading out in a billion tiny droplets which watered the plants below. The inspector was still at his shoulder.

'They've thought of everything, haven't they?' the inspector said. 'Just about.' He indicated a wall where someone had daubed: Jiménez for president. 'That's a new one,' he continued. 'The first time a name has been put forward anyway. What would I give to be a fly on the wall in the president's office right now.'

Xavier remained silent. The inspector smiled. He was a tall, thin man with a grey complexion. As he talked and stood, intently watching the people in the square at the same time, he reminded Xavier of a heron fishing in a river. His smile broke with a lightning flash and was gone again.

'I've only just been landed with this particular can of worms,' he lied. 'I was attached to the medical unit before. In a previous life I was actually a doctor.'

'That's where I am. I'm on the nursery wards.'

The inspector flashed his predatory smile again. 'Yes, I noticed from your ID. An important job. Guarding the future of our civilisation.'

Xavier moved on. The inspector stayed with him.

'And your friend Alara. She was important too.'

At the mention of the name Xavier stopped and looked the man in the face. There was no clue but that split-second of a smile.

'Just a work colleague. You know a lot.'

'I know too much.' Briefly it appeared that the inspector was going to share a confidence with him. Then there was a sudden change in his manner as he added: 'You haven't got much time left. If you want to buy anything for... anyone, let's say.' He gestured towards a gift shop selling a variety of plants. 'A miniature citrus perhaps. Beautiful and practical.'

'Thanks,' said Xavier. 'I'll bear it in mind.'

'What's economics got to do with it?' President Luis paced impatiently around the room as Lorca, Fernandez and Jiménez sat facing his empty desk. Lorca twisted his head round to look at him.

'We have people with not an awful lot to do, no incentive to work and too much opportunity to cause trouble.'

The president sat down. 'And why shouldn't we? This ship isn't a prison nor a punishment. This is our great enterprise, the start of a new world.'

'But this is human nature, President. People don't appreciate what they do not have to struggle for. I know we have more than enough resources for our ship. You know it. Jiménez knows it. But we must maintain some semblance of normal life, some aim, some goal for people to work towards.'

'What greater aim do we have than the survival of the human race?'

Fernandez sighed. 'With respect, President, that's all a bit abstract. That aim is hundreds of years away. What people worry about is tomorrow and the next day, but probably not the day after that.'

Jiménez spoke for the first time as if rousing himself from a deep lethargy. 'President, I will not mince my words with you. We have a serious problem of public order. We have tried to deal with it in a civilised fashion but it has not worked. When the forces who are now calling for elections are capable of interrupting a presidential broadcast then we have to assume that the rot has reached high among our ranks, perhaps even into our own security services.'

Their eyes met. Luis looked like a man who was feeling the political wind change direction. And here was his old friend, swaying in the breeze. He decided to meet it head-on. 'Perhaps into this very room, Colonel Jiménez.'

Jiménez stiffened visibly. 'President?'

'I expect you are aware that your name has begun to appear on the walls of the shopping mall. Jiménez for president.'

Lorca looked at the man sitting next to him and held his breath. Jiménez rose slowly.

'President, you are an idealist. In such times as these I believe that great ideals must be backed by strength.' The colonel bowed imperceptibly and strode out of the room.

'And you, Lorca? You, Fernandez. Will your names also appear overnight on the walls of our shopping mall?'

Fernandez remained silent. Lorca tried again.

'President, there is a need for forceful action. I will support you should you decide on that course. If not, I must seek another way to see it achieved.'

'Lorca,' said the president, pressing his eyeballs back into their sockets with his thumb and forefinger. 'Antonio. We have been through a lot, you and I. Is this the end of the dream?'

'The question is only who serves the dream best, President.'

'Jiménez is a dangerous man.'

'It is a dangerous dream, President, to play God with the human race.'

Alara jumped at the knock on her door. She sat up, her heart beating fast. She wasn't expecting anyone. She kept herself to herself. In fact, barely anyone knew where her apartment was. Barely anyone except perhaps somebody like Jiménez.

The door opened and Xavier walked in bearing his citrus tree like a lamp before him.

'It's you,' she said, springing to her feet . 'How did you know how to find me?'

He proffered her his gift in answer and she took it from him. 'It's beautiful. Look at that, so tiny. Citrus, obviously, a spiky little citrus.'

'Satsuma,' said Xavier, smiling at her combination of botanical knowledge and sheer enthusiasm.

'I knew that. It's in flower already, look. Smell that scent.' She breathed it in deeply and then shoved it under his nose.

'Ouch,' he said, rubbing his nose. 'It is spiky.'

'It's beautiful,' she said again.

'They said it will probably fruit in a month or so. It looks small but the satsumas are supposed to be as big as normal ones.'

'You shouldn't have,' she said, placing it on the table beside her bed.

'Why not? It's a present.' He shrugged. 'I earn more money than I can find things to spend it on.' He became suddenly serious. 'It's true of everyone aboard this ship.'

'So? We are on our way to the promised land, you know.'

'Yes, but... Moses spent years in the wilderness first.'

As she looked at him long and hard her hand went unconsciously to the cross which hung round her neck, visible now she was not wearing her uniform.

'Too much money and too much time on their hands,' he said. 'It's no way to run an economy.'

Alara breathed in the scent of her satsuma once more.

'Mmm. The scent of orange blossom, the land of milk and honey. Thank you.'

He waited. 'Are you going to ask me to sit down?'

'I'm sorry. I wasn't expecting you. I wasn't expecting anyone. I live a rather solitary life.'

'So I gather.'

She looked at him.

'I met someone today who seemed to know you. Or know of you at least.'

'Who?'

'Oh, some security guy. A bit odd. Very odd.'

'Oh.'

Xavier sat down finally, though he had still not been invited to. 'Alara, you puzzle me. I don't know what your story is, and you don't have to tell me if you don't want to. The truth is I never quite cut it as a dreamer at the Academy, but I do have some sensitivity you know. I guess that you need a friend and I,' he grinned, 'well I don't have an awful lot to occupy my time at the moment.'

Alara apologised again. 'It's not that I mean to be unfriendly. Or that I don't trust you. It's just that knowing me might not be the safest thing for you right now.'

'From what my security guy said to me I suspect it might already be too late to protect me from that.'

'Oh.'

There was a pause. And then at last the story began. All of it, every detail which Alara had turned over in her mind on so many sleepless nights poured out of her at last. And with each revelation, each explanation of what she felt, her burden lifted a little, until finally, late into the night, when she could find no more to say about it, they said goodbye and Alara slept the sleep she had craved for so many days.

In the mall the next day Xavier saw the Heron immediately, standing still as the current of humanity swept by him on either side. He pushed his way through the crowds towards the inspector and was met by a look of expectation.

'Inspector.'

'Pepe, please. Pepe Bascato,' he said with a smile. There was a pause. 'You wanted to say something?'

'I rather thought you would have something to say to me.'

The inspector began to walk away from the crowded central area. 'I've got my work cut out today. These price rises are bringing people out in droves. There are rumours of more to follow, everyone seems to want to stock up with things they don't need. Today it is panic-buying. Tomorrow they will turn disgruntled. Still it takes their minds off daubing the walls of our beautiful piazza.' He said it easily, as if he might actually believe it.

Xavier decided to take a chance. 'It's a cynical move by a cynical politician who is losing his grip on the reins of power.'

The inspector suddenly took notice. 'Good. Well said. There is too much cynicism aboard this ship. You said you thought I might have something to tell you.'

Xavier had caught sight of Alara across the piazza sitting outside a cafe where they had agreed to meet. The inspector's eyes followed his gaze, assessed the scene, then returned to Xavier.

'There is a feeling of change in the air, don't you agree?' Xavier nodded. 'In the next days or weeks or months, however long it takes, those changes will take place and when they do, things will be different. There are those, closer to the reins of power than myself, to whom you... ' and here he nodded across the piazza to where Alara was sitting, '... and others like you may be valuable.'

The questions began to form themselves in Xavier's mind, but already the inspector was turning as if to leave.

'We shall see. If those changes do not happen, I will not speak to you again. If I see you I will ignore you. If you ever claim to have spoken to me I will deny it. I will use the full force of my position and rank to make sure that any statement I make will be believed over yours.'

The smile flashed briefly as if to assure Xavier these words, despite the copious small print, were spoken in friendship.

Xavier's first question had finally reached his lips. 'Are you part of some sort of underground?'

'The underground, if it exists, will be wiped out. I intend to survive.' The Heron's smile flashed and was gone.

Xavier's heart beat fast as he crossed the piazza to Alara's table. He sat down unceremoniously, almost without greeting her.

'What's the matter?'

Xavier shook his head. 'There are huge queues everywhere. Everyone's buying before the next price-hike.'

'Yes, but what's the matter?'

Xavier's eyes scanned the crowds in search of the inspector.

'Xavier.'

His attention was brought back to her. 'I'm sorry. A strange meeting. The security guy I told you about.'

'What did he say?'

Xavier shook his head then laughed. 'I don't know. I'm really not sure.'

He turned towards her earnestly, leaning across the table towards her, his hands flattened out before him.

'Alara, these messages you get from Jiménez. Maybe it is time you answered.'

Alara leaned away from him shaking her head.

'Have you ever opened one even?'

'No.'

'So you don't know what he wants?'

'I don't want to know.'

Xavier sank back in his seat, his normally bright expression temporarily clouded by her inflexibility.

'I don't trust him,' she continued after a short silence. 'Whatever it is he wants, whatever he did or didn't do, I don't trust him.'

'But if you were prepared to see him...'

'No.' She got up violently and sat again just as quickly. 'No, Xavier.'

'What is it you want most, Alara?'

Alara looked down at her hands, a deep sadness welling up inside her. After a while she answered.

'To find Gwidion, to make sure he's safe, that he's all right.'

Xavier caught her hand across the table and pressed it. 'The only way to do that, the only way, is through the loom. And Jiménez has it.'

The tears began to roll down Alara's face. 'There must be another way.'

'I don't think so.'

'There must be.'

'Alara, we can't even move aboard this ship without someone knowing what we are doing.' He gestured across the piazza. 'The inspector, for example. If the loom is in Jiménez' possession, how can we possibly get to it?'

Alara's sobs made it impossible for her to answer, but still she shook her head.

'Alara, how else? At least listen to one of his messages. At the very least, find out what it is he wants.'

Alara could stand it no longer. She could not answer his logic, she could not control the sadness and guilt which paralysed her thoughts, she could only get up from the table and leave, shaking her head to rid her ears of his protestations as she went.

Alara was still in tears when Xavier found her in her apartment.

'Are you easy?'

She motioned him in and wiped her nose with the back of her hand.

'I'm sorry.'

From behind his back he produced a bunch of red roses with a flourish. Alara broke into a smile.

'That's better.'

She got up and took them from him, sinking her nose into the soft velvety blooms.

'I am your friend,' he said, a slight look of embarrassment crossing his face.

'I know.' The tears started again. She caught his arm and he cradled her head gently on his chest.

'Easy, easy.'

'I hate this place, I hate this ship, I wish I'd never come here.'

Xavier stroked her long black hair, smelled her smell and said nothing. After a long time her grip on him relaxed.

'I'm sorry.'

'Nothing to be sorry about. I figure. I feel the same sometimes. I feel the same too. We'll find a way.'

'Take me out.'

Xavier looked doubtful. 'Out?'

'Yes, out. I want to know what's going on.'

'Nothing much this time of night.'

'There must be something.'

'A few fast food places. Guinea pig in a bun, maybe?'

She looked at him to check that it was a joke.

She had a sudden doubt. 'Is it risky?'

Xavier shook his head. 'There are cameras everywhere. You can't do anything on this ship without it being recorded.' He shrugged. 'Security is suffering from an information overload. There aren't enough staff to watch everybody doing everything all the time.'

'Where are we going?'

'To a party.'

'I thought you said there wasn't much happening.'

'There's not.' Xavier laughed and took her hand. 'Come on, you'll see what I mean.'

Alara could tell from the heat that they were deep in the bowels of the ship. Now that they were away from the inhabited quarters there was a peculiar watery sound too, like waves hitting the hull of a small boat.

'Nearly there,' said Xavier as he led her to a small hatchway. It took some moments for Alara to take in the scene. Far below her, some forty or fifty metres, were more than a hundred people sitting or lying on the floor of the vast storage hold. Xavier indicated the metal ladder which was the only way down.

'I can't,' her breath was heavy and came in gasps. 'I can't.'

Xavier came back to her side and took her hand again. 'It's easy. It's not as bad as it looks.'

'It's so high.'

Xavier laughed out loud. 'Don't tell me our girl from the Andes has got vertigo.'

She managed a smile. 'No. It's just so high.'

'It looks worse than it is. We're not used to seeing things from directly above. It affects our judgment of distance.'

He led her closer to the hatchway. 'Come on.'

'What are they all doing? There's so many of them.' She looked more closely this time. They were all ages, but most of them probably her age or a bit older. She also noticed that they were facing in one direction towards something which, from this angle, she could not see.

'Come on.' Xavier put his foot on the first rung. 'I'll go first.'

Together they descended the ladder. Their entry seemed to attract no interest, everyone was seemingly still engrossed in whatever lay to their right. A few metres down it came into view. On a large screen which took up most of the huge side wall of the hold was a single, simple image consisting of orange and green horizontal stripes, exactly like the ones on the wafers Xavier had shown her. And now she noticed too a small number of people moving about among the crowd dressed in hooded robes in the same orange and green stripes.

At first she had thought it was the hissing sound she had heard outside the inhabited quarters, but now as she came closer she realised they were reciting something as they wandered around the crowd. At the bottom of the ladder Xavier took her hand again and headed for the most crowded part of the hold. It seemed to Alara as if there was no room here as they picked their way between the sprawled legs and bodies of the people watching the screen, but somehow they reached the central part of the crowd. Xavier appeared to know almost everybody. He smiled and nodded as he stretched and tiptoed his way forward.

'Out-side,' he said softly every now and again.

'Out-side,' came the reply.

Finally he stopped among a sprawl of bodies. He grinned.

'Space.'

'All around you,' said a girl of about Alara's age without taking her eyes off the screen. They sat down – an achievement which it struck Alara would have been impossible without Xavier being there.

'This is weird,' whispered Alara after they had sat some minutes gazing at the screen. 'There's nothing happening.'

The girl who had made room for them leaned forward and took hold of Alara's crucifix which had come out of her tunic as she climbed down the metal ladder.

'You go to church?' Her voice was friendly.

Alara said nothing.

'Nothing happens in church.' The girl leaned back again.

Xavier smiled at Alara. 'Be easy.'

Alara nodded towards the hooded people, one or two of whom were now making their way towards the newcomers.

'Who are they?'

'The chanters,' said Xavier. 'You'll see.' He looked across at the tall, stooping figure of one of the hooded figures and it struck him that he was familiar. Whoever it was seemed also to have recognised Xavier and stopped, turning his head sideways towards the screen so that his face remained shrouded. But Xavier did not need to see the face. That heron-like stance was unmistakable.

'Pepe,' he muttered.

'Who?' asked Alara.

'Somebody I know. Somebody I wasn't expecting to see here,' said Xavier, but the chanter had already moved on and was now heading away from them to the back of the hold.

Another chanter approached them from in front and for the first time Alara could make out what it was they were reciting, like some strange unworldly litany. A single word. 'Kicks.'

Xavier gave him a small amount of pesetas and took two orange and green striped wafers from him. He offered one to Alara. She had been a good girl once, for most of her life, in fact. And that had brought her nothing but trouble. For once she was going to be bad and hang the consequences. This time she took it and copied him as he placed it on his tongue and let it dissolve. It tasted of oranges.

'How long do I have to wait?'

'Not long,' smiled Xavier. 'Be easy.'

The minutes went by slowly as she waited for something to happen and stared with the others at the strangely uninteresting screen.

'I feel sick,' she said finally.

'No you don't,' said Xavier, still grinning. 'You can if you want, but there's not much point. You've come here to enjoy yourself, haven't you?'

Alara felt the girl's hand on her shoulder.

'Be easy,' she said. Alara noticed others around her were nodding in agreement, mouthing the words almost silently. 'Be easy.'

She had expected some sort of hallucinogenic effect, some rush of excitement, some light-headedness. But there was nothing like that. Only a feeling of warmth.

'Be easy,' she said to herself. And she was easy. And for the first time she saw what everyone else was looking at on the screen. A set of orange and green stripes. Except now they were so pleasing, so unbelievably pleasing. So pleasing that she suddenly wanted to laugh or giggle or share her pleasure with someone. But they were already sharing it, she realised as she looked around. And laughing and giggling were fine, but they were a lot of trouble. Looking at the screen was no trouble at all. It was no trouble. Absolutely no trouble. And so pleasing. So perfectly pleasing.

Rumours of the chaos and terror which reigned on Earth still managed to reach the crew of the Tierra Nueva. The chaos and terror which reigned in the higher levels of their own government were better concealed. Apart, that is, from the question of where exactly they were going. Free from the distortions of Earth's atmosphere and now well beyond the far reaches of the solar system, it was clear that Eridani, their closest target, was a non-starter. Its massive Jupiter-like planet orbiting close to its sun had been detectable from Earth. Hopes for the presence of smaller Earth-like bodies at greater distances away were quickly dashed by analysis of the data coming from the ship's huge satellite dish array.

At about fifty-five years' travelling time from Earth, Eridani had at first acquired something of a mystique. The possibility of a human being able to leave Earth and arrive at the new destination in his or her own lifetime was slim, but it was disproportionately alluring. Solar system after solar system exhibited the same depressing feature – a giant planet orbiting too close to the sun and no viable small planets. When that particular holy grail was no longer worth chasing, some people felt that somebody ought to pay the price. News of the disappointment leaked out. The astronomers, and those who supported them, had obviously got it wrong.

Fortunately, from the Tierra Nueva's point of view, so the story went, there was a new head of science aboard the ship in Jiménez. A head of science who not only had not been associated with the original choice of targets, but who had been actively proposing an alternative before they left Earth, but who had been over-ruled by the president.

Lorca and Fernandez seemed to recall having serious reservations about the president's standpoint on this issue too. And since neither were particularly hungry for more power than they already possessed, they were content to see things that way too.

And then there was Bascato. But Bascato was safely ensconced in the security department. And doing rather well, Jiménez thought. There was an old saying in the Republic: Keep your friends at arm's length and your enemies under your nose. Luis was old, and ready for a fall.

Besides, young Pepe had an idea that Eridani itself might not be sufficient to topple Luis. An unaccountable food shortage, along with a marked decrease in security presence, might help tip the balance.

On the day after the food rioters wrecked the mall and managed to break the security cordon surrounding the president's office, Luis fell from power. Lorca, Fernandez and Jiménez refused his request for a preliminary meeting in order to present a united front to the people. He had no option but to call an extraordinary meeting of the Senate.

Luis had faced death many times and many political foes, but it was with a peculiar feeling of nervousness that he made his way to the Senate in a last attempt to win over his colleagues. He thought somewhat bitterly of his days back on Earth when he had taken the reins of the Republic at a time when no-one else wanted the terrible responsibility of ruling over a dying planet. He had held the Republic together long enough to complete the huge and difficult Tierra Nueva project. Perhaps it was just old age that had come upon him. But he had launched mankind on a new beginning – he found it hard to believe he would not see it through as far as his natural life allowed.

The chamber was unusually silent as he made his way to the crescent-shaped table where Lorca, Fernandez and Jiménez already sat. Perhaps it was the fact that the cameras and microphones had been excluded from the meeting that made his colleagues so polite, he smiled to himself. And with that thought he recovered some of his old composure. If he was going under then he was going down in style and he wasn't going to give them the pleasure of watching him squirm as he sank. He looked around the room of expectant faces. For once his supporters and his enemies shared a mutual interest – to see how the great man would fall. He began his address in an unorthodox fashion.

'Friends, remnants of a once-great Republic, have you sunk so low that you cast off your leaders at the first whiff of trouble? I thought as I came here today of our last years on Earth – our cities crumbling, our civilisation in decay, our Republic under attack daily from rebels and terrorists. Yet we have come this far. And through worse times than these. The rioters of yesterday in our shopping mall will be caught and quelled. Set against such a great enterprise as we have begun, this is nothing. This is as nothing.'

And he sat down. Jiménez rose slowly, looking all the while at the president. Luis held his gaze, but his confidence wilted a little as his old friend murmured the first word of his speech.

'Senators.' Then his voice rose. 'Senators, we have riots at the heart of our great hope for the human race and the president gives us nothing but a few fine words to feed on.' He raised his arm towards Luis sitting high at the head of the chamber. 'Rhetoric. And then he promptly sits down in disdain.'

The chamber broke out in a buzz of chatter. The president's elation of a moment ago had vanished. Perhaps he had badly mis-judged the mood of his fellow politicians.

'We have a land of plenty, a ship built to last for hundreds of years and to travel unimaginable distances. And barely at the beginning of our voyage we have food riots in our shopping mall. What does our president offer? Arrogance and complacency.'

There were a few cheers among the chatter now. In an instant Luis had lost his composure and was on his feet again. 'The food shortages were not my idea.' Jiménez sat down and gave way. 'The price rises, yes. They were aimed at taking the public's mind off... off... anarchy and protest. A temporary measure to... to raise morale, to concentrate their minds. This was a policy agreed by the four of us. But the food shortages, no. This was a plot, a trick. Senators, for the love of Earth, let us hang onto democracy and decency on this voyage.' He finished abruptly, suddenly aware of the impression his words must be creating.

'May I?' asked Jiménez. The president sat down and the colonel again took the stage. The fatal blows would be easy now, the president himself had done the hard work.

'Senators, we have no time for experiments in sociology and politics and morality. We have no time for paranoia about plots and sabotage and dirty tricks. We have no time for democracy and decency dressed in the wolf's clothing of rioting and anarchy. What we need, Senators, is action and unity. The rest is idle luxury.' He sat down as the cheers rang round the chamber.

Finally, ex-President Luis got to his feet. He looked at Jiménez. 'For one who has so little time for democracy, I will spare you the necessity of a motion and a vote.' And with that he left the chamber.

At five o'clock that day all televiewers aboard the Tierra Nueva were automatically switched on. After five minutes of martial music, the sad death of President Luis was announced. He had died after a massive heart attack. Although doctors believed they could save him he had been allowed to die peacefully at his own request. His last words were reported to be: 'The Tierra Nueva is not a place for the old and weak. I am proud to have brought the last survivors of Earth this far. It is for you now to realise our common dream.'

After a minute's silence, new President Jiménez paid tribute to the life and achievements of his predecessor. 'We have lost a great man and great men are hard to find. President Luis may have gone, but I will serve his ideals and his dream of a new planet for the people of Earth,' he said.

The news programmes which followed were full of biographies of, and tributes to, the man who had put the future of the Tierra Nueva above his own future. It was also announced that problems in the supply of food had been corrected by technologists and officials working under the new administration. President Jiménez had taken direct control of the relevant department during the emergency.

Alara and Xavier watched the news reports on the screen in silence. Xavier sensed her unspoken thoughts but waited for her to speak first.

'So he's got what he wants.'

'For now, anyway,' Xavier agreed.

'Oh, Xavier, we'll never get anywhere near the loom. I mean, look at it. Jiménez is the most powerful man aboard the ship. How are we going to get to it?'

'I know. That really is the stuff. But, who knows? Things change fast here. We have to be patient.'

Alara laughed. 'Patience, yes. Time is on our side.'

'We said we'd find another way.'

'What, the chanters, the kick-addicts? I don't think so. It's all they can do to drag themselves away from those confounded orange and green stripes.'

'You said, just now, a moment ago... '

Alara recognised the faltering in his voice, so untypical of him. 'Yes?'

'You said we'd never get to it, the loom.'

She guessed which way his mind was thinking. 'Xavier, don't start that again. I won't see Jiménez.'

'No, listen. Something the soñador once said to me, when I was at the Academy.'

Alara was suddenly animated. 'What, what was it?'

'He said the loom was no more than an aid, like a candle is an aid to meditation. Maybe we don't need the loom itself. Maybe there's a way of doing it without the loom.'

'You think?'

'Well, I wasn't one of their star pupils, but yes, I connected.'

'Yes, so did I. Once or twice.'

'Maybe if we help each other.'

The pair were suddenly a flurry of activity and excitement, arranging cushions on the floor, placing a small low table between them.

'We need a point of focus,' said Xavier. 'A candle?'

Alara shook her head. 'I haven't got any. You?'

'No.'

They looked at each other, their initial frenzy subsiding again.

'Wait a minute.' Alara went to a small chest and pulled out the top drawer. Her hand found what she was looking for immediately.

'I'd forgotten all about it.'

'What is it?'

She turned it over in her hand, feeling the age-old feel of ancient paper.

'A notebook. I found it among Gwidion's things at the Academy just before we left. I picked it up, I picked up all his things.'

'Of course,' Xavier comforted her.

'I don't know why... I thought if I ever saw him again he might want it.'

Xavier took it from her hands and looked inside, scanning the rows of dates.

'How odd.'

'I don't know what it means, but I guessed it was important to him.'

Xavier placed it on the table and they sat cross-legged on either side, their hands resting lightly on the notebook. They closed their eyes, they breathed deeply, smelling the smell of ancient paper, letting the microscopic particles of timeless dust enter their nostrils.

Jiménez sat behind the presidential desk. The Heron stood before him. It amused him that fate had brought him and his old adversary Bascato together again, but in such different circumstances.

'You have seen them together?'

'Yes, President. I would say they are good friends.' His Adam's apple moved up and down his throat as if he was swallowing a fish whole.

'And?'

'The laser disks are available for you to view, sir. We monitored all activity.'

'Come, inspector. My time is valuable.'

The inspector swallowed again. 'They meet, they talk. No more than that.'

'No more than that?' Jiménez sighed. The Heron followed his

eyes across the room to the corner where the loom was on display. 'These two may be useful to us one day.'

'President?'

'Thank you, inspector. You may go.' He saluted. 'And Bascato, thank you for bringing this to my attention.' The Heron turned and bowed. 'We were enemies once, but that was another place and another time. I am in your debt. Have the laser disks brought up to my private secretary, will you?'

'Yes, sir.'

An interesting turn of events, Jiménez mused after he had gone. But after all Bascato was better suited to security than science. He could do with men like him. And men like him were more useful where he could see exactly what they were doing.

Xavier and Alara appeared not to have moved, though their hands were clasped together now on top of Gwidion's notebook. There was a smell. At first Alara thought it was the dusty paper of the book she had experienced earlier. But no. It was salty. And there was the noise of wind, but it was not wind. Too sharp, too keen, too constant to be wind. The hum of a ship sailing through space perhaps. And the unmistakable sound of water. Slap, slap against the shore. Shore? Or maybe not. What shore? They had heard that sound before too, in the hold in the bowels of the ship. She was fooling herself. She saw nothing.

Her disappointment after their initial elation at having something practical to do, some hope, however faint, was interfering with her meditation. Reality was impinging on her state of mind. Reality. The Tierra Nueva. An endless voyage. Reality was so devastating.

She was jolted awake by a crash as the table upturned into her lap, wrenching her hands from Xavier's and spilling Gwidion's notebook. In disbelief she stared at the scene before her as her eyes opened. Xavier was spreadeagled on the floor, his hands pulled behind his head, the unmistakable figure of the Heron perched on top of him, his long bony knee pressing against Xavier's neck.

She rolled away instinctively, gathering the notebook beneath her body and secreting it in a single reflex movement beneath the cushion she had been sitting on. Above her two guards stood by, but their eyes were on the brief battle between Xavier and their boss.

Bascato pulled Xavier upright by the scruff of the neck, his other hand bending Xavier's arm behind his back in an almost impossible position.

'Come on,' he barked as he pushed him out of the door. The guards threw her a cursory look and followed behind.

book four chapter one

Gwidion looked around. There was no sign of Cai. There was no sign of the tower or his village. Nothing was familiar. He closed his eyes and breathed until his racing heart began to slow and the fear and panic subsided. The loom was gone. He was alone. Home, he had said. But this was no home that he knew.

He was standing some hundred and fifty metres above a beach near the edge of a cliff. From his vantage point he surveyed the sweep of the bay – about three kilometres long – fringed with lush vegetation. At the foot of the cliff a single path clearly worn through the plants snaked its way towards the sea. The cliff itself seemed to be a plateau. It was rocky and bare – the constant wind appeared to have whipped the soil away, allowing only low stunted bushes to colonise pockets of deeper soil. In both directions it fell away almost vertically.

In the yellowy water he had noticed some black shapes, barely distinguishable from this distance, and had assumed they were rocks. As he watched he realised their positions were changing. In the shallows where they appeared to be congregating the water appeared calm. Beyond them he could see the angry white-capped waves whipped by the wind. He guessed that the waves marked the limit of the shelter from the table-top where he stood. If he could climb down he might find some relief from the increasingly irritating wind, but it was going to be a dangerous exercise.

He began walking to the right, leaning slightly into the wind which seared across the plateau towards the sea, sending a thin plume of dry soil out from the cliff edge like an unruly fringe. There were no gusts or sudden drops. It blew relentlessly at about 60kph he guessed, like a soft wall always falling against him. And it was bitterly cold and dry. Soon his right ear began to ache from the constant bombardment as he walked at right angles to it, and he was thirsty. The beach at this end melted away into a promontory, but there was no easy way down. The cliff was just as high and just as steep. In the other direction, facing into the wind, was a featureless plain. His eyes stung as he tried to stare into the distance. Between the watering of his eyes and the low haze of wind-blown dust, visibility in that direction was no more than a few hundred metres. Apart from the mystery of what lay that way, it appeared the plateau was cut sheer on all sides, like a piece of cake with a bite taken out of one sharp corner.

Instead of retracing his steps along the rim, he cut diagonally across the plateau to reach the opposite side of the slice of cake. The surface, apparently smooth to the eye, hid a number of treacherous obstacles. What vegetation there was, though thin and patchy, bore painful spikes which the shrubs gave up easily to passers-by. The needle-like thorns had to be picked out laboriously and where they pierced the skin swelled up almost immediately and began to itch. What had seemed like a shortcut was turning out to be the long way round as he was obliged to skirt the clumps of bushes. The pot-holes were even more difficult to avoid. Silted up with the soft sandy soil which was blown on the wind, they lay hidden until a falling foot discovered them and opened them up again in a cloud of swirling dust. It took him an hour, for the wind was taking its toll on his strength and determination and the constant stumbling and diversions made his progress much slower than at the cliff edge where there was no vegetation.

Finally he reached a vantage point where he could look along the coast. The view was the same, except that here the water lapped to the foot of the cliff.

He walked back towards where he had seen the group of black shapes, both ears screaming with pain, peering along the face for any hope of a way down. At one point, almost level with the group, was a small waterfall which had cut a shallow groove in the plateau and fell almost directly to the sand below. From close up he could see it was not as smooth as it appeared: it was pock-marked with erosion holes and small shelves, maybe enough to provide hand and foot-holds. Water marks could be seen on the surface. Gwidion paused and licked the fluid, then reached down into the trough and cupped handfuls of water into his mouth and over his burning face. It tasted chalky.

He let himself down over the edge, his first few hesitant steps at last taking him out of the relentless wind. The relief was indescribable, and suddenly he found the going easier. He let a foot dangle until it located one of the pock-marks or a small shelf, then eased his way onto it. He stopped to enjoy the feeling of still air and the sudden warmth it brought. More importantly than that, he seemed to be able to think clearly again. He rested a while, breathing gently, then metre by metre he descended the cliff.

His presence had now attracted the attention of the creatures in the shallows. The main group huddled together in the water while four or five had come out onto the beach. He could see now that they were bipeds. They were not unlike humans, except for their smaller size, the webbing on their hands and feet and their awkward waddling gait when they were out of water. Behind him, though he did not dare turn that far around, he was aware of the reddish sun setting. Night was falling and the dark came suddenly. On the horizon, above a short but spectacularly beautiful twilight, rose twin moons. With ten metres to go – almost at the level of the tops of the trees along the shore – Gwidion's foot slipped off a wet shelf. The sudden extra weight on his tired hands was too much.

Gwidion was woken by what sounded like the cooing of doves. For a moment his mind was filled with thoughts of his Academy room in Madrid, the sunlight streaming through the shutters, the soft touch of Alara's hand, her warm black eyes. But the smell was different, he could not place it.

He opened his eyes and saw for the first time the flattish faces of the creatures he had seen in the water. He appeared to be in a rude den made from the still-growing vegetation at the beach fringe. The bright sun filtering through its leaves was enough for him to look at his hosts, who surrounded him in a curious huddle. One leant forward and pressed a slimy slug-like shape into his mouth. The unfamiliar smell reached his nose again. Rancid mead. The food was slightly salty and he rolled it around his mouth before hunger conquered his squeamishness and his teeth sliced through its body. An inner sac burst, allowing a draught of fresh water to explode into his mouth.

Their webbed hands touched parts of him shyly, but when he sat up the huddle around him withdrew to a respectful, or perhaps merely safe, distance. He stood as best he could in the low shelter and smiled, the cooing began again. He took a few unsteady steps towards the shade of a large tree-fern growing on the margin and collapsed.

It was still light when Gwidion awoke and found he was surrounded by large flat shells bearing the sea-slugs he had been given earlier. A pair of creatures stood a little way off observing him. With some difficulty he tackled his meal. The slugs were encased in a soft flexible shell, like a thin paper wrapper. On his first attempt he failed to bite through it to the flesh beneath and struggled for some minutes to slit it open.

The creatures advanced on flippered feet, and picked up one of the slugs. The sharp talons on their three webbed fingers slit the casing open expertly. They re-laid it on the shell and waited. Gwidion took it, nodded, smiled and ate gratefully. The creatures cooed and with that moved from shell to shell performing the same operation on each of the slugs.

Gwidion stood and pointed at his head, then patted his chest with both hands. 'Gwidion,' he said, 'Gwidion'. The creatures moved closer. He tried again, 'Gwidion'. One of the pair uttered a guttural 'Cchooi'. It was unmistakably an attempt to imitate him. He repeated his name. Still the same sound came back to him. 'Cchooi, Cchooi.' Hard consonants were not their strong point.

'Gwidion,' he repeated touching his chest. 'Cchooi,' came the reply. He pointed at the creature's chest. The creature touched its head with a hand.

'Silu.' Then it touched the chest of its companion. 'Sili.' Gwidion pointed at them in turn. 'Silu. Sili.' They cooed excitedly. A group of three who had approached nervously, now stepped forward. One touched its breast, then the chests of the others. 'Hilu. Hili. Hilo.'

Gwidion nodded, smiled and repeated their names. Silu and Sili now turned and took a step towards the sea. They stopped to face Gwidion and waited again. Gwidion followed. They cooed. 'Cchooi.' Together they waded into the shallows. The strange scent assaulted his nostrils again.

In the shallows mothers with their broods of children around them moved discreetly away as he approached with the others, watching him all the while and making soft noises to their offspring. It had not been obvious out of the water, but now he could see the fringe of skin which flapped free from their waists and appeared to mark out the females from the males. As it spread and floated in the surf it provided an anchorage for the young. It reminded him bizarrely of a ballerina's tutu. As he waded by, the young rushed to cling to the safety of their mother's flap until he had passed, their excited cries much higher-pitched than the adults. They hung on to their mother, splashing and playing as the small waves broke over them.

He continued out until the water was up to his chest then dived into the waves. There was much cooing as he did so and his two guides also began swimming. They disappeared underwater, immediately surfacing about twenty metres ahead before he had even managed a few feeble strokes. They turned on their backs.

'Cchooi,' they called. 'Cchooi.'

Some two hundred metres out from the shore, his guides turned and swam towards him, diving and jumping like dolphins. This far out the protection of the cliffs was lost and the wind once more blew like a giant hairdrier across the surface of the sea. It was already significantly colder. As he swam on the creatures began to gesture to him and the cooing turned to guttural cries and growls. They called his name. He stopped and trod water. One of the guides dived, surfacing minutes later with a sea-slug. He showed it to Gwidion then in one amazing movement threw it in the air and struck it with his foot, as if playing a ball game. The creature landed far out to sea. The cries and gestures were repeated. Gwidion could not see what happened to it but he guessed it was a warning. Whatever was out there might be part of the reason they had moved into the shallows.

Life on the plateau, if they could ever find a way up there, would be distinctly uncomfortable for these creatures. It appeared that life in the deep water held its dangers too. He imagined he was on a large planet, its only life confined to this strip of water and beach, imprisoned by the inhospitable plateau above and the unknown perils of the deeper waters. Still, for all he knew this was no more than an isolated island far from the planet's true civilisations and these creatures were no more the dominant life-form than dolphins were on Earth.

His skin was beginning to feel sore: he guessed from too much sun, he had no idea what the ultra-violet levels were like on this planet. The smell still bothered him. He put a finger in his mouth and tasted. It was bitter, acidic.

What Gwidion had originally assumed from on top of the cliff to be a well-worn path through the vegetation turned out on closer examination to be no such thing. The creatures did indeed walk along it, but it was in fact a shallow trench dug laboriously out of the sand and stone by creatures ill-equipped for digging. He noticed too that the talons of many of them were broken or missing altogether.

Just as they had slit open the sea-slug casings for him, so he often saw them perform the same operation for others in the group who had lost their all-important finger knife. Whatever purpose this trench served was obviously of some importance to them. He followed the path to the foot of the cliff. On his climb down he had noticed the many water stains on the rock face. At the foot of the small waterfall was a large pool which appeared to have been excavated. It seemed that as fast as they did so the roots of the nearby tree-ferns gratefully spread out and drank the water as if through large straws. The dried-out trench was now above the level of water in the pool. Gwidion tasted it – pure, as far as he could tell. What fed the flow of water to the waterfall was unclear, but if there was any impurity in it when it fell from the clouds on the plateau above or rose from some vast underground spring, then it had been thoroughly filtered as it percolated through the limestone.

As night fell once more he witnessed their pilgrimage to the pool. For once they were quiet: dipping themselves in small groups

in the water before retiring to let the next group in. Gwidion began
to think that these groupings – twos, threes, seldom fours – were
something more than mere chance. After the first few hours in
their company he could recognise many of them well enough and
he imagined that there was more than a random facial similarity
between members of a group. Was it possible that these were
siblings? On Earth it would not be unusual in many species to find
multiple births. The idea grew on him that the groups were family
members, twins, triplets.

Gwidion too was ushered in by his guides. The atmosphere was
as reverent as at a baptism. He was grateful – his sore skin had now
erupted in burn-like blisters and even the temporary relief of dipping
into the water was welcome. His eyes watered constantly.

Gwidion puzzled over this gentle rite. Was it the place that was
so important or the water? Were the creatures attempting to fill
the pool from the sea along their trench? He doubted it. He could
see no evidence of any tidal movement – certainly not enough to
bring the sea flooding this far up the beach. On the other hand the
complicated gravitational effects of two moons could mean a period
of stability followed by enormous swings in tidal levels.

He attracted the attention of his guides and scooped up some
water in his cupped hands, gesturing towards the sea.

'Coo, coo.' His guides became excited and uttered guttural noises
which seemed to him like encouragement.

The next day Gwidion set about his task. He began by fashioning an
axehead from the limestone the creatures had excavated from their
trench. It was not the best material for a cutting tool but although it
blunted easily it was just as easily sharpened. It was a crude tool and
one which took him many hours to make. There was no sign of any
stone harder than the limestone axehead itself, so fashioning it was
a question of hitting it carefully with other pieces of limestone.
Inevitably it was sometimes the tool itself which chipped unhelpfully,
and not the stone he was attempting to shape it with. When that
happened he was obliged to start again with the surviving stone.

The result was a mis-shapen hand-tool which at first glance
might just as well have been gathered from the beach. In any event

the trunks of the tree ferns owed their strength to the fibrous web of strands of which they were made. It was laborious, but not difficult, to saw through them one by one with sharp shells which could be readily replaced when they broke.

He began by clearing the ferns close to the pool, cutting the root systems as well to provide himself with a straight piece of tubing. The maximum length was just under twice the length of his arm – this enabled him to scoop out the fleshy matter from inside. By the end of the first day he had enough tubes to take him halfway to the sea.

The twins Silu and Sili watched him constantly, chattering for long periods, examining his actions intently and attending to his needs. They seemed to hold some special authority in the tribe, though they exercised it without any apparent calls or gestures. When he was hungry or thirsty other sibling groups appeared bringing food and drink for him. When he was tired they came to him shyly, their sing-song cooing telling him of their approach, their gentle hands touching him lightly on his sore muscles.

Next he used the fibrous material to bind flat shells to small sticks of fern and showed Silu and Sili how they could scrape out a trench in the sand without breaking their talons. As the three knelt, engrossed in the task, an army of cooing sibling groups appeared as if from nowhere, eager to get involved. He straightened his back and looked around at them and smiled at their interest, then beckoned with his hand. They copied the gesture and came nearer. As they dug and made a shallow hollow, he laid the pipes as best he could along the trench. Silu discovered that the sea-slug casings made a passable seal where they joined. He mixed it with the fibrous soft flesh scooped out of the trunks and pasted it around the joints.

From one large tree Gwidion made an open chute which he propped underneath the waterfall to catch the water and bring it to the mouth of his pipeline. After two days' work the first gush of water from the cliff arrived direct and fresh at the sea's edge.

His new friends were ecstatic. They played in the waterspout like children. They brought him extra helpings of sea-slug and hung his neck with all manner of shells strung together with their new-found all-purpose material: slug-casing. Around the pool they decked the branches of the tree-ferns with shells which clinked together as they brushed their way through the vegetation. But Gwidion was too exhausted to enjoy his triumph. He had been careful to stay out of the sun during the day, working in the shade of the ferns and only venturing out for a refreshing swim. His skin continued to blister. It was so raw in parts that he could not sit or lie comfortably.

The days went by. Gwidion had little idea how long he had been there. He calculated it must have been a week or more. For much of the time he was alone, but curious sibling groups were never far away, watching him, attempting to help him in whatever task he had dreamed up. For those no language was necessary, it was always possible to show each other what was meant. But he chatted to them in Welsh as he did things, and they cooed back, and so the constant seesaw of language and actions began to link together and make sense.

Their language was much more highly developed than he had first thought. As he got used to hearing the soft cooing sounds which went on around him all day he began to discern different sounds and different intonations. The children had lost their fear of him very quickly, and as soon as their mothers allowed them they came to play with him. The females, and some of the other males, continued to keep a respectful distance.

The little ones though enjoyed playing with the remains of his Academy suit which hung in tatters on him and would spend long hours unpicking the tight matted knots in his hair with their talons. With them, picking up the language was easier. Their chatter was repetitive and the structure simple. From the range of sounds he guessed that their alphabet, if they ever developed one, would need no more than thirteen or fifteen letters. But the intonations, the sing-song way the syllables rattled in their throats added another set of levels to their meanings. It was, in effect, three-dimensional and its musical nature would require some new kind of notation.

What they did not appear to have was any way of naming the new tools and structures which Gwidion's building works were gradually bringing to the small patch of beach. For their part they picked up the Welsh words he used with great enthusiasm, cooing and singing over each new word, eliding the difficult consonant sounds they could not pronounce and replacing them with their multi-dimensional vowels. The effect was often quite comical to both sets of ears and interrupted their work with bouts of laughter and cooing.

The way they mangled the Welsh words taught him much about how their own language was constructed, but communication moved ahead more swiftly than sharing words.

Gwidion had stopped swimming in the sea, which away from the mouth of his freshwater pipe was acidic, and he was careful to keep out of the sun. Already his skin was getting better, but it was still crusted and flaky where the sun and sea blisters took a long time to heal.

The creatures' skin appeared to give them some protection from the acidity of the seawater and it was not a uniform grey-black as he had at first thought. When not in the water it was possible to see that each had distinctive mottling, subtle patterns and shades. In family groups these were quite similar, in siblings they were virtually indistinguishable. He was sure that even though they seldom ventured out into the deep sea, they had nevertheless built up a strong resistance to the acidity of the water in the shallows.

Gwidion's own skin mottling was a source of concern to them. They brought him the thick rubbery leaves from a succulent-type plant which grew at the beginning of the promontory where the acid seas almost lapped against the cliff. They slit the leaf neatly with their talons allowing a white sticky substance to ooze from the plant and covered Gwidion's sores in the lotion. Grooming, whether it was unpicking the knots from his hair, or soothing his skin, was an important part of their lifestyle.

Along the shoreline grew a stunted spiky plant not dissimilar to those he had seen on the plateau. They bore a bright orange fruit which the creatures loved. They called it rora. Its seeds hung outside the skin at one end on a short stalk and were coated with a clear sticky substance. When the fruit was eaten, the seeds transferred themselves to the new host and clung efficiently to the short sleek hairs which covered certain parts of their bodies. Cleaning and removing these was an integral and constant part of their daily grooming ritual and in the process the seeds were scattered along the beach to germinate.

The creatures were quick to accept Gwidion's new ideas and the possibilities which his crude tools offered to them. After the pipe had been constructed they began quarrying at the foot of the cliff where constant water erosion had weakened and cracked the limestone rock. With levers made from the tree ferns and picks made with shells, he showed small groups of the creatures how to dig out slabs of stone, working laboriously along the fault lines with their fragile tools where the water had already done the hard work.

He taught other groups how to make sand-sledges with runners of hollowed half-trunks. These moved easily across the beach for some distance before getting bogged down when the sand finally built up inside the trunks and they had to be emptied again. It was a primitive form of transport but it enabled them to move large lime-stone slabs to the outlet of their pipeline. Here, under Gwidion's direction, they began to form a small limestone harbour, a barrier which would one day provide a safe acid-free lagoon.

He shouted at them as they worked, using the sounds he had learned from them and Welsh wherever he needed a new word. 'Here, bring that over here,' or 'Good, put that there. Good.' And the creatures would coo to each other and attempt to repeat the sounds they heard and pat each other on the chest.

Now that his skin was getting better and his bowels had adjusted to his diet of sea-slugs and fruit, Gwidion oddly began to feel at home. During his first days he had thought often about his other homes, about Alara and Madrid, about Cai, about Lauren and about his mother. He had even hoped that he might reconnect with the loom in some way, that there might be a way to go back.

In the evening when the creatures went down to the seas for their final bathe and feed of the day, he would perform his daily ritual. He took his wrist clasp and placed it on the sand in front of him under the rude shelter of the shoreline vegetation. He breathed deeply, focusing on the energy which he drew up his spine and sent outwards to every part of his body.

He stilled his thoughts. He let the image of a cloaked figure walk away from him, through the arched doorway and up the white steps.

He felt sleep coming to him and focused once more on his breath. Sometimes the desire to sleep for his tired and battered body was too great even for his well-practised meditation techniques. At other times he would dream, but any connection with his previous life – Cai, the loom, Mimosa – seemed unattainable.

He tried to conjure up those images which had been his constant obsession, of skyscrapers, of falling, of the dome... They came as images only, without content, without presence, without reality. They were nothing more than memories, and as with all memories their emotional power was beginning to fade.

Exactly what had happened that day on the tower with Cai was a mystery to him, but he understood that he had made the first soma jump, the impossible jump. Across space. He knew that much. Across time? There was no way of knowing. He had no history, because for all he knew his history still lay before him. He had nowhere to go back to, because back was no longer a meaningful direction.

He tried to feel something about it. Sadness. Regret. He conjured up his mother's face, her smell, for these were surely the most potent memories he had to draw on. He thought of Lauren. But they were nothing to him. They were like pictures in a realie. They were not real.

Each evening he repeated the ritual. Each evening ended in sleep, or tears of frustration. Each morning began with the cooing of doves, the gentle presence of his new companions and new hope that tonight would be different. And gradually it was different, though not in the way he had yearned for.

His village was as far away from the here and now as it was possible to be. It puzzled him, but it no longer made him sad. When he had jumped, when he had made that incomprehensible step, he had felt he was going home. He began to understand that home was something to be created. It did not arrive in the world ready-made, by some act of magic. Home was an emotion.

His eyes opened on the setting sun filtering through the curved branches of vegetation, the cooing of doves returning to their cotes greeted him as the creatures waddled out of the sea. They laid their sea-slugs before him and stroked him gently.

He was young, he was happy, he had escaped. The next thing was to give his home a name.

He lay on the beach one evening watching the brief sunset as the others gathered in their dens in the undergrowth. He guessed the shortness of the twilight meant they were near the equator of this planet. So far it had been mild, but judging from the vegetation, no warmer than a sub-tropical climate on Earth. That might mean that north or south were less habitable. It might not. He had no way of knowing the size of the planet, nor its orientation towards its sun, nor its orbit. Not yet, at least.

How do you name a planet? The names he thought of, names from his village, names from history, Greek gods, Welsh heroes, Spanish leaders, seemed flat and silly. He returned to the dens and found Silu and Sili, sitting up waiting for his return. He was never unhappy to see them. Their doleful liquid black eyes, unringed by white, stared at him from their circular frame of long eyelashes – then the cooing began at the sight of him, the intricate interplay of hands and gestures and facial expressions.

Gwidion sat down and told them to look. He took a stick and drew a shape like the cliff behind them and the long slow curve of the beach. He put his hand on his chest. 'Gwidion.'

'Cchooi,' they agreed in unison.

He pointed to the picture and gave them a questioning look. Silu put his talon into the sand and drew a globe encircling Gwidion's drawing. He drew another globe above it and indicated that it moved across the sky. He drew two smaller globes and made the sound for night. Gwidion nodded.

Silu made a circle with his outstretched hands to indicate it all. 'Ama.' Sili repeated it: 'Ama.' It was their word for mother. There could not be a more appropriate name.

book three chapter two

And Jemin gave the people the fruit of the banana tree. And he said: 'Eat and you shall see'. And the people saw and they were at peace.

Alara wandered through the shopping mall. Things had certainly changed in the five years since Jiménez had come to power. Not just her own circumstances. She had lost her job, that much was true. But she hadn't lost her salary and she hadn't lost her freedom. She could not say as much for Xavier. She could not say anything with certainty about Xavier. Torture? Death even. She did not know. That, she suspected, was the particularly painful torture – more cruel than any other she could think of – to which Jiménez had sentenced her. She had half-hoped to see him again, somewhere, anywhere in the crowds, at the kick parties in the hold, though she had never again visited them except as part of her eternal quest to find Xavier. But even those gatherings no longer existed. Instead, in the main central piazza was a large vidscreen with the familiar orange and green stripes. A small group of people hung around it, patiently staring at the image. Among them the chanters moved as ever, whispering their wares. That was one of the unique things about the latest craze. Even without the wafers, once introduced to kick the orange and green stripes had the same calming, pleasing effect.

The authorities had not been slow to realise that this was an invaluable tool in maintaining public order, especially after the food riots that had led to Luis' downfall. But why stop there? It was only a small step to allowing the chanters to peddle their wafers openly in the mall. For a few pesetas you could enjoy the full kick, and no hangover in the morning. What's more, away from the magnet of the orange and green stripes, it didn't affect people's normal work routine. They could carry out an operation, fix a photon drive, even pilot a spaceship. Kick only served to lighten the load.

It appeared to Alara that the whole kick phenomenon was not after all an underground drug for rebellious youngsters. Kick had to be produced somewhere and there was nowhere aboard ship with the right facilities which wasn't closely supervised by the government. Out of habit, but without optimism, she scanned the group watching the screen. Just in case. Besides, without a job there wasn't much alternative to cruising the mall. Alara had time on her hands.

Amelia was her closest friend, and the only one who came to see Alara. They had met on Alara's one visit to a kick party with Xavier – she was the girl who made room for them. Amelia was a few years older than Alara, a graduate in molecular biology from the University of Buenos Aires.

It was she who had finally convinced Alara she should at least open one of the president's weekly vidcom messages. And under the pressure of her constant boredom and the chance, however slim, that perhaps, just perhaps, she could discover something about Xavier, she had finally relented.

And once one was opened – what stubborn pride was there left to hang onto? Well, why not the next? And the next?

He told her about his plans, his mistakes, his thwarted attempts to achieve this or that. He talked to her about Lorca and Fernandez and, of course, about his new-found ally Bascato.

In his anxiousness to restore her faith in him, he shared everything. And Alara listened. She no longer flinched at his descriptions of the reality of power, about his indiscretions and his manipulations. Was he somehow aware that at last she was listening? It seemed so. He grew more ready to tell her about them as if each confession, each display of honesty, might win her round. Each message opened seemed to serve to convince him that he was reaching her. He explained how he had stripped the security service of its intellectuals and free-thinkers and created a service whose primary interest was in security and whose loyalty was to him alone.

He told her of the success of his plan to relieve the Senate of the majority of its politicians. This, he said, was a response to the public cynicism about the number of senators in proportion to the size of the colony. In the process he created a chamber of some thirty senators who owed their allegiance, and probably their lives, to him.

He told her how he had overseen the large-scale production and cheap distribution of kick and how costly that had been in terms of the ship's resources. He explained how his plans to reorganise the security service and the Senate had reduced the population of the Tierra Nueva to below six hundred.

Such was the heady effect of absolute power. Or was this merely a display of power? He wanted something from her – she could no longer believe it was love. But she was his confidante once more, safe because – whatever she might know – she was powerless and he was invincible. And he had the loom, and he knew she wanted it. About Xavier he said nothing.

He even apologised – and he was not a man to say sorry easily or to dwell on his mistakes. He even had the courage and confidence again to remind her of his love for her, to offer her a place at the very heart of his new world.

In his self-absorption and self-righteousness he failed to understand what so many men fail to understand. That when a woman has been a mother – as Alara had been a mother to Gwidion – she has only one focus, which is neither past nor future, though it may include both; which is not the world men call reality, though it may encompass that as well, but is more real than all the reality ever created. And it is called trust.

The screen in the piazza caught Alara's eye as she walked across to her familiar table outside one of the cafés. The orange and green stripes gave way to the familiar jaunty tones of what passed these days for news coverage. These broadcasts were of a uniform type, anodyne upbeat bulletins of events aboard the ship – births, deaths, marriages, human interest stories, the soap opera of life on the Tierra Nueva.

This one was different only in the high-pitched frenzy of the announcer's voice, the grand music and sumptuous soft-focus intro. The wedding ceremony in the viewing gallery was unassuming and brief – the simple joining of two people who loved each other. It was also an intensely private occasion beamed, naturally, to everyone aboard the ship, and a masterpiece of film-making. The images of the president and his young, heavily-pregnant wife, set against the ever-approaching blackness of space, were transmitted constantly for twenty-four hours. A wedding is a great occasion. A wedding with the birth of a new life only days away is doubly great. A presidential wedding with the promise of a new dynasty born aboard a spaceship set on humankind's most monumental journey is nothing short of stunning. The honey-voiced presenters had a field day. Two photogenic lovers, separated by age and background, but finding their destiny on a historic voyage through space – the Spanish language barely seemed to contain enough adjectives or superlatives for such a script.

Despite herself, Alara could not help but feel a twinge of pain. That young girl on the screen could so easily have been her – in some sense had been her for a while. And the pregnancy... better not to follow that thought. She would only punish herself with that. She had lost one child, Gwidion, surrogate or not. She did not deserve another. Instead she fought to recover her strength and her cynicism, struggled to see Jiménez and his new bride through the eyes of Xavier or Amelia and not through those of her former self – a young trusting girl in love.

The couple and their beautifully-shaped miracle of life were tenderly filmed from every angle, their life stories – from their romantic first meeting through to their close working relationship on one of the Republic's most ambitious scientific projects – was told and retold.

The crowds in the piazza gathered around, nodded and raised their eyes and shook their heads. They laughed and cried and made sarcastic comments. Thankfully, from Alara's point of view, they gradually blocked her view from the café table and helped drown out the sugary fiction.

In his office, head of security and best man at the wedding Pepe Bascato smiled. Those who knew him well, or more correctly, those who met him often, were aware that he did everything with a smile, whether he was asking you to pass the salt or threatening you with the loss of your job. In the latter case the smile might even widen to a grin.

He grinned. It was a fine production, great footage. Of course it did not include the moment when Jiménez had lifted his bride across the threshold of his apartment. It was less graceful than the production team had hoped, given her size and weight at the moment and the flowing dress which caught in the heel of his shoe sending them both staggering across the room.

But the rest – wonderful, and all his own idea. Jiménez had not even taken much persuading. The fertility plague, this epic voyage, had made notions of romantic love the stuff of children's stories. As the Heron had pointed out there was love, and there was producing children, and the two were quite separate. And the greatest of these was producing children. And if you thought otherwise, then there was no place for you in the late twenty-first century.

Bascato flicked off the screen and looked at the watch he had acquired the other day from a new shop in the piazza. It did not tell the time, but the new thick green and orange stripes on its face certainly had an interesting effect.

In front of the vidcom in her room, where the wedding footage still played endlessly, Alara made her decision. Perhaps she had already left it too late, she chided herself. Perhaps she had been too stubborn, perhaps right from the start she should have been prepared to play the same two-faced games that Jiménez himself was prepared to play. Perhaps right from the moment she had held the blood-stained loom in her hand.

It was now or never.

Jiménez was tired after the day's exertions – and he still had his wedding reception to get through. He passed his palm over his bald head and sat down at the vidcom. All part of a president's life. Work never went away, even on your wedding day.

His eyes flicked over the messages. The usual stuff. Nothing he needed to deal with right now. He stopped in surprise, a slight smile spreading across his lips. Well, he hadn't expected to see that. Not today of all days. Just when he had finally given up hope. Just when he had resolved to put the future of the ship, the Republic – and, of course, himself – before his attempt to resolve the mistakes of the past, there it was. A reply from Alara.

The screen filled with her face and a small, soft sigh escaped his lips. Despite the years which had passed, despite the anger and frustration he had felt towards her, despite even his wedding day, he could not help it. He had made mistakes, he had been indiscreet, he had been less than truthful about many things, but his love for her... that was as real as the day he had first met her on the shores of Lake Titicaca.

She looked older. She looked tired. Her face bore no particular expression except perhaps resignation but it was as beautiful to him as ever.

'Where is Xavier?' she said simply and the message ended.

His reply was instantaneous.

'Meet me.'

book four chapter two

Gwidion had no idea how long he had been on Ama. It was months, that much he was sure of to judge from the growth of soft hair on his face. He must be a curious sight to the sleek-haired natives who were now frolicking in the shallows. He looked along the beach with pride. It had begun to look like a settlement. The lagoon was now well-established and provided a relatively painless place for him to bathe. And they had begun to move from the makeshift cover of the natural vegetation to something closer to small dwellings.

It was he who had begun the process, with no more in mind than providing himself with something approaching home comforts and a refuge from the sun. But everything he did seemed to fascinate the Amans and they were nothing if not excellent mimics. With his help, and with the tools he was able to show them how to make, they had begun to construct small round duggs. The limestone rock was easy to quarry and on low circular walls it was a simple matter to construct a roof from the woven fronds and stalks of the rubbery vegetation.

But something was bothering him – and as he observed regularly over many nights it bothered him more. He noticed that the two moons, which had been almost at opposite ends of the sky when he first arrived, had drawn closer together. The tidal movement, too, had begun to change. Not much, a metre maybe. But enough to cause him some concern.

The sun was now at its highest point. He took a stick and buried it deeply in the soft ground so that its shadow was as short as possible. Around it he drew a circle. When the sun set he would mark the position of the shadow, and again when the sun rose. And each day it rose he would mark a notch on the stick. His activity, like anything he did on this planet, immediately attracted a crowd of cooing spectators. He smiled at them. Tomorrow they would see what he did also. And the next day. And the day after that. And in time they would know the length of the year.

He sat down again and his collection of admirers drifted away, except for a pair of female siblings, who still hovered nearby. They walked the perimeter of the circle, holding hands and cooing. He watched them out of the corner of his eye for a long time, until the shadow had visibly moved and lengthened from its original position. He could tell from the frilly skirts which were not quite yet fully developed that they were on the verge of adulthood and when he looked at them directly they moved away shyly. He beckoned to them, calling out to them to come, but still they kept a respectful distance.

He pointed to his chest. 'Cchooi,' he said. The two looked at each other. He pointed to them with a questioning look.

'Lori,' sang one of them indicating her sister. Then pointing to herself. 'Loru.'

Gwidion smiled and nodded, and repeated the names out loud. 'Lori, Loru.'

The pair cooed at him, the pitch of their voices a sonorous interval apart. It was too hot for him in the open sunshine and he left them for the shade of his new dugg. When he woke they appeared to have lost much of their shyness. They had brought him food and gestured excitedly at the stick. The shadow had visibly moved a large distance. Gwidion smiled at them and nodded, thanking them for the food. When the sun set they should return, he tried to explain in a combination of words he had learned and sign language.

They cooed in answer, but left only occasionally to bathe or bring food. When the sun finally set they were still there and watched as he marked the circle. Then they went.

The next day the siblings were outside his dugg before he woke.

The morning sun had to rise reasonably high before it began to penetrate the shade of the steep cliff at their backs and the first rays were only just tipping its edge by the time Gwidion appeared. He had no idea how long they had been waiting.

Loru and Lori cooed in greeting. 'Cchooi.' They pointed excitedly at the stick which was finally casting a shadow. Lori, who appeared to be the more dominant of the two, took the stick in her hand and turned it. The shadow did not move. She looked at Gwidion in puzzlement.

He shook his head and indicated the sun and his own shadow on the sand, then turned a pirouette. Lori and Loru clapped at the sight and copied him. Gwidion shook his head again and indicated that they should watch the shadow, but the spectacle of their unusual visitor turning on the beach was evidently more interesting even than a sundial. He turned again, and again they clapped in delight and spun themselves around. Gwidion gave up the explanation and took them by their hands in a circle. Their simple joy and curiosity was infectious, and for the lack of a common language, he began to sing a simple chant. The Amans showed their pleasure again, and as he lost his self-consciousness and the rhythm of the chant became strong and clear, he began automatically to dance. It was one of the simplest circle dances of Mimosa and required nothing which might trip up the Amans.

And soon the others joined them, leaving the shallows or their dens to link in a growing circle. And as the dance grew, Gwidion's chant grew louder and more confident. He threw back his head and watched the blue sky circle above him, then closed his eyes as he came around to face the cliff. The strong sun blinded him through a haze of mist as it burned away the moisture from the shaded areas of the beach. At the back of his eyelids he watched the illumination and the red and yellow flare which stayed before his eyes like another sun each time he blinked.

The Amans stamped and their coos rose up to the sun, a sweet cacophony at first, which, as Gwidion grew accustomed to their unusual intervals, slowly harmonised with the tune of his chant. Finally he stopped, breathless from the dancing and the singing, and his choir stopped too, their new composition echoing against the cliff and fading out over the sea.

There was no mistaking the movement of the twin moons now, they stood at an angle of less than ninety degrees to each other in the sky. The tidal movement was also clearly growing and Gwidion began to fear for the safety of his dugg.

The plateau behind him offered no kind of refuge and the lagoon had ceased to be effective as the acid tides washed over the limestone barrier. Gwidion had no idea how serious the threat was. When the two moons finally arrived at their closest position, he theorised that the tide too would reach its highest point. How high that would be he had no way of knowing, nor did he know how often it might happen. As for the Amans, Gwidion supposed that they would be well able to cope with it. They were probably accustomed to the event and although they chose not to spend long periods far out at sea, they might be able to survive long enough for the tides to subside and for them to once more colonise the beach.

He attempted to talk to Silu and Sili about it. He showed them the advancing tidemark and drew the two moons in the sand. They cooed sadly. Silu rubbed one of the moons out. The two of them chattered excitedly. Some of the words Gwidion could understand, lots he could not. It had seemed at first as if their mutual under-standing of each other's languages would progress very fast, and so it had done. But abstract thought was a barrier which required time to cross. Silu's drawings in the sand were enough to confirm his fear that one of the moons would indeed pass behind the other and on that day their settlement would sink beneath the sea. Gwidion disappeared into his dugg and brought out his calendar. This was no more than a collection of notched sticks, but Silu and Sili had taken an interest in his daily time-keeping activities and understood well enough what the marks signified.

How many more notches before the moons pass behind each other? he asked. Silu picked up a stick with some fifty notches on it and shook it at him. Gwidion looked up the sheer cliff face behind him towards the lip where the sunlight illuminated tiny swirls of dust circling in the turbulence of the wind from the plateau. There was no alternative, time was running out.

As the sun cleared the cliff edge, Loru and Lori were there to greet him as ever, but today there was to be no singing and chanting to mark the start of a new day. The siblings cooed sadly and watched as Gwidion filled a rough bag woven from strands of plant fibre with some of the tools they had fashioned from the limestone rock along with a day's supply of sea-slugs.

It seemed like an age ago that he had first descended the cliff alongside the waterfall. With the fierce cold wind of the plateau at his back, he had barely contemplated the danger of the descent. Now, from the comfortable beach below, the way back seemed almost impossible. He slung the bag across his shoulder and over his back and began to climb. For the first ten metres he struggled to find hand and foot holds on the smooth wet limestone face. The thought struck him – was this the level the sea reached when the two moons passed each other? If so, how long would he need to be on the plateau before he could return to the relative comfort of the beach? Below him Loru and Lori still stood, their soft coos rising up to him, their figures strangely foreshortened by his vertical distance above them. His bag was uncomfortable and ill-fitting and scraped at his back through the remains of his Academy uniform.

One hundred and forty metres to go. The climbing was easier, the pock-marks and ledges more frequent, but his muscles already ached from his initial exertions and his bare toes felt stretched and torn by the unaccustomed gripping they were required to do to preserve his balance. He reached a ledge where he was able to plant his two feet side by side and achieve a semblance of standing upright. He wanted to cry, but there was no point in it. He wished desperately for company, human company. He breathed deeply and focused within in an effort to relieve the pain and silence the barrage of worrying thoughts that filled his head. Then he groped upwards with his right foot to find a new hold. And began to climb again.

The sun was reaching its highest point and the sweat covered him, making getting a grip even more troublesome. His exposed skin was sore and he noted that this was not a feat he should repeat so late in the morning. He had been climbing for an hour or more as he edged his way nearer to the summit. Below him he occasionally saw Loru and Lori, no more than dark dots on the beach, watching his progress. And then, almost without realising it for he had been concentrating so hard on studying the rockface, he felt cooler air. It propelled him up the final metres in a last flurry of energy and he flopped onto the dusty plateau. For a few seconds the cold wind was like a balm on his hot aching body, and then rapidly the chill of cooling sweat began to set in. He knew he had to work fast and he had to keep moving.

He cursed himself for his stupidity now that he was both in the full glare of the afternoon sun and whipped by the wind, but it was too late to do anything about it. He scrabbled in his bag for his rudimentary tools and began digging at the ground close to the waterfall. It was hard and rocky, for no topsoil or sand could rest here for long in the constant wind, but he hoped that water had achieved what he could not hope to accomplish with tools which were no harder than the material he was attempting to scrape away. His first limestone axehead was blunted within minutes and he felt the tears of frustration and hopelessness welling again behind his eyes. He shivered with cold as he looked out over the desolate landscape, the wind in his face allowing him to cry for real. Nothing but rock and a few stunted bushes.

He crawled to the nearest one. It was dense and spiny and tore at the raw skin of his hands as he felt for its roots. There, a few centimetres below the surface, was a pocket of what could pass for soil. Ignoring the blood running down his forearms, he scooped the soil away from the roots, watching it disappear instantly over the cliff face as it was caught by the wind. The bush appeared to be sitting in a small bowl in the limestone, less than a metre in diameter. Carefully, painstakingly, he removed as much of the soil as he could, then began the difficult task of cutting through the roots one by one. On almost three quarters of the circumference the work was easy. The roots reached the wall of the bowl and stopped or turned in on themselves or veered away to find a new source of nutrients and moisture. On the other quarter they were thick and strong and disappeared into the rock. That way, he felt sure, lay the water.

He had succeeded in removing almost all the soil apart from where it clung in the tight tangle of roots. He was tired, his muscles and joints ached, the sea-slugs he had brought with him had failed to satisfy his hunger, even less his thirst, and his blood-stained skin felt like a thick callous on his body. He was faced with an uncomfortable choice – to make his way back down the cliff in the heat of the day, or to work on until evening in the mind-numbing wind.

He pulled the spiny plant as far out of its pocket as he was able and jammed the tools he had brought with him into the bowl. At least the beach meant rest and food and company. He would let the wind do what it could to wrench the plant from its socket. He crawled the few metres back to the waterfall and drank greedily, his chin poking over the sheer face to where Loru and Lori still stood watching and waiting.

For a moment Gwidion felt nothing except an inability to move. Then as he stretched and rolled off his bed of woven plant material the pain began. It was in his shoulders first but his hands and feet too were curled as if paralysed in an attitude of grasping. He got up, shaking his limbs, and went outside the shelter. The sun had not yet cleared the cliff edge but Loru and Lori stood waiting for him. They gave a soft coo when he appeared, shivering in the cool shade of the morning.

'Olu,' they sang, the soft undulating notes making up for their lack of facial expression. The delicate mottling on their bodies seemed to glow. 'Olu, Cchooi.'

'Olu,' he sang back. 'Olu, Lori a Loru.' He smiled at them and stretched his aching body towards the cliff face. They scuttled away and returned a few minutes later with a small hollowed trunk they had filled at the waterfall.

'Diooch.' He took it and drank deeply until he had drunk enough, then let the rest of the water splash over his face and body. Loru and Lori cooed in a way he guessed passed for laughter and rushed up to him to rub the glistening water over his body. The massage felt good and his muscles began to move again without crying out at him. There was still some thirty metres of beach to the water's edge, but there was no doubt the tide level was rising. He looked back up at the cliff. He had woken early today and would have comfortably enough time to climb in the shade, but he did not want to waste any time.

He signalled to Loru and Lori that he wanted more water containers and told them to fill them from the sea, far out at sea. They chattered in alarm and touched his skin shyly.

'Fao, fao. Jheo.' Good, good, he assured them. Quick.

They waddled obediently towards the waterline. While they were gone Gwidion gathered some sea-slugs from the pile they provided for him every day and packed them in his bag, then set about pounding some thick rubbery leaves into a mash. Once dried slightly, these would serve to plug the water containers for the long climb to the plateau.

Once Loru and Lori had returned, he packed the containers of acid seawater with the plant mash and put them in his bag.

'Pen,' he gestured to the top of the cliff. Loru took his hand and led him towards the sun clock. Gwidion understood, and smiling, he put down his equipment once more and − sun or no sun − together they danced their morning dance.

The climb went quicker despite Gwidion's sore body. It was vastly more comfortable in the cool of the morning and his growing familiarity with the rock meant he was not so often obliged to cling on for dear life as he desperately tried to untangle his body and get to the next foot or hand hold. He also had time to look at the composition of the face more closely. The limestone varied from what appeared to be hard and stable to soft, chalky deposits which flaked and crumbled under his grip. The organic matter in these chalky layers was easy to see, almost complete shells were sometimes visible as well as small fossils of still complete invertebrates.

The chalky layers were the most difficult to climb, for although it was easy to scrape a hold in them, there was a limit to how much weight these makeshift ledges were able to bear before they collapsed and left his hands or toes frantically clawing the face. The harder rock was worn and cracked by the effects of water erosion and although the holds here were small they were at least dependable.

He could feel a damp patch on his lower back which he at first thought might be sweat, until the telltale itching confirmed that his water bottles were seeping the acid sea onto his skin. There was not a lot he could do about that, whether climbing the cliff or not. He took heart from the increased ease of the climb and pushed himself upwards in a renewed effort to reach the summit quickly.

The final few metres were a grim warning of what was to come. First there was the noise, the ceaseless low, angry whip of the wind across the plateau and the sudden chill. Then there was the brightness of the sun as he appeared over the top, and the shock as the full force of the wind buffeted him. It was enough to make him gasp for air and almost lose his balance. He lay flat on the top and looked for the plant he had started to uproot the day before, but it was nowhere to be seen.

Good. At least the wind had done that bit of work for him. He crawled forwards until he found the bowl. Already the tools he had left behind were covered in a thick film of dusty soil which piled almost to the lip at the side sheltered from the wind. He pulled them out and placed them carefully around the rim and scooped the earth out once more. The taproot of the plant had been left behind when it was blown away and still filled the hole which Gwidion supposed went through the rock to some source of water nearby.

Once the pocket was cleaned, he emptied his two containers into it. The liquid filled barely a third of it. There was a soft hiss as the acid reacted with the limestone and an acrid smell filled his nostrils as he pressed himself over the hole to escape the wind. Within two minutes the bowl was empty again, leaving a soft damp powdery deposit. Gwidion scraped at it with his axehead. The pocket had deepened by no more than a few millimetres before he was back to solid rock once more.

He lay for a moment, breathing in the sour smell, feeling the wind numbing his skin. Useless, it was useless. He hammered in frustration at the taproot which still filled the only weak point in the rock. His wrist and forearm caught against the sides of the bowl as he pounded out his anger in a frantic bass accompaniment to the howling of the wind. He would wait here to die. He would wait here until his skin peeled off or until the wind took his last breath away.

When his anger had subsided, he laid his tools once more in the bowl, crawled to the edge of the cliff and began his long climb down once again.

The next day Loru and Lori had not even arrived when Gwidion was out of his shelter contemplating the cliff face. He went to the fire he had made the evening before and collected the kindling he had gathered the previous day. From the ashes of the fire he picked out the lumps of charred trunk and packed them in his bag along with two pieces of thin stick.

As he was about to set out, Loru and Lori came rushing towards him, perturbed that they had missed him rising.

'Olu, olu.'

'Olu,' said Gwidion with a smile, throwing the bag over his back.

They touched him lightly, as if asking him not to go. Gwidion smiled and dismissed the cliff with a wave of his hand.

'Jheo, jheo,' he said. Quick, quick.

The climb was almost enjoyable. It was a vertical path, but a well-trodden one, and Gwidion took pride in the ease with which his hands and feet found their way up it. And he was sure that this time his idea would work.

Once he had reached his bowl and cleared it of his tools and the build-up of dusty soil, he laid the kindling at the bottom and arranged his charcoal around it. Then, lying over the hole so that his body protected it from the wind, he slipped his hands underneath his stomach and began to rub his sticks together. He turned his head to one side, shut his eyes and began to work. After the first few minutes his arms and fingers ached, but as he lay and breathed and allowed himself to become nothing more than an organism which rubbed sticks, he forgot the discomfort and his mind wandered to other times. What different times they were.

He remembered his first ritual fire in the village. Surely that had been more nerve-wracking than this, with all his family and friends gathered around him to watch. If he failed here, no-one would know but him. He felt the warmth against his stomach and attempted to peer under himself to see what was happening, but there was no fire yet.

So he thought back to the village again and remembered the nine sorts of kindling he had collected from the hedges of Mimosa. Then he reconstructed the intricate building of the layers in his mind. The effort seemed to allow his hands to move faster and faster and more freely under his stomach. His brow furrowed in concentration and he felt the sweat on his hands as he worked. Strands of music from Tabitha's fiddle drifted into his mind and for a moment it seemed that the infernal howl of the wind in his head had been stilled. Then he smelled the unmistakable smell of scorching, then smoke. He didn't dare lift his body to look in case the wind caught the kindling or spoiled his fire. He carried on, pressing the sticks close to the kindling, trusting there would be enough draught to turn the smoke into flame. And finally he felt the pain of burning on the skin of his stomach. And he was so grateful, he almost cried.

When he had loaded the charcoal onto the fire and lain on it like a broody hen for what seemed like an age and until he could bear the heat no longer, he rolled to the windward side of the bowl and positioned himself in a protective curve around it. The charcoal glowed red, fanned by the slight breeze which still managed to reach below the lip of the pocket. When he was satisfied there was no danger the fire could be put out, he crawled again to the edge of the cliff and drank from the waterfall. It was already afternoon and the sun beat down on the white face. Far below him were the familiar figures of Loru and Lori.

Gwidion was up before dawn the next day. The twin moons appeared less than an arm's length apart, chasing each other into the sea to his right. He needed no equipment today and as he marched purposefully towards the cliff he half-hoped to see Loru and Lori appearing from nowhere, their coos of greeting and concern marking the start of a new day.

By the time he reached his fire it was barely light but he could see it had been a success. All that remained was a thick layer of white ash, covered by the usual layer of dusty soil. He scraped the bowl clean and felt the rock. It flaked in places where the temperature had risen high enough to attack its structure and he picked up his axe-head eagerly. A centimetre this time, more in places where the fire had been very hot, but after quarter of an hour's work, the same impenetrable surface of limestone stared back at him. He sat up and stared around the featureless plateau, hoping against hope to see something he hadn't noticed before. He had to have somewhere to hide. He wondered how long he could survive in this landscape unprotected. Longer than he imagined, probably. Long enough to go crazy in the incessant confusion of the wind.

The effect of three days of activity in the open sun, added to the acid burns on his back from the leaking water containers, had taken their toll on his spirit as well as his skin. The large cooling leaves which Loru and Lori brought him each evening soothed the pain but did little to repair the damage.

He turned back to the pocket and hacked at it with his axehead until his knuckles and hands bled, until the axehead itself began to crumble and flake in his hands. Mad thoughts flitted across his brain. He could bring Loru and Lori to help. Perhaps their talons could help prise open the gap where the charred taproot still clung like a tight stopper. He could carry them on his back up the cliff, he was adept enough now at the climb, they were smaller than he.

And for the first time since he had made the decision to stay here, he regretted it. Maybe he could reconnect with the loom, or Cai, or the soñador. Perhaps his first attempt had failed for some reason he was unaware of. If he tried again, if he tried harder...

He had barely meditated since his the first weeks immediately after his soma jump. He had told himself that he did not need to, that it served no purpose here on Ama. But the truth was he could not. The same hormones which coursed through his adolescent body and gave him strength and endurance and the grim determination to scale the cliff day after day, they distracted him too. They drove wild thoughts through his silences and interrupted his breath. Their rhythms were like gunshot, startling, chaotic and when he was in their grip meditation made no sense. They laughed at him.

He staggered upright against the wind and walked to the edge of the cliff. The remnants of his Academy uniform fluttered like flags before him, announcing his arrival. He would fly. He would stand on the edge of the cliff and he would open his arms and he would stare out at the pale yellow sea which crept ever closer to him like a foul disease. And he would give himself up to it all. In one glorious, hopeless gesture, he would spread his hands wide and fall the perfect fall. Not the desperate leap of a man escaping a burning building, not the graceful flight of a seagull taking off, but the immaculate swallow dive of one returning to the earth from which he came.

He balanced a moment, his bare toes clutching the cliff edge, ready to propel him outwards. And his eye caught sight of two figures on the beach, their soft coos drifting up the hundred and fifty metres like the awestruck sounds of a child. Watching. Waiting. Wondering. If he lifted his foot so, just so; he could blot them out completely.

There was a rush of air past his ears. Then thud, his shelter shook. In an instant he was awake, rolling off his mattress and out onto the beach. The scene struck him as one of panic. All around him the Amans were leaving their dens higher up the beach, gathering their young and rushing towards the sea. The first wave had struck, bringing the water level almost to the door of his shelter. At the sea edge Silu and Sili stood, beating the sand in alarm. Loru and Lori were rushing towards him, their guttural cries warning him to move to the cliff.

'Jheo, jheo.' Loru took his hand and pulled. Gwidion looked out to sea. Far on the horizon he saw what appeared to be a wall of water, moving slowly, almost imperceptibly towards the beach. Loru had stopped pulling and was examining his scarred, bleeding hands. She pointed to the cliff.

'It's no good, I can't. I've got nowhere to go.' He knelt and scrabbled frantically in the sand then showed her his injured hands. 'The cliff. I can't dig.'

Loru cocked her head to one side.

'I know, you don't understand,' Gwidion said in frustration. He punched the sand, sending up a spray of fine white grains. Loru looked over to the others. The beach was almost empty as they took to the water and swam and bobbed expertly out to sea in a large shoal. At the centre babies clung to the frills of their mothers while the males circled them, shepherding them forward, keeping the shoal together.

'Aroo,' cooed Loru. Wait. 'Aroo.'

She took Lori and they waddled into the sea. Gwidion watched them go, then looked at the cliff. What did they mean? Had he understood? They swam away from the shoal towards where the small lagoon was now completely submerged by the rising tide and then further on towards the promontory. Beyond that it was difficult to follow them, but every now and again their two heads appeared on the crest of a swell. Then they disappeared beneath the water. Gwidion still waited. On the horizon the huge wave marched towards him slowly and relentlessly. Was this some strange inexplicable effect of the two moons, or was this something else altogether? Loru and Lori were still nowhere to be seen. He had no idea what to do.

He was about to pack his bag once more with food, charcoal and kindling and start climbing the cliff when he heard their excited cries and saw them once again dipping and rising in the swell. The wall of water was now level with the head of the promontory. He began to panic, they would never make it. He had to start climbing. He waved frantically at them.

'Mol, mol.' Go back, go back. But either they did not hear or they ignored his cries. He ran to the cliff and shouted again, then slung the bag over his shoulder and began to climb.

By the time they reached the beach, Gwidion was already ten metres up the face. He could see the size of the wave more clearly from his elevated position. It was at least as high as he had climbed and as it broke against the promontory further out it sent plumes of water arching into the air, reaching almost to the top of the cliff. Even worse he could see what was behind it. Another wave, just as big. And another. All the way to the horizon, pulse after pulse of water was moving towards the beach as if somewhere far away a giant stone had been dropped into the ocean and its ripples were now arriving.

Loru and Lori were still ignoring his cries to go back and join the shoal and were rushing up the beach, casting anxious glances behind them at the wave. Gwidion let himself fall back to the sand again, flexing his legs and rolling. He looked up to find Loru cooing excitedly and offering him two large objects, still shiny from the water. Flint. Gwidion took them and threw them in his bag.

'Diooch, diooch. Mol, mol. Cchooi fao.' Thank you, go back. Gwidion is OK.

Lori turned and made her way back to the water as fast as she could. As Gwidion began to climb he felt Loru pushing him from below.

'Jheo, jheo.' Quick, quick.

Gwidion pushed himself up as high as he could and clung there a moment. 'Mol, mol.' Then he looked upwards and climbed as fast as he was able.

He dared not look round as he heard a loud rushing sound, but flattened himself against the cliff face and dug every limb as hard as he could into the rock. He heard the horrible thud and felt the cliff tremble, then felt the water press him into the rock. He felt it drenching him, and as it hit the cliff there was a hiss like the sound of a blacksmith dipping a hot iron in water and the nauseating smell of acid and lime reacting. And as fast as it dripped away from his back he felt the familiar stinging.

The minute the pressure relaxed and he was able to move he started counting and began to climb again. One, two, three, four. His arms and legs fell into the rhythm of the numbers and propelled him upwards. At one hundred and seventy he heard the rush of water again, the thud, the cliff shivered and hissed and he felt the water on his back.

One, two, three, four. The interval between the waves was remarkably regular, and so it seemed, was their power. At one hundred and seventy he stopped and gripped the face again. The rush of water, the thud, the vibration, the hiss and the drenching. Less this time. And each time it grew less, until after half a dozen waves he could afford for the first time to turn around and look behind him.

Far out to sea he could see the shoal of Amans, still apparently safe, riding the massive waves like so much flotsam and jetsam. And still as far as the eye could see came wave after wave. Nearer to the shore he thought he could make out one of them heading out to join them. Lori perhaps. Nothing of the beach was visible apart from the plant debris which floated and churned at the base of the cliff. There was the roof of his shelter, spread out like a large parasol. And where the greeny-yellow water seethed and foamed white at the base of the cliff was a small black object. A body.

As Gwidion pulled himself up and over the edge onto the plateau he was greeted by a sight which momentarily made him forget Loru battered against the cliff below. Low on the horizon across the scrub was a single dark cloud. It was so singular, and so dark, it looked almost artificial, as if it might be a puff of smoke in the sky. The dawning sun was behind it and the slight relief that it gave to the glaring light of the sky enabled him to see something else, lower yet on the horizon and just disappearing out of view. Another moon. Even now it was so faint as to be barely visible, but there was no mistaking it. A third moon.

Gwidion's hands were bleeding again as he hacked at the limestone where the taproot disappeared. The flint was vastly more effective than his limestone tools, but nevertheless the work was slow. For once the buzzing of the wind in his ears was a blessing. It stopped him thinking about Loru. It was the second time that pair of siblings had dragged him back from the edge of absolute despair. If it had not been for her he might have given up, but she had paid for his crude flint tools with her life and he owed it to her to do his best.

The hours wore on. His back was raw and the ceaseless sound of rushing air in his head was accompanied by a deeper beat, the low thud which marked the arrival of a new wave at three-minute intervals. As night fell the taproot was at last dislodged and its hole was big enough for him to push his hand through. What lay beneath he had no idea. It could be no more than another small pocket, it could be anything.

By the time night came he was almost delirious with exhaustion. Too fatigued to sleep, he took fitful naps before returning to pound and pound the hole which was growing in the darkness beneath him. Then something gave way. His flint tool fell and splashed into water, the edges of his hole split and the pocket collapsed like a false bottom. He sat up and beat at it with his heels. The jagged rock cut him, but he didn't care any more, the stone was falling away. Splash, splash into water not far below. As soon as he thought it was wide enough, he put his feet through and lowered himself down as far as the hips. He explored the cavern with his feet.

The sides were smooth and wet and slippery but his bleeding feet could touch the cool soothing water. He let himself in as far as his chest and his feet touched bottom. He pulled himself down further until his head was the only thing pointing up into what had been the bowl. The wind still whipped the top strands of his hair, but suddenly his face tingled with the relief of having some shelter. The thud of the waves was now more audible than the hiss of the wind. He tucked his flint tool safely into his bag, propped himself as comfortably as he could against the stone and dozed to the gentle rhythmic thud of the chaos far beneath him.

Hour after hour passed. He dozed fitfully, waking to the twin accompaniment of the wind and the thump, thump, thump of the waves. Somewhere in the water were the Amans, somewhere in the water was Loru. Somewhere in the water Lori's sharp cries of pain were drowned by the sound of the maelstrom.

When morning came he heaved himself out of his dug-out, glad to be able to stretch himself upright despite the cold assault of the wind. He drank and relieved himself, and looked out over the sea, letting his eyes skim over the debris at the foot of the cliff without focusing, so that he would not see what he dreaded to see. And he hauled himself back into his hole and waited. He took the last of his sea-slugs in his hand and savoured it, letting his teeth play along its rubbery outside before slicing through into the cool, nourishing interior.

He remembered home, when the hot weather had come and the springs had dried and the water collectors lay empty and he felt his stomach shrink in readiness for the famine, felt the familiar tension as the sides of his stomach came to meet each other. It was not pain, it was an aching dullness of desire which could still be relieved by licking the rock, tasting its soft chalkiness, feeling his tongue sucked against it in its search for nourishment.

Soon there was only his stomach, the dullness growing sharper. He sank into himself and the light began to fade. With a start he looked up. Clouds. His heart leapt for a moment as if he really were once again in the village during the long drought, as if his prayers had been answered. The sun disappeared behind the tall grey plumes which drifted flat-bottomed across the plateau like a herd of huge animals marching across the land. For a while it broke through here and there, sending fan-shaped rays of light to the ground, illuminating a bush or an outcrop of stone in a ghostly fashion. Then the clouds closed ranks and rolled together, a gigantic silent stampede which sank closer to the earth under its own weight.

The fear followed close behind. He hurriedly took his bag and laid it on top of his head. Why hadn't he thought of it before to protect his head from the savage whispering of the wind? But it was not the wind he feared. The first few drops of rain spat into the dried soil around him, sending up small puffs of dust and forming miniature puddles which dried as quickly as they formed. Then the tiny damp craters multiplied, breaking down each other's walls and creating rivulets. For a moment he could fool himself that the earth was actually drying and cracking before his eyes like a mud pool. He listened for the terrible hiss he feared so much and sniffed for the bitter smell. And all the while the earth beneath his feet thumped patiently. He drew himself down in his hole, bowed his head and waited.

His confused mind turned things over and over endlessly as if his thought processes were suddenly set adrift on the sea below him. As the shock from each wave subsided, the thoughts would begin. What, he wondered, did the Amans think of him? Sometimes they appeared to treat him with reverence, as if he were some sort of god. At others he was merely an interesting, curious, but ultimately irrelevant arrival on their planet. Deity, he decided, was a concept as alien to the people of Ama as desert sand was to the Inuit. Thud. The thought was broken by a new wave shattering against the cliff. He started suddenly as if being shaken awake and peered over the lip of his bowl at the cold hell of the plateau.

If such a thing as a cold hell was possible. But then alien lands sometimes demanded alien constructions to describe them. Why should American be able adequately to convey the conditions on a planet on which it had no roots? Welsh had umpteen different ways of describing its valleys and their mountain formations. The extinct language of the Inuit was said to have a similar number of words for describing snow. Thud. A new shock distorted his inner conversation. And so time passed, until he had half-thought all the same half-thoughts a hundred times over and still they were no more than the jabbering confusion of the wind and he slipped briefly into sleep.

He woke often. His bag gave him some protection while the rain-water which trickled into his bowl and onto his skin, though less acid because of its contact with the limestone, still marked his skin in rings where it came to settle. The pins and needles in his legs were virtually unshakeable and soon he began to lose feeling in them.

Suddenly he was wide awake. It was night and the rain continued to beat the ground, and from his low position drowned even the wind to some extent. Something was different. He held his breath so that the pounding of his heart filled his ears, and he realised. The waves had stopped. The earth seemed uncannily quiet. Only now did he appreciate how loud and constant the beat had been. The slightest sound nearby, a particular splash of rain, would make him freeze a moment as he listened to see if they had returned. Then came the relief when he knew they hadn't and the craving to rush out of his hole and go and see the beach. If their ending was like their beginning then he knew it would be some hours before the sea level retreated enough for him to return, and meanwhile the rain continued to fall.

When morning came once more and he poked his head out of his hole, he could see the new landscape around him. Where before there had appeared to be a uniform flatness, the water had sought out its weakness and unevenness. It was as if some giant had been scratching the surface of the plateau with a large stick. Mini-ravines ran this way and that. Small crevasses, no wider than a man's foot, were cleared of soil by the advancing water and ran following the lines of the sedimentation. Boulders were exposed, and roots. Plants were washed from their secure pockets. The plateau had been transformed into a wrinkled skin ready to harden again in its new shape, until the wind and the soil and the dust soothed it and smoothed it and masked it once more.

He could contain himself no longer. Despite the rain he pulled himself free from his shelter and tried to walk to the cliff edge. His useless legs collapsed beneath him. He lay a while on the surface, willing the blood back into them, protecting his skin as best he could with his bag. At last, when they had enough life to drag him crawling to the edge, he was able to peer over. A thin strip of sand was now visible at the foot of the cliff. Unmarked, uncultivated, uncolonised, pristine. The waterfall where he usually drank had disappeared, diverted most probably by the rainstorms. He searched the clifftop to see if it had found another exit nearby, but there was no sign of it. No matter, the water must find a way out somehow.

The cliff provided some shelter from the rain, but the descent took much longer than usual. At first sight the face looked no different from what it had been before but the constant battering from the acid seas had subtly changed the details. Familiar hand and foot holds were missing or smoothed out. New ones had appeared or needed to be created with his feet and hands as he worked his way down. The last ten metres, where the action of the sea had been at its most forceful, was scooped clean, its slight concave shape providing an additional difficulty to negotiate.

Exhausted and relieved at the same time, he let himself drop the final part, bending his knees and rolling to break his fall. He gathered what debris had been left stranded on the thin strip of sand and fished what he could out of the shallows. When the sun appeared again he would need more shelter than the cliff could give him. He worked quickly, arranging several largish trunks in a wigwam and covering them with wet fronds and branches. By mid-day he had reconstructed a rudimentary shelter at the base.

The waterfall, he discovered, had found an outlet at the foot of the cliff not far from where he positioned his new shelter, but nothing of it was to be seen except at the bottom where it bubbled out of the rock like a spring. He had protection, he had water, he had a place to call home, but without the fruits of the shoreline vegetation, he had no food until the Amans returned. He sat cross-legged with the shelter at his back staring out to sea until the sun rose so high he was forced to go inside.

He was awoken by the most joyous sound. Outside his dugg Lori was jumping up and down excitedly, flapping her hands in imitation of the clapping Gwidion performed when he was pleased with them. At her feet was a small collection sea-slugs and flint.

'You made it. And the others?' He looked out to sea but there was no sign of the shoal.

Lori pointed excitedly. 'Mol, mol.' Back, back. She put her arms around him and hugged tight. Her head came no higher than his chest and the flushed and glowing mottled skin on her own front, felt surprisingly unslippery to the touch. Her snub nostrils pushed against his bare body where his Academy uniform was all but hanging from him like a tattered flag.

'Cchooi, Cchooi,' she cooed.

Gwidion held her at arm's length and looked into her round black eyes.

'Loru?'

She gave a sharp yelp unlike anything he had heard them utter before and struggled to come close to him again. They stayed so for a long time before the beating sun reminded Gwidion he needed to be inside. He was glad of her company and glad of the physical closeness of another living being. He was both indescribably weary and exhilarated. He did not know what the future held, whether the beach was safe for another long period. Loru had died trying to help him, but he had survived. And Lori had survived. It was not guilt he felt as they lay curled together in the shade of his shelter on the cool sand, it was not even sadness. It was awe and shock. Awe that a life could be taken away so easily, so instantly, so much without preparation. And the love he had not felt when Loru and Lori were two, he began to feel when there was only one. Her dependance on him was so obvious and complete, and where she had been two, now she was one. And he was one.

The child Soru was born after two hundred and ten days and was a wonder to everyone. His blue eyes fascinated the Amans and his body, though similar to their mottled moleskin, was lighter and more expressive. The clawed hands were not unlike Lori's but the feet too appeared more hand-like. The next day his twin sister Sora was born. Lori suckled them from swollen glands around her abdomen below her frills which secreted a rich fatty milk. She lay patiently with her belly exposed while the two struggled as best they could to reach the food.

Gwidion sat apart from them. The murmur of the retreating sea was like a balm on his mind after the long hours spent on the plateau. His contentment came from his feelings of relief and release, closeness and tenderness. It came because the sun shone and the vegetation on his shelter steamed and the world which turned, every jhara, into chaos and anarchy was returning to stability. It was an affirmation of life, whatever form of life that might be, because life was indivisible, it either was or it wasn't. And if it was, then everything that belonged to life and living was both pleasurable and pure. The beach outside was recolonised by the rora plants and their orange fruits hung from them like row upon row of coloured lights celebrating the new cycle of life on the shoreline. The dugg was a substantial dwelling, about five metres in diameter, big enough for the new family, but simple and impermanent, as it had to be. The proud father greeted the shy Amans as they wandered nearby in their sibling groups, hoping to catch a glimpse of the new arrivals. He invited them in and they looked in amazement at the pair, cooing over their unusual colourings and shapes, then in wonder at the dugg, which Lori and Gwidion had hung and decorated with strings of shells and flints. These sounded like wind chimes when brushed against or spun and twirled in the movements of air, fascinating the new babies and drawing their attention away from their constant obsession with their mother.

In one corner, near the sleeping area was a small table, built roughly out of trunks and bound together with fibrous strands from leaves. The remnants of Gwidion's Academy uniform were folded here, his wrist clasp laid neatly on top. The only things he wore, apart from his lengthening beard and hair, were a bag for his tools and, when he was outside, a woven cloak to protect him from the worst of the sun. It had taken Lori to make up this most simple and most obvious of objects. For all the care Gwidion took in constructing tools, for all the painstaking work he would put into inventing calendars or fashioning foot holds on the cliff face or building water pipes, he had let his skin take care of itself.

Lori had presented him with it soon after their first night together. A humble, shy offering of love. A token that she cared for him.

In the evening sky the proximity of the two moons indicated that the time of the great waves, jhara, was approaching once more. This time Gwidion was prepared. The cliff face bore the marks of his many journeys to and from the beach. In the softer chalk sections his hand and foot holds were worn almost like steps and on the plateau the tiny pothole in which he had jammed himself was big enough for two. Lori, of course, would never be able to make that journey, but one day, he hoped, his children might. It was not these things which preoccupied him. Lori and the others would take good care of his son and daughter, but the separation would be the first they had had to endure since Loru's death. The memories of that event would weigh heavily on them.

When the moons were the width of two fingers apart Gwidion gathered as much fruit as possible from the shoreline vegetation while Lori dived every day to bring him sea-slugs. Gwidion packed their few belongings, the shell hangings and chimes, his Academy rags, and slipped on the wrist clasp. Hazel, oak and holly. What foreign symbols they seemed on this strange planet, and yet how appropriate. Wisdom born from the eternal struggle for knowledge. He thought of Lauren. She seemed a lifetime or more away.

He had intended his farewell to Lori and his children to be brief and matter-of-fact, as if that might help their separation to be likewise. When the moment came, however, he could not disguise the tears. Lori wondered at them and traced their tracks delicately down his face with the talon of one hand. He was uncomfortable at being scrutinised in this way when what he had decided on was a brave, manly attempt at leaving, and as if sensing it she turned away and found something to do. She picked up his cloak from among his belongings and offered it to him. He had to stoop for her to reach around his shoulders and pull it tight. She turned the wrist clasp on his arm, following its intricate turns, then she clung to him, her upturned head beseeching him for something unspecific, undefined.

She spoke the only words which made any sense to her, the only ones which came near to expressing her deepest feelings for him. 'Now you are my twin.'

Gwidion was touched by the reverential tenderness, and shocked too by the unexpected impact the words had on him. He searched for his own with which to reply. Wife, husband – these were words he had read in books or realies, they had no currency in the place where he had learned to speak and even less here. For fear she took his hesitation to mean something else, he replied using her own words. And having uttered them, he realised that they were the truth.

'Popegh fao.' Everything will be fine. Gwidion kissed her and turned away to dandle Sora and Soru briefly above his head, one after the other. They squealed to be returned to their mother. Gwidion laughed.

'Pa jhwr, jhe ghefa, fach.' You too one day, little ones.

book three chapter three

And Ara turned to Jemin and said: 'I will not judge you, I will let others be your judge'.

In the shopping mall the crowds gathered around the new public vidscreen which covered a wall opposite the fountain and the statue of President Jiménez. It showed a series of orange and green stripes which held the attention of most of the crowd. Among the audience moved a group of people dressed in the characteristic orange and green striped hoods of the chanters. Their now perfectly legal wafer biscuits of kick still changed hands for a few pesetas each. These days there was no public gathering at which one could not find a chanter, the official dispensers of good times to the population.

The crowd found a place to sit or lean, or squatted or sat cross-legged on the floor as the broadcast began. The chanters still moved about muttering their liturgy. Occasionally they would stop and take someone by the arm and look deep into their face. 'Are you easy? Are you sure?' And occasionally they might press a free wafer into his or her hand – 'Take the weight off' – and move on again.

In terms of government, running the ship was a relatively small task compared to running a republic. Keeping the people's focus on their leaders was best achieved by ideas from earlier times – Ferdinand and Isabel, Emperor Xaviers, the Incas and Aztecs of South America, for example, provided the role models for a way of life which Jiménez found more conducive to preserving order on the ship.

Love, lust, relationships, births, deaths, family squabbles, all these were the stuff of the drama played each day on the ship's vidscreens.

If they did not exist, then they could be manufactured.

The screen faded into its pattern of orange and green stripes once more. There was clapping and some cheers. The chanters began to move among the crowd again, while behind them the fountain erupted in a cascade of orange and green watersprays.

Time and decay. These were the twin adversaries the planners of the Tierra had not accurately foreseen. Space ageing was a known phenomenon, but quite how devastating it could be when allied to the extended lack of stimulation of a long space journey had not been wholly appreciated. Time hung heavily on a tiny spaceship hurtling through infinite space. It stressed the bones and eroded the muscles. There was no escape from it, not in a healthy regime of vitamin supplements, not inside the gym or in the apparently busy offices of government. These were only diversions along the way. Days turned into daze. And weeks into daze, and years into daze.

Night-time was the worst – the artificial night that the Tierra Nueva had maintained throughout its voyage began at 9pm Earth-time with an almost imperceptible dimming of ship-board lights, waning slowly towards a twilight which lasted until 6am.

Alara sat in the chair next to her bed, as she did each day for many hours. Here, when she was alone with the notebook cradled in her lap, she had the time and the peace to reflect. Here, with his notebook before her, she had assiduously practised the techniques of meditation which she had hoped might one day enable her to contact Gwidion.

She thought of him often, his gentle innocence, his quickness of mind. She hoped he had found whatever it was he was searching for when he had disappeared that last day in the Academy in Madrid. She could never escape those memories.

Escape. What a futile hope. She, Jiménez, all of them aboard the Tierra Nueva, they had all made that mistake. There was no escape, not from their history, not from themselves. Most of all not from themselves. However much they had tried to reinvent themselves, they were always finally tripped up by... themselves. At least Gwidion had been in search of something that offered a hope of true escape. She wished with all her heart that he had found it. For all she knew he was back in his village now. Anything was possible. Anything.

She could not avoid the feeling that tonight was the time to put right whatever things could be put right, before they too perished before her eyes, each time dragging a little bit more of her with them. At least she should try.

Tonight she was finally to meet Jiménez. The negotiations had been long and she had bargained hard. The president had promised her Xavier was safe. The president's promises! This time she would not be so naive. Before she kept their appointment she had something important to do.

The president's care-worn look was becoming more obvious, thought Bascato as he waited patiently for Jiménez to look up from his desk. Maybe married life didn't suit him.

'We need some good news, Pepe.'

'President?'

'The wedding was fine, a great idea.'

The Heron dipped his neck in acknowledgement of the compliment.

'But it's not enough. We need hope. Eridani failed us. We need something to happen. Now.'

Bascato raised his eyebrows and held out his hands in a shrug. Even aboard the Tierra Nueva the impossible took longer than that to achieve.

Jiménez leaned back in his chair and put his hands behind his head, massaging the taut muscles of his neck. 'I know. There's no easy answer.'

'There's still kick. I'm sure the chemists can come up with something stronger.'

Jiménez nodded gravely. It wasn't exactly what he had in mind, turning his great new venture into a cargo-load of zombies. It wasn't what anyone had had in mind. His eyes roamed around the room, coming to rest, as they did so often, on the loom in the corner of his office.

He had once harboured hopes that Xavier might be of use in that regard, but he had chosen to leave the boy in the rather brutish hands of his head of security. If only. But if-onlys were no good to a president.

'See what you can do,' he said finally, dismissing Bascato with an impatient gesture of his hand. Then, 'and tell the guards to go'.

The Heron stopped. 'President?'

'I'm expecting a visitor. I have my reasons.'

'President, as your head of security I have to advise you that may be unwise.'

Jiménez did not look up. 'Thank you, Pepe.'

Still he stood motionless. 'May I ask who it is?'

'Not this time.' Then he relaxed, softening the tone of voice, appealing, man to man. 'Pepe, she's no danger, it's OK. Trust me.'

Alara followed the directions through the labyrinth of corridors which made up the ordinary quarters on the ship. Space was at a premium here and the closed doors which hid the living spaces of most of the people aboard were barely a metre apart, disappearing into the distance as if reflected in a hall of mirrors.

Deck 12, Room 113P. She made her way as fast as she could and knocked on the hard metal.

'It's open.' It was Xavier's voice all right. She pushed the door to reveal a room barely wider than the door itself and not much longer. There was room for a bed, a chair and a vidscreen. There was an acrid smell of body odour and soft music mixed with the sound of falling water.

'Ay, Xavier.' She was shocked at the sight of him. It was not the change in his physical appearance, though he was fatter and flabbier. It was quite simply that the spark had gone. He looked at her briefly and smiled.

'Alara. Out-side.' His eyes returned to the orange and green stripes on the screen.

She placed herself in front of it and he refocused on her, then sat up. She took him by the shoulders as if to shake him out of his stupor, but instead drew him towards her and kissed his forehead.

'Xavier, I'm so glad to see you.'

He nodded vaguely.

'What did they do to you?'

He tried to look past her at the screen again, but she blocked his path of vision with her head, trying to keep contact with his eyes.

He shook his head in an exaggerated fashion as if his neck was loose. 'I'm easy. I'm easy.'

'What happened, what are you doing?'

'Nothing much.'

'Are you working?'

He shook his head. 'But I get paid. Who cares? I'm easy.'

'Amelia sends her love.'

'Amelia. Out-side.'

His eyes were attempting to look past her again towards the orange and green stripes. She put her hand on his shoulder and turned his eyes towards her again.

'Xavier, you need help.'

'I'm easy.'

'You're not. You need help. Look at you, you're out of shape, you can barely keep your eyes off the screen. Xavier, let me help you.'

'I don't need your help.' It was said gently, with no hint of bitterness.

She held his shoulders again, forcing him to focus on her. 'I'm Alara, remember? We were friends.'

His eyes flicked over her as if he genuinely needed reminding. 'We were, weren't we? I guess I'm lucky to be alive.'

'I'm sorry.'

He shrugged. 'It's easy. I told you, I get paid.'

Alara's kneeling position on the floor was beginning to become uncomfortable. She stood up and Xavier's eyes returned to the screen.

'Sit down,' he said without looking at her. 'Have a wafer.'

She shook her head. He reached over and took one himself.

'I'm sorry, Xavier, I have to go.'

'That's easy. You take care of yourself.'

She had reached the door and was about to close it behind her. 'Love to Amelia. And nice to see you.'

He dragged his eyes away from the screen and for the briefest of moments she imagined she saw a flicker of the old Xavier, the one who had cheered her when she was down, the one who had, for a short time, made eternity aboard the Tierra Nueva seem fun. Then it was gone. Suddenly she didn't know why she had come here at all.

It was evening. The ship's light had dimmed, the corridors were quiet, even here in the higher echelons of government. The plain metal doors and walls gave way to something more reminiscent of life on Earth – the spacious corridors became carpeted hallways, wooden panelling gave a warmth to the surroundings and heavy oak double doors replaced the sliding partitions of the public areas. Jiménez was standing ready to greet her.

'Alara. At last.' His pleasure was genuine and he made to touch her hand. He was surprised at the way she recoiled, though he admitted to himself that he shouldn't have been.

But yes, it was possible to learn to despise someone, even if it was someone you had once loved. Love comes easily to those whose hearts are open to it, but hate can sometimes find a place to live there too.

'I want the truth.' She stood before him as proud as ever, as beautiful. More beautiful.

'Alara, sit down. I will tell you the truth.' He passed his hand over the top of his head. 'I loved you, Alara, I always loved you and I lost your trust.'

'Soñador Martín would never have allowed you take the loom. Never. Don't try to tell me he did.'

'I panicked. I was desperate about Gwidion. I thought we could carry on our work on board the ship. I thought I had to have the loom. I thought that was our only hope.'

'And Martín?'

Jiménez only shook his head.

'It would have destroyed him, losing the loom.'

Jiménez did not meet her gaze. 'I thought saving Gwidion was more important.'

There was a long silence.

'You killed Martín. And you left your son for dead.'

'No, Alara.'

'There was blood on the loom.'

Jiménez shook his head violently. 'I don't know. Mine, perhaps when I injured my hand as we left. Alara, we were under attack, there were troops all over the place.'

Alara's fairness, her ability to see his side, made her soften, made her listen.

'There is nothing hidden between us, Alara. Nothing, I promise.'

Silence.

'I did what I thought I had to do. Alara, you would never have done it but that doesn't make you a better person, only a different one.'

Yes, thought Alara. Always the politician.

'I know this must be very difficult for you. I know this isn't at all what you imagined or how you wanted it to be. For God's sake, Alara, it's not how I wanted it to be.'

'And Xavier?'

'Xavier... Xavier was not all he seemed. And besides, it was not my doing. Security would have had him killed. I at least made sure he was allowed to live.'

Alara merely shook her head.

'You are an intelligent woman. I won't insult that intellect with a speech of high ideas about the importance of this colony and our place in the future of the human race. Yet I believe in those high ideas, Alara. I believe in them as passionately as I believed in our work in Madrid. And I believe you do too, or you would not have come here.'

She remained silent, knowing that Jiménez the politician would find the words to fill the spaces.

'After Madrid you said you could not trust me any more. Well, perhaps I made a mistake. But if I did I wasn't thinking only of myself. What should I have done?'

'You should have brought Martín. You should not have abandoned Gwidion.'

'Martín refused to come. Martín was an old man who wanted to live out his days on Earth with his precious dreams. I wanted him to come.'

'And Gwidion?'

Jiménez sighed. 'Never a night goes by when I do not think about Gwidion. And that is why I have tried to reach you, that is why I invited you here. Please believe that. Maybe we can find him again. Maybe he is already where he wants to be.'

'I hope so.'

'I want you to trust me again, Alara. Not today, not tomorrow maybe. But I want you to believe in me again.'

In that moment she saw him as she had seen him before in his most private moments – suddenly smaller, suddenly vulnerable. She felt her heart soften and shook herself. She took a deep breath and reminded herself why she had agreed to come. She was a fool to be listening.

'If what you say is true, then help Xavier. Take him off the kick, give him a job to do, give him his life back.'

'And you will try to contact Gwidion?'

'Not here, not like this.'

Jiménez hesitated.

'I must be quiet. I must be alone.'

He nodded. 'As you wish.'

When she was sure he had left her, she cradled the loom in her trembling hands once more and studied its intricate crystal structures. Her heart beat fast as she dimmed the lights and sat cross-legged on the floor, placing the ball in front of her. Her mind still raced with the conversation she had had with Jiménez but she stilled them with her steady breathing. After some minutes those thoughts were replaced by memories of another time. Of Xavier and her small apartment.

She let the thoughts come and she let the thoughts go and felt her whole being relax. She took out Gwidion's notebook and placed it beside the loom. She remembered an occasion many years ago in an Academy room in Madrid, and she held onto the memory. As she stilled her breathing, letting her belly swell with air, lifting it through her chest and up to her collarbones, the memory of the presence of the soñador and Gwidion was almost tangible. She let her eyes close, holding the infinite connections of the crystals in her mind, and followed her breath until she found herself in a tranquil and peaceful place.

Occasionally the emotion of past events disturbed her. She felt guilty, she felt sad. Most of all she felt silly as though she was unworthy of this exercise. But she was not to be deflected. Her surroundings at last faded from her consciousness, today's events lost their presence. And yesterday's events. And all the events of her past. Still she followed the rhythms of her breath, letting it travel the intricate weavings of the loom, until sleep was imminent. And in that moment, in the twilight between wake and sleep, a single thought took hold of her, replacing the attention to her breath, replacing everything. Until she was the single thought and that was all she was.

'Gwidion, I am sorry.'

And she began to dream.

book four chapter three

Gwidion laid the sticks and roots inside the circle of stones outside the dugg and watched the sun set like a melting golden ball on the horizon. He looked over to the group of Amans playing in the shallows or stretched out on the damp sand close to the tide line. His hands moved absently but with automatic precision as he built the beginnings of the fire. It was not needed for either warmth or preparing food, for after the initial fascination with his activities even his own family had never truly taken to the idea of cooking. It was yet another of the interesting but useless quirks of behaviour that this stranger had brought to their planet. And increasingly Gwidion felt like a stranger.

He recognised the voices of Soru and Sora who were playing with the Amans. It was seven jharas since their birth and though the intervening time had brought him and Lori another set of twins, he found it hard to feel as he wanted to feel about his growing family. He looked over his shoulder into the dugg where he could hear the sound of Choru and Chora suckling at their mother's breasts. Before too long they would have to face their first jhara but they were far from ready to leave the warmth and security of Lori's attentions.

His hands had finished their intricate pile of kindling and now eyelessly searched the sand at the side of his thigh for the flints. He squeezed one in each hand, feeling the hard, sharpness dig into his palms. Despite Soru and Sora's differences from the original Amans they all played quite happily together. He had never seen any signs of rancour or cruelty between the youngsters. Of that much he was glad, but his emotions were not without a little jealousy. He wanted to be a father to them if they would let him. But with him there seemed always to be a shyness, a reserve, which he could not overcome. All too soon his new offspring would join the group too.

He struck one piece of flint against the other with a hard crack. That was the way. After the intensity of the first two jharas in their mother's protection he had hoped they would gravitate towards their father. It had never happened. He had hoped he might teach them the rituals of fire-making. He had hoped he could interest them in his attempts to measure the passage of time or unlock the secrets of the planet and its moons and the incredible tidal forces unleashed every year.

He hit the flints again and sparks flew aimlessly on his fire, dying on contact with the kindling. He did not care. Part of the problem, he mused, was language. Neither Lori nor his own children seemed to show any inclination to move beyond the most basic and practical forms of communication. Their interest in language seemed to stop at the point where they could understand what Gwidion wanted. Abstract thought appeared to be outside their ken.

He struck the flints once more, purely for the pleasure of seeing the sparks jump in the deepening twilight now that the sun had almost completely melted. He could not understand it. They showed no lack of aptitude, no lack of ability or intelligence or adaptability. Quite the opposite. And they did exhibit an effortless ability to co-operate, to do what must be done. He could not escape the feeling that he was simply an outcast in their midst. He was, very simply, not one of them.

His feelings placed an enormous strain on his relationship with Lori. She appeared as devoted to him as ever, and he to her. The taking of a twin was not something performed lightly on Ama. But he found it difficult to talk to her about the things he felt, so intense were her maternal duties.

Lori appeared at the doorway of the dugg. He waved. Chora and Choru must have gone to sleep. Soru and Sora should be here by now. Before he could turn back to the beach he heard the sound of them approaching. They hurried towards their mother, the orchestration of hand movements, gestures, and cooing already beginning as they passed their father.

'Soru, Sora,' he called. 'Come light a fire.'

The children stopped and looked to their mother, then Sora came back and sat on the sand. Soru went inside the dugg. Gwidion hit the flints fiercely, sending a spray of sparks across his fire, then set to in earnest, rubbing them together close to the kindling. Sora cooed and touched her father gently. Gwidion smiled back at her and looked deep into her black eyes. More and more, though it was not always easy to get beyond her alien-ness, he recognised himself in her face.

She was beautiful. It was not a beauty that Gwidion had been familiar with at any other time in his life. It was not a beauty that belonged to humans. It was her beauty alone, the beauty of the Amans. Sora glanced back at the dugg where her brother was. He sensed her discomfort, and he could no longer pretend to ignore Soru's snub. He got up and left the embryonic fire to catch.

In the gloom of the dugg Soru sat picking rora seeds from his coat and placed them carefully in his mouth. Sora, who had followed her father, joined him and took over the task of grooming, sharing the seeds between them. Gwidion squatted in front of them. He pointed towards the west.

'The moons are closing.'

Soru looked up and nodded, then found a clump of rora seeds in his sister's fur which captured his attention.

'At the time of the next jhara I would like you to climb the cliff face.'

This time they both looked up, then to their mother who lay with her babies a little way off. Gwidion looked towards her too.

'They are almost fully grown, they cannot cling to you when you have Choru and Chora to look after.'

Lori nodded her assent.

'But we do not need our mother. We can survive in the deep water.'

Gwidion looked at them, their almost human hands and feet.

'Perhaps you can, but can you survive the jhara too?'

Sora moved closer to her brother. 'We can. We will help each other.'

'I would like you to come with me.'

There was a pause.

'The cliff face is high and hard. We can swim better than we can climb,' Sora said.

'I will help you. We have plenty of time to practise. We will start tomorrow, and every day until jhara.'

'We have seen even you fall.' It was Sora again.

Gwidion gave a laugh. 'You must know how to fall. If I think by the time of jhara that you are not able to do it, then...'

Another pause.

'At least try.'

'What about our friends and the other Amans?' It was Soru this time who spoke.

'What do you mean?'

'They will go to sea as we have always done.'

'Yes. They could not climb the face. You can.'

The whimpering of the two babies disturbed the silence.

'We do not want to,' said Soru finally.

'You do not know what you want until you have tried it,' said Gwidion softly. 'If you are frightened I will help you. What if you cannot swim in the jhara waves because your hands and feet are not strong enough? And look at your skin, does that stand up to the acid water as well as the other Amans? To learn you must try.'

'Then we must try to survive the jhara too.'

For a moment the feeling of being an outcast returned to him and his temper frayed. He stood up straight, his tall figure an intimidating presence in the low dugg and his voice was hard.

'I am your father. I want you to come with me.'

Silence.

'You will come with me. Tomorrow we begin practising.'

Soru stood up quickly, his frame still only reaching to his father's shoulder.

'Why have you made us different from the others? You are not Aman. We are Aman. We will not go with you.'

Gwidion felt the tips of his ears grow hot as his anger rose uncontrollably. He leaned over his son so their faces came close and they could smell each other's smell. Gwidion's frustration at all his unspoken thoughts strangled his reason. Suddenly the lack of understanding between them was a wall that he could not climb. Instead he tried to batter his way through it.

'You are not wholly Aman. You will come,' he barked. Sora sat wide-eyed watching the confrontation as her father turned on her. 'And you too.' He looked at Lori. Nothing.

Soru almost spat the words at his father. 'We do not know you.' He turned away and sat again with his sister, comforting her. Gwidion swore and marched out of the dugg.

It was dark and the embers of his half-started fire glowed in the slight breeze. He sat cross-legged before it and listened to the pounding of his heart. The fire flared up momentarily fanned by a gust of wind, consuming the last supplies of fuel in a burst of flame, then died down again. Gwidion breathed deeply, stretching upright, filling his lungs from bottom to top. As he breathed out his anger, the hurt took its place. The feeling he had lived with all his childhood in Mimosa, the feeling of different-ness, was more acute now than it had ever been in all those years of being one boy among many girls. He wallowed in the feeling of loneliness for a while, until he began to gain strength from it.

He breathed in, and slowly and carefully out. Then he began to laugh. Softly at first, a small explosive chuckle that came from somewhere deep, deep inside him taking him by surprise, ambushing his pain and his self-pity. He remembered how desperately he had always wanted to know his father, how much he was determined his own children would know him. And now he had a family of his own, how much he didn't know them at all. His solitary laughter bounced off the cliff face behind him and echoed around the beach of sleeping Amans before fading away as it was consumed by the quiet sea.

As his eyes closed and he approached the shifting boundary between waking and sleep, he thought of the soñador. He would have liked to have been able to call him father. His eyes moved rapidly behind their lids, his breath was controlled and easy. The images of Madrid, Martín, Alara, Jiménez, came to him more vividly than they had ever done since his arrival on the planet, but they were not present, they were not in the place he was looking for them.

Much later, when the fire was out, and the gentle swish-swish of the sea's rolling was all that accompanied the complicated sounds of people sleeping, he got up and returned to the dugg. He slipped alongside Lori, the opposite side of her from the new twins and sculpted his body against her back. She murmured wordlessly.

He knew he could ask her to tell Soru and Sora to do what he wanted, he could ask her to reason with them and he knew they would listen. He put his free arm around her stomach and pulled tight up to her.

'I will find a way,' he whispered.

She stirred and clasped his arm closer. 'You will find a way.'

Soru and Sora stood before the cliff face and looked up. He sensed their hesitation. Sora was the more ready to do her father's bidding, but Soru wore a scowl. He seemed withdrawn, his voice silent, arms hanging loosely at his sides, an unusual stillness compared to the Amans' normal pantomime of gestures and soft cooings. It seemed an awfully long way. The distance, Gwidion reminded them, was not the obstacle, only the fear of the unknown. Lori stood with her babies a little way apart, her soft guttural noises soothing the nervousness of the atmosphere. One day when Choru and Chora reached maturity they would be required to do the same. But Soru and Sora were the first. After their father, of course. But they would be the first.

Soru looked nervously from the cliff to the family groups a little way off along the beach near their dens in the shoreline vegetation, curious at this strange ritual. Since Gwidion first arrived on their planet they had become accustomed to his eccentric behaviour and as his family had grown so had the eccentricities. It was not in their placid nature to do anything but coo and wonder at it, to help if they could and to accept the help that was offered them.

'I would like to spend jhara at sea.' His words were almost inaudible and his hands seemed to shake at his sides. Gwidion squatted so that he was smaller than his son.

'Are you frightened?'

Soru looked out to sea. 'Why should I be? I am not afraid of the jhara.'

'To me the jhara is more frightening,' Gwidion said gently, then guessing his son's thoughts: 'I thought fear was something we shared. It is better shared.' Soru looked away. 'But you will tell me I am different.'

'Do you fear the cliff face?'

Gwidion thought a moment before answering. 'I did.'

'But not any more?'

'Now I respect it.'

Soru desperately wanted to join the others along the beach, but the truth was that gradually he and Sora had become less and less a part of the shoal. What would he achieve if he walked away from this task? Soru steeled himself. He would do this thing that his father wanted, and when it was done he and Sora would have their own dugg and he would never do it again. Things would be different then.

They did as their father had taught them, closing their eyes, steadying the breath, focusing on the breath. Until their pounding hearts calmed, until their breath rates dropped. Then in their minds they began to march, as if up a set of stairs, pausing at each step to still the breath, smiling and feeling the joy of it. And when they had performed each movement in their minds, they began.

Their feet were much better shaped for climbing and walking than the original Amans, but for this genetic gift from their father there was a price paid each year at the time of the great waves. Such a natural disaster was an effective limiter of the population. The days the shoal spent each jhara out at sea – without shelter or rest, riding the giant ocean swells and often unable to feed because of them – weeded out the weak, the old, the sickly and the plain unlucky. Looking at their brother and sister gathered to send them on this new adventure, they knew that their family might have to pay a high price for a foot which could grip better than it could swim.

Soru and Sora let go hands and Soru took the first step onto the limestone face.

Seven jharas of Gwidion's constant pilgrimages up and down the cliff had marked the way well. More than that, with the flints that his family found for him on the seabed he had laboriously sculpted each hand and foot hold into a small shelf. His morning's work, as long as the cliff gave him shade, was to hack another small part of the pathway. A stairway it was not. Not yet.

Soru took the first step. They had been practising this for many weeks on the first section while their father worked high above them to complete the preparations for their climb and there was a chorus of appreciative coos as they quickly scaled the first few metres. Though almost fully grown they were a head or more shorter than Gwidion and needed more holds than he. Their webbed feet could provide no more than a solid platform, while their hands were much better adapted to the gripping and climbing required to take them higher and so took most of the strain. It was the arms that tired first. Once Soru and Sora were a few metres ahead, Gwidion began to follow. At ten metres came the hardest part of the climb where the previous jharas had pounded with their full force and sculpted the rock in a gentle concave. In order to traverse this lip which led to the rest of the climb, it was necessary to take the full weight on the arms and swing the legs free, out and to the side, to land them on the next section. While the hands found new holds above, the whole weight of the body was momentarily taken by the legs and feet. Soru struggled. His first attempt to swing his legs up and over the lip missed the new foot holds above. His grunts could be heard echoing back from the cliff face as he hung a moment, all his weight taken on his hands, gathering his strength to swing again.

Again he swung and lifted his hips. Again his feet landed above the lip and failed to find their grip, slithering back and bringing a shower of chalky dust with them which landed on the head of Sora below him.

Higher up Gwidion saw his difficulties and began to climb quickly down to reach him.

'Aroo, Soru. Cha, cha.' Wait, Soru, I am coming, I am coming.

If he could reach his son then he could support his hips for long enough for Soru to find his balance and get a good grip. Soru did not wish to wait for his father's help. He swung again, but his tired arms were beginning to tremble with the exertion of holding his weight. Again his feet scrambled over the lip and failed to find a grip. In desperation he lunged with one hand for a hold higher up in the hope of hauling himself up by brute strength alone, but his flailing feet gave him no propulsion.

There was a cry of despair as his body sprawled diagonally across the face, his hand missing the new hold higher up, his body turning over to face the sky. Above him Gwidion felt the pit of his stomach collapse, depriving him of breath as he braced himself to jump. The summit and the blue sky swung before Soru's eyes for a moment and then he was rolling, tumbling over the lip, his limbs like a doll's.

From the beach there was an anguished guttural cry as Lori watched the appalling scenario unfold.

'Fi fach, fi fach. Ajha fi fach.' My baby, my baby. Save my baby.

In another place, an unknown number of light years distant, in another time, another woman who knew the pain of loss was also transfixed by the scene. In the quiet of her room aboard the Tierra Nueva, the loom in front of her, Alara's apology faded on her lips. This was no dream she had slipped into, this was a nightmare. She struggled against the jolt of shock which threatened to disturb her meditative state. She understood nothing of what she was seeing. She did not recognise the place, or the dwellings or the creatures, but she recognised Gwidion.

'How he has grown.' The thought came to her involuntarily, like a reflex, and she could not help smiling to herself at its triteness. But it was true. He had always remained the same in her memory – a fourteen-year-old boy whose air of piercing innocence and fragile intelligence stared up at her from his clear grey eyes. This was not the figure she saw before her. His body, though still bearing the lithe and attractive leanness of a young man, was thicker and stronger and bore the scars of life. If she stood next to him now it would be she who must lift her eyes to look at him.

Alara watched Sora flatten herself against the cliff face and cling on for dear life in case she too was caught up in her brother's avalanche of skin and bone falling towards her. Alara knew nothing of these people. She barely knew Gwidion any longer. Her hands trembled before her, but they moved with decisive swiftness. She had no time to think as she grabbed at the loom, the only physical form of what she saw in her mind. There was an intake of breath then she sprang upwards and sideways, flinging her arms around Soru's waist and clutching him on top of her. The two hit the beach with a thud and a shower of sand.

It seemed for a moment as if the world had stopped. In the sudden silence which followed the dull sound of falling bodies and the aftershock of a million grains of sand returning to earth, Soru's mother ran to her son. High above them Gwidion checked his own impulse to jump. He rocked against the cliff face, fighting to regain his grip, then he jumped too, bending his knees as he hit the sand, rolling and coming to rest sprawled on his back, his eyes closed against the new spray of sand, panting.

Soru lay on the beach beside him, staring into the blue sky until the figure of his mother reached him and threw her arms around him with a cry. Sora, who had jumped after them copying her father's fall, put her arms around them both and the three lay in a heap on the beach, savouring the blood which pounded through their veins in wave after wave after wave.

Gwidion picked himself up and crawled towards the fifth form which lay a little way apart. Her arms were folded in an odd and ungainly attitude beneath her back as if she had tried to break her own fall at the last moment. Her head was turned sideways at an unnatural angle and a thin trickle of blood stained the whiteness of the beach an incredible red which turned just as quickly to black as it soaked into the powdery limestone sand. Her long black hair had freed itself from a silver clasp at the back of her neck and lay in strands across her white dusted cheek.

'Alara.' Gwidion bent his ear to her nose and mouth. He took her wrist in his hand, and shyly, hesitatingly, pressed his ear against her left breast. Nothing. He slid his hand gently under her face as if to turn her head towards him, but recoiled at the limpness of the neck. He released her eyes from their expression of terror and stroked the white sand out of her hair.

Slowly he became aware of the others gathering around him. Their soft, uncomprehending noises made him look up at his son Soru who knelt now beside him. His webbed hand was on his father's shoulder in a gesture of comfort and questioning but his face was illuminated with the exultation of someone who has experienced the extremity of fear and yet survived. Lori tucked her small frame beneath Gwidion's arm, both seeking and offering comfort.

Gwidion regretted every instant of his life. He had lost everything.

Lauren, his mother, his father. Now Alara. And to these people of Ama it seemed he had brought nothing but suffering and tragedy. Perhaps after all he was wrong. This was not where he belonged. This was not his home.

Gwidion looked around at the faces which surrounded him and at the unforgiving whiteness of the cliff behind which at once defined their shapes and threw their features into shade. They looked to him as to someone who would answer their questions and offer them guidance.

Next to Alara's prone body Soru had noticed something else besides the grief in his father's face. He reached under the body, digging with his hand and pulled out the globe which had broken the lower part of Alara's spine as she fell. The wildness in his eyes, the blood pounding through his veins, turned from exhilaration to an anger he dared not vent on his father.

The loom rolled on his outstretched hand as it shook before him. His whisper was almost inaudible beneath the fury in his voice.

'If you fall I will catch you.' He clenched his fingers around the loom, turned and flung it at the cliff face. There was a high-pitched crash as it shattered, the countless tiny shards falling onto the sand below like glittering raindrops.

Gwidion watched as if everything was happening in slow motion. It took place before his eyes with such clarity and detail that he felt as if at any moment he could stop it. At any moment. From when the loom had first trembled in his son's hand – from when he had first sensed Soru's anger, his desperation to do something, anything – until it finally made contact with the limestone. And even then, even as the rock itself yielded imperceptibly under the impact, and while the cracks in the loom were no more than a millisecond old, even then it seemed to him that he could stretch out his hand and stop it. But he did not.

His family, the other spectators, looked at him to see what he would do, whether this was of any significance. Soru himself turned, suddenly sober, suddenly aware that he had acted. Sora too, as if it was she herself who had thrown the loom. Gwidion's nostrils flexed as a whiff of pulverised lazurite was brought to him on the warm air.

Gwidion's eyes met Soru's. And in that moment something

extraordinary happened. More extraordinary even than Alara's jump through space. Gwidion turned to Sora, and Lori and the rest of his children. There was a connection which had not been there before. It reminded him of the feeling he had experienced when he first met the soñador, but this was deeper, this was intense. It was as if in that instant everything was revealed, everything known. It was a connection that was without language, it was a language. Now he knew how these people felt. Now he knew what it was to be an Aman. He knew suddenly that if he wished he could discover anything – where they went at jhara, how they smelled, how they tasted, any trivial detail he cared to think of. But it was not in those details that the knowledge came. It came like an inspiration. Complete. It came like a single intake of breath, like an emotion. The rest, the details, were not contained within it though they followed from it, stretching into the distance like a landscape waiting to be explored. And by the same token, they now knew him.

Neither Gwidion nor Soru could sleep that night. As Gwidion sat before the dying fire outside the dugg he breathed in, enjoying the scents of rora flowers which hung in the still air. As he breathed out he let his mind wander through its new landscape. Suddenly, without knowing, he knew.

He knew the currents of the sea, he knew their warmth and their coldness, their acidity and their freshness. He knew the topography of the deepest water, the skeins of rock. He felt the pull of the moons and the surge of the tide held in delicate balance as Ama circled its sun and let loose once a year at the time of jhara. He knew the movement of the winds and the gathering of the rains.

He sensed, without thinking, the existence of the other Amans, in their dens on the shoreline, out at sea, the snufflings of their sleep, the gentle snores. And he knew that they sensed him too. It was a glorious feeling, it was a feeling of completeness. And it made perfect sense. Out at sea during the time of jhara, in the noise and chaos of the planet's natural forces, speech would be next to useless to them. For the shoal to survive such a catastrophe, it had to have more than a spoken language.

Soru joined him at the fire silently, and silently they spoke the words that had been missing between them.

'What happened? Why did she save me?'

Gwidion paused. 'Because she felt responsible for me being here.'

'She did not know me.'

'She would not have seen it that way. She saw someone who needed help.'

Soru thought for a while. 'It is like that too among your people? As it is with us?'

His father bowed his head. 'Not always.'

'I did not know it was like that with you. Until now.'

Gwidion looked his son in the eye. Soru's hands flew back and forth, touching, gesturing. Gwidion looked away and picked a seed from his son's coat. Shyly his throat made a soft cooing sound. 'I never knew how it was with you.'

'And we did not know. We thought that you were different, we thought you could not be one with us.'

'I never knew what it was to be twin.'

'All our names mean twin.'

Gwidion turned his head to look at his son once more. He picked at a clump of rora seeds clinging to his arm. The conversation continued, but it was not in words. Sometimes words accompanied it, sometimes gestures, sometimes only a soft sing-song cooing.

'What do you mean?'

'The intonation of all our names means twin.'

And now that Gwidion thought about it, it was true. He hummed the tune the Amans always hummed during the ritual dance that he and Loru and Lori had first developed. Soru cooed in a particular pitch that signified laughter and agreement. The tune had always struck Gwidion as strange and particularly haunting. And it struck him as he hummed it that this was not a tune at all, but a scale. The scale of their language. Soru cooed again.

The thoughts in Gwidion's head began to run away with him as he did the mathematics. Nine notes of a scale, thirteen, maybe fifteen letter sounds. So each letter could be sung on nine different notes – a potential alphabet of... He stopped, stunned. A potential alphabet of thirteen multiplied by nine: one hundred and seventeen separate letter-notes. And he had thought their language skills were limited!

The scale played on in his brain until something else slowly dawned on him. That irritating habit they had when they called to each other. Not irritating because it was annoying, but irritating because it seemed to have meaning and yet its significance had always eluded him. It was as if they adopted a special strange voice for speaking each other's names. He had put it down to being a tone of affection or endearment, indicated by the particular pitch.

He sang the scale in his head again. Then for each note he substituted a name vocalised in that peculiar 'affectionate' way. Then he sang them out loud: Silu, Sili, Choru, Chora, Lori, Soru, Sora, Loru. He knew it now. It was the scale itself, the scale of a people living in harmony, a people who communicated on so many different levels that there could scarcely be any misunderstanding, only mistakes. The mistake had been all his.

A little way off Alara's body was laid out on a small raft of rora trunks. Gwidion looked at her body lying there black against the white sand. She had known the meaning of community, he pondered, though it had taken her death for him to learn it. Tomorrow they would float her body to sea as the sun set.

'I'm sorry.' It was Soru. Gwidion nodded.

'I did not know about the loom. I did not know then.' They looked at each other. 'Now I know you, as you know us.'

'The loom was less important than anyone ever imagined.'

'But it was full of your planet's history.'

Gwidion nodded. 'It had no place here.'

'I am sorry.'

'I don't blame you, Soru.' His son looked up doubtfully. 'I blame myself for not being there to catch you first.'

Gwidion smiled. He felt Soru's arms encircling him as the tears began to fall.

'Cchooi.' His name rang out in that particular intonation he now understood. 'After today we will climb again, Cchooi.'

book three chapter four

And the people turned to the Heron and spoke. 'Sleep is but a little death and dreams only are the way to life.'

If you have the choice, never let history be your judge. Of the first two presidents who ruled the Tierra Nueva, history judged Luis to be a weak man without vision or ideas, a power-seeker who committed the ultimate sin of not being strong enough to hang onto that power.

The loss of Jiménez, on the other hand, was mourned. Here was a man who had ruled with an iron fist, a man of action who had brought order and stability to the developing chaos aboard the ship. Here was a leader who had stripped government of bureaucracy and unnecessary politicians and had given the people what they most desired – contentment.

But he made a fatal mistake. He ignored the advice of his security chief, lost a member of the ship and, most importantly, the Tierra Nueva's most prized relic. It was an error of judgment that even he could not get away with.

Bascato was woken by news from the ship's astronomers of a new Eridani. A small, unnamed and previously undetected star system had been located by the on-board arrays. Its mature sun was circled by at least five planets, the second of which, although slightly smaller than Earth, showed promising signs of supporting an oxygen-rich atmosphere with liquid water on its surface. At just over thirteen light years from their present position it was further distant than Eridani but they could still reach it within seventy years.

President Bascato was ready to milk the new planet's public relations possibilities to the full. A day of celebration was announced and crowds packed the mall to share the occasion on the public vid-screens. Scientists speculated wildly on the possibilities this new find offered. They dreamed of the wonders of life on a new planet with less gravity and more oxygen than on Earth. They even postulated the positive likelihood of finding alien life. Whatever fears that notion might raise in the minds of those on board the Tierra Nueva were quickly offset by the hypothesis that on the new world the citizens of the republic would have the powers of superhumans.

Commentators eager to fuel the new wave of hope and excitement which swept the ship calculated, with very little real scientific data to support them, that the average man would be able to jump ten metres from a standing start in the lower gravity and would have the strength to lift ten times his own weight. The crew of the spaceliner might by then have spent nearly eighty years of their lives travelling through space, and the effects of space ageing meant that none were likely to see their new world, but for their descendants a rare paradise was waiting.

In a shrewd display of sentimentality Bascato named the planet Alara, in honour of the honest hard-working galley assistant who had been lost overboard by the disgraced ex-President Jiménez and to wild cheers from the fascinated and jubilant crowds of the shopping mall. The details of this mysterious tragedy were sketchy, but more than enough to satisfy an excitement-hungry public fed on a diet of trivia. Suffice it to say that they involved some dubious goings-on behind the back of the president's pregnant wife, along with some psychic and esoteric rituals performed in the presidential office. Here was a story which could run and run.

In private Bascato had to admit Alara's jump disturbed him. He did not like the unexplained, it gave him feelings of paranoia. But all that was some time ago. As a wheeler and dealer, as a back-street brawler and as a political chameleon, he was, in all respects, the perfect successor.

One of the Heron's first acts as the new leader of the Tierra Nueva was to turn his office into a sauna and pool. He now undertook whatever official business he could not avoid in the chamber itself, which was, he argued, a nearly obsolete room in any case. His visitors approached him as supplicants to an emperor's dais and were obliged to stand throughout the interview. The Heron found it helped hurry business matters along enormously.

'What the hell have you been up to, Pepe?' The chief of security had known the president a long time and even the echoes of his words around the empty chamber failed to curb his familiarity.

'Nothing I can't handle,' said the Heron, making himself comfortable in his throne.

'Well, I hope you can handle this,' said Miguel. He took off his coat, rolled up his sleeves and put his hand-vid on the president's desk. Then he put both his fists on the table and leaned over, further invading the Heron's presidential space. 'You've got a problem. We've got trouble on the streets again. Murmurings of discontent about this Alara business. We haven't seen this sort of thing since we first got on board this ship. We've got knots of protesters gathering and talking about it. The next thing it will be graffiti and leaflets and God knows what else.' He stood upright and his head was level with the Heron's.

The president dipped his head as if taking a drink from a pool of water. 'Get some more kick on the streets, Miguel.' The chanters were now part of the security services and came directly under Miguel's direction.

'There isn't any. The biologists are growing the stuff so intensively they are having problems with a new strain of viruses.'

Kick was a derivative of the fruit of the banana tree. Its production took up valuable resources in terms of space and horticultural care.

'It's got to the point where kick is endangering other food supplies. They can't get enough of it, and every time they want a little more than the last time. People want their kick, but Christ it doesn't spoil their appetite. Remember the food riots under Luis?'

The Heron remembered them well. He also knew what the implications of Miguel's question were. The Heron felt a little sick, and very angry. Jesus, he'd never really wanted this job, it had never been one of his ambitions. He didn't even really believe that he was right for it – or that anyone else thought he was. But he'd been flattered into it. Cajoled by people like Miguel himself; people who didn't want it themselves either but wanted to make sure the wrong man didn't get it.

'Synthesise it.'

The chief of security shook his head slowly as if he had won that particular round.

'The scientists say it can't be done. At least, they've come up with something. But it's not quite kick.'

'Does it do the job?'

'There's the possibility of side-effects.'

'Such as?'

Miguel shrugged. 'They don't know.'

'Such as getting me out of a hole.'

Miguel smiled. 'Yes, that side-effect, I suppose.'

'What is the alternative?'

'I don't know.' His eyes narrowed. 'A smaller population, more resources diverted to kick. They have their problems too.'

Miguel felt quite pleased with himself as he left the chamber. He had given the president the solution as well as the problem, without appearing to have forced it down his throat. And he had not had to offer the third possibility, because the president had never asked for it. Not that Miguel particularly favoured another innovation from the chemists. They only seemed to cause more problems.

The fourth possibility, however, did appeal to him. Maybe he was something of a puritan after all – a population weaned off kick voting him into office on a wave of democratic gratitude. A new deal, a new age, a new pure beginning for the people of the Tierra Nueva. Yes, he liked that idea. It was the reason he was happy to see the Heron hold the interim presidency, a period he felt sure would produce just the right amount of decay and decadence to produce the conditions for his own rise to power. As a man of thirty-two time was still on his side. Now he could return to his troops and execute the president's orders while at the same time expressing his own serious reservations – and his own idealistic aspirations – in the right quarters.

For the moment he was pleased with his handling of the president – the exercise of power by the subtlest of means. He had, after all, learned at the feet of a master. The Heron himself would surely have been proud of that.

The Heron returned to his pool and sauna. Before he stripped off his clothes and jumped into the welcoming water, he made a single com-call. By the time he completed his third length of the pool his chief of security was a small canister zooming unseen into limitless space and the presidential order to carry out the synthesisation of kick was in operation.

Xavier was pleased to see the chanters out in force again at the piazza. Sometimes lately it was impossible to get your hands on any wafers at all. He wasn't one for taking part in the huge communal gatherings around the public vidscreen in the square, that was more for the young people. These days he found it difficult even to drag himself out of his room down to the shopping mall.

'Give me a ton,' he told the chanter. He had decided to stock up this time in case there was another shortage. The chanter held his face and looked into his eyes.

'Sure, sure. Are you all easy?'

'Yes, I'm easy,' said Xavier impatiently, 'I just need a good stack.'

The chanter took his money and handed him the package. 'Take it easy,' he said, but Xavier was already on his way back to his room.

The new stuff was good, he decided, a real kick to it. So much of a kick, in fact, that it made him feel sick for the first half-hour. That was probably because he hadn't been able to get hold of any for a while now. He just wasn't used to it. But it was good, very good. He took another one and sat down in front of his screen letting the colours and the music wash over him.

'The cause of his death in the medical unit the next morning – along with two other men in their sixties – was recorded as "natural causes due to respiratory breakdown compounded by a latent asthmatic tendency".'

Bascato scanned the report on his hand-vid and gave a tut.

'My old friend Xavier,' he murmured. 'What a waste.'

He forwarded the report to the head of his special investigating team along with some extra details.

By the afternoon, the public screens in the mall were carrying little else. A spurned lover from Alara's past whose jealousy had turned to violence after years of a wasted life of drug addiction. Another great story in the continuing drama of life at the top. A sad tale rather than one of unmitigated evil. A moral tale for the crew of the Tierra Nueva. A fitting end. Almost worthy of Miguel, he mused.

One day followed another day. And still planet Alara was a lifetime away. After the initial euphoria, the lethargy and disgruntlements returned. So much was the same that no-one took the trouble to think differently. Seventy or eighty years was plenty long enough to change the Tierra Nueva's great new adventure into an old, old adventure. What's the point in getting in training for a race you won't be taking part in and which may be centuries away?

The Heron had something to say about that as well. 'Philosophy was never my strong point. Life is a playground. Jump in, let's have some fun. Kick – it's no different from cryogenics, is it? I mean, everyone goes to sleep for a few hundred years, and hey presto, they're all up and about in time to arrive at the new world. Give or take a percentage in losses. Well, kick is the same, except we're not totally asleep. Come the time, we'll wake up. You wait and see.'

book four chapter four

Gwidion, Soru and Sora huddled together in the darkness of the cavern. Above them, at the head of a steep incline of broken rocks, the only shaft of light came from the bowl Gwidion had laboriously fashioned and where he had spent his first jhara. It was comfortably big enough now for a man to climb through. His own efforts, and the yearly ravages of erosion which the changing water courses wrought on these underground labyrinths, had enabled them to find this refuge from the wind on the plateau. Behind them their crude ladder of bound rora poles lay ready to lead them out again.

Despite their fatigue, Soru and Sora cooed excitedly after the elation of their first climb. They had practised well, but their digits and joints ached after the exertions of gripping and their heads swam with their achievement. Gwidion was weary too, not with the effort of the climb but with the responsibility of fatherhood. As the light began to fade Soru and Sora released their grip on him and stood up attentively as if listening for something. Far out at sea where their family and the other Amans now bobbed and rode the giant waves, they sensed what was coming.

'It is the beginning,' said Sora softly and sat again by her father. 'What will we do?'

'We must wait,' said Gwidion and he beckoned Soru to join them.

Through the tensed bodies of his children, Gwidion felt the first wave arrive. The tremors reached them, shaking the massiveness of the cliff as if it was a rora tree moved by the wind. Then came the sound, low, almost beneath hearing. A thud followed by the lighter clash of spray and debris. Then the recoil, a terrible silence which seemed to suck the air out of their caves.

In the twilight between waking and sleeping, between the huddle of life in the cavern and the raging of death from the ocean, Gwidion's mind began to wander. He looked at his son and remembered their conflict over climbing the cliff face. He appeared fearless now, as Gwidion had to the original Amans. At the time of jhara however, and more so as his dependants grew in number, fear tested him again. A different sort of fear.

He feared for his family, he feared for his tribe. He feared that when the waves ceased and they tried to return to the plateau, the passageway would be blocked and collapsed, the exit lost. He feared that without him they might not be able to continue this pilgrimage jhara after jhara. However far that day might be away, he feared that they might have to do it without him sooner than he wanted.

What had he done? He had created a people who could no longer survive on the open sea during this great upheaval like the original Amans could. He feared he had created a people who might not find peace on land either.

Alexander the Great once asked Gwidion's ancestors, the Celts, what they feared most. They replied that they feared no-one, only that one day the sky would fall to the earth. Gwidion thought of the Old Testament prophets, of the Mayan astronomers and the Hindu scientists who had once witnessed such events when Venus first became a part of the solar system and collided with Earth. When the land groaned and swallowed up cities, when the sky was illuminated by the thunderbolts and battles of primitive gods, when the sun stood still and the world was covered with a layer of darkness. And the sky came so close to the ground that men could not stand up and walk around in the choking clouds.

As the waves hit and shook the cliff these were the visions he had of what was happening to his foster planet and he could only comfort himself with the thought that they had lived through so much calamity and disaster, perhaps even now they could still survive. His memories became confused. Life in Mimosa, his crystal clear recollections of life in the village, seemed no longer ago than yesterday. And now they seemed to meld with life on Ama, a complex mix of past and present.

He was not old enough to remember life in his village before the dome, when men and women walked their way through wind and rain and tucked themselves up at home in the evening secure against the elements and listened to the wind whistle under the roof tiles. Yet now he imagined he knew what it was like.

The howl of the storm penetrated the frail soft rock of the cliff, echoing and booming upwards. And in the cavern, bound to his children, he listened to the deathly sound, the most dangerous sound in the world, the primeval breathing of the wolf at the door. It chilled his blood.

That night Alara came to him as he lay with his head full of the sound of the waves. It seemed to be filling him up inside and his brain struggled to expand to allow it in, yet still above it all, he could hear the pump of his own blood.

She was no more than a silhouette in the gloom, her black hair falling over her face. When she was naked she slipped under the cover beside him and kissed him. He could feel her warm body against his, the exquisite shape of a woman's body, the slope of her back and the fullness of her hips. Her hair, mixed with her breath, fell on his face; her fingernails dug into his skin. Then it was not Alara at all. It was Lauren and Bethan. It was Lori. For a moment he thought again of the wolf.

It is not possible to make love in a foreign language. The words which express the deepest and keenest emotions are those learned in our mother tongue, the words our mothers taught us. *Cariad – mi caro, dere – ven.* The words fell from his lips with their kisses. It was only later as she climbed on top of him and let him feel the indescribable secrets of a woman; later, when the sweat began to mix together on their bodies and their breath came in inelegant bursts; that they shared the common language of pleasure. The baying of the wolf, the cries of fear and ecstasy.

Soru and Sora bent low over their father, trying to make sense of the whispered ramblings which came from his throat. Soru brought water to wet his brow. They did not understand their father's dreams.

With a start, their father sat upright.

'*Wyt ti'n siarad Cymraeg?*' Do you speak Welsh?

Sora smiled and shook her head as she tried to lie him down again.

'Na ash, cha,' she cooed softly. I don't understand, father.

He struggled against her so that his breath was tortured and harsh above the sounds in the cave and she had to let him sit. His eyes were still closed.

'*Un o ble wyt ti?*' Where do you come from? Well, not precisely. One of what place are you? The question which begins every conversation between two Welsh-speakers meeting for the first time. And those who are not in the place they are of, are condemned to the life of an exile. Is that what he had forced on his children? That they were exiles in their own land? It was a hard thing to bear.

Perhaps not. Perhaps that was the fate he had chosen for himself – both its suffering and its exhilaration. A punishment and a privilege. He let the rhythm of the waves break against his brow, blending with the drip, drip of water from the roof of the cave. His breathing stilled, his eyes moved back and forth behind his lids. And in that dim twilight where dreams begin and sleep has not yet come, he began to fall.

First there was heat, a terrible heat, a heat so tangible it was unbelievable. Smoke clouded the blue sky and gripped his chest like a panic attack. It entered his nose and masked the smell of sweat, it submerged all other scents under something darker, impenetrable and more terrible. It was the smell of fear.

There was a noise, a roar, a pounding which seemed at the same time to be both inside his head and outside it, in a dream and in the real world. This, then, was dying, this was death. He felt someone's arms around him, somebody was whispering to him.

In his mind the sky was blue again, the air was fresh and clear, and it rushed past his ears and up his nostrils so he could hardly breathe. Yet he was desperate to breathe. The arms gripped him, their rough clothes giving life to his skin, awakening his senses.

Still he fell. How far did he have to fall? How long does death take? But he knew the question was meaningless. Whether it came in an instant, or whether it came after an interminable time of terror and suffering, made no difference. In the moment of death, time had no meaning. Death was the end of time.

The episodes of his life passed him as if they were the ones falling, not he. His mother, Lauren, his father, the mentor, Alara, Martín. There were Silu and Sili, Loru and Lori, his children, his first-born and those who came after. And perhaps someone unnamed, unknown to him, Bethan's child. And Cai, who held him tightly in his arms and whispered in his ear, 'I will save you, I will not let you fall.' Cai was his brother, Cai was his twin.

Then suddenly there was nothing. Silence.

Once, a long time ago – and he had no way of knowing how long ago that was – there had been a day, September 11, when he was born, when time was born, when the story was simple, uncomplicated and immediate. A singular moment of truth. There were other September 11s too. Somewhere, some time. Then out of the blue, something happened, and it was never September 11 again.

Gwidion opened his eyes, something was coming. There was a rushing of water. For a moment he thought it was the echo of the jhara still ringing in his ears, then the three of them watched as the wall in front of them, grey in the darkness of the cave, bulged and cracked and was replaced by a wall of water. They felt the floor of the cavern move and sway and scrambled further towards the safety of the shaft of light above them.

The water fell with a white crash into the open space and flooded the floor of the cavern. They watched for what seemed like a long time as the level crept higher, then there was a new crash and a gurgle. Large bubbles of air broke the surface in a boiling mass and the flood began to recede again. They stayed where they were, listening to the trail of the new river, hearing it wind its way through the crevices and hollows beneath them until they could hear it no more.

Gwidion rose and stretched out his hand to Soru and Sora to help them up to the plateau again, but Soru pulled him back.

'Follow the water.'

They climbed down the tumble of rocks to the floor of the cavern and began to follow the course of the water. It exited through a small opening in the far corner. From there it was a three-metre drop into another cavern below. Soru took the ladder from above them and placed it in the opening, leading the way while Gwidion and Sora followed.

The second cavern was barely high enough for them to stand and the water washed around their knees still supplied from some-where above them and across the plateau. Or perhaps it had risen through the faults and passageways under the force of the constant pounding of the jhara and was now receding. They continued away from the cliff face almost level for what seemed like a long time, occasionally stopping to clear boulders from their path, sometimes obliged to wait as the water level fell, at other times forced to turn back and seek out a new route.

In the darkness of the interior Gwidion could see barely anything and had to feel his way along. Sora and Soru's night vision was better than his and they took it in turns to lead him, slow and stumbling, through the twists and turns of the voyage. The exertions of the cliff climb were a long time behind them and after two days of inactivity their journey was an exciting adventure. At every turn there were new wonders, stalactites and stalagmites hundreds of jharas old hung from the cavern ceilings or grew from the floors or lay shattered by the flood of water. In this way they climbed and walked and scrambled through a network of caves, pools and sink-holes which took them forwards and backwards behind the face of the cliff so that sometimes they imagined they could punch a hole through the thin walls and emerge into open air. But downwards, always downwards.

Then there was light.

'We've done it,' shouted Soru, and the three laughed and cooed, hurrying to be first to emerge through a small opening at the base of the cliff.

They stood blinking in the bright sun on the white sand, blinded after so much time underground, until they could see again. There was nothing to see. The pristine sand, unmarked by footprints, led down to the receding sea where the debris of their home washed untidily at the edge of the water. Far out at sea a shoal of black dots told them what they already knew. The others were returning.

On top of the plateau Gwidion straightened his back and peered over the lip of the cliff. It was a familiar and comforting sight. The rora trees, rich with purple blossom whose heady scent drifted even as far as the plateau before it was whipped to sea by the wind, were already thick enough for the Amans to have started fashioning their small dens. The dugg looked no more than a drawing in the sand.

A group of Amans plied their way back and forth to the sea collecting shells and flints. These were transported to the plateau by another group who, with the help of new ladders positioned at difficult points, were able laboriously to wind their way through the network of caverns which now led from the beach to the clifftop just below the plateau. In the cavern where Soru and Sora had spent their first jhara the shells were ground down to powder and mixed with smaller shards of flint to provide mortar.

Gwidion descended once more into the cave. From the piles of broken limestone boulders he had selected the ones that were needed and had marked them with the orange dye of the rora fruit. The ladder which led from below to the bowl on the plateau would serve both as a climbing frame and as rails for moving these rocks to the surface. This was not easy work for the native Amans, but many had gathered to help, along with Lori and Choru and Chora, who were now able to walk unsteadily among the rocks, fascinated by this new enterprise.

Soru stood on the plateau, bracing himself against the wind, a long woven rope stretching from his hand down into the cave and around the first boulder. Sora and Gwidion stood on the first rung of the ladder ready to help, and a crowd of willing helpers positioned themselves along the slope ready to add their weight as best they could. Sora and Gwidion pushed and the rock moved a few centimetres. It was harder than they had thought. Gwidion drove a pole over the rung of the ladder and underneath the limestone to prevent it slipping back and the two paused for breath.

Sora smiled at her father and wordlessly they heaved again. Gwidion was so engrossed in his work that at first he did not hear the sound which came from the other workers, a deep, bass note, almost outside the range of his hearing, which resonated through the cavern. He felt it at first in his body and it fuelled and toned his muscles. The rock moved another rung and he drove his pole in once again. This time there was no stopping.

At first the sound was like a ground-out, constant, low. He began to listen to it as the stone slid rung by rung up the ladder. Then it seemed to have a beat, a long beat. Like an emphasis, a single push, like an undulation, like a breath. He joined in, letting himself feel the sound, letting the sound do the work of pushing. And as the pulse came he felt it in every part of his body, as if every molecule in his body coiled for a moment, then released. The rock slid further, he drove the pole on top of another rung.

The workers were scrambling up to the opening as their rhythm and harmony sent the load further upwards, until finally its end peeped over the surface of the plateau. Soru held the rope taut, standing at right angles now to the wind, leaning back into another imaginary wind which came from a different direction. The stone slowed, balanced, swayed. And as the pulse came it slid effortlessly into the air and over the side of the bowl as if suddenly set free.

Everybody scrabbled out of the cave before the momentum was lost, guiding the stone across the plateau surface, lifting it over hollows and dips, swapping sides to share the discomfort of the wind whipping into their faces. And all the while the low bass rolled stronger and stronger as the final position was in sight. Gwidion counted. Of course. It was the pulse of the jhara. One hundred and seventy seconds. And as he and the others straightened their backs and turned them to the wind, smiling out across their settlement to the sea beyond, he understood why they did not fear the great waves.

The low roll of the jhara, the thunder and cymbals which clashed through the limestone passageways, the vibration in their bodies, these were things the Amans understood. This was their heartbeat, this was the music of their planet.

book three chapter five

In long-ago time there was Tierra and Tierra became dust and the dust was silver and the silver dust was spread over the universe in all directions in equal measure. And the dust was like the seeds of plants, each grain of dust a seedpod. And we are the seed within the pod which is no more than a grain of dust in the universe. Where we settle, there will we spill and there will we grow and we will become Tierra again. And of all the dust that flies through the universe only we are the true seed.

'Master.' The man's fingers flew over the touchpad of the screen before him as he gave an imperceptible sigh. It was always Col who had the questions. He pushed his hand through the small amount of greying hair he could still call his own.

'Yes, Col.'

'If the probe won't launch why don't we send someone down to look at it?' Then, in a gesture towards the politeness which was due to one's elders and betters: 'Sir. I only mean...' She looked up at planet Alara which filled the viewscreen across the front of the command centre. 'I mean, if anything goes wrong this time...' She drew her finger across her own touchpad and blew the thin layer of dust away.

The master looked over with a sardonic grin and shared it with the rest of the crew. He was beginning to feel his age – all twenty-four Earth years of it. Col didn't need to tell him how important this was, but he appreciated that her first day on the bridge was a big occasion and she wanted to get it right.

'Fancy a go yourself, Col?'

Col shifted in her seat, embarrassed. 'I'm not an engineer.'

'No. Who is?' The words were not unkind.

'Doesn't anyone know how this ship works?'

'Oh sure,' said the master returning to his touchpad.

'I mean does anyone really know?'

The master's good humour was shaken slightly by the persistence of the question. 'We can read the manuals.' He turned to a boy on his other side. 'Andre, re-direct the probe through the exhaust tubes, that'll get it launched at least.'

Andre obeyed silently. 'Probe launched, master.'

'Good, keep it tracked.'

They sat back and gazed at the planet. It was a beautiful sight to people who had never known any life apart from the Tierra Nueva. It was swathed in white land masses and yellowy-green seas and flimsy white clouds swept across its surface. It was such a big day the master's good mood couldn't stay buried for long.

'I'm sorry, Col.' There was no reply. 'I cannot blame you for asking the questions you do, I asked them myself once.'

'Don't you always teach us to find out the truth?'

'Col, you are a very bright girl, the brightest we've got. Isn't that right, Andre?' He looked over his shoulder at the boy. He was sixteen, a quiet, amenable type. He did what he was told and he didn't make mistakes, and the master knew well that he had a soft spot for Col.

'Bright enough,' Andre agreed, stealing a shy glance towards the girl and enjoying his role as the master's buddy.

The master turned back to Col. 'You are fourteen now. Whether we land on this planet or whether we go on, in a year or two I will be gone and it is likely that you will be master of the pod. It is a great responsibility to bear and there are many things you must learn. In the short time that is left to me I will try to tell you everything I know. One day you will do the same for your successor.'

'But that's why I ask these questions, master. I want to learn.'

The master waved her quiet with his hand. 'I have said that I will tell you everything I know. The first thing you must know is that we know next to nothing.' He waited a beat and saw it was having the desired effect on Col. As the girl recovered enough to formulate another question, the master intervened with a question of his own.

'How long we have we been in this pod?'

'We can count the generations,' Col shot back proudly. 'I am Col descended from Col Jemin who is my five-father. On average we have our first child by sixteen which means we left Tierra about eighty years ago.' It was a sum she had calculated and recalculated many times before. The master smiled and nodded. It was a sum he himself had calculated many times when he was Jemin's age.

'A generation was not always sixteen years. We believe that originally it was much longer, perhaps twice as long.'

He watched Col do the maths in her head. 'It makes quite a difference, doesn't it? When we left Tierra there were many more than the seventy on board now. A thousand, at least.'

He paused again to let Col begin formulating her questions. 'In those days it was necessary to control the population very strictly, only certain women would have been allowed to have children. In addition the average lifespan was three times what it is today – a small number of children to a small number of women around the age of thirty would have been the norm.

'When our forefathers sent this pod out from Tierra, it was with a single purpose, a fantastic enterprise, and they equipped this ship to achieve it. Imagine, a colony of people, technicians, scientists, leaders, people who knew how to operate this pod and carried with them the history of Tierra.'

'Where is it now?'

The master gestured helplessly. 'We don't know. Or rather it is all around us. The secrets to our past, and our future, are still here somewhere among the blinking lights and the whirring machinery. It was built by men and women to sustain us on our long journey. Somewhere within, it carries all their knowledge and expertise, but we have lost the key and we don't have the resources to recover it.'

The silence echoed around the command centre. It was true, thought Col, this room alone would hold many more than the half a dozen children who came here to assist the master.

'I know all this.'

The master's laconic expression returned. 'You've read the manuals.'

'Yes.' It was a proud and self-satisfied reply.

'The problem is the manuals are only a fraction of the story. We've had so many system shutdowns it sometimes amazes me the tub still flies at all. You can't even begin to imagine what it must have been like originally. We operate the machinery as best we can. There's no point dwelling on the things we don't know. It is the only hope of surviving.'

The master came down from the console at the head of the command centre.

'There are many places on our pod which I will show you. Vast spaces which have lain unused for generations, many times bigger than the rooms we live in now.'

Silence.

'It'll be a while before the probe starts transmitting. Come with me.' The master led Col out and along a corridor. They came to a portal and the master unlocked a small flap at the side of the door.

'We're going out into the void?' Col asked in horror.

The master pressed keys inside the flap. He expelled his breath in annoyance and then tried again. The door opened.

'See, no void. The command centre where you have grown up is only a fraction of the pod, though not everywhere is safe to go. This will take us down to the other levels.'

They got into the lift. For Col it was exactly like disappearing into the void except that she could still breathe and her limbs were not torn from her body and turned inside out as they were told would happen. She gasped as the shock of the descent hit her in the stomach. They got out and entered a huge domed area. In the centre was a huge bowl, around it were walkways and stairways leading to the many levels stretching up to the struts of the glass roof. On every side were empty rooms with windows looking onto the central square. Col's neck began to ache with looking up and around. All she could do was give a low whistle.

'This was a place of entertainment, a focal point for the many people on our pod to gather. This bowl was once able to spurt water in great showers into the air and there was coloured light and music.'

'The Water Mother,' whispered Col in wonder. 'I thought that was just a bedtime story.'

'These rooms,' the master gestured at the blank windows, 'were also places of entertainment, places where you could buy things – food and gifts, all sorts of things.'

'What happened to all those people?'

'We don't know.'

'It must be in the logs.'

'Maybe it is. Some have been wiped. By mistake mainly. Some have been lost during shutdowns. We have barely a third of the ship's systems online. Maybe the answer is out here somewhere.'

'Then we should find it.'

'We've got better things to do, Col. We concentrate our resources on keeping the pod flying. You may have noticed we're a bit under-staffed.'

'But we knew where we were going.'

'We managed that much. As I say, we concentrate on the things we do know. Our priorities must be clear. These unanswered questions are fascinating but we have no time to deal with them. It gets us by. That and getting this far, those are the things that really mattered.'

He watched her as she stared around the mall, biting her lip. He sensed her distaste at his reasoning.

'What would you do, Col? If you were the master? Tell the others how much you don't know? Leave them without hope or belief? It's not what we've lost that matters most, it's what we've still got. It is the only knowledge we have.'

Back on the bridge Col gazed through one of the side screens and thought about what the master had told her. So she was one day to lead their small group – and soon, too. The thought didn't frighten her but it was sooner than she was ready for. There were so many questions which needed to be answered and there was no-one to answer them. There was only blackness – the sort of blackness into which she had gazed so many times at this viewing screen, limitless, infinite, impenetrable.

But today at least there was something else filling the main viewscreen. It was a body such as they had been taught Tierra must once have been. And across the face of the globe swept wisps of white fluff, barely obscuring areas of the land below. Further off lay three smaller bodies, grey and lifeless moons like so many she had seen before. And it was as if they belonged to this larger body, as if they were attracted by its beauty and yet stood a little way off in awe of it.

For a moment she was filled with an indescribable excitement. She held her breath. Was this to be the place where they would finally settle? Was this the ground to which the true seed had been flung?

Her fingers flew over the touchpad as the probe entered the planet's atmosphere. Her voice was high-pitched with excitement.

'Habitations.'

The master sat up at his console. Streams of data were flowing into his computer from the probe and he could barely keep up with it. He transferred his attention to the screen where Col was zooming in on the planet.

'Near the equator. You see the central plateau, beneath the mountain range?'

The master stared at the three shapes clustered at the edge of a strangely-shaped promontory.

'They could be anything. Rock formations, anything.'

'They're the only feature on the plain. Look at them.'

The master turned back to his console. 'Maybe. We'll investigate it. Don't let your imagination run away with you.'

The screen shifted to the area of the cliff face. What they saw there captured their attention. The master gave a low whistle.

'Tsunami.' He pointed at the pulses which rippled across the ocean surface, visible even from orbit. 'At least ten metres high. Look at them, wave after wave. The coastline must surely be uninhabitable. Let's see what else we've got.'

The data was depressing.

'High acidity in the oceans,' said the master. 'And look at these weather systems, wind speeds of sixty kilometres an hour or more. Ultra-violet levels are outside the range.'

'What about the mountains?'

The master shook his head. 'Doesn't look any better. Acid rain, the vegetation must have adapted.'

'So could we.'

A score of answers ran through the master's head as Col waited for the one he would choose. His heart beat fast and his throat was dry. He had never set foot on a planet before. All he had known was the pod. And for all its deficiencies at least the pod came with a manual. His fingers moved across the touchpad.

'The life data analyser says no.'

'Life data analyser? What's that?'

'A sim. It tells the computer to compare the probe readings with the pod's data banks on life-supporting planets. You don't have to be a scientist to make a scientific judgment. I wrote it myself.'

Col's hands moved across the touchpad. 'You wrote it? Why

didn't you just tell the computer to do that?'

The master gave her a questioning look.

'Voice-activation,' said Col airily.

He shook his head. 'If it was that easy why are there all these manual consoles?'

'Perhaps they just wanted something to do with their hands. Eighty years is a long time. Look.' She transferred her screen to his. 'It's in the manual. Voice-activation capability. I thought you were good at reading manuals.'

The master skimmed the text on his screen and raised his eyebrows. 'You're right. I don't know, maybe it got damaged in one of the shutdowns.'

Their minds returned to the planet still filling their viewscreen.

'The sim still says no.'

'We should at least take a look.'

The master took a deep breath. 'If we could get a ship down there, there's no guarantee we'd get back. We may only ever have one chance at this. We need to be more certain.'

There was a silence.

'Can you guarantee we would get down?' said Col.

The master was busy at his touchpad.

'I mean to any planet. Can you guarantee we can get down?'

'I'm working on a sim. If you want to take a look at it you're welcome.'

Col was about to give him a biting reply. Instead she satisfied herself with: 'I will. Or I'll get the computer to do it.'

The three stared a little longer at the beautiful sight before them. There was a lump in Col's throat as the master spoke to Andre.

'Set a course. We have another target less than two light years from here. There's no point wasting time.'

Col turned away. And Ama became no more than a speck of dust on the screen. A tiny speck of dust in the huge, huge universe.

book four chapter five

Gwidion rolled onto his back in the warm water of the lagoon watching his long grey beard spread out around him like some strange jellyfish. He stared into the clear blue sky and attempted to calm his breath. Even the exertion of swimming half a kilometre required some minutes' recuperation, but it was a daily ritual he would not give up. He barked an order to Soru and Sora who ducked and dived effortlessly nearby, but they ignored it and cooed soothingly in reply.

This behaviour in their father was not unusual when his frailty was exposed in this way. He hated inactivity, he disliked not being in control. As his eldest son and daughter it was their duty and their honour to take him to safety at the time of jhara, and they were glad to do it. Not for the honour, but simply because it meant their father still lived, he had survived another jhara. Sora surfaced at his side and stroked the beard on his chest, cooing softly as she did so. Sometimes, in his worst depressions, he would shy away from being touched. It reminded him of the ravages that one hundred and twenty-one jharas of acid water and burning heat had wrought on his skin. But those moods never lasted long. He lay silently, still trying to recover his breath, his body crusted and flaking under her hands. But he did not push her away or snap at her angrily.

Gwidion let his gaze wander across the rora groves along the cliff edge. He could not help the feeling of pride which rose inside him. They were a hive of activity as the pickers hurried to harvest everything before the time of the waves. In the half-light of dawn against the white background, the fruits appeared like strings of orange lights, while the pickers, small black beetles, moved slowly among them, extinguishing the lights one by one as they loaded them into the bags on their backs.

The plants, the irrigation channels and pathways which turned the beach into a huge abstract painting, would soon be lost and the process of rebuilding would begin again. In the centre of the beach, with the tide almost lapping at its foundations, was the ceremonial dugg, its roof of woven vegetation stained orange from the juice of the skin of the rora. All these would be washed clean by the waves.

Gwidion watched the sun rising over the clifftop as its first rays hit the three dhoomas on top. These low limestone shelters had been built painstakingly over many jharas. Like igloos with a slice taken out, with their backs to the searing wind of the plateau which had softened and shaped them, they appeared like three moons rising over the beach. He lifted his head to see them better, then his leg. He lined his sight along his knee. If he raised his foot just so, he could... The shift in weight caused his bottom to sink in the water, his body jack-knifing and dipping his mouth and nose into the sea. He could not help laughing at the result and turned over coughing and spluttering as the water entered his nostrils. Then he began to swim in slow strong strokes to shore.

Soru and Sora took their father's arms and covered him in his woven cloak stained orange with the dye of the rora fruit and coated his bare skin with the same mixture of flint shards and crushed sea-slug casings that served as mortar for the small half-domes on the plateau surface.

As his children finished their preparations the rest of his family gathered to start the procession – his family by Lori, and his families by his second and third mates. And their families. And their families. Among them too were the fisher-Amans who would spend this jhara at sea. Gwidion stood a head or more above the tallest of them, a striking figure even without his dyed cloak, and when all the things that they needed to salvage from the waves were packed and ready to be carried into the caverns, he sounded the first note. The others joined in, starting on the note of their choice, until the complete scale could be heard strung out in a glorious discord, ringing out from a choir of seventy voices, rebounding from the cliff face, ever-changing as the singers moved up and down the scale.

They joined hands in a long and weaving line, dancing the simple dance that had begun its life on another planet in another time and was now adapted for the peculiar hopping gait that flippers imposed on sea creatures walking on land. The column wound in and out of the small nest of duggs which hugged the cliff base along the shoreline, a tribe on the move.

The younger members carried small hollowed trunks with a

diaphragm of thin flesh stretched across one end and pierced by a long thin piece of wood. At a signal from Soru, the line began to split into two as the fisher-Amans, the ones not of Gwidion's line, made their way towards the open water. The youngsters worked the pieces of wood up and down, providing a strange-sounding rhythmic beat below the song which still harmonised and clashed above it. In front of them was the arched doorway in the cliff which led into the cave labyrinth behind. For a moment, as Gwidion had to let go of hands and stoop to go through, he turned and looked back over his tribe. Emotion stopped him singing for a moment, and in response the voices of his family swelled and rose towards him. Then he led the dance up a boulder stairway through the opening and out of the light.

Many years of work had transformed this route through the cliff. The rora ladders had been replaced in time by rude steps, greatly refined by subsequent generations, until finally it was possible to climb in relative comfort from the beach to the plateau to escape the waves. For his ageing body ascending them was an arduous task. The flights of steps were regular, but narrow and high. He braced himself against Soru and Sora as best he could, letting them take his weight when the climb was too much.

At the end of the procession a small group stopped to lever several large boulders into the archway, blocking it as securely as they could. These would inevitably be thrown aside by the force of the waves as the lower caves flooded. The route followed the faults and seams which water had already worked and widened, took them deep under the plateau and back near the face again as it wound its way upwards in the dark to the accompaniment of the drip, drip of water from the rocks.

Near the top of the ascent the way opened out into a large cavern. The original pocket where Gwidion had spent his first jhara was high above them, the only shaft of light in the darkness. Another passageway led out of the cavern and up steeply to the plateau above and the refuge of the dhoomas.

By the time evening came the bombardment had begun. The first wave was shocking, bursting through the pathetic barrier of the archway and flooding the caverns below with a fierce rushing noise. As Gwidion had done when building this refuge, the water followed the line of least resistance, bashing and whooshing along the passageways, spurting up in huge sprays so that it seemed as if the waves might threaten to reach them from below. Plumes of water and spray did indeed reach the top of the cliff where they were instantly whipped back on themselves by the wind, a visual echo, the ghost of a wave returning out to sea. The drummers took up their hollowed trunks again and began to play so that it was almost possible to believe each thud of a new wave seemed only an extra uplifting beat to the rhythm.

In the shelters the tribe members clung to each other for warmth and comfort as the sound of the jhara bounced around the ear-like structure of the dhooma. It magnified the sound, enveloping the tribe in its vibrations, and sent it back out to sea where it belonged. The cold reached Gwidion's bones quickly and made breathing harder than ever, but its harsh rasping was drowned now by other more awesome sounds.

It was the custom to fast during the days of jhara, but Gwidion was so weak that he was excused. Sora had brought a small supply of sea-slugs and berries which she mashed in a small bowl and attempted to feed him every so often. He ate nothing, whether from respect for the fast or lack of appetite, she did not know.

She offered him a small beaker and he sat up to drink. Rora and water. He tasted the acid fruit and the chalky water. Orange and lime. He watched the darkness from where the waves rolled endlessly towards the cliff. Finally he sank back into the music of the planet and the music they themselves made and the thump, thump of the waves possessed Ama once more, until a kind of sleep came. It was not a sleep like he had ever known, it was not an absence of consciousness, nor was it a lapse into sub-consciousness. He was buoyed by their joint consciousness, he was rested. It was like floating on water.

Gwidion opened his eyes to see a patch of blue sky. A perfect blue. The sort of blue that things were destined to come out of. He sat up, sipped the rora and water and smiled, turning his silver wrist clasp absently on his arm. He took a notched stick from beside him and passed it to Sora. She hesitated.

'It is your time,' said Gwidion. Sora looked at Soru and the unspoken words confirmed what her father had said.

The story she was to retell to her people was one she, and every member of the tribe, knew by heart. She held the story stick, fon shara, straight in front of her, her arm at full stretch so that her wrist was bent at ninety degrees to her forearm. Her fingers fell flat against the stick.

Gwidion rose, refusing the offers of help from his children, and stepped outside the shelter. The shock of the wind made him totter on his weak legs and he clutched his cloak around him as he bent forward into it. At the rear, built into the thick walls of the dhooma was a series of steps worn smooth and curved by the constant erosion of the wind. He picked his way carefully up them and stood unsteadily on the top shielding his eyes from the rising sun. The third moon was faintly visible above the plateau, a semi-transparent disk which appeared to roll briefly along the horizon in a low arc before dropping out of view. He turned his back to the wind.

From here he could see the most magnificent sight. Far out to sea wave after enormous wave rolled towards the beach as if they would never cease. It was as if someone had taken an infinite sheet by two ends and flapped it. He stared at it a long time, aware in his mind of the fisher-Amans who bobbed and tossed and rode the storm.

The majesty and wonder of the sights which greeted his eyes dispelled the doubts which had once tormented him. From the people on the plateau who had shared the days of his terror, from the fisher-Amans who gleefully rode their challenges out at sea, and most of all through their connected-ness, he drew strength and inspiration.

Then he braced himself to turn in the other direction. The extra elevation of the dhooma enabled him to see over the thick haze of dust which lay like a fog above the ground and restricted visibility. Far in the distance rose the snow-capped peaks of a mountain range, the greenery of forests and vegetation, a new country, a new set of challenges. But Gwidion did not see them. He was staring into the dust storm. One day their dhoomas would stretch to the end of the plateau, metre by metre as the tribe grew larger, as new families added their own dhoomas to the three of Gwidion's line. Like white ears growing across the plain, a city of shells.

When he was younger he had believed it might be possible to understand the world, or rather he had not believed it, but had taken it for granted. And for some brief moments in his life before coming here he had glimpsed the pattern in the chaos, he had been granted a vision of its warp and its weft. And then, just as quickly, the light had changed and all was confusion again.

For so much of his life things had never been what they seemed. But this... this was exactly what it seemed. And so were its people. And so was he.

In the dhooma beneath him Sora had begun her story. As she spoke in a strange, lilting sing-song voice, her hands felt the notches and marks along the length of the fon shara from the top down, and each indentation, each scratch, though not a complete record of her words, was a reminder of what she had to say. Neither Gwidion nor any other of the Amans needed to listen, just as Sora did not need to remember. But every one of them heard.

This is the story of the people of Ama. In the time of no-time came the traveller. And he was single and alone, a broken wing, a wing without a brother or sister, and yet he could fly. He spoke the words of no-words from deep within his throat and the sounds he rolled about his mouth fell like pebbles on the beach, round and formed. With these pebbles he began to shape the world, and they fell on us and we felt their weight. And with these pebbles he began to build, and there were three things that he built.

First he built the dam, and the dam was against the evil water and it took the good water which was twin of the evil water from the plateau and made it do battle with the evil water. And this battle still goes on. It is the battle of good and evil, it is the battle of twin against twin. Still it goes on, and will go on forever.

Second he built the shelter and he alone lived in it. For he said that the sun was his evil twin and he must not always be in its view. For he had many things to do and he must not always be fighting with his twin if he was to accomplish many things.

Third he built time. Outside his shelter he drove a stick into the ground and forbade us to move it. And he drew a shadow from his evil twin the sun and laid it on the ground from the bottom of the stick. And this shadow only he was allowed to move. And with the pebbles from his mouth he marked the shadow's movements and these were time.

But the greatest of all the things the traveller accomplished was still to come. For one of our people who had lost her twin came to him and was crestfallen. And she said: 'Release me from time, for I am heartbroken and wish to return to the time of no-time when my sister was alive'. And the traveller took her into his shelter and said: 'There is no way back to the time of no-time until time itself takes you there.'

And she lay with him and when she returned to her people she bore twins in his image. And the twins were a wonder to our people, for they too marked their deeds with small round pebbles formed from their mouths. And so the single traveller became our twin, and his people became twin to our people, and our people were twin to his.

So was paradise created.

About the Author

Eifion Jenkins is a freelance writer and journalist living in west Wales with his wife and two children.

As well as a stage play, *Nightshift Blues,* he has written comedy sketches for television as well as a radio play and short story for BBC radio. His short stories and poems have appeared in anthologies of writing from Wales. He is also the author of a social history of South Wales in the 20th century. This is his first novel.